CHASM

CHASM

BOOK TWO

The characters and events portrayed in this book are products of the author's imagination and are used fictitiously. Any similarity to real persons, living or dead, is coincidental and not intended by the author.

Cover and interior design by We Got You Covered Book Design

WWW.WEGOTYOUCOVEREDBOOKDESIGN.COM

book two

CHASM

L.L. STANDAGE

To Bret, Ella, Caleb, Joshua, and Kate.

Hoping if I dedicate one of my books to you,
you'll forgive me for so many hours at the computer.
And for my terrible cooking.

I love you a million back-scratches.

Author's Note

The characters and events portrayed in this book are products of the author's imagination and are used fictitiously. Any similarity to real persons, living or dead, is coincidental and not intended by the author.

Except for Darci. And she gave me permission.

On that same subject, many of the settings in this book, especially in and around the University of Maryland, are real places. I've done my best to capture the incredible beauty and dignity of the college with as much accuracy as possible. For reasons of clarity and simplicity in description, I did take some artistic license and there are a few differences in the fictional versus the actual setting.

In other words, yeah, I know I got the interior of Cambridge Hall wrong. This decision was intentional. I hope those who are familiar with the college can forgive me and still enjoy the story.

Go Terps!

1

The Aquarium

Dear Samantha, I typed into my cell phone. Then I looked up. Sharks swam behind the glass of an enormous aquarium exhibit. The gray-blue light from their water cast a dim glow in the nearly empty corridor. A woman passed in front of me, rubbing her arms.

I continued my email.

At the aquarium. That season pass I splurged on a few months ago was a great idea. I'm sitting in front of the sharks again. I know how much you like them. In answer to your last question, yes, the aquarium does give them names. The big tiger shark is Rufus. And there's a white tip they named Hannah. She's pregnant with twins. And that's all I'll say about it because I know how much my aquarium travelogues bore you. Haha. Do you keep pets where you are?

I sighed and lowered my phone. If Samantha had been here with me, she'd either whine about being bored, suggest I add highlights to my hair, or imagine all kinds of horrific things the shark named Rufus could do to a person if they fell into his sanctuary.

I'd give anything to hear her.

School started several weeks ago. Midterms are coming up soon. I'm applying for an internship that I hope will bring me closer to where you guys are. It's in Hawaii! Maybe then we can sneak in some visits without having to write letters.

To answer your other question, no, I haven't spoken to anyone from Eamon's group recently. Before they all left San Diego last year, I asked Eamon if I could join them. Wouldn't that be great? I could run around with them, saving people, kicking butt. But he said no. He said I needed to go to school and live my life first. I wrote to him for a couple months, but stopped a long time ago. You can only hear the word "no" so many times.

The woman paced in front of me again, this time murmuring to herself. I returned to my email to keep from staring.

I know what you're thinking, Sam. And no, I haven't talked to Calder either. That ended even before Eamon's letters. I've said it before and I'll say it again: the distance was too much. He and I both agreed. We haven't spoken or emailed since…well, I can't remember. Anyway, I don't want to talk about them. It's for the best.

I always said that in my letters. It's for the best. Because it was. I couldn't wait around for a life that probably wouldn't happen. I needed to move on. So why was it so hard to do? I sighed again, finished my message, and sent it off to Samantha's mom, who knew how to get them to her. Samantha wouldn't get it for several more weeks.

I glanced down at my phone again to check the time. In order to catch the last train back to the University of Maryland, I needed to go. I stood from the bench and watched as a stingray glided by.

"E-excuse me?" came a voice from behind. I turned. The small woman who had been pacing back and forth stood there. With eyes too big for her face, she glanced between me and the glass encasing the rippling sea life. Her fair hair, very similar to mine, hung wet and limp around her face and long down her chest. She clutched a scarf around her neck.

"Uh, I was just leaving," I said.

"No, wait!" She held out one hand. Taken aback, I blinked at her a few times. My nerves tingled in my shoulders.

"Can I help you with something?" I asked slowly. She rubbed her arms again. Wetness from her hair spread a watermark over the blue tee-shirt she wore. Had it been raining outside?

"Are you Olivia Owens?" she whispered. "Please tell me you're Olivia Owens."

How'd she know my name? I studied her, trying to remember if I'd seen her in a class or somewhere on campus, when a few drops of water fell from where her fists gripped the ends of the scarf resting on her neck. I looked at the floor where the droplets fell. Her scarf was soaking wet.

Should I answer? She seemed a little bit crazy. But also sad and anxious. I'd seen that look before, on a woman with long, red hair. Delfina. Back in San Diego, over a year ago—the summer everything in my world changed forever. Something like a popped soda can fizzed within me. Was this woman a…

"What do you want with Olivia Owens?" I asked.

"I need her help. Someone I love…is in terrible trouble."

I hesitated. "Okay. Yes, I am Olivia Owens. Can I ask who told you I could help?"

She took a breath, her face drawing down as though she struggled not to cry. "I've been looking for you for days. I know I shouldn't intrude on you like this, but I'm desperate. I was told I'd find you here every afternoon."

I had to chuckle a little. "No, only on Fridays. Who told you?"

"E-Eamon O'Dell."

My stomach dropped. Gazing at the woman, I watched as she raised her hand to brush some strands of wet hair from her face. Dark purple tinged her fingernails.

For a moment, I forgot about the train. I forgot about the waning day and the dangers of walking at night in downtown Baltimore. The woman watched me, her icy eyes pleading. She rubbed her arms again. The moisture from the scarf spread over her skin.

"What help did you need?" I whispered. "I can't promise I'll be able to do much, but I'll do what I can."

She let out a lungful of air. "Thank you. Thank you. I need to get to this address." She reached into the pocket of her ill-fitting jeans and pulled out a crumpled piece of paper, where an address was written in scrawling numbers and letters:

8 Thornwell Way, Hanover, Maryland
The Pond

Hanover. One of the stops along the route back to the university was in Hanover.

"I'm pretty sure I can get you there. But it'll take a while. Are you sure you don't want to hire someone to drive you?"

She shook her head. "I don't have any more of your currency. I used the last of it to get in here."

I tried not to cringe as the limited numbers in my bank account came to mind. "Okay, I'll do my best. But we'll need to hurry."

She nodded and followed me through the halls and floors of the aquarium, toward the exit. Outside, the early evening sunset stained the sky orange. Chilled breezes blew in from Chesapeake Bay. Behind me, the woman gasped and panted as she tried to keep up. I hung back.

"I'm sorry if I'm walking too fast. Have you had any water?"

"Not since I entered that place." She pointed to the aquarium behind us. "They wouldn't let me bring such a large container inside."

"Okay." I looked around. There was a pharmacy on the corner less than a block away. "I can get you more water, but we need to do it quickly. We have to ride a train to get us to where we need to go and if we don't hurry, we'll miss it. What's your name?"

"Naia."

I led Naia to the pharmacy, bought some water with a little bit of cash I had in my wallet, then the two of us continued the walk toward the train station. She stayed silent the entire way while staring up at the tall buildings and jumping at every horn and screech of tires on the street.

"How'd you get here?" I asked as I used my debit card to buy her a ticket for the train to Hanover. She finished gulping and lowered the bottle.

"I climbed out. The sea comes close to that place where you keep your fish."

"You mean the aquarium? Yeah. Humans love to look at fish. They're really pretty and interesting. The animals are well taken care of at that place."

She nodded and drank more water.

Soon, we boarded the south bound train at Camden Station. I headed to the back of the train car, away from every other passenger. Naia and I sat facing one another next to the window.

"Can I ask what happened?" I said. "Who are we trying to help?"

Naia stared out the window, watching the buildings as the train began to move.

"My sister. She's trapped in a pond."

"How do you know?"

Her face crumpled in misery. "She was taken. Being held for research by a terrible person who knows about my people. My sister isn't quite… right. She's wild. She doesn't understand what has happened to her."

My mouth fell open. "I'm so sorry. That's terrible. I didn't think anyone on this side of the country knew about your people except for me. Do you know who has her?"

Naia shook her head.

"I'll help you get her out. Your people can always trust me."

She turned her orb-like eyes on me. "Thank you, Olivia Owens."

I smiled a little to reassure her, while inside, I marveled. San Diego felt like it had happened a lifetime ago. A dream. But no—at this moment, very much awake, I sat across from a living, breathing, mermaid.

2

The Pond

A train ride, two bus rides, and a short walk later, Naia and I crouched beside a tiny pond in a small Hanover neighborhood surrounded by copses of trees and low bushes. A little, red-brick apartment building stood nearby. The sun had set and the shadows darkened the water to ink. Not a ripple moved on the lily pad surface of the pond. Bullfrog calls strummed in the night. I pointed to a dark-windowed two-story house on the other side of the pond.

"That house is number 8, according to this map on my phone," I said. "Are you sure she's here?"

Naia closed her eyes. After a moment, she opened them again and nodded.

"She's in the pond. I can hear her."

Amplified hearing. Somehow I'd forgotten merpeople had that trait.

"Is she in human form?" I asked, knowing merpeople could still breathe underwater whether or not they had their fins. "Getting her out of there will be a lot harder if she's not."

"I'm not certain," she replied, closing her eyes again. "Yes. She still has her human form. I don't know how much longer that will be. But I'm terrified I'll get caught along with her if I go in there."

"Do you think it's a trap?"

She closed her eyes again and shook her head. "She's in a cage. The pond isn't deep. But she'll be confused when she's freed. I need to wait for her out here to help her home." She looked at me. "I know you can't breathe under the water. But…could you…could you please free her? I can take care of her once she's out of the water. We'll make our way to the river from here. It'll take us both back to the ocean."

"I can't go in there," I said. "I've brought you here. You'll have to do the rest."

Naia shut her eyes for a moment, biting her lower lip. "All right." She took a breath and looked at me again. "What if we—"

A light on the house's back patio flipped on. She gasped. My heart jumped to my throat. We darted for the bushes surrounding the pond and crouched low. Someone came out of the house. I swallowed, my pulse pounding in my neck. I peered through the brush. A man stood on the backyard deck.

"Who's out there?" he called out. Naia whimpered and took off running.

"Naia," I whispered. "*Naia.*"

She disappeared through the trees. I clenched my fists and let out a sigh of exasperation. So much for that. I looked back at the house, where the man still stood, gazing toward the pond. Had he seen Naia run away? He looked left and right, scanned the pond, and scratched his head. He seemed normal—just an average man in average clothing. How in the world did he capture Naia's sister, and why was he keeping her in the pond behind his house?

He couldn't get away with it. I couldn't let that happen. And if I succeeded? I could tell Eamon. Maybe he'd been more open to letting me join his team instead of making me wait until after I finished school.

Amid my thoughts, my phone beeped. I grabbed my bag and shot a glance toward the house. The man on the deck didn't look in my direction. Heaving a sigh of relief, I opened my bag and checked my phone to see who had texted me. The name on the notification said *Jenna Beck*. It would have to wait. I put my phone down and watched the man.

He searched around the pond for a moment longer, then went back inside the house. The porch light flicked off. Crickets and bullfrogs resumed their calls. The man didn't return. I looked back at my phone to read the text.

Hey Olivia! Where you at? Wanna hang out? I just got done with a monstrous essay and I need some food!

The little nudge of reality from my school friend yanked me out of my daydreams. Who was I fooling? I was a college student. I had a life. I couldn't drop everything and dive into some random pond just to try and impress Eamon. I shook my head, typed out a response for Jenna, and turned away from the water. Marine biology was my future. Obtaining an internship, studying the ocean, finding my place in this weird world—these things made more sense. They felt secure, real, safe. And yet…

I turned back.

I couldn't just leave the poor creature trapped in the pond. If Eamon and the others *were* here, they'd jump in without question. A pang twinged in my heart. What would Samantha tell me to do?

The pond's leafy, lily surface sat placidly in the darkness. The songs of nocturnal wildlife grew louder. The early October temperatures weren't terribly low. A little pond water wouldn't hurt anyone. All I had to do was slip in, find the cage, and let her out. Naia herself said the pond wasn't deep. It couldn't be that hard in the dark, could it?

Several breaths went by. I glanced between the woods, the pond, the house, the empty road leading back to the city—where I'd have to hire a ride to get home—and back to the pond. I came this far. I might as well finish it. A burning of anticipation and fear engulfed my stomach. I took off my shoes and sweater and hid them with my cell phone and bag in the underbrush. Then I crouched down and crept closer to the pond. The frog calls lessened.

I dipped my hand into the cold water.

"If you're in there," I whispered, hoping she could hear me, "I'm here to help." Pressing my lips together and squeezing my eyes shut, I stepped into the pond. I gasped in the water—colder than I expected. My feet sank into the mud. The water soaked through my pants and shirt. I slipped under the surface. Night and murky water blinded me. Lily pad stems tangled around my outstretched hands. I pushed them aside and swam deeper into the pond, pausing once to take a breath before diving back under.

Soon, my fingers brushed metal. I felt along the thin bars of the cage—similar to a huge dog crate—when it rattled. A bubble of air burst from my mouth. I swam to the surface to get another breath, then dove under the surface again and swam back toward where I'd first felt the cage. I patted the metal bars as though to calm a wild animal and began searching for a latch. Why hadn't Naia's sister simply undone it herself? Then I remembered how Naia had described her. Maybe she didn't understand.

There. I'd found the latch. The cage rattled again, stronger this time. Something within it eked out a squealing call. It made me jump, but I continued working at the latch. A length of wire secured it. I untwisted it but ran out of breath before I could finish.

When I went up for air, the light in the house's back patio was on again. I gasped and buried myself under the water, hurrying as fast as I could to untwist the wire and undo the latch. The cage door opened, but only a few inches. The mud on the pond's uneven floor stopped it from opening all the way. I pulled hard, but then the prisoner squealed again and slammed through. Something scraped my arm.

"Ouch!" I cried. It came out as a huge bubble. Someone kicked past. I could feel the double current of two legs as she swam away. I pushed off the bottom and came through the surface just in time to see a person crawl out of the pond along the bank, get unsteadily to her feet, and stumble away. Her wet, filmy hair clung to her body down to her knees. She looked back once, only for a second. Her eyes flashed in the light from the patio. Then she ran.

"Who's there?" the same man from earlier shouted. He ran toward where the woman disappeared. Then he turned toward the pond. I ducked back into the water. My heart pounded. I couldn't stay in here long. I had to breathe.

I swam closer to the lily pads and poked my head above the shallow water to try and find the man. The area around the pond was empty. The frogs and crickets made no sound. I had to get out of here before he came back. Standing, I stepped as quietly as I could. Water dripped from my hair and clothes. I shivered and searched for my shoes and bag.

"Hey!" the man shouted from the trees across the pond. I scrambled into the bushes, frantically rifling through the branches to find my stuff. There! I grabbed it and ran, slipping on grass and bruising my feet on stray pebbles.

I came to the road. Streetlights lit the way. Would I be easier to spot under the lights? I checked over my shoulder. No one was in sight among all the foliage, but I couldn't stop. I kept running, keeping to the side of the road and out of the streetlights.

Ten minutes later, I sat on the curb outside a fast food restaurant to put my shoes on, but only found one. The other had fallen somewhere between here and the pond. I rubbed my face in frustration, then got my phone out to look up a ride service. It would set me back thirty bucks, but the last train south toward the university left long ago. I needed to get out of here fast. While I waited, still damp and smelling like pond water, I looked up at the sky and hoped Naia had found her sister, and that they both had found their way back to the ocean.

With my heart rate calmed, a missing shoe, a scraped arm, and small cuts on my bare foot, I took a deep breath and smiled.

I'd had misgivings. But I did it. And I had to tell Eamon.

3

The Loch Raven Strangler

Fluorescent lights hummed overhead in the Cambridge Hall student lounge, while a news program chattered from a television in the corner. The room smelled like day-old pizza. My unfinished lab write-up on the reproductive process of earthworms blurred in my notebook as my eyes glazed over. I shifted and leaned one elbow on my knee.

"I thought invertebrate zoology meant we'd get to study something cool," I said. Jenna chugged on an energy drink while our lab partner, Nathan, stretched from his spot on the couch.

"What, you don't like earthworms?" he asked.

I tossed my textbook onto the coffee table and kicked my legs over the chair's arm. "I'm sorry, but any animal with a sex life this boring that *still* gives us an extra three hours of lab work is not worth it."

They laughed. Jenna leaned her head back to look at me.

"At least it's not the writing class we took last semester," she said. "Remember that catastrophe?"

"How could I forget?" I said with a snicker, remembering the torturous class I took in the spring semester of my freshman year. I turned my head toward Nathan. "Our teacher smelled like B-O and compared everything to Shakespeare. Jenna was the only thing that kept me sane."

Nathan laughed again and stood. "I'm getting some food." He stuck his lab write up into his textbook and set it on a side table. "You ladies want anything?"

"No thanks," said Jenna, who took another gulp of her energy drink. I smiled and shook my head, my thoughts drifting as Nathan walked away. This was what I wanted, wasn't it? To be here, studying boring earthworms, instead of running around, helping Eamon solve the world's problems? I sighed to myself. Who was I kidding? Ever since the adventure at the pond, everything I thought I knew had flipped on its head. I pulled out my phone and checked my emails again. Nothing.

Two weeks had passed since the night I'd helped Naia rescue her sister from that pond. But instead of thanks, or even acknowledgment, the man I'd hoped would one day become my mentor had ghosted me. True, it had been a long time since our last communication, but that shouldn't matter. He had told me to contact him if I ever needed help. Why would he ignore this?

I looked back at my write-up but didn't really see it. Words from Eamon's previous emails came back to my mind: *You're too young. Get an education. My work is too dangerous. You're not ready.*

Well, he didn't need to say it this time. I could take a hint. The little adventure with Naia at the pond was just a fluke. A blip. Now that it was over, I could go back to finding my own life.

Shifting my position on the uncomfortable chair, I reached for my textbook on the coffee table. My gaze caught the television mounted in the corner. *Breaking News* flashed across the screen.

"What began as a shocking double murder near Loch Raven Reservoir early in September has turned into a stream of deadly attacks and a state-wide manhunt. After the initial attack, the assailant, nicknamed The Loch Raven Strangler, struck again in Hanover on October 2nd. The unidentified victim was the first in a renewed killing spree spanning through Baltimore and Howard Counties over the last few weeks."

I didn't hear the rest. Did she say October 2nd? I grabbed my phone and looked at the calendar to double check. Sure enough, October 2nd was a Friday—the day I was at the aquarium. The day I helped Naia's sister escape the pond. A serial killer had murdered someone in Hanover that night. Dread tingled in my chest.

"Olivia?" Jenna rapped the coffee table in front of me.

"Hm?" I looked away from the television and realized I still sat with one arm reaching for my textbook, my hand on the cover.

"You okay?" she asked. Nathan chewed on a candy bar, watching me with concern.

My pulse pounded in my throat as I nonchalantly picked up my textbook. "Fine. Why?"

"I said your name like three times. And your face just got really pale."

"Did I? I mean it? I mean…"

"What's wrong?" Nathan asked. I pretended a smile. I couldn't tell my friends why the news story had freaked me out. They didn't know I was in Hanover that night. What would I say? An unplanned detour to Hanover, for no reason, sounded bad enough—add the whole "trapped mermaid in a pond" thing and they'd either laugh or recommend a good therapist.

"Nothing," I said with a fake yawn, bottling up my fears and secrets yet again. "Just tired. I think I'll go up. You guys going to stay?"

"Yeah. I don't wanna go home," said Jenna. She took another sip from the tall aluminum can. "My roommate keeps nagging me to organize my shoes."

I gave a forced laugh. "At least you have a roommate."

"Are you kidding?" she asked. "I wish I had my own room."

"No, you don't," I said with more fake humor. "My room is so small, it's like someone dropped the ball on room assignments, so they made a dorm out of a supply closet."

She tilted her head with a thoughtful frown. "True."

"You sure you're okay?" Nathan asked me, scratching his auburn head. "Do you need someone to walk with you?"

"I'm fine," I lied, but gave him a grateful smile all the same. "Thanks though." I stood and gathered my things, then walked out of the student lounge and made my way to the dorm stairwell.

I neared the top of the last flight of stairs, lonely in my thoughts despite having just been with my friends. Then I hurried down the hall as though the loneliness and worry biting at my heels would jump up and make a grab for my neck.

Once in my room, I carelessly tossed my backpack to the floor, took off my sweatshirt, and slumped into my desk chair.

Deep breath.

I looked around my room, at my huge orca poster near my bed. Dozens of travel postcards from my free-spirited Aunt Shannon wallpapered the space beside it. I gazed at my betta fish, Minerva, in her little tank on the shelf above my desk, her blue fins flowing in the water.

A sudden weariness fell over my shoulders. I turned to my desk. My gaze strayed toward one of the drawers. I pulled it out and reached underneath a small stack of folded flyers, old syllabuses, and a letter from the school. Beneath them sat a bundle of emails I'd printed out so I could delete them from my computer, but still have them to reread. Leaning back in my chair and propping my feet on the desk, I started to read through the letters one at a time, even though I had read them many times before. The most recent one had arrived just before my adventure with Naia at the pond.

Hey Livvie-le-skivvie!

How's your summer going? I'm glad you get to go to the aquarium a lot. It sounds amazing! Do they name the sharks there? We don't get many sharks in our area. It's too cold and dark for them. They like the water nearer the surface, where all the food is. We get other pretty wicked fish though. I wish I could send you a picture! Lots of teeth.

Have you heard from Eamon at all?

I'd answered that question in my last letter to her. And I still hadn't heard from him. I scowled and read on.

...or anyone else from our insane adventure in San Diego? I miss you like crazy, and I wish I could tell you more about life down here.

Every letter had something along those lines mentioned at least once: "*Weather doesn't change much, but I won't go into detail.*" "*The you-know-what of you-know-where invited me to this sporting championship next week.*" "*I went somewhere so incredibly cool yesterday, but I'll have to wait until I see you to tell you about it.*" "*I can't say as much as I'd like to, but*

I'm really getting the hang of this new culture."

Even though every letter that arrived from my bestie brought me all kinds of excitement, they never brought me much solace. All her dancing around specifics was maddening.

I came to the next letter, one I'd received last year before going home for Christmas. A little over a year ago, a big explosion had occurred in the Mediterranean Sea. It had worried me, so I'd written to Sam asking about it. I'd written to Eamon too, but he never responded.

Liv,

Hey, bestie. To answer your first question, yes, we did hear about the explosion. I don't know who was all involved, but I do know some people died. No one we know. It was unbelievably sad. Everyone is shaken up about it, but don't worry. We're all okay. I can't go into much more than that in a letter.

And now for the next thing: What on earth is that stupid Scottish Neanderthal thinking? Too far of a distance, phsaw! And don't you give me that "it's all for the best" attitude because you're not fooling me for a second, Olivia Owens. What I want you to do right now is go put on your comfortable, holey sweatpants, get the most gigantic carton of peanut butter fudge ice cream you can find, and eat and curse Calder's name until you feel better.

I smiled to myself as I read the letter. Even from so far away, Samantha could read me like an open magazine. She even knew I had pigged out on peanut butter fudge ice cream after things between Calder Brydon and I had fizzled out. And I admit it...I cried into my pillow for days, skipped classes, and let my grades get crapped on. When my GPA suffered too much, I got a notice from the school saying if I didn't get my act together, I could kiss my scholarship goodbye.

That kicked my butt back into gear.

Jenna helped too, though I couldn't confide in her the entire truth about my best friend—or about the memories constantly gnawing at my soul. I never told her specifics about Calder, but she still helped to pull me out of my woe-is-me funk and swear off dating for the second time in my life.

And life went on, just like it always did after getting dumped by an adventurous, intelligent Scottish hottie. I wrinkled my brow for a moment at the thought. *Dumped*...can someone be dumped if there's nothing to be dumped from? I was never his girlfriend. Not really.

"I've moved on," I said aloud, looking up at Minerva. "Don't look at me like that. Hanging on to that guy was a mistake. And I barely even think about Calder anymore."

I sighed, picked up the stack of Samantha's letters, and threw them in the trash. Then I went back, pulled them all out, and put them back in the drawer. Collapsing my face into my hands, I longed for the one thing I couldn't have in this wide world: someone I could talk to—really talk to—without having to lie. Someone on my side of the planet. Someone besides an anti-social invertebrate.

4

The Visitor

Things hadn't improved much by that next Tuesday. Professor Seeley, my zoology professor and chief decision-maker of Hawaii internships, called me "Miss Olsen" after class. Again.

"It's Owens," I said, my heart sinking.

"Right, I am so sorry," she said, blinking her dark eyes as she gave me an apologetic smile. I sighed and shuffled toward the classroom door. I'd been in her class for two months and still she didn't know me from the next nameless student on her roster. I went out the door and walked sullenly up the hall. Jenna followed after me, holding a forty-four-ounce soda.

"What's with you?" she asked. She sipped from her straw.

"Professor Seeley keeps calling me 'Miss Olsen.'"

"So?" said Jenna. Nathan then joined us.

"*So?*" I went on. "She's on the marine biology board. She helps pick people for the Hawaii internship. I'm never going to stand out to her if she can't even remember my name."

"You'll get the internship," said Nathan. "You run circles around all of us."

I raised my eyebrows at him. "It's easy for you to say. Professor Seeley loves you."

He shrugged. "She knows my dad from their college days. It's not anything I did."

We walked outside and I folded my arms against the cold. As the weeks had passed deeper into October, an unseasonable chill had crept into College Park, Maryland. The sun struggled behind thick cloud cover and a frigid breeze blew the red and goldenrod leaves on the sidewalk.

Nathan turned to go to his next class in another direction.

"Oh, and Olivia, thanks for helping me study for that quiz," he said as he backed into the direction he was going.

"No problem," I replied with a smile. "See you later?"

"Definitely," he replied.

Jenna and I continued down the sidewalk. "Wish I had connections like he does. Test scores only get you so far. Most of my professors treat me like I'm invisible."

"Then quit being invisible," said Jenna. "A girl in my philosophy class last year went at it with the teacher about organized religion—she ended up acing her final with 106%."

"Wow. So, all I have to do is stand up and argue?" I wrinkled my nose.

"No," said Jenna. "You need to tell the teacher what they want to hear. Sometimes they want an argument, sometimes shameless butt-kissing."

Oh, was that all?

"But how do I know which one it is?" I said, kicking at pebbles on the sidewalk with more force than they deserved.

"Practice?" Jenna offered. She looked at her phone. "I gotta go. Don't let it get you down, girl."

I smiled gratefully as she turned down an adjacent sidewalk. Then I sighed.

"Practice."

I never thought I was bad at reading people until I had to do it without Samantha. Maybe I could write to her and ask for advice. But a letter would take weeks or even months to arrive. By then, the internship application would be long overdue.

Your best friend is gone, said my head. *Put on your big girl pants and deal with this.*

Hitching my bag higher on my shoulder, I quickened my stride. I had thirty minutes before Organic Chemistry, and I would probably need to remind that professor what my name was too.

Wednesday. Blueberry muffin day. Footnotes Café, just off the McKeldin Library, always baked fresh ones on Wednesday mornings. I got up early to get ready for school, looking forward to munching on a muffin while breathing fresh, book-scented air. I hurried down the stairs, my footsteps echoing on the steps. When I passed the dorm lounge on my way to the front doors, I heard my name.

"Hey Olivia," said Darci, the resident advisor for my floor. "Did you see this?" She nodded toward the television in the lounge, her brow knit. I stopped to watch.

"*The murder in Laurel Monday night and the attack at Greenbelt Lake last night have both been linked to the work of the Loch Raven Strangler.*"

Uneasiness quirked in my stomach. The serial killer was getting closer. The news anchor continued:

"*We have no further details at this time, but we urge the citizens in Prince George's and Anne Arundel counties to be on their guard. Avoid going outside alone after nightfall. Police want to reassure the community that they are doing everything they can to keep us safe.*"

Darci shook her head with a frown, tossing her blue-streaked hair and fiddling with her black-rimmed glasses.

"Let's just hope the police catch that psycho before he hurts anyone else."

"Yeah," I said with another twist of anxiety. "I gotta go, Darci, I'm going to be late for class."

"Be careful out there."

"I will."

"Oh, and Olivia?"

"Hm?"

"I almost forgot. Someone came by late last night looking for you."

A thousand questions took over my brain. Who would come looking for me? Besides Naia. Holy crap, did she come back? Did she need help again? How did she know where I lived? Had I told her? I couldn't remember.

"Olivia?"

"What? Oh. Um, who was it?"

Darci shrugged. "I don't know. She came in and asked if you lived here and wanted to know which room you were in. I didn't tell her though. We never give that information out to strangers. I think she snuck in with a group of people because she didn't have a key card."

"What did she look like?"

Darci looked up in recollection. "Um, about your age. Brown hair, about this long." She gestured to a spot just below her shoulders.

"Oh." Didn't sound like Naia. "She didn't leave a name?"

"Nope. Just said you didn't know each other and she'd try back later."

I frowned. "Weird." I didn't care about the weirdness though. The weirder the better. As frustrated as I had been with Eamon, I still missed him and the others. Seidon, Captain Cordelia, Walter, Natasha, Uther... and Calder. No, not Calder. But I longed to hear from everyone else. Because of the amount of secrecy that always surrounded my old friends, maybe this meant they were back. Hope flared even brighter inside me.

"She seemed friendly enough," Darci continued, "but we have a policy. And with these news reports..." She jerked her head toward the TV again.

"Right," I said. "Maybe she's from one of my classes or something."

"Should I have security keep an eye out?"

"No, it's fine. Thanks, Darci."

I headed off to Footnotes to grab my muffin and ate it on the way to Calculus. But with my pile of worries now mounting higher, I couldn't enjoy the sweet combo of blueberries and cake as much as I normally would have.

As I walked, I wondered about my mysterious visitor—who it could have been and why they'd come. Worries about my professors and what Jenna had said about people-pleasing also took up space in my thoughts.

Did my calc teacher, Professor Cunningham, prefer fighters or sycophants in his kingdom of formulas and functions? When I walked into his class, I sat down and watched the balding man with glasses that made his eyes really small. Then I watched for clues. He never paused from talking, except to fire a question at unsuspecting students. He never acknowledged anyone by name, just pointed at them with two fingers and said "you," whenever he wanted an answer. My head felt like a swirling bowl of numbers and cold mush by the time class ended.

Literature, way off across campus, started soon after Calc.

I suffered through—I mean, *listened*—to Professor Trafford's lecture and tried to do the same unqualified behavior assessment I'd done in Calc. Argue or butt-kiss? I got nothing. Her smooth cheeks and light eyes made her look like a suburban soccer mom, while her short, styled white hair gave her the look of a strict fashion mogul. When class was over and the flurry of departure began, Professor Trafford moved from her lecture podium to the table beside it.

"Don't forget, due next week: five-page analysis on the underlying themes behind the first half of our readings of Brontë," she said.

I stuffed my paperback copy of *Wuthering Heights* into my bag with a silent snarl. Even though the class had nothing to do with my animal sciences major, I still had to take it to appease the quacks on the board of education. I'd rather stare at a specimen in a glass tank all day than analyze the pointless woes of Catherine what's-her-face.

"Olivia?" said Professor Trafford. The only teacher who remembered my name. My stomach growled, but I turned and put on an *I'm-not-hungry-or-cranky-or-hating-your-class-at-all* face.

"Yes?"

"I noticed you sent me a request for a letter of recommendation," she said as she shifted a stack of books on the cluttered table next to her podium.

"Yeah…I needed a character reference from someone outside the field. It's for a marine biology internship."

"Oh." She looked up. "How impressive. When is this internship?"

"Next semester."

"Well, I'd love to hear more about it when you get a chance. And I'll make sure to get you that recommendation." She shuffled a stack of papers on the table, shifted another stack, looked under a textbook, and patted the pockets of her khaki suit pants. "Now where did my glasses go?"

"On your head," I replied, pointing. She grabbed them and laughed.

"My goodness, where is my brain? Thank you."

"Anytime," I said and hurried out as fast as my food-deprived legs would take me to the nearest club sandwich.

I walked into Footnotes to order the blessed sandwich and spotted Nathan at a table, reading from a book and nibbling on potato chips. He looked up and waved. I waved back before going to the counter to get my food, then took it back to his table.

"Hey," I said sitting down. "This seat taken?"

"It is now," he replied. He closed the book and placed it next to his bag of chips. I sighed, dropped my backpack from my shoulder, and slipped into my seat.

"Studying for midterms?" I asked, nodding to his book, titled *Hawaiian Coastal Flora*. He shrugged.

"It's a book Seeley gave me for 'light reading.'" He made quotation marks with his fingers.

"Ha. Yeah." I didn't admit I'd read that book last summer. For fun. "Are you going to go for the internship?"

"It's *Hawaii.* Of course I'm going for it."

"But aren't you studying to be a vet? For horses?"

He shrugged with a sheepish smile. "It'll still look good on vet school applications. Imagine if we both got it."

I huffed as I unwrapped my sandwich. "Put in a good word for me when you do get picked. If I don't get enough professor recommendations, I'm not going. And if I don't go, I..." I trailed off and took a bite of sandwich. I didn't want to think about not getting the internship. Studying the ocean, living in paradise closer to Sam—it was the only logical thing for me to pursue. Thinking about Samantha made me remember the mysterious visitor who'd come looking for me at my dorm. Had it been Sam? No, it couldn't be. She'd have called first for sure. Unless she didn't have access to a phone.

"Come on." Nathan interrupted my reverie. "You'll get it." He dug a chip from the little bag on the table. I smiled, mouth still full. Nathan fingered the bag of chips, a pensive look on his face.

I swallowed. "What's wrong?"

"Oh, nothing," he replied. He cleared his throat and shifted in his chair. I paused from taking another bite of my sandwich and watched him. With a scowl, he wet his lips and started cracking the joints in his fingers one by one as though preparing to throw a pitch in a baseball game. Jenna and I had been friends with Nathan since we were assigned lab partners in Zoology this semester. I'd never seen him so nervous.

"So..." He began.

"So," I echoed with a slow nod of encouragement. "Is everything okay?"

"Are-you-busy-Saturday-night?"

He said it really fast. I wanted to burst out laughing but held it in. His question wasn't funny at all—only the way he said it.

"Um, no," I said. Was Nathan asking me out?

"Because I just was wondering if you wanted to go get some dinner. With me."

He *was* asking me out.

"Oh. Okay."

"Yeah?" his face brightened. "Great. I'll come by around seven."

"Sounds good."

"Good." He nodded. "Great. Uh. I'll see you later?"

"Sure," I said, still trying not to laugh. He gathered his things, left me with a small smile, and darted out of the café. I looked back at my sandwich with a mixture of confusion and amusement. I had no idea Nathan was interested in me that way. He was a sweet guy. We seemed to have a lot in common. But it was only a casual dinner. It didn't mean anything was going to come of it. We were just friends.

Wait. I frowned at my sandwich. Was I making excuses? Desire for dating had been thin to nonexistent my entire freshman year. Maybe I was just out of practice. Or…

Calder's face just *had* to sail into my mind at that moment. I did a gentle shake of the head as though to clear the mental picture like a vapor. *Snap out of it, you dummy. He lives across an ocean. You haven't seen him for over a year.*

No, the real reason I made excuses was because I needed to focus on my school work. I had to keep my priorities straight. Right. That was it. Nothing more.

Calder was never coming back.

5

The Other Visitor

"Please remember, the application for my internship next year is due by the beginning of next week," said Professor Seeley at the end of her lecture Thursday morning. "The sooner the better, people! And another reminder that office hours have changed from Tuesdays at two pm to Mondays at ten am."

"So, Saturday?" said Nathan, as though I'd forgotten in the last twenty-four hours. I nodded as I packed my stuff into my backpack.

"Yeah, definitely," I replied with a smile.

"Awesome." He dashed off, his ears red.

"Finally," Jenna asked. She grinned at me over the plastic cover of her large latte.

"Finally?"

"He's been wanting to ask you out for weeks." Jenna sipped the latte and flung her bag over her shoulder. "Glad he finally manned up. I was getting a little tired of him asking me for advice."

"Really? I—"

"I gotta go, I have to talk to my anatomy professor before he leaves his office hours. See you in lab?"

"Okay." What I wanted to say was something like *how long has this been going on*? Or *I'm really bad at dating, how about some pointers*? I wished for Samantha. And time. I needed time to process.

Professor Seeley started packing her briefcase. I approached her desk, wondering yet again what kind of student she preferred. Ew, that made her sound like a college-level cannibal.

Get your head in the game, Liv.

"Professor Seeley?" I asked.

She looked up at me. "Yes, Miss Olsen."

I tried not to let my shoulders sag. "It's Owens. Olivia Owens."

"Right." She waved a manicured hand and chuckled. "What can I do for you?"

"I was wondering if I could include time at the aquarium on my application for the Hawaii internship? I wanted to write a paper on it."

"Oh. Yes, you can include that."

"Great. Thank you."

"Just make sure it's turned in by the end of next week." She picked up a briefcase and stood.

"Oh, and I just wanted to say I really enjoyed *Hawaiian Coastal Flora*," I said quickly. "I read it last summer."

Shameless butt-kissing it is.

She nodded slowly. "Good, I'm glad you liked it." She turned and walked out the door. I cringed.

Shameless butt-kissing it isn't, I guess.

At long last, just two minutes before the clock chimed the café's closing time, I typed a lackluster conclusion to my essay for Lit. I saved the stupid thing to my files, chucked my copy of *Wuthering Heights* into my bag, and walked out of Footnotes.

Outside, the night air hit me like a bucket of cold water. I hurried down the sidewalk toward Cambridge hall, passing buildings with windows staring like bright, square-shaped eyes. Lampposts covered in old stickers cast their circles of golden light over the sidewalk.

As I cut across a wide square of grass around the northwest corner of the Cambridge Community, a chilled breeze rushed by. I hugged my coat tighter around me, hurried up the steps to the entrance, swiped my key card, and pulled the handle of one of the big oak double doors. But it didn't open. I tried the other door; it wouldn't move either. Nonplussed, I swiped my card again and pulled on both handles at the same time. Someone had locked up early.

I groaned in frustration.

"No! Come on!" I tugged on the doors again, then turned on my heel and trudged over some soggy grass along the building to find another entrance. Passing window after dark window, my mind went back to the conversation I had had with Darci and the advice the newscasters had given everyone: *Be careful. Don't wander alone at night.* But I was right outside my building. Nothing to worry about. No one was going to attack me in the middle of campus. I rounded the corner to the building's side entrance. Light from the lampposts didn't reach here. The shadows fell deeper. Sudden urgency to get inside came over me.

"Calm down," I said to myself, swiped my card, and pulled the door handle. It was locked too. I knocked again. No one came. Turning quickly to go back to the front door, I stopped and cried out.

About twenty yards away, someone stood watching me from beside a large, decorative shrub. The sight of the person had startled me, but I shrugged it off. I needed to get a grip.

Then the figure moved. Slow at first, but gaining speed, she limped across the sidewalk toward me, keeping in the shadows. She seemed familiar. Her long hair hung almost to her knees like a silvery mantle. Naia's sister. Why was she here? Why wasn't she back in the ocean with Naia? I backed into the door and tried to open it again, to no avail.

She came closer. Her bare feet slapped on the pavement. Then I gasped. Her face—had it always looked like that? Her eyes bugged out like two huge moons beneath a ridge of hairless brow. Her teeth looked like shark teeth—rows of jagged, mottled spikes sticking out from a wide, dripping mouth. Slack and nightmarish, her face sent my heart into a panic rhythm. I pounded on the door. A smell arose, like rotting fish and bad breath.

"Let me in! Someone, please!" I looked back. Her mouth opened in a grotesque leer. "*What do you want?*" I cried. Her only reply was a gurgling growl.

"Help!" I banged my fists on the door as the woman closed the space between us with lopsided but quick loping strides. I whimpered. Her hands curled claw-like in front of her. She growled again. I shrieked.

The door fell open behind me. I stumbled back, scrambled around it, and crumpled as the door banged shut. Snarling screams sounded on the other side of the door for a moment, then went silent. I looked up from between my arms.

"What the hell was that?" said my savior. Her streak of blue hair came into focus first. Darci.

"Uh...uh..." I replied in a choking whisper.

"This door is locked earlier these days. Your key card will only work on the front doors."

"They were locked too."

"Really? I'll have to check into that. They're not supposed to be locked until one. Are you all right?"

"Yeah." I stood. She listened at the door for a second, then opened it a crack. An immediate surge of new panic shook me. "No!"

Darci peeked out the door. "Well, whoever it was, they're gone now. What a sick joke to play on a person. Might've given you a heart attack."

My breath came fast. The fishy smell lingered even though there was no sign of the strange, terrible monster. Darci shut the door and looked at me.

"You sure you're okay?" she asked.

"Yeah. I'm fine," I lied.

"I'll walk with you." She must have noticed me still shaking. She led the way down the long corridor. I followed, trying to force my heart rate back to normal as I pondered on what I had just seen.

That person outside—that *thing*—was horrible. Naia's sister didn't have a face like that. Did she? I racked my brain, trying to remember back to that night. She'd looked back at me after leaving the water. I saw her eyes flash, reflecting the light from the house. But beyond that...she'd been too far away.

She couldn't have been Naia's sister. Could she? Or was it just a nasty joke like Darci suggested? Either way, I hurried up to my dorm room and locked the door behind me. I stripped off my bag, coat, and shoes, and buried myself in my bed. Shivering, I continued to wonder—what *was* that thing?

6

Purple Fingernails

Every time I closed my eyes to attempt sleep, I saw that face snarling at me from behind my eyelids. I tossed and turned, my mind buzzing with a combination of trepidation and puzzlement. Why did she come after me? Was she really after *me,* or could it have been a random attack?

Of one thing I was certain: with a face like that, she couldn't have been human.

And then there was the person Darci had sent away. Maybe someone had come to warn me. Cordelia? No, Darci said the woman's hair was medium length, and from what I knew of Cordelia, she would never have cut her waist-length locks. Someone else? Maybe…but I couldn't begin to guess who. It didn't make sense.

Well, nothing ever made sense when dealing with creatures that weren't supposed to exist. If I hadn't gone to San Diego that summer, I'd never have known they existed either. It was a secret I'd kept since the moment I saw them break the surface of the ocean two summers ago. A secret that kept breaking the surface of my mind and tormenting me at unexpected moments.

Sometimes, even after so long, I could still hear their voices. Faint, more like a memory than anything else, but still there, in the back of my mind. It reached me when I stared out at the ships crossing the horizon of Chesapeake Bay on a quiet morning. Sometimes it came before I fell asleep at night. Every time I visited the Baltimore Aquarium, I stared through the thick, cold glass into the blue-gray water and wondered if the life behind the window had ever heard them. Even now, my mind searched back to the time I had been there, listening, marveling at the songs of the creatures from the deep.

I didn't notice that I had fallen asleep until my alarm clock jolted me out of a dream I'd been having about the merpeople—Captain Cordelia with her stern arrogance and loyalty, Prince Seidon with his eager curiosity about human life, and Samantha...

I blinked several times in the dim dorm room, half-seeing the faces of my old friends swimming in front of me. Exhaustion clawed at my brain, but I couldn't force my watering eyes to close. Again, the image of the thing that had come after me last night jumped out of my imagination.

There was nothing else to do. I had to try contacting Eamon again. Maybe this time he would answer.

I sat down at my computer, opened up my email account, and began drafting another message for the old Irish doctor/mermaid guardian. It took me a long time, trying to make the situation sound as dire as I felt it was, without naming specifics.

After several drafts, I reread the finished product:

Dear Eamon,

You must be pretty busy, and I hate to bother you again, but I needed to write to you about something that happened last night. I hoped you might be able to explain it.

Someone paid a little visit. I don't know who she is or what she wants, but she doesn't seem very nice. I can't be sure, but does Cordelia have any relatives that are on the meaner side?

I'd like to help out wherever it's needed. Please let me know what I should do. Say hello to the others for me.

~Olivia

In my last letter to Eamon, it had been a lot harder to describe helping Naia without actually coming out and saying the word "mermaid." I looked over this new email several times. I couldn't say too much in case it was intercepted by someone like Doran Linnaeus, who thought a mermaid exhibit would make a great addition to his failing theme park. Linnaeus had been willing to kill anyone who stood in his way. Linnaeus was dead, but I couldn't take any chances in case there were more people in the world like him.

"I'm not being paranoid," I said to Minerva. "You'd feel the same way if you'd seen what I've seen."

The letter seemed okay to me, so I hit *send*, hoping that wherever Eamon was, he'd be able to check his emails soon. And that this time, he'd reply.

I sighed and shut my laptop.

I faked sick to avoid going outside that day. Jenna and Nathan both texted me a couple times. Lying to them made my skin crawl. And every time I thought about the assignments I'd get behind on, my gut twisted a little tighter. But I couldn't go outside. I checked my emails about once a minute that day. Still no reply from Eamon.

After seeing the empty inbox again Saturday morning, I slumped back in my chair with an angry huff. I glared at Minerva.

"I don't care if it's only been twenty-four hours," I said as I got up to drop some fish food into her tank. "What does he have against answering emails? Even if he's off on some mermaid rescuing mission, he should at least take two minutes to find a Wi-Fi signal every once in a while."

I sighed at my fish and put her food away. Someone knocked on my door. I got up and answered it. Jenna stood there, holding a flowery shirt in one hand and a tall, metal coffee tumbler in the other.

"Hi," I said and stepped aside to let her in.

She smiled and tossed her long brown hair. "Just bringing your shirt back. You feeling any better?" She went to my closet to hang up the shirt. It had once belonged to Samantha. Jenna didn't know that. Jenna didn't know anything about Samantha.

"Yeah. Thanks," I said, trying to swallow down my frustration with Eamon's silence so she wouldn't ask why I was so grouchy. I went back to my desk, shut my laptop, and reached down to plug it in to charge.

"Whoa. Have you always had that scar?"

I froze and looked down at my tank top. Preoccupation with the email and the scary shark-lady drove the exposed scar on my shoulder completely from my mind.

"Always had what scar?" I asked, even though I knew what she referred to. The round, nickel-sized, puckered scar wasn't exactly hard to miss. I reached for a sweater laying at the foot of my bed and slipped it on.

"On your shoulder. It's huge! I've never noticed it before. What happened?"

"Nothing," I said. She sipped her coffee with a snort.

"Right, a pimple scar is nothing. *That* looks like a..."

"*It's just a scar, Jenna,*" I snapped. She closed her mouth, her eyes wide.

"Sorry."

Guilt dropped like a heavy coin on my head. I sighed.

"No, I'm sorry," I replied in a quiet voice. "It's just not something I like to talk about."

"I hope nothing bad happened."

I smiled a little, even though the fact was, a horrific thing had happened. But I was never going to tell Jenna, or anyone, the truth about the gunshot wound. One of Linnaeus's men had done it. Though Eamon had stepped in and helped it to heal with miraculous speed, I still carried the bullet's mark.

"I've got one on my arm," said Jenna quickly. She bent her arm and showed me some jagged pink lines circling her elbow. "I got it from barbed wire, but this cute guy in my anatomy class thinks it looks like a shark bite."

"Ooh, stick to the shark bite story," I said, trying to make up for snapping at her. "Way more interesting."

"I haven't been in the ocean much. I don't know if that'll work."

"Wait, aren't you from Boston?" I asked. "You're near the coast."

She shrugged. "Too much sun gives you wrinkles."

I laughed. "That didn't stop me. I lived six hours from the ocean growing up, and I couldn't get enough of it."

"Well, you'll make a good marine biologist." She kicked back on my bed and sipped her coffee. "So, are you excited about your *date* tonight?" she asked with a grin and a wiggle to her eyebrows. Grateful she seemed over my outburst, but confused at her question, I frowned.

"Date?" It took a second to remember. "Right! With Nathan." My eyes slipped out of focus. I couldn't go out with Nathan! That thing was still out there. I relaxed my face to hide my inner foreboding.

"Yeah," Jenna continued, oblivious to my scattered thoughts as she looked at the postcards on the wall from Aunt Shannon. "He told me he wants to get to know you. Figure you out."

"Figure me out? What's that supposed to mean?"

Jenna shrugged. "I don't know. We're girls, not Sudoku puzzles. So, you excited?"

"Yeah. Nathan's a nice guy."

"Where are you going?"

"Um, just dinner I guess."

Jenna gave me a sideways glance. "You sure you're excited?"

"Yeah," I said quickly. I cleared my throat. "It's just...been a while since I've gone on a date. What should I wear?" I got up to go to my closet, grateful that the subject had safely moved on from my scar. Next step: figuring out how to get through tonight without getting mauled by a shark-woman.

I couldn't fake sick this time. Jenna knew I was "feeling better." So, at seven, I answered another knock on my door.

"Hi, Nathan," I said, my eyes immediately drawn to the long-stemmed rose in his hand. Oh, wow. He was going all out.

"Hi, Olivia. You—you look pretty." He gave me a nervous smile as he handed me the rose.

"Thanks. It's beautiful. Um, let me put it in some water." Water. I looked around my room until I spotted a half-empty plastic bottle of water. I grabbed it, unscrewed the lid, and stuck it on my desk with the rose looking out of proportion both in size and in elegance inside it.

Awkward. That's how the rose looked—and how I felt as I walked along the dorm hallway next to Nathan in complete silence. We were friends. We always had stuff to talk about. But now, it was as if some unsettling cloud of dumb had drifted over us. And ever-present, lurking behind me like a stalker: the dread of going outside. The vision of the terrible shark-faced woman reared again in my head.

"So. How was class this week?" Nathan asked.

"Um, good. You?"

"Good."

"That's good."

Cue the chirping crickets. This was a bad idea.

We continued down the many flights of stairs till we got to the ground floor. He held the door open. Cold air rushed at me and I shivered, hesitating on the threshold.

"You okay?" he asked.

"Yeah. Fine." I stepped outside, folding my arms against the cold and the fear. I looked in all directions.

"How are you doing with your internship application?" Nathan asked.

"Good," I replied. "I finally got one of my professors to write me a letter of recommendation. She's a little absentminded, but she's the only professor who's given me the time of day. She seems supportive."

"That's great. You'll be training dolphins in San Diego in no time."

I smiled but shook my head. "Actually, I think I'll try to stay in Hawaii once the internship is over. The East Coast is too cold, and California is too...overrated. How's the application for you?"

He talked about his own application, as well as some of the undergrad work he did on the campus farm to the east of the Cambridge Community dorms. We walked along the aptly named Farm Drive, and past the big, red barns and brown fences enclosing the land animals on our way to the nearest student parking lot. The smell didn't bother me too much, especially since it had lessened in the colder weather.

"And there are some fistulated cows there too," said Nathan. "They have holes in their stomachs so we can study their anatomy and their digestion."

I cringed. "Doesn't that hurt them?"

"Nope. You should come see it sometime. It's cool."

"I wonder if they can do something like that on a dolphin," I said as we continued walking down the sidewalk, past the farm, to an adjoining street called Regents Drive, and toward the parking lot. The weird, first-date-between-just-friends iciness started to melt. A little. But always on the back of my mind was that face. The snarling, the clutching fingers, the crazy eyes. I thought of my email to Eamon and wondered when he would answer it. I couldn't wait much longer.

"Olivia?"

"Hm?"

"What's the matter?" Nathan stood holding the passenger door of a blue sedan open for me. I'd been looking over my shoulder, searching.

"Oh. Sorry." I slid into the car, noting Nathan's confused expression. He got into the driver's seat without a word.

"I hope you like seafood," he said as he backed the car out of the space. I held back a snort at the irony.

"Yeah, it's great. Thanks for taking me out."

"No problem."

The silence trickled on as we drove away from the university, while I wondered if things would ever be normal between us.

"Um…any plans after midterms?" I asked. Nathan shrugged.

"Not really. You?"

"Oh I don't know. I'll probably just hang out by the coast like I usually do."

"I've never known anyone so obsessed with oceans," Nathan said with a grin. I smiled back.

"If only you knew." I didn't mean to say it out loud. And did it sound as wistful to him as it did to me? I wanted to palm my face.

"What?"

I shook my head. "Nothing."

We sat for a few minutes, Nathan driving in silence and me feeling guilty that this night was turning into a disaster.

"I've just had lots of cool experiences with the ocean," I began, then tensed. I couldn't reveal too much, so I backpedaled. "It fascinates me. You know."

"It fascinates me too, but on breaks, I like to *take a break*. Like a normal person."

I shrugged. "For me, the ocean is my break."

We pulled into the parking lot of a restaurant. "There's so much we don't know about it. Ecosystems within ecosystems. We've barely scratched the surface. Doesn't that make you wonder?"

"I've never really thought about it." Nathan pulled the car into a parking space. "But yeah, I guess so." We got out of the car and walked to the entrance, where he held the door open for me. He approached the hostess's station in the center of the entrance. No one was there, so we waited. Nathan leaned against the wood and drummed his fingers."Wonder where the greeter person is."

"Who knows, maybe they're just—" I stopped cold. I caught sight of Nathan's hand, fingers tapping out an unheard beat on the hostess's station. Fingers that were unremarkable except that they ended in fingernails tinged with dark purple.

Purple fingernails.

I gasped.

"What?" Nathan asked, looking around as if I'd seen a spider. I swallowed, still staring at his hand. Then I looked at his neck. He wore a coat and scarf. Had he always worn a coat and scarf? No. But I'd never noticed. How did I never notice?

"Nathan?" I squeaked.

"What's the matter?" he asked, concern now creasing his forehead. I had to ask. But I couldn't ask outright.

"Um..." I stammered, looking back at his fingernails. "Are you thirsty?"

"Uh, a little but I'm fine, thanks."

"What about shrimp?" Merpeople didn't eat shrimp.

"Yeah, you can get some shrimp."

"No, for you," I said.

"Ugh, no. Shrimp is gross. I love salmon though." He laughed. What kind of game was he playing? Anger boiled in my chest as I grabbed for his hand and looked again at his fingernails. Purple. I let go. Nathan held on. A hostess approached us and asked if we wanted a table.

"Yes, for two," said Nathan without looking away from me. The hostess turned to gather some menus while Nathan held onto my hand. "Are you okay?"

"No, I'm not," I finally admitted. "Why haven't—"

"This way," said the hostess. Nathan let go of my hand and followed the hostess. I followed too, but numbly. He kept glancing at me over his shoulder. I stared at him, studying for any more signs that my assumption was correct.

How could I have been friends with a merperson for half a semester and not known it?

7

In Which I Freak Out

My menu shook in my hands. I kept looking up at the guy sitting across from me. I watched him sip his water as he perused his menu. *All this time.* Why hadn't he told me? How did I not notice until now? His fair skin. His light eyes. His interest in marine biology even though he wanted to be a vet for land animals.

He looked up. "What?"

"Where are you from again?" I asked.

"Long Island. I've told you before, haven't I?"

"Oh. Yeah, you have." I lowered my eyes to my menu and scanned the entrees while trying to figure out a way to clue him in. He needed to know he could trust me. *I know about merpeople. I'm safe to confide in.*

"And you're from Arizona, right?" he asked. I nodded. "That's pretty cool. I've never seen a cactus before."

I huffed. "And you never will."

He put his menu down. "What's that supposed to mean?"

"Sorry." I just realized how rude that sounded. "I mean, Arizona is *really* dry. It rains, like, seven days out of the whole year."

"Ugh."

"Yeah." Now I was getting somewhere. "It'd be uncomfortable for... someone like you." I watched him for his reaction. He knit his eyebrows.

"Someone like me?"

Stop denying it already!

"Have you ever been to Zydrunas?" I asked.

"Uh, where?" His face went blank. I'd hoped he'd recognize the word.

"Why don't you just come out and say it, Nathan?"

He frowned and tossed his menu aside. "Say what?"

"You can tell me the truth. I already know about it."

He sat back in his chair, a slight flush coloring his face. "You do?"

Finally, he was admitting it. I huffed in disbelief.

"Yes. And it's kind of incredible."

Several seconds passed. He smiled and shook his head. Then he reached across the table for my hand. I let him take it, looking at the purple fingernails and wondering where he'd come from and why he was here. He must have come for a reason. It couldn't be a coincidence that we became friends. Maybe he came here because the merpeople knew me, and that I could be trusted. The thought warmed my heart.

"So, what brought you here?" I asked.

"I don't know. Luck, I guess." He laced his fingers through mine. "But I'm glad it finally happened." I gave his hand a squeeze, then let go.

The waitress approached.

"Are we ready to order?" she asked.

"Nothing with shrimp," I said with a grin at Nathan. He laughed. After that, he changed the subject, so I followed his lead and talked about other stuff.

After dinner, we drove back to campus. I got out of the car and met Nathan in front of it, where he put his arm around my shoulders.

"Thanks for dinner," I said. "You didn't drink much water, though. Are you sure you're okay?"

"I'm fine."

"I guess spending enough time here makes it easier, right? You'll still be able to go home whenever you want, won't you?"

He looked a little confused, but nodded. "Yeah, why wouldn't I?"

"Things must be different where you're from."

"Or maybe Arizona girls just need to get out more." He hugged me to his side. We continued walking down the sidewalk near the barns and fences, and had reached the corner of Regents and Farm when it happened:

"*Olivia.*"

"Hm?" I said, looking at Nathan.

He shook his head. "I didn't say anything."

I stopped walking and looked around as if someone had just tapped me on my shoulder and ran. The chilled breeze lifted my hair. I shivered.

"What's wrong?" Nathan asked.

"Nothing." But still, I kept a wary eye on our surroundings as we continued. The shark-woman was still out there somewhere. Did Nathan know her? Did he know Naia? I opened my mouth to ask when I heard it again:

"*Olivia.*"

I whirled around.

"What's the matter?" Nathan asked, a note of annoyance rising in his tone.

"That voice," I said. "You didn't hear it?"

"No."

"It's like it was…" I trailed off. *It was in my head.* I kept turning, searching every shadow, every tree, every golden-leafed shrub. Nothing.

"Olivia, you've been acting weird all night. What is going on?"

"I don't know. But I really did hear something. Maybe they just weren't talking to you. But why are they talking to me?"

"You're not making any sense."

I looked around, backward and forward, left, right, searching. He grabbed my hand.

"Olivia."

I stopped. He took a step closer to me. Then another, until he stood a breath away. Whoa. Was that what all the hand-holding at the restaurant was about? I thought he was just being nice.

"Nathan…"

He let go of my hand and put his hands tentatively on my waist. A low simmer started somewhere in my stomach as his eyes flicked to my mouth. I'd been so lonely for so long. Was I about to kiss a merman? Wait, did I even want to? What was I supposed to do? This was Nathan. I didn't want to lose him as a friend. And I couldn't let any distractions—

He leaned in. I put my hand on his chest with a pang of longing. I couldn't tell if it was for Nathan or physical closeness in general. Just then, Calder's face rose to the surface of my mind. I shut my eyes as though trying to shut him out. It didn't work.

"Wait." I shrunk away when I couldn't figure out my battling emotions. My hormones beat me with a stick, and my brain frowned like my strictest professor, as if waiting for me to screw up. I swallowed, looking away. Then I saw something: moonlight glinting on a silvery head. Behind some bushes on the other side of the street, two wide eyes, like lamps, shone out of the darkness. My stomach jumped to my throat as I gasped.

"What's the matter?" Nathan asked.

"Run!"

I grabbed his hand and yanked him to a run. We hurried down the street to our dorm building. Any minute now, I'd hear snapping, shark-like jaws, feel the harrow of talons in my back, or hear Nathan scream if she got him first. I scurried up the steps, nearly tripped on the last one, and pushed Nathan toward the doors.

"Get inside!" I shouted. He swiped his key card and pulled the door open. I darted inside after him and slammed the door behind us. I held my back against it, my chest heaving. Nathan watched me in alarm. And he wasn't the only one. Several other people standing around the lobby stared at me as though I had just puked live birds.

"What was that about?" said Nathan as he caught his breath. I couldn't explain right now—not with all these people watching. I stepped away from the door.

"I'm sorry. I just saw something. It scared me."

"What was it?" Nathan asked, looking out the window. I shook my head. Then the door opened and I shrieked like a rusty hinge while bemused but innocent people walked in through the door. I rubbed my forehead with a prickle of embarrassment. Nathan went outside.

"No, don't!"

After a minute, he reappeared. "It's okay. There's no one out there."

He led me to a chair. "Sit down."

"What's her deal?" someone sneered from across the room.

"I'll have what she's having," said another, earning more laughter from his friends. I shook my head and covered my face.

"What did you see out there?" Nathan asked.

"I saw," I began, trying to ignore the listening ears and snickering. "I don't know; maybe I just imagined it. Maybe it was just shadows. I've been paranoid lately."

"You know," a guy wearing his hat backwards and a too-tight tee shirt said nearby, pointing toward me. "I've got more if you're looking to buy. Great stuff. Real high quality."

I rolled my eyes in disgust and stood. If the person I saw in the bushes had been the mer-malformation, she'd have come after us. Maybe I had been seeing things.

"Stay here," I said. "I'll be right back."

"No, wait," he replied, grabbing for my hand. "Just stay."

"I'm fine, I promise. I overreacted." I stepped away. "I'm just going to go double-check."

"Why? Double-check what?"

"Uh…" I looked at the people nearby again. "I'll have to tell you later."

"What was it?"

"I'm not sure. That's why I need to go check."

"I'll come with you."

Having a merman with me might be a good idea. "Yeah," I said, casually pulling my hand free from his grasp. "Come on."

We stepped back outside. The night air closed around us. Fear hit me as hard as the cold. I ignored both, folded my arms, and marched toward the stairs leading down to the street. A car passed. On the other side of the road, a student walked toward the bus stop along the sidewalk. Nothing else seemed out of place. Maybe I had imagined it. Lack of sleep could be the culprit.

"Anything?" Nathan asked. I shook my head. The girl across the street passed beneath a lamppost. I turned to go back inside but stopped. I looked back over my shoulder. Something about the girl cried out with familiarity. The shoulder-length brown hair, the way she walked with a slight sway as though ready to conquer the runway—even the way she held her cell phone to her ear. I took a step closer to the edge of the sidewalk. As she continued walking, the girl bent her face toward me. My heart stopped. It couldn't be. That girl—she looked exactly like...

"Samantha?" I whispered.

8

The Return of an Old Friend

My eyes had to be playing tricks on me. Or maybe the fear of attack made me delirious. I rubbed my eyes hard and looked again. The girl put her phone in her pocket and kept walking. I marched into the street to follow her. She increased her pace. Maybe it wasn't Samantha after all. She wouldn't just walk past and ignore me. I stared after her, took some running steps, and opened my mouth to call out her name.

"Olivia!" Nathan called out just as someone rammed into me, dragging me away from the screech of a car slamming on its brakes. I screamed and stumbled. The person who pushed me out of harm's way held me up. The car's driver shouted several choice words before continuing down the street. I gasped over and over, sinking to one trembling knee.

"Is she hurt?" Nathan asked, running closer.

"No, she's fine," said a voice I hadn't heard in so long, I'd almost forgotten what it sounded like. I looked up.

"*Seidon?*" My old friend, the prince of Zydrunas, and Samantha's boyfriend (or whatever merpeople called their significant other) stood there, out of breath. Seidon! *Here!* He grasped my elbow and helped me stand.

"Are you all right?" he asked. "I'm so glad we finally found you."

I looked from Seidon to where the girl that resembled Samantha had disappeared around the corner, and back and forth again, still unable to believe it.

"Seidon!" I threw my arms around him, laughing and almost crying, then pulled back. "What are you doing here? Was that Samantha?" I pointed down the street.

"Yes," he replied, frowning. With another half-laugh, half-sob, I turned to go after her.

"Olivia." Seidon grabbed my arm to hold me back.

"What's the matter?" I asked, tugging my arm away. How dare he prevent me from raining affection on my long-missed best friend? "What's going on?"

"Can we talk in private?"

"Can't I go after Sam first? I haven't seen her in forever! Why did she just walk away? Didn't she see me?"

"Olivia?" Nathan asked, standing at the edge of the sidewalk and looking both confused and angry. The sudden collision of worlds made my head spin.

"Oh, um." I heaved a breath, trying to control my shaking. "Sorry. I, um, Nathan, this is my friend Seidon. Seidon, this is Nathan. He's... like you."

"What?" said Seidon.

"What?" said Nathan at the same time. I could almost see Seidon's thought process as he looked at Nathan's face, neck, fingernails, and legs.

"Where are you from?" he asked, looking back at his face. "Coralium?"

"No, Long Island."

"Oh. Right." He nodded slowly, then put a hand on my shoulder. "Uh, do you mind if I steal Olivia for a while? She has lots of catching up to do with me and my fiancé."

"Sure," he said. "I'll just...see you later, Olivia."

"Couldn't he come with us?" I asked, but then Seidon's wording hit me. "Wait—*fiancé*?"

His face lit with a smile. "That's what Samantha calls it. Back home, we call it a match, but I like fiancé better. We made it official several cycles ago."

"Cycles? How long is a cycle?"

"Uh...I think you call it a month?" He looked at Nathan. "Olivia and my fiancé are dear friends. You understand."

Nathan nodded, looking slightly calmer, but still a bit confused.

"You go ahead, Olivia. I'll see you tomorrow." He put his hands in his pockets and turned to go back to the dorm.

"Hey," I said. He looked back. "Thank you for tonight. It was really nice."

He smiled and nodded, then walked away. I turned back to Seidon.

"You're engaged?" I asked. He smiled, but something about it seemed off—almost sad.

"Yes. Samantha wanted to tell you in person, rather than in a letter. She should have been the one to give you the good news, but under the circumstances..."

"What circumstances?" I asked. "What's going on?"

He waited until Nathan had walked back into the dorm building, then looked down at the ground, hesitating before he spoke again. He sighed, his dark blue eyes earnest.

"Samantha doesn't remember you."

I stared back. "Wait, what?" My brain spun, still reeling from seeing Samantha, the almost-crash, and Seidon's shocking reappearance. "What do you mean? She remembers me fine. I have all her letters. We've been writing to each other this whole time."

He bit his lower lip. "Do you remember the last time we were here? On land. In California, I mean."

"Are you kidding?"

"Right, stupid question." He paused again. "You remember that our people have to leave a sacrifice to…you know…come here?"

I nodded, thinking back and remembering the things Seidon had once told me about merpeople and their ritual to transform into temporary human form.

"Yeah, you leave something like collateral at your god's temple, recite the Prayer, then you become human, and you can go back and claim your sacrifice when you return. What does that have to do with Samantha not remembering?"

"Samantha was determined to see you, to make sure you were safe. But since she was born a human, her sacrifice to come on land had to be extra precious—something she'd do anything to get back, something that would ensure she'd keep our secrets and return to her new life."

I stayed silent, suspecting the answer but hoping I was wrong. Seidon continued.

"She had to leave her memories of you."

I started crying before Seidon finished. He took my shoulders.

"She'll get them back. I promise, when we return, she'll remember everything. All she knows right now is that she can't remember most of her life before coming to the ocean. She knows she left memories behind. She just doesn't know what they were. She feels it every moment."

Though I heard him and understood, I couldn't stop crying. Seidon watched me with a sympathetic frown and pulled me in for another hug. Every fear, worry, startling surprise, and emotion of the last few days weighed on me and poured out at once. First, Eamon ignored my emails, then some crazy mermaid attacked me...wait, the mermaid! I gasped amid my tears.

"I can't believe I forgot." My voice shook. "We need to get inside, *now*. There's something out here. I don't know what it is."

"She's not here. We're safe."

"Wait, you know about it?"

"We've been here for three days. We've been doing a security sweep of this area all day."

"Three days? How could you be here for three days without telling me?" I cried. "That...that *thing* tried to kill me!"

Seidon's eyes widened. "You mean she attacked you?"

"YES!" I shouted. He shushed me. I dropped my voice. "Two days ago. That's what I've been trying to tell you guys." The horrible memory of her sharp, rotting teeth and snatching fingers flashed in my mind.

"Did she hurt you?" Seidon asked. I wiped my nose with the back of my hand and shook my head.

"I sent Eamon an email about it."

"He never said anything about an email. All I know is he and the others have been looking for you for weeks."

"What? They knew where I was; they were the ones who gave me this scholarship in the first place."

Seidon shrugged, looking helplessly perplexed. "All I know is what Samantha told me before she lost her memory. She knew you were in a place called Maryland. Do you have any idea how big Maryland is? We had to ask a Corresponder for your location."

"Ask a what?"

Seidon looked around us before answering. "It's not illegal, but my people don't exactly approve of it either. The Corresponders are merpeople who maintain human form to help merpeople and humans communicate. It's how we contacted Eamon last year."

"Samantha never said anything about a Corresponder. Is that how she got my emails? I always thought I was sending them to her mom."

"You were. Her mom sent them on to the Corresponder, who sent them to Samantha. It's a long story; I'll have to explain the process later. We asked him about your specific location. All he had was your email. Uther tried to use it to track your location. But he couldn't find it. Something blocked him."

"How? He's a hacker! And *why*?" Something was very wrong.

"I don't understand all the details," said Seidon. "The important thing is, now that we've found you, we need you to come with us."

I wiped my eyes again. None of this made any sense, but at least I could get more answers soon.

"Okay," I said. With a pat to my shoulder blade, Seidon urged me to walk. We headed down the sidewalk on Farm Drive in the same direction Samantha had gone, then turned right at Regents Drive.

9

True Loyalty

Seidon and I kept walking. Even though he told me we were safe, I knew I didn't imagine the pale eyes flashing in the darkness. I listened hard for any sound of bare feet slapping on the pavement or a guttural snarl.

And then…footsteps. Behind me. I turned so fast, my neck cricked. But the sound wasn't of bare feet. It was of booted feet. Striding up the sidewalk, long, dark tresses flying behind her like a flag, came Captain Cordelia. She wore a brown parka over a tee shirt and jeans tucked into brown leather boots. I gave a nervous, disbelieving laugh. Cordelia! I' was sorely tempted to hug her but held back because people don't hug mermaid captains. They just don't.

"Hello, Captain," I said, self-conscious that the sight of my mermaid friend had lifted my depressed spirits so much. Well, sort of friend. More like an acquaintance who might kind of probably respect me a little. Maybe.

She gave me a quick nod.

"Seidon, go on ahead," she said. "I need a private word with Olivia before we rejoin Samantha."

Inwardly, I quailed a bit. A private word with the mermaid captain could contain only one of two things: a threat or an order.

Seidon nodded and continued walking. I chewed on my lip and fidgeted with my hair. She walked back the way we'd come a few yards. I followed her until she did a quick about-face with her hands folded behind her back.

"Am I in trouble?" I asked. I couldn't help it. The woman looked like a drill sergeant.

"No. I just wanted to give you some important instructions."

Ah. An order, then.

"Okay," I said, folding my arms to keep from nervously playing with my hair.

"I understand Seidon informed you of Samantha's condition," Cordelia went on. "I know this must be difficult for you. Ties of friendship run deep. For Samantha to forget everything about you must be a lot to take."

"Mhmm." I looked at the ground. Don't cry in front of Cordelia, for the love of all that is holy.

"It was either that or leave behind all memories of ever having been human," she continued. "Which, of course, still includes you."

I nodded again.

"It was necessary," she said. "She was willing to make that sacrifice to be here. To help you."

"But *why*?" I exploded. "Seriously, why? Haven't we done enough for your people?"

"*Shh!*" Cordelia slapped her hand over my mouth. It kinda hurt, so

I backed away from her and lowered my voice till I could barely hear myself.

"Shouldn't she be allowed to keep her memories of me, especially because I'm the reason she's here? And part of the reason she became a mermaid in the first place?"

"The decisions of mer-councils cannot be questioned. It is for the good of our people. Samantha was once a human. For her to be allowed to walk on land at all is an *astounding* privilege. You must understand our point of view."

"No, I don't understand. It's stupid and it isn't fair."

Cordelia raised an eyebrow. I shut my still-stinging mouth.

"What's done is done. What I need from you is to not try to jog her memory. To do so would result in devastating consequences. Once she returns to Zydrunas, her memories will be restored and you may correspond as you once did."

"But every time she comes on land, she'll forget all over again."

Cordelia paused, her face softening. "I'm afraid so."

I shook my head at the ground. "Then what's the point? What's keeping her here if she doesn't know me?"

"She knows she's lost something. And it was either stay under the ocean and worry, or come and fight for someone she doesn't even know. She chose the latter. That should tell you something about true loyalty." Her tone wasn't condescending, but full of something I'd never heard from her before: admiration. I looked up in surprise. Cordelia smiled. Tight-lipped and small, but definitely a smile.

I sighed. "Okay. I'll, um, play along. Or whatever you want to call it."

"We'll get this mess straightened out. I promise." She patted my shoulder and walked on. Stunned by her kindness, it took me a minute to follow her toward where Seidon and Samantha stood on the sidewalk, waiting for us. Samantha looked happy and stylish in her green bomber jacket and jeans. She hadn't changed at all. Not even her hair. I'd have thought she would grow it mermaid-long like Cordelia. But no. She wore it maybe an inch longer than the chin-length bob I remembered. She gazed at Seidon with adoration while he wrapped one arm around her waist.

"Our ride should be here soon," said Cordelia once we had joined them. I held back, trying not to stare and make it weird.

"Good," said Seidon. "While we're waiting, Samantha, I'd like you to meet Olivia." He held a hand toward me, then grasped my elbow to pull me a little closer to the group. She smiled and held out her hand for me to shake.

"Hi," she said.

"Hi." My heart split open a little wider. I needed a hug from my bestie. But she didn't know me.

"Olivia is the friend I told you about," Seidon continued. "We can trust her."

She smiled at him. "You'd never introduce me to someone I couldn't trust." She looked back at me. "Nice to meet you, Olivia."

"Nice to meet you too."

This was cruel. How many people in the world can say they've met their soul-sister twice? In fact, now that I thought about it, I couldn't remember the actual day I met Sam the first time. We might have been five or six.

"Something wrong?" she asked.

Only everything. I shook my head and tried to erase any hint of the complete loneliness brought on by standing next to the person who knew me better than anyone else. We waited on the sidewalk, warding off the cold while the silence between us stretched on. I looked down at Samantha's left hand to see the glimmer of a ring on her finger. I longed to grab her hand and squeal with her and admire it. But I couldn't.

She doesn't know me.

Ever since she fell in the water that night off the California shore, all I wanted was to see her again, to laugh with her, get her advice on stuff. But now, in her mind, we had never met before. More tears leaked out my eyes but I kept them quiet. Even though Seidon had rescued me from getting run over by a car—and they were all here to keep me safe from whatever lurked on my college campus—I had never felt so abandoned in all my life.

Well, no…the time I thought Samantha was dead ranked worse than this.

Soon, a sand-colored car pulled up and parked beside us. Cordelia climbed into the front seat while the driver came out. Tweed flat cap and all.

"Eamon!" I shouted, dropping decorum and hurrying around the car to hug him.

"Hullo, lassie," he said with a chuckle, returning the embrace. Then the unanswered emails burst into my mind. I let go of him and stood back, suddenly awkward. Eamon looked down into my face. "Are you all right? You've given us a scare."

"I'm sorry."

He smiled and pointed a thumb at the car. "Get in."

I slid into the back, next to Seidon and Sam. All three merpeople guzzled from huge water bottles like they hadn't had anything to drink in days. Eamon pulled the car away from the curb.

"So, what's going on?" I said. "All I know is some crazy shark-lady came and attacked me, then you guys showed up."

"The creature made contact?" Cordelia turned sharply in her seat.

"Uh. *Yeah.* I'd say it was a little more hostile than 'contact' though. She looked like she wanted to claw my eyes out."

Seidon shared a worried glance with Cordelia.

"I emailed Eamon about it," I went on. "I kept out the specifics though, just in case."

Eamon looked at me from the rearview mirror. "When did you send the email?"

"Two days ago."

He shook his head. "I haven't received any emails from you since last year."

"What? That's impossible. I've emailed you since then."

"Do you have your cell phone?" he asked. I pulled it out and opened up my email app. Then I scrolled to my sent mail folder. But none of the emails were there.

"That's weird," I whispered.

"What?" Seidon asked.

"I sent Eamon an email two weeks ago. I sent another one two days ago. But neither of them are in my sent folder."

"Are you sure?" Eamon asked.

"Yeah. Seidon said Uther was blocked from finding my location. Could someone be hacking into my email account?"

"It's possible, but I hope not," said Eamon. "Someone would need a specific reason to target you and the reasons couldn't be noble."

"Should I stop using that email account?"

"For now, yes. We'll have Uther look at it."

Cordelia turned to look back at me. "You said the creature attacked you?"

"Yes. I was walking back to my dorm building late at night. She..." A shudder ran through me at the memory. I could almost smell it—that rotting fish odor. "She ran at me. I barely got inside in time."

"Could she be after Olivia?" Samantha asked. Hearing her ask the question in such a calm, detached tone startled me. I had to peek at her face. If she had been the old Samantha, she would be freaking out right now instead of looking at Cordelia with mild unease and puzzlement. This whole memory-loss thing was getting more bizarre by the minute.

"It's doubtful," Cordelia replied, "but not impossible."

"Why, though?" Eamon asked. I sat straighter. He had a point. Why *would* some wild mermaid incarnation want to hurt me?

"For now, I can only guess," Cordelia replied. "We don't even know how she got here."

My spine prickled as my thoughts turned back to that night in Hanover. Time to confess. They had to know.

"I think—I set her free."

10

The House in Berwyn Heights

The car stopped fast. Every eye turned to stare at me. Cordelia looked too angry to speak. Eamon's shock and disapproval made me shrink in my seat.

"What do you mean you set it free?" Eamon asked.

"I was trying to help," I said. "A mermaid approached me at the aquarium in Baltimore. She said she needed me to help her."

"Who was this person?" Cordelia asked, her voice deeper than normal.

"Her name was Naia. She said the mermaid in trouble was her sister. I told Eamon about it in that email."

"An email that I never received," he said. He turned forward in his seat and the car moved forward again. "Start from the beginning. And tell us everything."

I relayed the story to him, from the time I first spoke to Naia at the aquarium until I'd run from the pond where her sister had been kept in a cage.

"I don't know if the mermaid in the cage and the creature who attacked me are the same person. But they both had the same hair. And the way she moved was..." I trailed off. Matching up the person from the attack to the mermaid-in-human-form crawling from the pond created a dark, heavy weight on my chest.

How could I have been so stupid?

After I finished talking, everyone else in the car stayed quiet. Soon Eamon turned into the Berwyn Heights neighborhood a few miles from my school. The houses here were modest and quaint, with trees lining the lanes and trim yards of green grass.

He turned into the driveway of a little brick house with a gray-shingled roof and a garage beside it with white siding. The front porch had concrete steps and thin, column-like poles supporting the porch roof. The lush landscaping surrounding the house displayed a spectrum of changing leaves, from deep green, to yellow, and tinges of orange.

Eamon clicked a remote garage door opener, waited as the door rose, then pulled inside the garage. Everyone else disembarked, half-empty water bottles sloshing with the merpeople. Cordelia led the way into the house, but I stayed in the car.

It was my fault. I'd set that terrible creature free. She was supposed to go back to the ocean. But Naia had run off before her sister got out of the pond. I shut my eyes and rubbed my face. If only I'd stayed behind long enough to make sure Naia had found the creature. I could have ensured they made it back to the river, or at the very least been reunited with one another. Instead, I'd run away, congratulating myself.

The door next to me opened.

"You don't have to wait in here," said Samantha. I looked up. She smiled. "Come inside."

I nodded and slid out of the car, holding my breath to keep from crying. All I'd ever wanted was to be part of this group of people. Now that I was here—all I wanted was to go back to my dorm to try and forget any of this happened. *Why did they have to take away Samantha's memory?*

Eamon held the door to the house open for Seidon and Cordelia. I walked in next. Sam and Eamon followed behind. In the gloom, I couldn't see well. It might have been a pantry or storage room. Up ahead, Seidon opened another door, where a little more light filtered through. The garage door closed behind me and I looked over my shoulder. Samantha's eyes flashed in the reflection of the light. I jumped.

"Problem?" Cordelia asked from ahead.

"Sorry. Samantha's eyes were glowing for a second."

"Night vision," said Samantha. "It's reflective, like a cat's."

"I may have given you a similar scare earlier this evening when you were walking to your dormitories with your male friend," said Cordelia. "You saw me and then hurried for the indoors."

"That was you? Captain?"

She smirked and took the lead through the door, bringing the water bottle back to her lips. Yep, same old Cordelia. She still got a kick out of freaking me out. I followed her and came into a clean kitchen.

"How'd you guys get this house?" I asked.

"It's a rental," said Samantha. Then she giggled. "When I first met Seidon, these guys were squatting at an empty house in Imperial Beach, California."

She spoke as if I hadn't been at that house in Imperial Beach with her the entire time. Did she remember everything about that summer except for me? How was her mind working?

"We've brought Olivia," said Seidon's voice from a room up ahead.

I braced myself for a happy reunion with Uther, Walter, and Natasha...and possibly an awkward one with Calder. My heartbeat quickened. I told it to shut up.

When I turned into the room, only one person stood from his seat at a dining room table.

"Uther," I said, smiling despite my terrible mood. I made my way around the table to hug him, whether he liked it or not. He smelled of aftershave and cigarette smoke. He cleared his throat and patted my shoulder. I didn't care. When I let go of him, he wore a grateful, if not bashful, smile.

"Good to see you, *meine freundin*," he said, his German accent as thick as ever.

"Come, come, sit down," said Eamon. I sat in one of the wooden chairs surrounding the table and looked around the room. Wooden blinds blocked the windows, a wrought-iron chandelier hung overhead, and pictures of seascapes decorated the walls. Where were Walter, Natasha, and Calder?

"Where's..." I turned around to ask Eamon and saw someone unfamiliar standing against the wall near the door, his massive arms folded across his wide chest. He was so quiet, I didn't notice him until now. With his small golden beard; prominent forehead; and long, straw-colored hair, he looked like a Viking. Or a professional wrestler.

"Olivia, this is Lieutenant Adrian," said Cordelia, noticing my staring. "He accompanied us from Zydrunas to ensure Seidon and Samantha's safety until the matter of the savage has been resolved."

I smiled and gave a stiff wave. Lieutenant Adrian did a slow blink, his eyes turning on me with a slight wrinkle in his nose. He blinked again and stared forward.

"The creature went after Olivia," said Seidon.

"What now?" said Uther, his face dropping. Yet again, I had to relate the entire story. Telling it over and over made it sound worse. A dull blush burned in my cheeks as I admitted my part in the creature's appearance.

"What was her name again?" Eamon asked. "The mermaid who approached you."

"Naia."

Cordelia and Seidon exchanged glances with both Samantha and Lieutenant Adrian, but all of them shook their heads.

"None of us have heard of her," said Cordelia. "What about you, Eamon? Do you know anyone named Naia?"

"No."

I furrowed my brow. "Wait, you should know her," I said, realizing I'd forgotten to tell them about that part. "She said she asked you for help, but you told her to find me."

He shook his head. "I did no such thing. I'd never send a merperson to someone with so little experience." He spoke to the room in general but kept his eyes toward his interlocked fingers resting on the table.

"I didn't have any experience in San Diego. I still broke into Linnaeus's office for you."

"That was different," said Eamon. "You weren't working to free a trapped mermaid. You were getting information from another human."

"I was able to help Naia though. That should count for something."

He shut his eyes.

"Olivia," he began, sounding tired. "I know you felt that you did the right thing. And I know you've wanted to be part of our tasks with the merpeople ever since you aided us back in San Diego." He brought his eyes up to mine. "But at this point, all we know is that a stranger approached you and got you to set an uncontrollable killing machine free."

"I didn't know. I—"

"That's precisely my point," Eamon continued. "You were trying to help, but there are now some major complications that have to be dealt with. This creature killed people."

"What? She killed people?"

Uther opened his laptop and turned it toward me. The screen showed a headline talking about the Loch Raven Strangler. I raised a trembling hand to my mouth. My heart, cracked and sore from losing Samantha all over again, now bled freely. The mermaid I'd rescued was the Loch Raven Strangler? Wait, no. I shook my head.

"The creature couldn't possibly be the Loch Raven Strangler. The Loch Raven Strangler has been killing people since before I set her free. And it was from a pond in Hanover, not Loch Raven."

Eamon sighed.

Seidon looked at him. "The Coralians said Loch Raven, didn't they?"

"What are Coralians?" I asked.

"Merpeople from Coralium," Eamon replied. "It's a reach in the Atlantic Ocean. They sent word of the mermaid's escape. From Loch Raven."

"I didn't know there was ever a mermaid in Loch Raven. It's a man-made reservoir. How could she get in there?"

"We don't know, but I think the Coralians might," said Eamon. Cordelia straightened.

"They knew of the creature's escape and tried to track it down," she said. "The first thing the creature did once it took human form was murder two teenagers near the reservoir."

I stared at her in horror. "That's…" I trailed off, unable to finish.

"The Coralians were able to find it several weeks ago, after it first escaped," Cordelia continued. "They kept it caged in a pond until they could find somewhere for her to go. It had lived in fresh water, so they didn't know whether or not salt water would be habitable for it."

"But…" I tried to breathe through the growing desperation. "Naia said she was trapped in that pond. She told me a human had trapped her for research."

"Where is this pond?" Eamon asked. I got out my phone and showed him the address. He typed it into his phone.

"Whoever this Naia is," said Seidon, "she lied to you." I leaned on my elbows and brought my hands over my face. Seidon went on. "We've been looking for you ever since we heard about the first escape. We knew you lived somewhere near that place."

With my hands still covering my face, I squeezed my eyes shut. Dread simmered in my belly. I'd set free the Loch Raven Strangler. All its victims from the time it emerged from that pond—I had their blood on my hands. My eyes welled up. I couldn't breathe. I stood, hurried out of the room, through the kitchen and the garage, and didn't stop until I had sky over my head. The night air chilled my skin. Wrapping my sweater more tightly around me, I stared at the ground.

How could I have screwed up so badly? I massaged my temples with despair. The door to the house opened behind me. I turned. Cordelia's eyes flashed in the reflected light from the outside lamp as she came out of the garage.

"Your phone. It chimed." She held it out to me, along with my bag. I turned and wiped my eyes before taking my stuff and looking at my phone. It had a text from Jenna.

Hey, where u at? Nathan said u almost got hit by a car, then took off with some dude who saved you from getting smashed! What's going on? U ok?

I smacked my forehead. "Nathan." I typed a message back:

I'm fine. Just had a close call. Came across some old friends. Wanted to catch up. Be back later.

"Who?" asked Cordelia. I looked up and saw her still standing there. I put the phone in my pocket and folded my arms.

"My friend. I could have just brought him with us. He's a merman from the Atlantic. He could help."

Cordelia gave me a weighty scowl.

"A merman in human form attends your school?"

"Yeah. His fingernails are purple. He doesn't eat shrimp."

"That doesn't mean he's a merman," she said with a shake of her head.

"But I sat talking to him about it at dinner."

She put her hands on her hips. "Did he actually say who he was? Did he tell you what reach he was from?"

"Reach?"

"Our kingdoms."

"Oh, right. I knew that." My hands twisted together.

Cordelia continued. "What did he say when you asked where he came from?"

"He…said he was from Long Island." I paused, chewing my lip and averting my eyes. "But that was before I told him I knew what he was. I think." My stomach soured at yet another mistake on my tab. Had I been so determined to have some kind of connection with merpeople that I made one up?

"Humans can have purple fingernails too," said Cordelia. "I've seen it before."

I covered my burning face and wished she would quit staring me down like a CIA interrogator. What next, waterboarding?

"First I set free a serial killer, and then I could have blown your secret," I said from under my hands.

"Did you tell your friend about us?" she asked. I lowered my hands.

"No. Not outright. Just talked to him about shrimp and oceans and..." I thought back on our date. "Drinking water and stuff."

"Hm. Well. Hopefully, there was no harm done."

"No harm done? I've already done terrible harm. I was only trying to help."

But my so-called help had not just hurt—it had killed people. A chill crawled up my spine as my knees locked and my heart squeezed. I paced, rubbed my arms, and cast a bitter glare toward Cordelia.

"So, did Eamon send you out to make me feel better?"

"No," she replied, the lack of sympathy in her voice startling me. "I came out here to tell you to quit being childish. You tend to flee from confrontation."

I stopped pacing and clenched my fists. "I do not 'flee from confrontation.' I've done nothing but run toward it ever since I met you people."

She chuckled. "That's more like it."

I looked away with a scowl. Cordelia sighed.

"I don't know why this Naia person came to you for help. But you answered the call and did what you thought was best."

I shut my eyes. "People died because of me."

"And would they have died if that fool of a mermaid had not convinced you to free the creature?"

"No. They'd still be alive if I hadn't been so stupid and gullible."

All those people who died—they all had families and friends now facing unbelievable loss. My shoulders slumped under the weight of guilt. Cordelia let out a long-suffering sigh.

"If you'd consider the facts for a moment, you'd see that it isn't your fault at all. This Naia—she approached you. Was she in great need?"

"Yeah. She was terrified."

"And you did what she asked because she said Eamon sent her to you."

"Yes."

Cordelia raised an eyebrow, looking just like one of my professors at school whenever they waited for someone in the class to answer a question.

"But she lied," I said. "She never talked to Eamon." I looked down in contemplation. "Why would she lie though?" Cordelia pointed a finger at me.

"Exactly." She turned to go back inside. "It's getting late. You should come back inside."

"Wait, you didn't explain anything!"

She kept walking. I sighed. I needed answers, not new questions. I turned to follow Cordelia back inside and through the kitchen. Pushing through the door heading into the dining room, I nearly collided with Eamon.

"Sorry," I said, clearing my throat. "About everything."

"It's all right," he said and stepped aside to let me in. I headed for a chair when Eamon's phone chimed.

"Ah. Calder's landing." He pocketed his phone. My brain buzzed and my breath thinned. Calder. Here. On this side of the Atlantic. Was he thinking of me? *No, stupid. Snap out of it.*

"Want me to go get him?" Uther asked.

"No need. I'll go. Olivia, you're welcome to stay here with us," said Eamon. "It isn't safe on your college campus until we catch the creature."

"Yeah, stay with us," said Seidon. "Calder will want to see you."

Uther snorted. A flush crept up my neck and felt everyone's eyes on me. I scratched my forehead. Part of me wanted to stay, for it to be like last time. But it wasn't like last time. So much had changed. Everything from Samantha's blank smile, to the glint of mistrust in Eamon's eyes, pushed me farther toward the door. And I wasn't ready to see Calder yet. I needed time to think and figure out a way to fix the damage I'd done. I'd already lost Eamon's confidence in me. I couldn't lose Calder's too, even though anything we had between us was over.

"I should probably go back. I've got a big internship I'm applying for and midterms are coming up soon."

"Are you certain?" Eamon reached for a set of keys on the table. "It's not far for us to drive you to classes."

"Yeah," I said, even though the commute wasn't my actual issue. "I'll be fine if I stay indoors."

"If that's what you want," said Eamon.

"We'll come too." Samantha stood. "Make sure you get back inside okay."

I forced a smile.

"You still have the same cell number?" Eamon asked. I'd sent him my number once I got a new cell phone in San Diego, hoping I'd get a call for a task. How naïve I'd been.

"Yeah."

"Right. I'll text you the number for my burner." He pulled out his phone, sent the text—which consisted of a thumbs-up emoji—and beckoned to me. "Let's be off."

I exchanged farewells with everyone but the lieutenant merman. He made no effort to say goodbye except for the disdainful glare he bestowed on me as he unscrewed the lid of his water bottle. Annoyed, but unsurprised by his behavior, I followed Eamon, Seidon, and Samantha out the door without looking back.

"Canon!" Seidon cried with a proud smile when the car came into view.

"Uh, what?" I asked. Samantha laughed.

"The word is 'shotgun,'" she said.

"Oh. Shotgun!"

I laughed too. How I'd missed Seidon's misuse of human words. We got into the car, Seidon taking the front seat, and Samantha and I taking the back. Safely out of Lieutenant Adrian's sight, I looked back at the house as Eamon drove off and shuddered.

"He's scary," I said.

"Who?" Samantha asked.

"That lieutenant guy."

"Oh, Adrian?" said Samantha. "Nah, he's all right. Just got his panties in a wad because he had to come to the surface with us."

"What are panties?" Seidon asked. I looked at Sam and we both snorted with laughter. My tension eased a little. After Seidon kept asking what was so funny, Eamon piped in.

"Human ladies' underwear," he said with all the solemnity of the medical professional he was.

"Why would Lieutenant Adrian have human ladies' underwear in a wad?"

Sam and I laughed harder.

"It's an expression," said Sam once we'd gotten ahold of ourselves. "'Panties in a wad' means in a bad mood."

"Humans should find a better way to describe a bad mood," said Seidon.

"Sorry, love. Sometimes I still use human phrases." She turned to me. "I, um…used to be a human. I don't know if they told you."

No. No one told me. I'd been witness to most of her human life and played a part in her transformation to her mermaid one.

"Yeah," I lied. "Uh, Seidon told me. So this Adrian guy is a real human hater, huh?"

"Unfortunately, yes. And"—Sam gave me one of her typical wicked grins—"he didn't like being taken from his *previous* assignment. He was on security detail for Seidon's sister, and I think he's hot for her. He'll deny it up and down the ocean, but he's been a pain in the fins ever since we left Zydrunas."

I laughed again. The old Sam shone through the amnesia.

"There's no basis in that rumor," said Seidon with an uncharacteristic growl in his voice. "Adrian admires Daxia, but he's not 'hot' for her."

I laughed yet again.

"Seidon also told me you're engaged," I said to Sam, trying to keep my tone casual. Sam's engaged! *Engaged!* As in, she's getting married to Seidon. I should be squealing with delight and jumping up and down. I ground my fingers into fists trying to stay calm.

"Yeah." She grinned and held up her left hand, where a ring set with a pearl gleamed.

"Aren't you supposed to marry a princess?" I asked Seidon. Both he and Samantha laughed.

"Honestly, it's the twenty-first century," said Sam. "Do your parents pick out who you have to marry?"

"Ha! No, I'm nowhere near that stage of life right now. College first."

"I always thought I'd go to college," she continued. "But I'm happy where I ended up instead."

I tried so hard to keep my face politely impassive, but Sam noticed the flicker of pain.

"Is something wrong?" she asked. Seidon looked at me over his shoulder and Eamon glanced through the rearview mirror.

"No." I sighed and recovered myself. "Not at all. It must have been a very high honor to join their society. What are your wedding plans like?"

She took a drink of water. "Well, we have to have it on land so my mom and my sisters can come. It'll be on a private beach somewhere, probably near some deep water. That way Seidon's family can come and go easily and no one will have to change." Sam continued chattering while my heart crumbled.

Her wedding would be on land. But I'd get no part in it. The person sitting next to me, happily going on about plans, didn't remember the times we'd planned our weddings as children. All our lives we'd imagined everything from the flowers to the groom, picturing exotic destinations and gorgeous gowns. A girl's wedding day was the biggest day of her life and a wondrous thing to share with her best friend. But now, because of some stupid mer-law, I wouldn't get to be a part of any of it. None of the planning, not even the wedding itself. To her, I was a total stranger. The merpeople may have saved her life the day she took a bullet for Seidon, but they also stole her life. They stole her from me when they should have trusted me. I'd once stood between them and their enemies too. How quickly they forgot.

I stared dully out the window, watching the trees on the side of the road as we drove closer to UMD. I'd broken a lot more than trust these last few weeks. What could I do to fix the damage done when I set Naia's sister free? Either prove she wasn't the one who killed those people or find her myself.

11

Guard Duty

I lay awake on my stomach, staring at the red glowing letters of my alarm clock as it changed from 5:59 to 6:00. The alarm buzzed. On a normal weekend, I would have turned it off, but I'd forgotten. Was it only Sunday morning? Last night seemed to last forever. I slapped the alarm off, then tightened the covers around me.

I couldn't shake the images in my head. The creature's snarling maw. Eamon's frown when I told him about freeing her. And Samantha's happy smile as she told me about her wedding plans. I spent half the night in nightmares and the other half wallowing in regret.

I needed hot chocolate. And a bacon, egg, and cheese burrito. Too bad no one at the University of Maryland had ever heard of a decent bacon, egg, and cheese burrito. And even if I could get one, I'd have to go outside to get it. And that creature was still out there. I shut my eyes. It didn't help. I checked my phone. No new texts.

Why didn't I just take Eamon up on his offer to stay with them? At least for the night.

"Because I'm an idiot," I answered myself, looking up at Minerva. Her fins rippled innocently. I scowled at my fish as though she agreed that I was an idiot.

I thrust myself out of bed. A hot shower called. At least I could get one of those.

An hour later—showered, dressed, and starving—I went down to the vending machines in the student lounge. But the junk food just wouldn't cut it today. I needed something hearty. I looked behind me, toward the building's main entrance. I shivered. Seidon said they'd done a security sweep and that the creature wasn't on campus. But the thought of going outside froze me to the spot. Those eyes, that mouth, and that growl were like a living horror film.

I turned back to the vending machine and put some coins in for a bag of chips when my phone buzzed. It was a text from Nathan.

Hey, Olivia. Jenna and I are going to the Diner for breakfast. Have you eaten?

Not yet, I replied. I couldn't tell him I was too scared to go outside because some insane creature had snarled at me. Nathan texted again.

Come with us! I went to get Starbucks, but I'm headed back your way. We can go together. Jenna's already there.

I breathed, looked at the vending machine, back at the doors, and bit my lower lip. Then I pushed the coin return button, gathered my change, and walked to the doors. Still, I hesitated. What would I find out there? Sundays usually meant lazy mornings for most people. Campus might be empty, unsafe, unwatched. Or it might be just fine. Either way, my stomach growled and comfort food called. Nathan was coming. And we would soon meet Jenna inside the diner. I wouldn't be alone. I pulled the door open.

Brisk air greeted me, more like January than October. Heavy skies gave off leaden light and a chill wind rustled the changing leaves in the trees. A few people walked the sidewalks, heads ducked into collars and hands in pockets. Nathan wasn't here yet. I scanned my surroundings, keeping an eye out for anything strange. Anything out of place. Anything that shouldn't be here—

I stopped. My breath, my searching, and probably my heart—for a second, it all stopped. Across the street, at the bus bench, someone stood. Blue jacket. Tousled brown hair. Even from a distance, even after so long, I could tell it was him. My ears rang. My throat dried. My paused heart now beat faster. He took a step forward as though he'd been waiting for me.

Calder. The real reason I didn't accept Eamon's invitation stood in the flesh across the street.

My first impulse was to run. Not away from him, but toward him. As fast as I could. A vision sprang to my mind involving tight, whirling embraces and a melty Scottish voice in my ear. That lasted about a second before fear, common sense, and memories of the last year shoved the vision aside. Memories of saying goodbye, emails and phone calls that stopped happening, sweatpants, and too much ice cream. Months upon months of nothing.

That's what I would get. Nothing but tears. Loneliness. Putting my education in jeopardy. A square jaw with a hint of stubble. Ocean-gray eyes.

Stop it, Liv.

He stood there, waiting. I waited too, until my hesitation became embarrassing. Then I walked down the building's front steps. Once I started, my legs wouldn't stop. He smiled and crossed the street. What would happen when we reached each other? I smiled as the idea to either hug him or slap him equally appealed to me. At the sidewalk, I stopped as though hit in the face with an invisible wall. He stopped a few feet in front of me.

"H-hi," I said.

"Hi."

Silence.

"Um…" I looked around. "What are you doing here?" Ugh, that sounded rude.

"They told you I was coming, didn't they?"

Oh, that accent. Wait, did Eamon send Calder here? I blinked.

"No. They didn't tell me."

His eyebrows rose. "Oh. Well, Eamon thought you needed looking after."

I chortled. "Looking after?"

"After what happened to you. He filled me in on everything last night."

This brought the events of last night back in full force. I pressed my mouth together. We stood there for a long minute. He put his hands in his pockets. I shuffled one of my feet. Okay, protection was nice. But why did Eamon have to send Calder? Was he trying to torture me?

"Are you okay with that?" Calder asked. I shifted.

"Yeah. Yeah, it's fine. I just—"

"Olivia!"

I turned. Nathan approached from up the sidewalk. His expression faltered a bit when he saw Calder, but he stepped up next to me without acknowledging him.

"How'd it go last night?" Nathan asked. Even though I knew I wouldn't find anything, I glanced at Nathan's neck. No sign of gills. What about his fingernails? I looked down at his hand holding a disposable coffee cup. The fingernails were still purple.

"Last night," I murmured.

"With your friends," said Nathan. "Did you guys catch up?"

"Oh. Yeah. It went fine." Biggest lie ever.

Nathan looked at Calder. Calder looked at me, then at Nathan. I shut my eyes. I needed to talk to Nathan without Calder. I needed to talk to Calder without Nathan. I needed to talk to Samantha. The *old* one.

"Calder Brydon," he said, holding out his hand. Nathan shook it.

"Nathan Buchanan."

Silence. Can I go now?

"Breakfast," I said, stepping away. "Jenna..."

Calder glanced at Nathan again, then nodded. "I'm sorry," he said. "You've got things to do. It was nice to see you again, Olivia." He walked away. I cringed.

"Friend of yours?" Nathan asked.

"Uh, yeah. Another old friend." A friend that was supposed to be protecting me. Even though, with Nathan here, I didn't have to go to the diner by myself, watching Calder walk away brought on a wave of anxiety. I should probably explain to Nathan, but...wait. I blinked at my train of thought. I didn't need to explain anything to Nathan. He wasn't my boyfriend. And if he wasn't what I thought he was...if we weren't what *he* thought we were—what exactly were we? I pinched the bridge of my nose as an ache began between my eyes.

"Hey," Nathan called after Calder. I looked up in surprise. Calder turned. "We were just going to meet our friend Jenna. Why don't you come with us?"

"No, it's fine," he replied.

"No, really," Nathan said again. I stared at him, then looked back at Calder.

He glanced at me, gave a half shrug, and walked back to us.

"I s'pose I could go for a coffee."

"Do you go to school here?" Nathan asked.

"No, just visiting."

"From Scotland," I said, trying to say something intelligent while my mind whirled. Nathan—my friend, who I thought was a merman but wasn't—was now being all nice to Calder, who I used to be super into, and who used to be into me, but maybe isn't, or wasn't or…what was I saying?

"…so I thought I'd stop by," said Calder. I'd missed everything else he said.

"Cool," said Nathan politely. I kept quiet and wished I wasn't starving so I could just go back to my dorm and figure stuff out. I sneaked a peek at Calder as we walked.

He met my eye but didn't say anything.

Nathan led the way into the Diner, an indoor food court in one of the other dorm buildings, where Jenna waved at us from a corner table. Then her eyes fell on Calder following behind us. Her jaw dropped.

"Jenna," said Nathan, "this is Olivia's friend from Scotland. Callder."

"Calder," he said, correcting Nathan's pronunciation. "Short 'a.' It's okay, happens all the time." He held out his hand. "Nice to meet you, Jenna."

Some kind of strange choking noise came out of Jenna's throat as she shook Calder's hand. I kicked at her foot under the table. She snapped her mouth closed.

"Nice to meet *you*. Calder." Her eyes glittered. I looked over at Nathan and saw an amused smirk cross his face. When he noticed me looking, he put on a mask of innocence. I rolled my eyes. *That's* why he invited Calder along. Smooth, Nathan.

"I'm going to get food," I said. "I'll be back."

"If you don't mind, I'll join you," said Calder. "Can I get you anything, Jenna? Nathan? It's on me."

My brows shot up. Since when was Calder so accommodating? This day was getting weirder by the second.

"No thanks," said Nathan as he slid into the booth. Jenna just cocked her head to the side. I blew out a sigh and walked across the room to order some food from a pastry and sandwich shop. I leaned an elbow on the glass encasing the pastries and cold drinks, one hand splayed across my face.

"Uther, Eamon, and Cordelia searched your campus again early this morning. No sign of the creature," said Calder as he peered at the food through the glass.

"Good," I said through my hand.

"You okay?"

No.

"Fine. You?"

"I sort of wish we could have had a little more time to talk. But I can see you're busy."

What was that supposed to mean?

"Calder…"

"Just stick with the story of me visiting my aunt and uncle." He spoke to me out of the side of his mouth as he looked up at the large menu display behind the counter.

"Your aunt and uncle?"

"That's what I told your friend." He looked at me. "Just a minute ago, remember?"

"Oh." I shook my head. "Guess I wasn't paying attention."

He chuckled. "A lot on your mind?"

"Where do I start?" I replied with a snort. "Samantha doesn't have a clue who I am. Eamon doesn't trust me. And there's some psycho-murder mermaid after me who, ironically, I set free."

"Eamon is just worried about you. Your friends don't know about your attack, do they?"

"No," I said.

"Good. Keep it that way."

I sighed again, stepped up to the register, and ordered a bacon and egg sandwich (closest thing I could get to a bacon, egg, and cheese burrito on this side of the Appalachians). Calder ordered coffee and a bagel. His phone rang as my order came up. I took my sandwich slowly, dying to hear what his phone call was about before going back to the table. I got nothing.

"Olivia, me and Jenna were just talking about going out tomorrow tonight," said Nathan as I approached.

"With midterms coming up?" I asked.

"Oh, come on," said Jenna. "We have to eat, don't we?"

"Very true. Well, have fun."

They both laughed. With that same dazzle in her eyes, Jenna looked across the diner to where Calder leaned against the opposite wall, still talking on the phone.

"We thought you and Nathan could set me up with Calder and we could go double," she said. I stopped mid-bite of my sandwich.

"Oh. Yeah, that's a great idea," I said, trying hard not to let any sarcasm leak through. Real great idea. Let's just carry this uncomfortable situation into tomorrow.

"Perfect," said Jenna.

Perfect. Maybe by tomorrow night, I could have my head figured out. Or my heart, or whatever it was that was making me want to crawl back into bed for the rest of the day.

Jenna went on chattering while I zeroed in on Nathan's purple-fingernailed hand. Here was my chance.

"What's wrong with your fingernails?" I asked, trying to give off concerned intrigue rather than a *holy-crap-are-you-part-fish* vibe. Nathan splayed his fingers and looked at his nails as though he'd never noticed something was wrong.

"My fingernails?"

"They're kind of purple." I held up my hand for comparison. Jenna looked at our hands.

"Oh, that happens in cold weather," she said, drumming her hot-pink painted nails on her coffee cup. "You probably just have poor circulation."

"Poor circulation?"

"It's common. Nothing to worry about." She smiled in adoration toward something over my head. I looked around. Ah. Calder was back.

"Olivia," he said. "You remember my Uncle Eamon? And my Aunt Cordelia?"

Right, the aunt and uncle thing. "Yeah, I remember them. How are they?"

He sat. "Well, they wondered if you'd come for some tea. You know how my aunt is. I'm sure she'll want to tell you all about that thing they've been looking for. That animal?"

"They found it!?" I exclaimed without thinking. Calder's face fell with annoyance.

"No. They thought they—never mind. Can you go or not?"

Torn between wanting to get back on Eamon's good side and needing to tackle my unprecedented homework load, my reply came out lukewarm. "Um, yeah. I can't stay long though. I have a lot of homework."

Jenna cleared her throat. I looked at her. She flicked her eyes toward Calder, as though trying to point without pointing.

"Oh, uh, what are you up to tomorrow night?" I said. He shrugged. I went on, "Because we, or at least Jenna and Nathan were thinking—"

Jenna kicked me. I stopped and looked at her. Her nonverbal communication powers continued with pursed lips and bugged eyes. I didn't care. If I was going to be shoved into this mud hole of awkwardness, she could dive in with me.

"—it'd be fun to go on a double date. You and Jenna and me and Nathan."

She blushed. "Only if you want to, no pressure." She reached across the table and touched his forearm.

He shrugged again. "Sure, why not? What time?"

Jenna glowed.

"Seven?" said Nathan.

"All right."

While everyone else chatted, I ate my sandwich with both hands and watched as Jenna stared at Calder. Why did I agree to another date with Nathan if I didn't want a relationship? At this thought, my stomach clamped with shame around the bacon and egg. Why couldn't I just be happy hanging out with Nathan? He was normal, nice, and cute. And present. No oceans to cross. But something held me back.

Calder and Jenna laughed at a joke I hadn't paid attention to. I squirmed.

"Well, I'd better go," said Calder. He stood. "I'll see you lot tomorrow at seven." He picked up his coffee and turned. "Oh, Liv, did you want a ride to see Eamon and Cordelia?"

He called me Liv. He'd never done that before. But it didn't matter. He could call me sweet Livvie, lover of my heart, but it wouldn't change anything. He'd still be that guy who dropped me like an unneeded class once we no longer had a mermaid task forcing us together.

"Oh. Uh, yeah, could you? I don't know where they're staying." I scooted out of the booth. "I'll see you guys later."

Jenna wriggled her fingers at Calder in farewell.

"Have fun, uh, drinking tea with Aunt Cordelia," said Nathan, pressing his lips together and arching a brow. Great, now he was annoyed. He had no reason to be. I'd just set Calder up on a date with Jenna; I wasn't running off to marry him. I stood there, looking stupid while Nathan bent his face toward his food and Jenna typed on her phone. So, I turned and walked after Calder. My phone buzzed. I pulled it out and read a new text message from Jenna:

He's HOT! When you get back, you have to tell me everything about him!

I rolled my eyes and put the phone away.

"What did Eamon want to talk to me about?" I asked as I kept pace with Calder's brisk walk.

"He didn't. He was calling to let me know he and Walter are going to that pond where you found the creature and—"

"Walter's here too?" I asked brightly.

"Yeah, just got here."

"Is Natasha coming?"

Calder's mouth tilted with disappointment. "No."

"Aw. Why not? I was hoping to see her too."

"We all were. But she didn't do well after San Diego. She hasn't been on any tasks with us since. She's still dealing with some PTSD."

I frowned. "Oh. That's—that's terrible." This news had me questioning whether I underestimated the dangers of what we'd done back then. Had I handled it too lightly? And Natasha…I hoped she was okay. "I wish I would have known," I went on. "I haven't talked to her in so long; I feel like I've let her down or something."

"Not at all. Everyone deals with trauma differently. Natasha asking to stay behind is a good sign that she knows her limits. Eamon assured us she's getting help and doing okay. We'll see her again."

I sighed. A visit from Natasha would have been such a relief. With her easy humor, her kindness, and her banter with the others, she brought a sense of feminine comfort to the group.

Calder continued. "Eamon also asked me to go check out a few of the nearby lakes to see if I can find where the creature is hiding."

I stopped. He didn't. After a few steps, he looked back and noticed me not following. "You all right?"

I shook my head. "I can't go looking for that thing."

"It'll be fine."

"You didn't see it."

"No, but I can manage."

I still couldn't move. I shut my eyes for a second.

"Hey," he said. I opened my eyes and bit my lips together. He had stepped closer. "I promise I won't let it hurt you. The sooner we find it, the sooner you can put this behind you." He gave my shoulder a gentle pull and started walking. "Eamon said the closest body of water is a place called Lake Artemesia."

"Yeah," I replied, grateful he stepped away so I could breathe again.

"We'll start there."

"I think I'd rather go drink tea with Aunt Cordelia," I said. He snorted.

"You think Cordelia would invite you to tea?"

"No. I just thought maybe they needed my help and you were using code or something."

"You're half right. I was using *code* if that's what you want to call it. But I don't really need the help. I'm just supposed to look after you, and I can't if I don't bring you along."

Oh. Ouch. I scowled and watched the ground as I followed him. So, he and Eamon still thought me useless? Well, I could prove them wrong. I could handle the creature, couldn't I? I could overcome the nightmares. And even if I never joined their group, they could use a little more courage on my part. I'd survived worse dangers before this. And I wouldn't be on my own.

I folded my arms, set my shoulders, and raised my chin.

"I'll come," I said, even though my subconscious thoughts of looking for that thing's habitat still made my blood run cold. "But not as baggage. I'm going to help."

He looked at me and smiled.

"Then let's go."

12

Loch Raven

Calder parked the car in front of an iron gate bearing the words *Welcome to Lake Artemesia* welded in the gate's design. Another sign stating *Authorized vehicles only* hung below the metal lettering. Thick trees and foliage bordered the road on either side and a tall hedge of overgrown plant life bordered the lake shores. Calder turned the car off.

"I don't think we're supposed to park here," I said. He shrugged.

"We won't be long." He got out. I followed, but kept my eyes open for any "authorized vehicles" nearby that might not like visitors taking liberties with parking spots. I walked toward a footpath curving around the gate and looked toward the lake.

The footpath ran around the overgrown shores of the wide, glassy Lake Artemesia. The surrounding trees and dense clouds overhead cast their reflections on the water in a perfect replica. I had never been here before, but it was beautiful. Just the place for an avid fisherman—or anyone, for that matter—to come looking for a little peace and quiet. Until a snarling mermaid violently interrupted their peace and quiet. I shuddered.

"Don't like it?" Calder asked. In one hand, he held the handle of a black case about the size of a handheld toolbox. He used the same one on the beach that summer in San Diego—the day I first met him.

"No, I love it. It's gorgeous. I just hate thinking that the creature might be here." The area would make a perfect hiding place. I couldn't see where land ended and water began due to the hedge and the collection of surface flora growing near the shores.

"Well, we're about to find out." He led the way down the footpath and toward the hedge bordering the water. The top of the plants grew taller than him. A sign poked out, nearly hidden by leaves, that said *No going in or on water*. Calder pushed aside some of the plants in the hedge to get a better look.

"Watch out for water snakes," I said. He recoiled. I pressed my lips together to keep from laughing. He looked around and noticed my face.

"What?" he said. "Water snakes are poisonous."

"Not all of them," I replied. "But, yeah, I wouldn't want to take a chance."

"Let's just..." he looked around and pointed across the lake, toward a metal dock just visible between the stalks and leaves, "go test the water from there." He backed away from the hedge and started down the path toward the dock a few hundred feet away.

I followed after him, still trying not to smile. I always thought Calder was so fearless. To see him worry about snakes made him seem more... real somehow.

Once we got to the dock, he knelt, opened the case, and brought out a glass beaker and a test tube with a rubber stopper. I peeked into the case to see what was inside it. There were a few beakers in varying sizes, and small, dark glass bottles with lids—all packed in snug foam compartments. There were medicine droppers, small red and blue plastic cases, pencils, a ruler, a writing pad, and a couple test tubes.

I watched while Calder set the beaker and the test tube's rubber stopper on the dock's aluminum surface. He reached down, filled the test tube halfway with murky lake water, put the stopper back on, and put it in the case. Then he filled the beaker with water.

"Would you hand me some litmus paper from the blue box?" he asked, pointing to one of the small plastic cases. I opened it up, pulled out a strip of paper about two inches long, and handed it to him. He dipped it into the beaker.

"Testing the pH levels?" I asked.

"Yeah," he said as examined the wet end of the paper. "I'll take a sample of the water back to the house for full analysis, but I can get a pretty good idea from a few basic tests."

The strip of paper stayed the same.

"Take this, put it in a bag. They're in the side pocket on the case."

I took the strip of paper, careful to hold it on the dry side so my skin wouldn't contaminate it, then found the pocket containing little plastic baggies.

"What does it mean, not changing?" I asked.

"Nothing. Normal. I suspected that. But at least we have something to compare. If a merperson lived in this lake, it would make the water more acidic."

I relaxed. A little.

He took out a dark bottle, unscrewed the lid and used a medicine dropper to deposit a few drops of clear liquid into the beaker of lake water. Nothing happened. He dumped the rest of the water in the lake, put the bottle and dropper back, then closed the case.

"Done. Let's go."

"What did you put in the water?" I asked as he hefted the case and began walking back to the car.

"A catalyst. Makes the acids in the water change color. It's harmless."

"So, Lake Artemesia doesn't have any acids in it?"

"Not the kind we're looking for."

I followed him back to the car and slid into the front seat while he put the black case back.

"Where to next?" I asked when he got into the driver's seat.

"We've got some options. I'd like to go see the location of the first attack."

"Loch Raven," I said. "It's north of Baltimore. It'll take a while to get there though. Do you think the creature would have gone all the way back there?"

"No, I don't." He reached over, opened the glove box in front of me, and pulled out a notepad. I couldn't help catching a whiff of him. Deodorant should not trigger memories in a person. Or be an attractive smell. I bit the insides of my cheeks.

"Okay, we've checked Lake Artemesia." He wrote it down. "What other places should we check?"

Distraction. Good. "Um…there are dozens of lakes and rivers around here. We can't check them all today."

"Right, so stick to the ones you're most familiar with."

"Well, Eamon said the creature is likely from Loch Raven," I said. "And she was definitely in the pond where I—where I first found her." I looked down at my hands. The guilt weighed hard on me again. How could I be so selfish to worry about all the things happening to me, or stupid stuff like the smell of Calder's deodorant, when I had allowed people to get murdered?

"What's wrong?" Calder asked. I twisted my fingers.

"I set it free. It killed people." My voice became a whisper. "I'm a murderer."

"Olivia," Calder said, his voice hard. I peeked at him. "You know that isn't true, right?"

I shrugged. He continued.

"If a mermaid convinced you to set the creature free, and she knew the creature was unstable, then it wasn't your fault."

I sat still for a moment. Cordelia had said something similar. In her cryptic, condescending way.

"Breathe," he continued. I did. He started the car and backed it out from the gate. "We don't know all the facts. Whoever Naia is, she's the one we need to find, after we catch the creature so it doesn't hurt anyone else. Let's head up to Loch Raven and check the water. If we can confirm a merperson had lived in it, then we can use this first test as a baseline and track the creature's course down through more bodies of water in Maryland. If we cross-reference the locations of the Loch Raven Strangler attacks with the closest water source, it might lead us to it."

It made sense. His logic was both comforting and seriously attractive. After a minute, I nodded. He was right. I didn't kill those people. The creature did. It wasn't my fault.

So why did I still feel so awful? Probably because I was duped into setting the Loch Raven Strangler on an unsuspecting public. Why would Naia do that? The minutes passed by while I stewed and took a few more deep breaths.

"How's school going?" Calder asked. Not at all what I currently worried about, but okay.

"Um—it's good. How's...Scotland?"

"Fine."

"Your mom?"

He smiled. "She's good."

We fell into silence. The strangeness of the situation hit me again; I still couldn't believe I sat here, now, next to him.

"Your friends seem nice," he said.

"They are. We're all in the same zoology class."

He nodded. More silence. After another hour of on-again-off-again talk, we pulled off the highway in a suburb north of Baltimore. Soon, a sign reading *Loch Raven Reservoir* marked a turnoff to the right. I Googled the Loch Raven Strangler on my phone to find out more about the first attack.

"Park at the fishing center," I said. "It's closest to where the first victims were found. Calder took the roads leading to the log cabin-like buildings near the lake, where long wooden docks led out to the water. Little fishing boats floated next to the dock. One or two boats with fishermen in them sped away on the water. Calder parked and got out. I stayed in the car, anxiety creeping, wrapping itself around my heart.

The scenery around the reservoir was just as picturesque as Lake Artemesia, and twice as accommodating. The reservoir had a jagged, rocky shoreline and lush trees. A knock on my window made me jump. Calder opened the door, his bag of tricks in his other hand.

"You coming?"

"No. You go ahead."

He squatted next to me. "She's not here. We're just going to test the water."

I looked at him. A voice in my head that sounded a lot like Eamon reminded me again that if I wanted this kind of life, I needed to stand up and live this kind of life. I had to show them I could do it. With a steeling breath, I turned to get out. Calder stood and moved out of the way.

"Let's go this way."

We walked away from the parking lot, along a path lined with wooden beams. Several signs stating "No Swimming" lined the railing. We continued toward an observation deck with a shady, wooden picnic gazebo casting reflection in the water. Aside from our thumping, creaking footsteps on the wooden deck, the area was strangely quiet for a Sunday afternoon.

Calder set the black case down and leaned over the railing to look into the rippling water. I rested my hands on the railing as well.

"What are you looking for?" I asked. Calder shook his head.

"It's too murky. Can't see anything. All the more reason I think this is for sure the place where the creature is from. It's a big lake, no swimming allowed, the site of the first attack." He straightened, then abruptly pulled his hand away from the railing with a whispered curse and a cringe.

"Splinter," he said.

I turned to look at his hand. "Let me see. I can get it out."

"No, it's fine." He pulled his hand away.

"Just let me *look* at it."

"No."

"It needs to come out." I reached for him again, but he turned more.

"No, it doesn't."

"Yes, it does."

"I like it where it is."

"Oh stop it, you big baby," I said, snatching his hand with irritation.

"It's a little fleck of wood." I picked up his hand and held it close to my face to examine the damage. Sure enough, there was a dark sliver of deck railing lodged in his palm. "Are you going to need some rubbing alcohol, Mr. Biochemist?" I said with a cocked eyebrow, remembering the time he had insisted on using the hateful liquid to clean some road rash on my knees.

He tried not to smile. "No."

I huffed and started to pick at the splinter with my fingernails, expecting him to whine. He didn't make a sound.

"Almost…" I said. At last, after pinching, picking, and squeezing, my nails grabbed a hold of one end of the splinter. I eased it out of Calder's skin and studied it between my fingers. "Got it." I looked up at him and smiled with pride. "Be more careful next time."

"Thanks." He stood close. Too close. A million memories rushed at me at once. My pulse quickened. Was I ready to go back to that place? Even if Eamon did let me become part of their team, it didn't mean this would work. We still had an ocean separating us. I let go of his hand and stepped back.

"So. More tests?"

He cleared his throat. "Yeah." He knelt next to the case and opened it up. Using a clean beaker, he reached through the gaps in the railing and scooped up some dirty, cloudy water. Then he took a slip of litmus paper, dipped it into the water, and we watched as it slowly turned red.

"I think we have a winner," said Calder. He looked up at me with a glint of success in his eye. But instead of feeling victorious, I looked over the water with foreboding and hugged my arms around myself. The creature had come from this place. Someone had given it the power to gain human form. Who, though? And why? I closed my eyes and fought off a shiver. Calder, meanwhile, performed the second test by dropping the catalyst solution into the beaker of water. It turned transparent red.

"Hm." He looked out at the surface of the reservoir. "You know, there could be some valuable plant life growing at the bottom."

"Really?"

"Yeah." He untied his shoes.

"Wait, you're not going to *swim* in that, are you?"

He pulled off his shoes and socks. "There are plants that take on certain properties in water that has been fertilized by mermaid waste."

"Mermaid...waste."

"Yeah. The plants are hard to come by, especially in a freshwater lake. Natasha could use it."

"Natasha's not even here."

"No, but she'll be glad I got it. Remember the medicines we used when you took that bullet in San Diego?"

I reached up and gripped my scarred shoulder. "I don't think I'll ever forget."

"Well, they came from plants like this. Natasha, Eamon, and I all develop medicines to help speed healing in case merpeople need it, so they can avoid hospitals."

"Why don't you make more of it and give it to humans? It worked on me. You could save a lot of lives."

Calder shook his head. "The merpeople won't let us. None of them ever found out we used the stuff on you. If they did, well...kiss the medicines goodbye." He took his jacket off next.

I grimaced. "Calder..."

He ignored me and lifted the layer of foam packing out of the case. Beneath it was a long length of thin rope, a flashlight, a pocketknife, and a gun. I stared at the contents with a rush of fear down my spine. My breath slowed. I shook my head.

"Don't go in the water."

"I'll be fine." He picked up the rope, tied one end of it loosely around his waist, and handed the other end to me. "If you feel a tug, you can pull me up."

"No, I can't!"

"Yes, you can."

"I'm not strong enough to pull you up. Don't do it. Please. The water's freezing."

"Thanks for caring so much," he said, giving me a toothy smile. I narrowed my eyes at him. He turned and pulled off his shirt. My stomach dropped with a splat at my feet and my breath caught at the sight of his tight, athletic upper body. He swung his legs over the railing. He stood on the other side just long enough for me to see a smattering of freckles on his shoulders before he dove in.

The slack on the rope shortened more and more until I had only a few feet left to hold on to. I gripped it tight and watched the water while the vision of a shirtless Calder remained pasted in front of my eyes. The seconds ticked by and every little twitch of the rope made me want to pull with all my strength.

A splash in the distance caught my attention. I looked up the shoreline, and toward the docks to search for the source of the sound, but couldn't see anything out of the ordinary. Ripples fanned out in the water.

"Calder!" I shouted even though he probably couldn't hear me. "I think we should go."

How long had it been? One minute? Two minutes? It felt like forever.

He couldn't hold his breath much longer. Where was he? Maybe he was in trouble and couldn't pull on the rope. Or maybe the rope was caught on something and he wasn't on the other end at all. I bit my lower lip and waited until the rope jerked violently from my hands. I screamed.

Several yards out, something splashed and struggled in the lake. I stepped toward the railing, but someone grabbed me from behind, wrapped a strong arm around my waist, and held a hand over my mouth and nose. I clawed at the hand while screaming away all my air. In the lake, Calder wrestled with two others, making their way closer to the shore.

"I can't breathe!" I shouted, sounding more like "Mmcmmbff!"

"Stop squirming," hissed the person into my ear. "And I'll let you have air."

I stilled. The hand moved from my nose. I inhaled over and over. Oxygen couldn't come fast enough. My head pounded as my captor dragged me away from the railing.

"Let her go!" Calder shouted. He twisted in the shallows of the lake and threw off his attackers, dodging them and splashing up a storm.

My captor didn't listen. He dragged me away from the deck and threw me onto the ground lot like a sack of lawn fertilizer. I fell hard, grazing my elbow and the side of my forehead. I looked up at the person who had dropped me. He was tall, with wide shoulders, chiseled cheekbones, and brown hair hanging long past his shoulders. He wore jeans and a tight tee-shirt that showed off a physique belonging on the label of a protein supplement. He stared down at me with piercing eyes and a curl of distaste to his lip.

Calder shouted from the shore, where a third attacker joined the onslaught. He said something, but the scuffle and splashing and voices from the others muffled it.

"Quiet, you worthless land-walker," the guy standing over me said to Calder. "And get a hold of him, for the love of Nereus!"

Nereus? I stared in awe at my captor. These guys were merpeople.

13

Kai of Coralium

There were five of them. It took one to subdue me, but it wasn't until the other four ganged up on Calder that he finally quit struggling. They deposited him on the ground next to me. He shivered, dripping wet and stinking like fish.

The guy with the long hair glared at his companions.

"Weaklings. Four of you against one of them?" He shook his head. The others, three males and one female, glared at us as though *we* had insulted them instead of their leader.

Calder looked at me.

"Are you all right?" His eyes settled on my forehead. I nodded, though my heart still palpitated.

"And what were you doing," the long-haired guy asked, standing over us, "diving into this place when the sign clearly says no swimming?"

"Why do you care?" said Calder. "You're not the park ranger."

They laughed.

"What do you want?" I whispered. The long-haired one stepped closer to me.

"What are you doing here?" he asked.

"We're—" Calder began but the leader cut him off.

"I asked the *female*," he growled. I swallowed, trying to get some liquid into my dry throat.

"We were investigating," I said. "Horrible things happened. Just trying to help."

"Who are you?" said the merman.

"Olivia Owens. I know your people. Captain Cordelia and Prince Seidon from Zydrunas are my friends."

His brow quirked. "Is that so?"

I nodded, wiped my hand over my stinging forehead, and found blood smeared on my fingers. Why did the sight of my blood always make the wound hurt more? I took a deep breath and clamped my teeth together to keep from letting them see my pain.

"Who are *you*?" Calder asked, still shivering. The ringleader lifted his chin.

"I am Kai. Son of Captain Samudra of Coralium. And you will show proper respect where it is due."

Proper respect? Was this guy someone important in the ocean?

"We're not your enemies," I said. None of them even acknowledged I'd said anything.

"I've heard of you, Olivia Owens," Kai said. My heart took courage until he continued. "You're the only human still alive that has heard the Prayer. How interesting."

His silky tone made my shoulders tense. I thought no one else knew I had heard the Prayer. All the others frowned at me. One flexed his fingers as though waiting to wrap them around my throat.

"Are you thirsty?" Calder asked. I glanced at him in bewilderment. How could he be asking about their thirst when they were about to murder us? But as he spoke, all of them eased back. The leader even licked his lips. Calder went on. "I've got water in the car. The water in the reservoir isn't the cleanest. You're welcome to all the water you want if you let us go."

"Or we could just kill you and take it ourselves," said the female from behind us.

"That sounds like something Captain Cordelia would say if she had no honor," Calder continued. She kicked him in the back. He arched and winced.

"We can take you to Cordelia," I said quickly, trying to distract them so they wouldn't try to hurt Calder again. "And Prince Seidon. They aren't far, only about an hour's drive."

Kai stared at me long enough to make me even more uncomfortable. Should I flatter him or argue with him? Maybe if I kept making promises, or warned them about possibly being spotted by other people, they'd leave us alone. My brain and my gut couldn't agree.

"Master Kai," said one of the other males. Kai turned toward him and the group huddled. They whispered among themselves for a few moments. Kai looked around and shook his head, then gestured to us. Two of them picked up the rope Calder had tied around his waist and used it to bind our hands behind our backs. I cringed as the rope tightened around my wrists.

"Cordelia won't be happy about what you're doing," I said, my voice unsteady.

"Cordelia has no power here," said Kai. "Not here, and not where we're from."

Anger flared in me. "All we've tried to do is help your people."

"We don't need your help."

I glared at him.

"Don't argue," said Calder. Still soaking wet and missing his shirt, jacket, and shoes, he shivered in the cold. "It'll only make things worse."

I looked at him with concern, wishing the merpeople would have at least let him get dressed.

"Do you think they know Naia?" I whispered to him.

Calder didn't answer, but all five merpeople looked down at me as though I'd just confessed to being the Loch Raven Strangler.

"Naia?" said Kai. His eyes narrowed. "What do you know of Naia?" He stood right in front of me, looking down at me with his arms folded, making his muscles bulge. The rest of them paced around us, staring at us like cruel, oceanic vultures.

"She came to me. And I helped her."

He glowered. Calder nudged me, a wordless warning in his eyes. I clamped my mouth closed.

Kai stepped closer and bent his face close to mine. He squinted, as though trying to look through me. I shrank back, wondering what thoughts went through his head. Based on the way he reacted to my mention of Naia, he must have known her.

His lip curled. "Humans are liars." He leaned closer to me again and winked. "Especially the pretty ones."

I scowled at him. "If all humans are liars, then all mermen are cowards."

He straightened and his smile widened. The female darted forward and slapped me across the face. I gasped.

"You insult our king," she growled. I gaped at her.

"No, I didn't, I just—"

SMACK.

"*Ow!*"

"Oy lay off!" Calder shouted. I lowered my face so they wouldn't see my watering eyes.

"Our contact isn't coming," said the female with irritation. "I say we either kill the humans ourselves or leave them to freeze to death."

Kai regarded us again, tilting his head and pursing his lips in contemplation. I frowned defiantly at the too-handsome merman. My eyes streamed from being slapped in the face twice but I couldn't wipe my cheeks with my hands tied.

"Leave them," he said. Even though his words gave me relief, I held my scowl and wished the murderous creature was here so I could sic her on that creep. He chuckled and turned to walk away.

"Are you sure?" one of his cohorts asked. Kai looked over his shoulder at us.

"CHASM will decide their fate."

He and the other merman smirked and walked away with the others, vanishing into the trees. I looked at Calder, who sat, shivering, with a bruised cheek and blood gathering in one of his nostrils.

"Are you okay?" I asked. He nodded and tried to maneuver his wrists around the rope.

"Here," I shifted so my back faced him. "Scoot closer and I'll try and untie you." He moved closer until we sat back-to-back. I fumbled over his fingers, seeking the knots in the rope. The merpeople had tied it too tight.

"Let me get my knife," he said. We clumsily got to our feet, trying to leverage off each other's hands and backs. Did he feel the same heat

I did when we sat back to back, our hands a tangle of rope and fingers? Or the same rush every time our hands touched? Whether he did or not, I couldn't let my pathetic loneliness complicate things further. I wouldn't. I shut my eyes to focus on looking for Calder's toolbox—not on the rope digging into my skin or wanting to warm his cold hands.

We found the toolbox where he'd left it on the deck, but all its contents were emptied and smashed. The foam divider lay cast aside. There was no sign of the knife or the gun. I stared at the mess and heaved a breath in discouragement. Then I peeked at Calder. His jaw tensed. Then, still barefoot, shirtless, damp, and tied up, he turned and started walking. I had no choice but to follow.

We trudged to the car with our hands still tied. Calder blindly opened the door. With my hands behind my back, I struggled to find my phone, but at last, I managed to dig it out of my bag and get Eamon on speaker. Calder did the talking while I tried again to untie the ropes. I still couldn't make any headway.

"We're on our way. Be there as soon as we can," said Eamon.

14

Courtesy of Eamon O'Dell

We resorted to asking a fisherman returning to the dock if he had a knife we could borrow to cut us free. The bespectacled man with the army green bucket hat and khaki fishing vest gave us a look—part incredulous, part frightened—before turning and hurrying away.

"Hey, come back! We just need a hand with these ropes!" Calder shouted after him. The man ignored us and increased his speed, but cast us several suspicious glances over his shoulder as he scurried away with his pole and tackle.

"He's probably never going to fish here again," I muttered. Calder didn't reply though. Instead, he looked toward the fishing center.

"Come on," he said with resignation. We made the walk past the docks and boats, to the little, brown cabin bearing the sign *Loch Raven Fishing Center*. Advertisements for bate, tackle, and boat rentals were posted on the wall beside the entrance.

Inside, a thin man stood behind a counter wearing a red flannel shirt and a wry expression. After we did some explaining, apologizing, and leaving out specific details, he finally cut us both free. I rotated my hands and rubbed the skin. My hands tingled as the blood rushed back into them. The man cut Calder's ropes next.

"First a double homicide, and now a hostage situation," he said with a grunt. He threw the cut rope into the garbage.

"Can I ask what you know about the homicide?" Calder asked while rubbing his wrists.

"Nothin'," the man replied. "Wasn't here when it happened."

"You didn't see anything suspicious?" I asked.

"We get hundreds of people coming in and out of here," he replied. "Never seen nothin' more suspicious than you comin' in here tied up and lookin' like a frat hazing gone wrong."

He gestured for us to leave. I was only too happy to obey.

Still shirtless, shoeless, and damp, Calder headed back toward the wooden deck past the docks. I had a hard time looking at him—and *not* looking at him. We got back to the deck, where I knelt and gathered whatever remained of the black case while he put his shirt, shoes, and jacket back on.

"Should we wait for Eamon, or...?" I handed him the black case. He took it and walked back to the car without answering. The loss of the things in the case must have upset him. I followed him back to the car. He opened the trunk and put his black case inside. When he shut the trunk again, he held a first aid kit.

"Let me see your head," he said, coming closer to me and reaching for my face. I shrank away, but his fingertips found my chin before I could get very far. He turned my head to the side, gently prodding the area around the graze. "It's not swollen, but I'll need to clean it."

"No, it's fine." I stepped back.

"It's got dirt in it."

"No, it doesn't."

"Who's the big baby now?" He put the first aid kit on the roof of the sedan and opened it. I glowered at him. He had a lot of nerve.

"I didn't use rubbing alcohol on your splinter. Your version of first aid hurts a lot more than mine does."

He opened up a small, square packet from the first aid kit. "Come here."

I huffed and stepped closer to him, readying myself for the sting of alcohol on my forehead. He took the square and daubed it on the scrape. Sure enough, the pain instantly flared. I flinched.

"Sorry," he said with a grimace. As he gently applied the alcohol, memories of him cleaning my wounds from other misadventures came just as vividly as the burn of disinfectant. It got harder to keep my breath even. My heart stretched and jumped. I couldn't help it. I watched his face, inches away. A bruise had formed under his right eye.

He lowered the alcohol swab and held still for half a second before another car pulled into the parking lot behind us. He let go of my face and waved a hand toward the approaching car.

"It's them," he said. I turned. The car pulled up next to Calder's. Enormous Walter Andrus climbed out of the front passenger seat. He wore a straw Panama hat and his signature Hawaiian button-up shirt. His bright smile contrasted with his black skin. I smiled too.

"Walter!"

"Olivia!" he said, holding his huge arms out wide. I gave him a bear hug. He jovially rocked me left to right as he returned the embrace.

"It's so good to see you," I cried.

"Good to see you too!" he said as he let me go. His smile turned into a frown of sympathy. "I heard about Samantha. I'm sorry. Damn merworld sacrifices."

His compassion warmed my heart. He was the only one to really acknowledge how hard it was for me to have her back, and yet not have her back.

"Add it to my laundry list of problems," I said with a humorless laugh to keep my eyes from welling up. Walter then caught sight of Calder, who spoke with Eamon near the other car with their heads bent down. Calder was shaking his head.

"Bad run-in with some Coralians, eh?" Walter said to him. "Did they push you in the lake?"

"Jumped in," Calder replied.

"He was trying to get some plant life from the bottom of the lake," I said. "The merpeople attacked us before he could get any though."

"Are you both okay?" Eamon asked. Something about him seemed off though. Darker. More somber.

"We're in one piece," I replied. Eamon looked back at Calder.

"I appreciate the gesture, but please stop trying to get yourself killed," he said. The lack of his usual cheerful demeanor gave me pause.

"What's wrong?" I asked. "We're fine."

"It's not that," Walter began with a glance back at Eamon. "We went to that pond. The one in Hanover you told him about, where you found that feral mermaid?"

"And? Did you find anything?"

He didn't answer. Eamon strode slowly toward me, looking at the ground and pressing his mouth into a line. Then he stopped, folded his arms, and met my eye. His expression didn't soften.

"The house and pond are both empty," he said. "No cage. No sign that anything had even been there."

"Did you test the water?" I asked. He nodded.

"Normal."

I frowned. "But—I was there. The cage was *there*. And someone came out of the house. Number—"

"Eight, right?" Eamon replied. "We checked it. It's been on the housing market for the last six weeks. No one's lived there since."

My mouth dropped open as my brows met. "But that's impossible."

"The last owner was a widow named Helen Wood. She now lives in a care facility in Baltimore. Does that name mean anything to you?"

I shook my head. "There has to be a mistake. A man came out of that house when I was there. He chased after us. Naia told me—"

"Enough."

I shut my mouth and drew back.

"Eamon," said Calder in a rueful voice. "Maybe the creature wasn't in the pond long enough to affect the water."

"It's possible," said Eamon. I looked from Calder to Eamon's stern face.

"You don't believe me?"

"No, of course we believe you," said Walter quickly. "He's just frustrated that we haven't found any answers."

"Seidon and Cordelia came all the way from Zydrunas for this. Samantha as well. All of us made sacrifices to be here. Now, I know you must miss your friend a great deal. We talked this over last night, and I hate to rehash old arguments, but—"

"You think I made all this up?" I almost shouted.

"No, I don't. The creature is certainly real. And you and Calder were just accosted as well. It's just very suspect. You disappeared off the face of the earth and only turn up again when there's more trouble with the merpeople."

"What do you mean, I disappeared? You knew where I was. You're the one who gave me the scholarship to UMD in the first place."

Eamon stared at me. All of them did. Dread hitched in my heart.

"Didn't you?" I asked. He sighed and shook his head.

"No."

"But—but your name was on the letter from the school. I remember. You sent it to my Aunt Shannon's house at the end of the summer last year. It said I was awarded the scholarship, courtesy of Eamon O'Dell and associates. I sent you an email to thank you for it."

I waited for comprehension to dawn on his face. It didn't. He shut his eyes.

"I never got an email about any scholarship," he said. I scowled in confusion and opened my mouth to argue, but he spoke again. "Olivia, we were indebted to you for your help last year. We were all very grateful. But I have nowhere near the means to award you a scholarship."

I kneaded my forehead with one hand and stared at the ground. How was this happening? It had to be a joke. But Eamon wasn't laughing.

"If you didn't...then who did?"

15

Concealing, Harboring, Armament, and Security of Merpersons

Eamon hadn't given me the scholarship to UMD. Someone else—some other extraordinarily generous person—had done it. And they wanted to remain anonymous. Whoever it was, they knew Eamon, otherwise, they wouldn't have given him the credit. But who?

"We should go," said Walter. "Meet back at the house." He patted my shoulder. Then he climbed back into their car with Eamon. I couldn't feel my legs enough to move.

Calder put the first aid kit back into the trunk of his car, then shut it. I could feel him watching me, so I got into the car and buckled my seat belt. He climbed into the driver's seat and turned the car engine on. For a moment, I watched his hands move the steering wheel to guide the car out of the parking lot. He smelled like fish and pond water.

"You don't think I'm making all this up, do you?" I asked.

"No," he replied without hesitation. "And neither does Eamon. He's just scared of something happening to you. He had a task go sideways last year and ever since, he's been extra cautious about stuff."

"What happened?"

"Same story as it always is. Merpeople were in danger of exposure. He succeeded in preventing it, but...some merpeople died."

"Oh, no." I frowned in sorrow. "That's awful. I'm so sorry."

He lifted a shoulder. "I am too. But it's a dangerous job."

I stayed silent for a long time, trying to sort through all the new information and unanswered questions.

"And Eamon hasn't been getting my emails?" I asked.

"I'm not sure. Sometimes he'll tell me stuff, but often he's not very, er, forthcoming with information. But we can find out what's going on."

I sighed. "At least now we know where the creature came from. That's a start. And we know Naia was from Coralium. Those merpeople knew her. They just didn't want to admit it. And they knew us too."

"Yeah, and the one called Kai said something about a contact. They had to be meeting someone there." He leaned against the window's armrest and scratched his head. "And for them to set up a meeting here? It had to be about the creature. It's all connected somehow."

"I just wish they would get over themselves and tell us," I said. "When are they going to understand we're here to help them? Why can't they trust us?"

"To them, we're either destroying their world or out to collect them and put them on display, like Linnaeus tried to do. They don't want our help."

I snorted in derision. "Well, that's stupid. We all share the same planet. As long as merpeople and humans live here, we're going to have to work together, whether they like it or not."

"I agree, but they won't ever see it that way. They don't care if you've never polluted their ocean, or if you've risked your life to protect them. They'll look for any excuse to blame you for their problems or even kill you if they can."

I looked at him in surprise. "They weren't *really* going to kill us, were they?"

"We were lucky. You think Cordelia was dangerous and judgmental when you first met her? Or those Atlantic ones? I've had nights where I couldn't sleep because of some of my encounters. And honestly, their prejudice isn't wholly unjustified. Uther once told me the king of Coralium hates humans so much because years ago, when he was still really young, his mother was killed by humans and his brother was stolen for a carnival side-show."

I looked at Calder in horror. "That's terrible. But all merpeople aren't like that. Look at Seidon. He's friendlier than anyone I've ever met, even a human."

"And if his people found out how fascinated he is by humans, he'd be a laughingstock at best. An outcast at worst. Add the fact that he's about to marry a former human? I'm surprised he hasn't been tossed out of the ocean on his arse already."

"*Calder*," I said indignantly. "You're talking about our friend and one of the only merpeople who actually trusts us."

"Wait a second..." Calder put out a hand, his eyes gaining thoughtful intensity as he looked from me to the road ahead. "Samantha and Seidon are getting married. The rest of the merworld can't be happy about that."

"Probably not."

"They'd probably do whatever it took to get her out of the way."

I shut my eyes and brought my hands to my temples. "No. Don't say that."

"I don't mean killing her. I mean getting her to leave the ocean. What is the one thing that would make Samantha want to take human form?"

It took half an instant for the idea to come to my mind, but several seconds to admit it out loud. "If someone she loved was in danger. Like someone from her family."

"Or her best friend." He looked back at me.

"You think the merpeople hatched some elaborate plan to lure Samantha out of the ocean?"

"It's possible."

"Yeah, it's possible. But why? She can just go back."

"Not if something happens to keep her out of the ocean for good."

"Like what?" I dreaded the answer.

He sat silent for a second. "I don't know."

I shook my head. "If all they wanted was to get Samantha away from Seidon, they could have done it a lot more easily without involving the creature, or humans, or getting anyone killed."

He shifted in his seat. "There's got to be something connecting all these pieces. Naia convinced you to free the creature. Then it went after you specifically. And this group of merpeople at Loch Raven just happened to be here when we came?"

I looked behind us, where the road and trees receded in the distance.

"We have to find Naia again," I said, turning back to face forward. "She may be the one who released the creature from the reservoir in the first place. She might even be the one controlling it."

"We can send Cordelia to Coralium to find out more information. In the meantime, you need to be careful. Someone must be watching you—may be following your every move."

I stared unseeingly through the windshield. Someone could be watching me, even reporting about me to the merpeople. Was that how they knew we had come to Loch Raven? Could they be doing something to my email too, so I couldn't communicate with the people who could help me?

"Hey," said Calder. I looked at him. "It's going to be okay. We can't let any of this get to us, especially if it means losing focus."

I sighed. Focus. So many things needed my focus right now. The internship, all my classes, my friends, a murderous mermaid—and the person controlling it could be anyone, anywhere.

And yet, as I looked sideways at Calder watching the roads, merging onto the highway, giving me a quick, reassuring glance—I let myself believe that things might, one day, be okay.

"Why don't you come back to the house for a little while?" he said. "Get some food."

"Okay," I replied. "I need to ask Cordelia and Seidon about my scholarship too. Maybe they're the ones who arranged it."

When we got back to the house, we walked through the garage door and got hit with the smell of fast food. I followed the aroma through the kitchen and into the dining room, where Walter unloaded bags of Styrofoam boxes to Eamon and Uther.

"You made it," said Walter, handing Calder a box. He didn't take it though.

"I need a shower," he said. "Be back in a mo'." He walked out the opposite door in the dining room.

"You survive?" Uther asked me. I sat down and pulled a Styrofoam box toward me. Inside, there was a gyro and some thick fries.

"Yeah, we're okay. Uther, could you take a look at my email account?" I asked. "I think there's something wrong with it."

"Consider it done," he said, pulling a gyro from his box. "What happened to you? Eamon said you got a little roughed up at Loch Raven."

I swallowed my bite and wiped tzatziki from the corner of my mouth. "We found the lake where the creature is from. Then we got attacked by some merpeople from Coralium. They tied us up and left us there, after saying something about a chasm."

"A chasm?" Uther's face blanked.

Eamon paused before biting into his gyro. "You never mentioned that."

"Didn't I? Oh. Yeah, the main guy—Kai, I think—he said something about a chasm deciding our fate."

Uther cast a confused scowl toward Eamon. "You ever heard of a chasm?" he asked. He and Walter both shook their heads.

"Well, in the ocean, a chasm is usually called a trench or an abyss," I replied, "like the Mariana Trench or the Tonga Trench."

All three of them looked up at me.

"Just saying," I said. Pounding footsteps came from the other end of the hall. Seidon burst into the dining room.

"Did you say CHASM?" he said, his eyes wild.

"Yeah," I replied. I gave him the short version of what happened that afternoon. "The leader—he said his name was Kai—he said CHASM would decide our fate. Then he walked off all smug."

I'd never seen Seidon so angry. His face soured as his hands clenched into hostile fists. Samantha came into the room behind him.

"What's wrong?" she asked. He turned and walked out of the room without another word. Samantha looked straight at me, a question in her eyes, then blinked in confusion, folded her arms, and looked away. I tried to hide my disappointment; she almost looked like she wanted to talk to me the way we used to talk.

"You've never heard of any special chasms, have you?" Uther asked her. She shook her head.

"No. They don't always trust me with information." She looked down. Cordelia and Adrian walked in. Adrian took his stance against the wall while Cordelia folded her arms and looked at me, her face a mask of military blankness.

"Seidon overheard your conversation. He said Kai of Coralium accosted you at the reservoir," she said.

"Yeah, Kai, son of…a captain, I guess? He said something about a chasm. Do you know what he's talking about?" I asked.

Seidon burst through the dining room door yet again. "Kai is a slimy old goby who loves to preen in the shadow of his mother's power. You can't trust anything he says."

"Seidon," said Walter, picking up a Styrofoam box. "Why don't you have something to eat?"

"I'm not hungry."

I gaped at Seidon. Anger and loss of appetite? Whatever it was about Kai, it must have really bothered him.

"What's a goby?" I asked.

"A coward," he replied, still scowling.

"You mentioned CHASM," Cordelia continued. In the corner, Adrian cleared his throat. Seidon looked at Cordelia, then at Samantha. His scowl turned to a panicked wrinkle in his brow.

"What is it?" Eamon asked. "I've never heard of it."

"Nor have I," said Uther.

"It's a council," said Cordelia. "It convenes every few years and its main purpose is to keep our world a secret and our people safe."

The door to the dining room opened again and Calder came in clean-shaven and wearing fresh clothes.

"What'd I miss?" he asked as he reached for a Styrofoam box.

"CHASM," said Eamon. "But Cordelia, if you're not comfortable telling us secrets of the merworld, you don't have to."

She shook her head. "It's not a secret. It's just not common knowledge. I've attended CHASM councils before, but only as an observer."

"Why is it called CHASM?" I asked. Adrian looked at me, his eyes so full of hateful warning, I had to look away.

"A chasm represents safety—the deepest part of the ocean is a haven for our people," Cordelia said, moving to stand at the head of the table. Her new position blocked Adrian from my view. "It's also an acronym. It stands for the Concealing, Harboring, Armament, and Security of Merpersons. High-ranking officials and royalty from each of the ten reaches are part of the council."

"Why are you telling them all this?" asked Adrian. I'd never heard him speak until now and his voice took me by surprise. Though I expected a much deeper tone to come out of such a huge dude, instead, his voice came out reedy. Whispery. It somehow made him even scarier.

"I'm telling them, *Lieutenant*," said Cordelia, "because I trust every person in this room."

Adrian scowled, but I had to hold back a smile. Cordelia trusted me? Wow. She went on.

"The fact that Kai told Calder and Olivia about CHASM tells me everything. It was an intimidation tactic. He wants us to feel like he and his people have the upper hand. But CHASM isn't due to convene for another year. Did he say why they were meeting?"

I shook my head.

"Blood of Nereus, it's none of their business!" Seidon shouted.

"Watch your language, Seidon." Cordelia gave him a sharp glare. "And what do you mean? What's none of their business?"

"Half the Hedron are classic human haters," Seidon continued. "Their opinions mean nothing to me."

Cordelia turned her body to face him, her face blazing. "Explain yourself, at once!"

Seidon looked at Samantha, his heartbreak and longing startling me. He sighed.

"I've been..." He paused, as though searching for words. "...*warned* that CHASM could meet to discuss our engagement."

My mouth dropped open. Calder was right. I glanced at him first, then looked at Sam with worry. She didn't notice though; she had eyes only for Seidon.

Cordelia let out a short breath. "If what you say is true, and CHASM is convening, this does not bode well."

"You don't think they'll keep us from getting married, do you?" Samantha asked Seidon in a small voice.

"*No.* Laws concerning marriage only apply to the heir to the throne. And that's my little sister."

"But why would these Atlantic merpeople bring it up?" said Eamon. "The issue at hand is the escaped feral mermaid murdering humans, not your engagement. Why give some obscure hint about their politics?"

"And what about Naia?" I asked. "She claimed that the creature was her sister, but no one has seen her. I asked the merpeople at Loch Raven about her, but they wouldn't tell me."

Cordelia shook her head and sighed.

"I wish I knew. The only way to know is to catch the creature or find Naia. Or, we could try attending CHASM ourselves."

"I'm not going anywhere near those shrimp-eating sea-devils," said Seidon.

"I believe your mother is on the council, is she not?" Cordelia replied sternly.

"Yes, well…she's the exception."

"Think they'll let us in?" Calder asked with an incredulous huff.

"You humans? No." Cordelia folded her arms. "And anyone observing is not allowed to contribute. But that's just during the meeting itself. We might be able to speak with the Hedron before CHASM officially convenes."

"What's the Hedron?" I asked.

"Short for Hendecahedron. It's what we call the delegates that meet at CHASM. A hendecahedron is an eleven-sided figure. The council is supposed to have eleven to break the occasional tie during votes, but Coralium recently absorbed Okeanos Ektasi. So, now there are only ten."

My mind reeled. Ten reaches—so ten submarine regions. All had their own politics, their own rulers, and their own culture. How much did the cultures vary? Did they have different languages? All the merpeople I'd ever met spoke English. Did all of them speak it? I had a sudden yearning to dive into the ocean to see what a reach looked like. I wanted to swim through buildings of coral and endless, water-filled caves. So much to explore and observe, so much to learn. With a stab of dismay, I realized though marine biology intrigued me, what I really wanted to be was a merworld anthropologist.

Life was so not fair.

"So what do we do now?" Samantha asked. I came back to earth with a jolt. This wasn't about me. Samantha and Seidon's future was at stake. She might not remember me now, but the old Sam would punch me in the face if she heard my wandering thoughts.

"We need to find how all this fits together," I said. "The creature. Naia. CHASM. Samantha and Seidon's wedding." Not to mention my missing emails, but I didn't want to bring up something that could've just been a technical issue.

Eamon nodded. "Maybe one of you merpeople could make contact with the Coralians and see if you can find out more about this Naia," he said.

"I agree," said Cordelia. "I'll head to Coralium. It'll take several days. I trust you'll keep things in order while I'm gone, Eamon?"

"Always."

"In the meantime," said Seidon, taking Samantha's hand, "everything continues as planned." He looked at her. "You do anything you need to plan our wedding. I bet Olivia would be willing to help." He glanced at me with a small smile. Taken aback, I didn't reply.

Sam nodded. "Sure. If you don't mind, Olivia." I gave her a tiny smile and a nod, then scratched my nose to hide the unexpected jolt of gratitude clashing with sadness.

"Then I'd best be off," said Cordelia. "I would appreciate a ride to the coast. Lieutenant Adrian, you'll accompany me."

"I can take you, Cordelia," said Calder.

"I need to get back to school. Could you drop me off?" I asked.

He nodded.

"Thank you for the food," I said without looking at anyone. I turned to go. Sam didn't say goodbye, which stung a little. We made our way through the house, to the garage, then to the car. Adrian and Cordelia took the back, leaving me to slide into the front.

"How are you holding up?" Calder asked. It took all I had to keep from exploding. I kept my teeth clenched, my eyes on the floor, and breath even. Don't fall apart. Not now. I unglued my jaw just enough to lie for the millionth time.

"I'm fine." I couldn't talk openly with the audience in the back seat. He stayed quiet. I stared out the window as he drove me back to campus, thinking of my to-do list: 1. Figure out why the feral mermaid was after me. 2. Find out how to convince this CHASM council to let Samantha and Seidon get married. 3. Help my best friend plan her wedding, while pretending I'm just a polite volunteer instead of her default maid-of-honor. 4. Somehow, fit in all my schoolwork. I grimaced.

Soon, we pulled into the front drive at Cambridge Hall. Calder parked the car and got out with me. We walked up the steps and to the doors of my building. He hung back as I swiped my key card and opened the door. Before I went in, however, I turned back, biting my lower lip. He looked at me with sympathy softening his eyes.

"You can call if you need anything," he said.

"I don't have your number." I pulled out my phone. He leaned closer and told it to me. My fingers fumbled a little on the digital keys while I struggled not to take a deep whiff of his freshly showered smell. I put my phone back in my bag once I'd entered his number. "Thanks."

"Try not to worry. Just don't go anywhere alone and you'll be fine. I'll be back here in the morning."

I peeked up at him. "Promise?"

A corner of his mouth lifted. "Promise."

I nodded, lingered for a second longer, then went inside. Ready to shrug off the day's problems and heartaches, I trudged up the flights of stairs and to my room. I stopped with my hand on the doorknob, saw my pile of homework on my desk, and smacked myself in the forehead. I'd forgotten to ask Cordelia about the scholarship. I got out my phone and called Calder.

"Olivia?" he said as he picked up. "What's wrong?"

"Nothing. I just need to ask Cordelia something."

"Sure, hang on." His muted voice repeated what I said, then Cordelia's voice came on.

"What is it?" she asked.

"I need to know if you or Seidon gave me my scholarship to the university," I said. She didn't reply for a moment.

"I know nothing about any ship, scholar or otherwise."

I laughed silently at her reply. But then the reality sank in and my mirth melted into a frown. "Okay. Let me talk to Calder."

A short pause, then his voice came back on the other end.

"No scholarship from the merpeople, then?" he asked sounding like he had been as amused by Cordelia's answer as I was.

"No. But if they didn't, who did? And why?"

"I'll get Uther on it."

I sighed. "Thank you."

"I'll see you tomorrow."

"Bye."

I hung up the phone and frowned, the worry weighing on me while I wondered yet again who would hand over thousands of dollars for a college education and not take credit for it. In the meantime, perhaps

I just needed to be grateful. Without the scholarship, attending a university would have been a lot more difficult.

After another shower to wash off the blood and dirt from my latest adventure, I came back into my room to my mountain of homework. Amid the essays, lab write-ups, and study guides, my brain kept running back to the things I needed to shut out. Calder. Nathan. Samantha. CHASM. Naia. I closed my eyes. But then the face of the creature leapt to the forefront.

We still hadn't found her. If what Cordelia said was true, that she wasn't smart enough to act on her own, then who was controlling her? Naia? The Atlantic merpeople? Calder had the idea of creating a trail based on bodies of water. Maybe instead of a water trail, I could try following a news trail. If the news tracked every attack from the Loch Raven Strangler, maybe I could find some clues to where the creature was hiding. I pulled my laptop closer and began a search.

Several news articles and media feeds came up. None of the information was new. I scrolled through, mapping out the course she made according to the attacks. Wait. I reread the last paragraph:

The attack at Greenbelt Lake follows the same pattern as the Loch Raven murders; however, police are no nearer to finding a suspect. The victim's name has not been released, due to the ongoing investigation.

Attack. It said attack, not murder. I pulled out my phone to text Calder:

Have Uther check out the police records on the Greenbelt Lake attack. I think the victim survived. Whoever it is, they might know something helpful.

I sent it, put my phone on my nightstand, and grudgingly went back to my homework.

16

Writing Notes

My phone buzzed, jolting me awake. I lifted my head and squinted around. My laptop sat open on one side of my bed. My O-chem textbook lay under my arm. I reached for my phone. The clock read almost midnight. There were two new text messages.

The first read *I'm on it,* sent about a half-hour after I sent mine this afternoon. I'd been so focused on my homework, I'd missed it. The second one had come in a few seconds ago.

You were right. The Greenbelt Lake victim survived. He lives just a few miles away from your school.

I sat up, staring at my phone, and typed back another message.

Are you going to go talk to him?

After a minute, the reply came.

Uther would like me to. What's your schedule like? Do you think you could come along? I worry about leaving you on your own.

I smiled. He worried about me?

I blinked and shook my head. Of course he worried. He was my friend and there was a crazy killing machine on the loose. I looked over at my stack of textbooks and homework folders on my desk. I took a slow breath and felt a little more grounded.

My first class starts at ten in the morning. I'll need some time to get homework done tomorrow too. How about around three?

Send.

Buzz.

I'll be there at 9:45. Stay inside until I get there.

I smiled again and, now that I was awake, went back to grind out more assignments.

By nine the next morning, I couldn't stand my room anymore. I went down early, sat cross-legged on the couch downstairs, and ate vending machine cereal while attempting to read more *Wuthering Heights*.

"Hey, Olivia!"

I looked up. Jenna came toward me with a latte in one hand, her school bag over her arm, and a huge smile on her face.

"Hi," I said. "Having a good morning?"

"Totally! I am *so* excited for tonight." She settled on the couch next to me.

"Tonight?"

"The date! Remember?"

"Oh. Yeah." The date I didn't want to go on. I took another big bite of cereal with half a mind to get a second bowl—something marshmallowy.

"What should I wear?" Jenna asked. I shrugged, staring at my book but not reading the words.

"You'll look pretty in whatever you wear."

She tsked. "You are no help at all. Can I meet you up in your room to get ready before we go?"

"Sure."

"What's the matter?"

I looked up at her concerned expression and quickly smiled. "Nothing, just trying to finish this terrible book."

She laughed. "Glad I finished Literature my freshman year. I'll see you tonight!"

"See you later," I replied, trying to infuse my voice with more enthusiasm. I took another bite of cereal and read on. An outburst of "*Hi Calder!*" made me look up.

Across the lobby, Calder had come into the building. How'd he get in? Had he swiped my key card? I grabbed my bag and found my card attached to its lanyard inside it. I looked back up. Jenna stood in front of Calder, flipping her hair and giving off a dazzling smile. He said something, then ran his fingers over his bruised eye. She laughed and lightly hit his chest. He smiled. I threw my empty cereal bowl in the garbage can next to the couch and stuck my nose into my book as though it were the most thrilling display of the human condition that ever graced the pages of the written word. Ooh, that was pretty good. I pulled out a pen and wrote "thrilling display of the human condition" in the margin of my paperback.

"Good book?" said a Scottish voice above me. I looked up. Calder stood there, looking way too cheerful for someone on his way to sit in a Literature class he wasn't even enrolled in. Then again, he'd just been furiously flirted with by my pretty friend.

"How'd you get in?"

He gestured behind him. "I waited outside until someone walked out. You ready for class?"

"Are you?" I asked. "It'll be pretty boring."

"Eh, I'll be fine. Is the book for your class?"

"Yep." I held it up so he could see the title, grabbed my bag, and stood. "Ever read it?" Maybe he could explain the hype.

"Nope. My uni Lit professor had me reading more Dickens."

We walked out of the building and toward my class. Like any other Monday morning, scattered groups of students meandered their way over the sidewalks, crossed the grassy expanse of the McKeldin Mall, or sat on the front steps of the various buildings, scrolling through their mobile devices. Nothing seemed off. But as we walked, Calder kept a lookout around us.

"What other classes are you taking?" he asked.

"Besides Literature, I'm taking Invertebrate Zoology, Calculus, Sociology, and Organic Chemistry. And a few labs."

"Ah, I loved O-chem when I was in school," he replied. I smiled.

"Yeah, it's not bad. Zoology is my favorite, now that we've moved on from earthworms."

"That's quite the schedule."

I shrugged. "I don't have to work because of my scholarship, so I fill my time with classes."

"And Literature is this morning?" he asked.

"Yep. Get ready for a good time," I said dryly. He laughed.

I sat in the back of the class, Calder next to me, and tried to avoid attracting too much attention from Professor Trafford so she wouldn't ask questions about him. During the lecture, he looked at his phone and scrolled a bit, sent a text, then picked up my pen and tore a sheet of paper from my notebook.

The victim of the Greenbelt Lake attack is Timothy Hawkins. He works for UMD as their landscaping coordinator. He was fishing early in the morning at Greenbelt Lake when he was attacked. The hospital released him yesterday.

I picked up the pen and wrote a reply: *Writing notes in class, Mr. Brydon? Shame.*

He grinned and wrote, *your teacher is looking at you.*

"Olivia?" Professor Trafford said, her arms folded. I looked up.

"Hm?"

"Did you hear my question?"

"Umm..."

She frowned. "How do you feel about the relationship between Catherine and Heathcliffe as it has developed in the chapters from the reading assignment?"

"Umm," I said again. In truth, I thought Catherine and Heathcliffe needed either a giant carton of peanut butter fudge ice cream or several therapy sessions. But I doubted Professor Trafford would accept that as a good answer. I flipped open my paperback, desperate for anything. "I think it's"—I read my scribbled commentary in the margin—"an *interesting* display of the human condition." I changed my wording a bit.

"Really? How so?"

Next to me, Calder held his fist in front of his mouth, trying hard not to laugh. I resisted the urge to glare at him and pretended to gather my thoughts.

"Well, they care about one other. But they can't come out and say it." Was that right? Did the two characters even like each other? Most of the time I couldn't understand what they said, much less how they felt.

She nodded and looked at another student. "And why do you think that is, Miss Campbell?"

I breathed. Calder snorted. I picked the pen up again.

See? Torture. Also, shut up. You're making it worse.

He took the pen. *She must like you. She let you off the hook just now.*

At least one of my professors does, I wrote. *The others can barely remember my name.*

He frowned sympathetically. *College is hard.*

Chasing merpeople and bad guys is more fun, I wrote back.

And sometimes terrible for life expectancy, he wrote. I grinned. He wrote on: *I'm serious though. Be careful with this stuff. It may seem exciting, but it's what got my da killed. You and I have both had a lot of close scrapes. That's why I'm here. I don't...* He stopped writing and scribbled out the last part. I took the pen, underlined the sentence about his dad's death, and wrote *I'm so sorry.*

He looked at me. His mouth lifted—not quite a smile, but I could see the gratitude in his eyes. I returned it with my own. Hesitantly, I reached over and patted his arm, then sat back and wrote another note on the page.

Wish we were studying Harry Potter instead. That's a discussion I could get into. He smiled and picked up the pen.

What do you think about the friendship between Harry and Hermione? An interesting display of the witch/wizard condition?

I chortled and took the pen from him to reply. It was probably the most fun I'd ever had, or ever would have, in a Literature class.

17

Psych Students

We left the classroom the moment the lecture ended.

"Where did you say Timothy Hawkins lived?" I asked.

"Not far. Close to the house we're staying in."

"Great! Let's go now."

"What about all that homework you had to do?" he asked with a teasing smile.

"I'll get to it," I muttered. He laughed.

"My car or yours?" he asked.

"I don't have a car anymore. I sold it when I started school for the extra cash."

"Oh, okay, we'll take mine then." We continued on the long walk toward the visitor parking lot.

"How are we going to do this?" I asked. "Pretend we're the cops or something?"

"I don't think he'll believe a Scot and a twenty-year-old girl are the police."

"Criminology students? Or maybe psychology. He works for the school. We can tell him we heard about his attack and we wanted to see if we could help. We can say it's for college credit or something."

"I like the psychology idea, but anything that makes it sound like we're trying to get something out of him might make him shut down. Let's go with counseling. You be the student and I can be the supervising GTA."

"What's a GTA?"

"Graduate Teaching Assistant," he replied.

"Oh. Here it's just TA."

"Okay, I'll be that."

"Why can't I be the TA and you be the student?" I asked, holding back a grin.

"Erm..." He frowned in thought. "Because I have a degree?"

I gave him a shove. "Quit your mansplaining. I was teasing you. I don't care who's in charge as long as I don't have to do all the talking."

"The thing is, you do have to do most of the talking. He might not trust a foreigner."

Oh great. More people reading. I wished Samantha were here.

A ten minute walk and a short drive later, we pulled up in front of Timothy Hawkins' house, a red brick, Cape Cod–style home with a cozy stoop. The well-kept house sat on a quiet lane just a few streets away from where Calder and the others were staying. An ash tree in the yard shed its leaves over the square lawn.

I stared at the cute little house and swallowed. Could I do this? I gripped my hands together and bit my lip. Then a sudden memory came to me: one of me walking the beach in La Jolla, California, pretending to be something I wasn't, to freak out a really stupid guy who thought of me as nothing more than exotic eye candy. This situation was a little different. But I could do it.

"Okay," I said with a deep breath. "Let's go."

We got out of the car. With a sudden idea, I pulled my school bag from the back seat to use as a prop. We walked up the sidewalk, up the front steps, and to the white front door. I rang the bell.

After a few seconds, the door opened. A woman with umber skin stood there, her gray hair feathered around her head. She peered at the two of us behind a pair of glasses.

"Can I help you?" she asked, holding on to the door with a protective air.

"I'm so sorry to bother you," I said, trying my best to sound kind instead of curious. "But is this the home of Timothy Hawkins?"

"He's not able to come to the door right now."

"Oh," I said. "Um, okay."

Calder cleared his throat and looked at me. He nodded his head toward the door.

"It's just...we're, um, we're students over at UMD," I said. "I'm Olivia, and this is my program's TA, Mr. Brydon." I clenched my teeth a little. *Mr. Brydon?* I wasn't in elementary school. "I, uh, I'm in the program for—post-traumatic stress disorder recovery counseling. The, uh, the school asked to send someone out, so my professor suggested we come. We just wanted to help."

The woman stared at me with a scowl. She wasn't going to buy it. I took a small step back, preparing for the dismissal. She sighed and pursed her lips together.

"Come in," she said in a gruff, resigned voice. She opened the door wider and stepped aside. Calder and I walked into the house. It smelled like fabric softener and toast. A set of stairs rose from the entryway to the second floor. Through an opening to the right, I caught a glimpse of a dining room with a table covered in a blue tablecloth and wooden chairs sitting around it. A grandfather clock ticked from the other side of the table, its pendulum swaying. The woman gestured to the left.

"If you'll take a seat, I'll get Tim." She turned to go up the carpeted staircase. Calder and I went to the left, through another open entry leading to a living room. Floral couches sat on either side of a wide fireplace. A braided rug lay on the floor between them. Family pictures covered the mantle on the fireplace—progressively aging versions of the woman who answered the door, pictured with a smiling, thick-set man. They had children, whose pictures hung on the wall, in dated clothing and hairstyles. Mr. and Mrs. Hawkins had grandchildren too. Framed photos of fat-cheeked, dark-eyed babies and toddlers decorated a side table.

The tick of the grandfather clock across the house's entryway sounded louder in the silence.

"How are we going to do this?" I whispered to Calder. "We're supposed to be PTSD counselors. I don't know the first thing about therapy."

"Be grateful for that," he whispered.

"But how are we going to get any information out of him if we're just here to talk about his feelings?"

"Just ask him if he's comfortable telling what happened. Tell him it's therapeutic to talk about it. We have to find out who's controlling the creature. He might have seen something."

I blew out a breath. Footsteps came down the stairs in slow thumps until a man emerged onto the floor. He wore sweat pants and a plaid button-up shirt, with thick socks on his feet. His skin was slightly darker than his wife's, his hair a touch grayer. He walked gingerly, leaning on a cane and keeping his neck stiff. My heart ached for him. He had no idea why this happened and now he had to deal with it.

"Hello," he said, sounding like he greeted friends instead of lying intruders. Behind him, his wife came down the stairs, glared at us, and turned to go down the hall. Sounds of running water in a sink, as well as moving pots and dishes, came from what must have been the kitchen.

"Hi, Mr. Hawkins," I said, trying to bat down my embarrassment and anxiety. He shuffled into the living room and eased himself onto the couch opposite us. He looked at us through bloodshot eyes, his thick neck mottled with bruises. I caught myself staring at the injuries and looked away.

"I'm sorry I'm so slow-moving these days," he said. "My wife said you were from the university?"

"Yes. You look like you're doing well, considering what you've been through," I said. He waved a slow hand.

"Takes more than a crazy homeless lady to do me in," he said.

"A homeless lady?" I asked.

"Yep," he replied. "Some ragged old thing. Long, long hair. Looked like she hadn't seen a dentist in her entire life."

I glanced at Calder, then looked back at Mr. Hawkins. "They said you were fishing when it happened. Could you tell us any other details? It helps the healing process if you release it. The memories, I mean."

Calder coughed. He held a fist over his mouth again—trying not to laugh at me. I leaned closer to him.

"You question him then if you think you can do better," I hissed through my teeth so only he could hear. Mr. Hawkins, on the other hand, rubbed his chin, staring toward nothing.

"Well, can't say I remember much. I told the police all I know. I was minding my own business, casting my line, when the lady pulled me back and squeezed my neck so hard, my eyes nearly popped out."

I waited for him to continue. "Is there anything else?" I asked. "Any other people? Any voices, sounds?"

He leaned back. "Well, now I do remember one other thing, now that I think about it," he began, but stomping footsteps came down the hall and into the living room, where Mrs. Hawkins appeared, her eyes blazing and her mouth curved in a furious sneer.

"You're journalists," she spat. She jabbed a finger toward the front door. "Get out of here. We don't need you rehashing this horrible ordeal for your dirty newspapers!"

"No, no, we're not journalists," I said, holding my hands up. "I'm not even writing anything d—"

"I said *get out*!"

"Betty," said Mr. Hawkins, "they're just—"

"OUT!"

We stood and walked to the door. Calder stopped before we went out and turned back.

"You're right, we're not psych students," he said. "But we're not journalists either. If you could just tell us what it was you remembered, we could help you get the justice you both deserve."

But Mrs. Hawkins wasn't having it. She opened the door, grabbed Calder by the arm, and pushed him out. My mouth hung open. I'd never seen anyone handle him like a schoolboy before. She then ushered me onto the stoop with a heavy grip on my shoulder.

"If you ever come back here, I'm calling the police!" she shouted, then slammed the door. I stood on the front steps, still gaping.

"Come on," said Calder, plucking my hand. "We're not going to get anything else from them."

I scowled. "No." I rang the doorbell. "She was rude. And he was about to tell us something."

Nothing happened. I rang the doorbell again and knocked on the door.

"Mr. Hawkins!" I shouted. "Mr. Hawkins, it's really important!"

"We can figure out another way, Liv. Don't keep pestering—"

The door opened. Mr. Hawkins stood at the door, looking bewildered but not angry.

"We're trying to catch the person who did this to you," I said. "Please, just tell us what you know."

Mrs. Hawkins shouted something from inside the house. Mr. Hawkins ignored it and came out onto the porch.

"I'm sorry," he said. "She's just terrified."

"I understand," I said. "I've seen the woman who attacked you. We know who she is, but to find her, we need any information you can give."

He looked from me to Calder and back again. He cleared his throat and rubbed his chest.

"Well," he said, scratching his dark, balding head. "The only other thing I remember is another voice shouting. I remember hearing the name 'Elspeth.' The lady let me go after that and took off. I rolled over and saw a black car driving away like a bat out of hell."

"Did you see the make?" Calder asked, stepping forward.

"Mercedes, I think," he said. "Didn't catch the license plate though."

Calder and I shared a quick look. "Anything else?"

Mr. Hawkins shook his head. "I'm afraid not."

“That’s okay,” said Calder. “You’ve been very helpful. I hope you recover quickly.”

“Thanks,” said Mr. Hawkins, turning to go back inside. “Oh,” he stopped, “don’t take this the wrong way. You seem like nice kids, but I seriously doubt you can do anything more than the police. I told them all this too and they’re still at a loss.”

“It’s all right. You’ve been very helpful. Thank you,” said Calder.

“Thank you,” I echoed. He went into the house and shut the door.

“Know anyone named Elspeth that drives a black Mercedes?” Calder asked.

“Wish I did.”

18

Double Date

After getting back to school, Calder walked me to my building. I stayed silent, wondering about the clues Timothy Hawkins had given us: A black Mercedes and someone named Elspeth. Not much to go on.

"Do you need to go anywhere else today?" Calder asked as we came to the front doors of Cambridge Hall.

"No. I can finish my homework in my room."

"Okay. You're sure?" He raised his eyebrows in question. Dang, he was cute.

"Yeah. It's fine."

"All right then. I'll see you later tonight."

I nodded and went inside. That stupid date. Why did I agree to it? I obviously still had feelings for Calder. This wasn't fair to Nathan or Jenna. Unless…

A terrible thought occurred to me. Did Calder want to go out with Jenna? Was he hanging around me for more than one reason? He seemed pretty open to the idea of going out with her, even though he was here to protect the merpeople, find the creature, and make sure I didn't get murdered. What was it he said before we went to Lake Artemesia? *I'm supposed to look after you, and I can't if I don't bring you along.*

It all made sense now. As I plodded up the staircase, my heart sank lower. Calder didn't see me the way I saw him. He probably thought Jenna was prettier. Which she was. She was smarter too. And better at flirting. In fact, I realized with surprise as I reached the first landing, Jenna was a lot like Samantha. I stomped up the next staircase, my sadness turning to anger.

But when I emerged onto the fourth floor, my anger fizzled back into sadness. What was wrong with me? What kind of person was I to jump right into the pit of jealousy just because Calder agreed to go out with my friend? I wanted to smack myself.

Wait, though; this could be a good thing. I had so much I needed to accomplish right now. I had so many goals that would bring me to the ultimate goal: getting paid to study the ocean for my day job, maybe answer Eamon's call to help merpeople on the side—if he let me—and live closer to Samantha. The real Samantha, not the stand-in with self-imposed amnesia. Calder going out with Jenna would help get my mind off him. He'd fulfill his duty, I'd stay safe from the creature, and when he went back to Scotland, I'd be no worse off than before. We could stay friends. This was good.

I wish it made me feel better.

A few hours later, Jenna walked into my room, looking pretty with her hair in loose curls and her pink sweater complimenting her complexion.

"Hey, you're not ready yet," she said. I looked at the clock. It was just past five.

"I've still got tons of time."

"I'm just too excited to go out with Calder," she said with a wide grin. "I've been looking up stuff about Scotland all day!"

"I have to warn you," I said as I finished off a problem for O-chem. "Calder takes a long time to warm up to people. He might be a little standoffish at first."

"Really?" she knit her eyebrows. "He seems so nice."

"Oh, he's cordial and everything. But when I first met him, he was pretty hard to get to know. I'm just putting you on your guard."

She pulled her smile back up. "Thanks for the tip."

I finished homework while Jenna passed the time by showing me funny videos on her phone and asking questions about Calder. The questions got harder to answer—partly because the answers involved merpeople, and partly because...I didn't know. What *were* Calder's favorite food, color, and movie?

"Girl, do you know the guy at *all*?" she asked. I laughed darkly. Did I know him?

"I guess not." That should make it easier to let him go, shouldn't it?

At seven, Nathan knocked on the door.

"You ladies ready?" he asked. Jenna jumped up and skipped out the door. Nathan and I had to hurry to keep up with her stride.

"How was afternoon tea with the Scottish aunt and uncle?" he asked me. I hesitated a beat.

"Oh. Fine," I said. "Boring."

He laughed. "Do they do that often? Invite you over for tea?"

"Every once in a while," I said blandly, hoping he didn't ask about something I couldn't explain away with an easy lie. We continued downstairs and outside, where Calder waited. The second I laid eyes on him, I wished he were my date.

He's not your date, so get over it and be normal.

"Jenna, nice to see you again," he said.

"Nice to see *you*." She giggled and threaded her hand through the crook of his arm. "How's your eye?"

"Better, thanks." He touched it with his fingers.

"How'd that happen?" Nathan asked. Calder shrugged.

"Took a hit during a rugby game yesterday," he replied without a hitch.

"That must have been so painful," Jenna simpered. I rolled my eyes when no one was looking.

"Are we ready?" said Nathan, pulling out his car keys with a jingle.

"Yeah, let's go," I said, and raised an eyebrow at Calder. He gave me a tiny shrug. Jenna clutched his arm and pulled close to him as they walked.

"So do you like Japanese food?" she asked.

"I love Japanese food," Calder replied.

Normal, I told myself again. *Be normal.*

"Japanese food sounds great," I said.

"Great," said Jenna, "because I know this awesome place. Super delicious. And a great atmosphere."

"I'm in," said Nathan, who kept brushing his hand against mine. I folded my arms.

Nathan led the way to his car. He opened the passenger side door for me. Calder did the same for Jenna in the back seat. I stayed mostly quiet during the car ride, while the other three did the talking. Once we got there, Nathan led me to my seat by the small of my back. We sat in a corner booth with black leather seats, muted orange lighting, and candles on the shining tabletop. All the while, Jenna made conversation with Calder. He responded with uncharacteristic warmth. Like Prince Charming. Or his evil twin.

"I'm majoring in health sciences," said Jenna, "but I guess they want me to know about animals that don't have a backbone as well as the ones that do. That's why I'm in the class with Olivia and Nathan."

"That's cool," said Calder. "My brother did health sciences. I did biochemistry."

I nearly spat my water. "You have a brother?" I said loudly. Calder and Jenna both looked at me.

"Yeah," said Calder. "Laith. He lives in England."

"You never told me you had a brother," I said, struggling to keep my voice even. I knew about his mom, his late dad—but he never brought up a brother. Not knowing his favorite food or color was one thing. But this...how could he not tell me?

"He keeps to himself," Calder said. I continued to stare in wonder, a little hurt that he hadn't clued me in on something this big.

"The teriyaki chicken looks good," said Nathan. I quit staring and looked at my menu.

"What about the sushi?" said Calder. "Ever had raw fish, Jenna?"

"No." By the look on her face, you'd have thought he had whispered it sensuously into her ear. "But I'd love to taste it."

I balled my hands.

"Don't places like this have those chefs who cook the food right in front of you?" I asked. "And throw it at you if you're *being weird*?"

Calder glanced at me while Nathan laughed.

"I'd pay to see that," he said.

"Why would they throw it at you?" Jenna asked with a puzzled frown.

"To catch it in your mouth," I replied. Obviously.

"What does that have to do with being weird?" Calder asked.

"I'll have the shrimp tempura," I said as though he hadn't spoken. "You know; the cockroaches of the ocean? The *bottom feeders*."

"What'd the shrimp ever do to you?" Calder muttered and gave me a pointed look. I shrugged.

"Maybe the shrimp is pretending to be something it's not."

"Okay," Nathan interrupted, "I'm going to add a bowl of yakisoba to the table. Get a little variety. We ready to order?" He looked around.

"Ready when you are," Calder replied. "So Jenna, have you ever seen a rugby game?"

I ground my teeth as their conversation continued and stayed quiet as Jenna beamed at her date and Nathan ordered the entrees. This different, outgoing Calder was *not* the moody know-it-all with whom I had once run from the cops and dodged flying bullets. The one who treated me with nothing but distrust and borderline hostility when I first met him. I had to fight tooth and nail just to get him to look me in the eye. *Now* he was all sweetness and gallantry.

Jenna was right. I didn't know him. Was anything we had in San Diego real?

"Are you okay?" Nathan asked. He put his arm on the back of the bench behind me. I hitched on a smile.

"I'm great!" I said. What a hypocrite I was. A fake. Faking that this was fine, that I was having a good time, and that I didn't seethe every time Jenna made Calder smile. It shouldn't bother me so much. *He isn't mine.* I shoved those pestering feelings back down to my soul's abyss where they belonged. Then I opened my mouth and chatted away the attempts at eating with chopsticks as if nothing in the world could dampen my happiness.

Before we finished, Calder's phone rang. I scowled at him as he answered it—not because I thought he was being rude, but because I knew who was on the other end of the call. Had something happened? Had they found the creature?

"Hello?" Calder said. "Eamon."

I sat straighter in my seat and gazed at Calder, then remembered Nathan and Jenna and tried to hide my concern. *Be normal.*

Calder continued. "Yeah. I'm at dinner." He met my eye for a split second before looking away. "Yes. Okay. On my way." He hung up his phone. "I'm sorry," he said with regret. "It's my uncle."

I fought the impulse to react from a wave of urgency. Was Eamon all right? I took a sip of water and tried to sound calmly curious.

"Is something wrong?"

"He said it's an emergency. I have to go."

"Now?" said Jenna.

"I'm afraid so. I'm really sorry, Jenna. It's been fun. We'll have to do it again sometime." He stood and opened his wallet. "I'll just take a cab. Here's for me and Jenna's half of the dinner." He left a couple twenties on the table.

"No, no, we can take you back," Jenna said quickly. "You don't have to take a cab, that'd be silly." We shuffled out of the booth after leaving enough money for the bill. As we walked out of the restaurant, Jenna took his arm again while I grimaced and tried to think of a way to ask Calder about what Eamon had said. After several failed attempts at telepathy, I tried something else.

"Did they figure out what happened with Elspeth?" I asked.

"Elspeth," he said, sliding into the car's back seat. Jenna slid to the middle, closer to him.

"Remember?" I went on. "When...we were at tea yesterday, they said something about Elspeth." Wow, was that only yesterday?

Understanding dawned on his face.

"No. They haven't figured out what happened with Elspeth." He looked at me. "He's worried about my cousin Naia. He wants me to meet him at the parking lot of his apartment as soon as I can."

My eyes widened. Had they found Naia?

"I hope everything's okay," said Jenna, putting her hand on Calder's bicep. He looked over at her. I turned back to face forward.

"Thank you. I'm sure it'll be fine. Just some unexpected family problems."

"Is anyone hurt?" I asked, looking back again.

"Eamon is fine. But I do need to go. You know how it is. Sometimes you get called away for a big emergency, and it turns out there was no real issue to begin with."

"I'm sorry it had to interrupt our night," said Nathan in a loud voice. I turned back around, glancing once at him. He cast me a suspicious glare. Had I been paying more attention to Calder than to him? Probably. I wrapped my arms across my chest as if taking up less space would make me feel less guilty.

We continued on the drive back to the school with Jenna and Nathan talking about some big play the school's theater arts program was putting on soon. Jenna kept dropping ocean liner-sized hints about wanting Calder to take her to see it while I stole glances at him through the rearview mirror.

We arrived at the university and got out of the car. Nathan and I walked ahead, while Calder and Jenna stayed behind.

"We're pretty good matchmakers," said Nathan. "Look at them. I think he might kiss her."

I jerked my head over my shoulder. They stood close together, Jenna's face turned up in adoration. Calder patted her on the shoulder, then turned and walked away. After a moment, Jenna caught up with us. She gave a swoony sigh.

"Olivia...you are the best friend *ever*!" she said, linking her arm around mine. "Where did you meet him?"

"California. Before college."

"He's so *amazing*. That accent. Wow." She smiled at me as if tonight had destined them for eternal bliss.

"You two seemed to hit it off," said Nathan. "I think he really likes you."

"I'd love to go out with him again, but he didn't get my phone number. Could you put in a good word for me, Olivia?"

"Sure," I said with a gritty smile. "I'll put in *lots* of good words."

19

Looking Inward

After we walked into the dorm building and Jenna swept off to her room in a smiley sort of daze, I tried to think of how to get away so I could go find out what was so important with Eamon.

"Well, I guess I'll call it a night then," I said when Nathan started for the student lounge.

"Now? It's still early."

"I'm kind of tired, and I still have things to do tonight."

"Didn't get all your homework done today?"

I wasn't talking about homework, but I'd take that.

"Is homework ever really done? What about your Statistics class?" I continued. "You've always said it was kicking you in the butt."

Nathan gave a long-suffering grin. "Yeah. You're right. Can we hang out again soon?"

"Sure."

"We'll set Jenna up with Calder again."

"Yeah," I lied.

He smiled, bent down, and kissed my cheek. I cleared my throat and stepped away. I needed to talk to him about keeping things friendly. But there wasn't time right now. So I kept quiet while my stomach writhed. He waved as I turned to go up to my room. I needed a jacket. And I didn't want him to know I was leaving with Calder. More guilt took up company in my gut.

As I neared my room, I felt a buzz of vibration coming from the inside of my bag. I dug my phone out of its depths and looked at the new text message.

Heading your way. Coming?

I typed, *yes in a min*, and sent it back. Then I hurried into my room and swapped my light sweater for my jacket. When I started back down the stairwell, I stopped. Nathan stood on the landing one floor below, talking to some other friends. I backed up and took the staircase on the other side of the building.

As soon as I was outside alone, I paused in a sudden wash of fear. The creature could be waiting around the next corner with her bony, throttling fingers and broken, razorblade teeth. But, as Nathan had said, it was still early and people came in and out of Cambridge Hall as though nothing frightening had ever happened here. I folded my arms and took slow strides. Then a few more. Then I went down the steps. My breath fog blinded me. I shivered and stopped.

Eamon has news. You can do this. You have to.

I looked down Farm Drive. In the sudden silence, my heart thumped. Shuddering panic began brewing in my chest. What if she was back? What if she waited around the next corner? What if she was right behind me?

I whirled around, but there was nothing there. Releasing a sigh, I turned again to walk down the street. The icy wind tossed the trees and brought a faint odor of the nearby farm animals. Leaves blew, scraping like fingernails as they skittered on the pavement. I couldn't move.

Calder would have to go without me. I reached for my phone to text him when a car pulled up along the street in front of me. The passenger side window rolled down.

"You coming?" Calder asked. I nodded fast, hurried to the car, and jumped in. The warm air released the tension in my muscles. The immobilizing fear melted away in the safety of the car. I took two long, slow breaths.

"I wasn't sure you'd be able to get away," he said. I glanced at him, and all at once remembered the date. His charm and friendliness. The sickening sight of him getting cozy in the back seat of Nathan's car. Jenna's love-stricken face as he bade her farewell. I bit my lower lip. He looked at me.

"What's the matter?"

"Nothing," I replied automatically, staring out the windshield. I folded my arms. He continued driving toward the house on Berwyn Road. I stayed silent. Soon, he parked in the driveway and turned the car off. For a moment, I didn't move. He got out without a word. I ground my teeth, opened the car door, and got out. Before he could reach the front steps of the house, I stomped over.

"Why didn't you tell me you have a brother?" I asked. Calder stopped and turned around, his eyes wide with dewy bewilderment.

"Because he asked me not to. When our da died, he wanted nothing to do with merpeople tasks."

"You could have told me after our last task was over."

"I'm sorry?" It sounded more like a question than a statement. "I guess it just never came up. His wife doesn't know about merpeople, and he wants to keep it that way."

"His *wife*? He's married?"

"Yes."

"So you kept the fact that you have a brother a secret while you're on tasks to help merpeople. Until now. *On a task.* Oh, no, I'm sorry," I gave a sarcastic chuckle, "You were on a date, so that made it okay. You had to impress Jenna. Let her into your life a little. Right?"

"What are you talking about?"

"I'm talking about this whole..." I fought to search for the right word, "*charade*, this—this *lie* you're telling."

"Lie? What do you mean lie?"

"Jenna! You're leading her on. You put on this act as if you're some suave Don Juan or something and now she's going to get her hopes up thinking you're all into her."

"Because I let it slip that my brother has the same major she does?"

I narrowed my eyes. "So you *are* into her."

"I'm sorry," said Calder with mocking severity. "I seem to remember *you* suggesting that I go on a date with a nice girl. Was I supposed to treat her like dirt?"

"Why not, it's what you're good at."

Calder's face darkened. I shut my mouth quickly and looked away. A grating silence followed.

"Why do you have to bring that up?" he said. "That was a long time ago. I made a mistake and I apologized. Get over it."

"Fine." I held up my hands. "You're right. I'll get over it." I stepped closer to him. "Just stay away from my friend. Unless you *mean* it."

"It was one date!" His volume grew.

"Yeah and she's going to want to make it two, then three. Then what? Are you going to string her along until you go back to Scotland and add another notch to your belt of ex-girlfriends?" My breath caught as I spoke.

"*No.*"

"Then you'd better quit."

"This whole stupid thing was *your* idea."

"No, it wasn't, it was Nathan and Jenna's! And anyway, it doesn't matter whose idea it was."

"Yeah, *right,*" he shouted. "Why don't you tell me what this is really about?"

I swallowed as a spasm of foreboding raced up my spinal cord. He knew. Of course he knew. But I wasn't going to give in. I refused to spill my heart out, only to be left alone the moment he and the others finished with me. No. I would conquer this. I took a deep breath.

"I have no idea what you mean."

Calder scowled at me, his face hard, the lines and muscles pulled taut as though they'd snap.

"You say I'm leading Jenna on. Maybe you should take a look at yourself and your besotted friend Nathan."

I froze. I opened my mouth to retort, but I had nothing. Shame engulfed my chest.

The front door opened. Eamon looked out at us. I looked away.

"Oh, good," Eamon said. "You're back." He turned into the house. "Let's go, Walt." Eamon came down the steps, followed by Walter. He gazed at us as he approached.

"What's the matter?" he asked.

"Nothing," said Calder and I at the same time. Walter looked between us, his eyes a little wider as he, too, sensed the tension.

"Everything okay?" he asked hesitantly.

"We're fine. Let's go," said Calder, passing the keys to Eamon. I frowned, but this time in confusion. We'd just gotten here. I'd hoped to see Samantha, despite her condition.

"Where are we going?"

Walter looked at Calder. "You didn't tell her?"

Calder shook his head and ducked into the back seat. Both Eamon and Walter looked back at me.

"We're going to the Baltimore City Morgue," said Eamon. "We need you to help identify a body."

20

The Morgue

Walter took the front seat. Which left me to sit in the back with Calder. I buckled my seatbelt and folded my arms without looking at him. An icy silence sat between us. From the driver's seat, Eamon turned on the car and backed it out of the driveway.

"Uther discovered a report of a Jane Doe murdered in the Hanover area near the pond where you said you freed the creature," he said. "The body's description matches what you told us about Naia."

"What?" I looked between Eamon and Walter. "No. No, it couldn't be her. She got away."

"We set up an appointment with the morgue for tonight. If we don't get out there, identify the body, and claim it before they do an autopsy, they're going to know something is off the second they see her blue blood."

I shut my eyes. No. It couldn't be Naia. I thought back to the day I went to the pond. She ran off before I freed the creature. What if she didn't get far? A shudder crawled through me.

"Was there a picture?" I asked.

"No. Only a description on the website," Eamon continued. "It says the body is of a young woman; early twenties; blonde hair; blue eyes; five feet, four inches tall; and about one hundred and twenty pounds."

I swallowed. A few different numbers and a mistaken eye color, and it sounded like it could've been my body lying in that morgue.

"Um…" I stopped, trying to shake off the thought of lying on a cold autopsy table. "The description matches her. But it couldn't be her."

"The only way to know for sure is to go check," said Walter. I massaged my knuckles and bit my lower lip. There had to be a mistake. I needed Naia alive. She needed to help us figure out why all of this was happening. She was my only link.

"When did the police find the body?" I asked. Walter looked at his phone again.

"Early in the morning on October 3rd."

"That was weeks ago," said Calder. "If they think the body was a murder victim, wouldn't they have done an autopsy already?"

"They may have," said Eamon. "Let's hope they haven't yet."

"So we just have to go to the morgue and make sure it isn't her?" I asked.

"Do you think you can?" Eamon asked.

I'd never seen a dead body up close before. The thought sent another shudder up my spine. But I nodded.

"When we get there, I need you to pretend to be her sister," said Eamon. "It's the only way they'll work with us."

"Okay." I kept quiet after that, repeating in my mind, *it can't be her. It isn't her.*

The orange street lights passed in a hypnotic rhythm as we took the highway north. Walter and Eamon talked in low voices. Calder and I said nothing. I stole a few glimpses of him, but he sat looking out the window. The space between us felt bigger than just an empty seat.

At length, we neared downtown Baltimore. A text came through on my phone, which shook me from the macabre hole I wallowed in. I checked the text. It was from Nathan.

Where'd you run off to? I thought you went up to your room.

I cringed.

Studying, I replied. Lying again. My already sour stomach did an uncomfortable twist. Another text came in.

Where? Jenna's at the library. She said you weren't there.

I sighed in irritation. *Why'd you go up to my room? I told you I had stuff to do.* Send.

I wanted to help, he replied. *Clearly, you don't want or need it.*

I scowled and turned my phone off. We rode the rest of the way to the morgue in silence. Once we arrived, Eamon parked along the street in front of a glass and brick building. The windows near the front doors listed the business hours: 8–5, Monday through Friday.

"Eamon, they're closed," I said.

"They're here," he replied and got out of the car. I got out slowly. The others walked the short distance to the glass doors ahead of me but stopped before going in until I got there.

"You ready?" Walter asked.

I nodded.

Please, don't let it be her.

Walter opened the door. Eamon, Calder, and I filed in. It didn't look like a morgue. No dim lights, no creepy passageways. It looked and smelled like the lobby of a nice hospital. Our footsteps tapped on blue vinyl tile. Artwork hung on the walls. A long, empty reception counter sat in the middle of the room. We waited a few minutes before a side door swung open and a man walked in. He had a dark complexion, a wide forehead, large ears, and a sympathetic expression. Under one arm, he held a manila folder and a clipboard.

"Hello." He reached out his hand to shake each of ours. "I'm Dr. Moretti. I understand you have a missing loved one."

Eamon turned and looked at me. My cue? Okay. I took an unsure step forward and a shaky breath. "Um. Yeah."

"If you'll follow me, please," he said, gesturing to the door he'd just come out of. "We have a room ready for you." He spoke in a soft, kind voice. Not at all what I expected. I followed Dr. Moretti through the door, the others trailing behind me.

"Thank you for seeing us after hours," said Walter. "It's been a difficult time."

"Happy to help," replied Dr. Moretti. He led us down a hallway. Any second now, someone would wheel a gurney with a body bag toward us. Or we'd walk into a dark, stainless-steel room with refrigerated drawers, and a sheet-covered corpse, where Dr. Moretti would reveal the face of someone I hoped beyond hope *wouldn't* be Naia.

Instead, he guided us to another, smaller room. It contained couches, chairs, and a coffee table in the middle. He held his hand out toward the couches.

"Please, have a seat," he said. He took one of the chairs while the rest of us settled onto the couches. "Now, before I share with you the pictures of the deceased, I need to ask you a few questions."

"Okay," I said with a scrap of relief. No sheet? No corpse? No lab reeking of formaldehyde?

"What is your relationship with the deceased?"

"My sister."

He nodded and made a note on a form on the clipboard. "And was your sister on any sort of medications?"

What should I say? I glanced at Eamon. He shut his eyes for a second, betraying a hint of frustration.

"Um, I…no," I replied.

Dr. Moretti frowned a bit but kept going. "Did she have any health problems? Blood oxygen issues?"

Calder, Eamon, and Walter all exchanged significant looks. Dr. Moretti had seen her blue blood. Dread curled in my chest.

"Could I please just see her?" I asked. Dr. Moretti nodded, opened the folder, and pulled something from it.

"First, I need you to prepare yourself," he began. His voice, if possible, grew even more kind. Low, and quiet. "This victim died from strangulation. There will be some severe bruising and discoloration. It may be shocking. Do I have your permission to show it to you?"

I nodded. *Please don't let it be her.* He laid the picture face down on the table. I reached for it and flipped it over. It took only a second before I had to look away. Gray skin blotched with purple bruises. Long blonde hair. A lifeless mouth and half-open eyelids. My stomach roiled.

"Yes," I gasped. "Yes, that's her. That's Naia."

21

Another Attack

I stared down at my palms as we drove back toward College Park. I dimly recalled Eamon and Walter thanking Dr. Moretti for his help and explained away Naia's blue blood with a bunch of medical and chemical words.

"Poor Olivia was unaware of the medical issues," Eamon had said.

"And the gashes on the sides of her neck?" Dr. Moretti had asked. "They weren't scars, but they weren't new wounds either."

"Ah, yes. A birth defect," said Eamon without missing a beat. "Our Naia was always self-conscious about them."

Dr. Moretti went on about the murder investigation and something about transferring Naia's body to another morgue until the case closed. I was too stunned to listen well.

The creature had murdered Naia. She had come to me for help and instead, she lost her life. She'd been my hope for explanations. Redemption, even. I'd failed. Worse than failed. I slouched in the back seat, too worried to cry, too tired to talk.

"The Coralians won't be happy," said Eamon. "If Naia was one of their people."

"The merpeople at Loch Raven seemed to know her," said Calder. "Where else could she be from. Eldoris?"

"It's possible," said Eamon. "Either that or Tetra. But Coralium is closer than any of the others. Cordelia will have more information when she gets back." He sighed. "I only hope we don't have any repercussions."

"Why would we have repercussions?" I asked, my defensiveness spurring me out of silence. "The creature killed Naia. Naia was the one who told me to free it."

"Yes, but we have no proof of that," said Eamon. I shut my mouth. "All we can do now is hope that we haven't burned any bridges. We've dealt with unexpected deaths of the merpeople before, but not like this."

"What about Delfina?" I asked. It had been a long time ago, but I wouldn't easily forget her haunting eyes, her long red hair, or her fleeing form the last time I saw her alive. "Did her death cause you any trouble?"

"Cordelia confirmed her cause of death before they took her body. Back then, we had Linnaeus to blame."

"So you're saying I'm the one to blame this time?"

Eamon sighed again. "I very much hope not. But since we still don't know who taught the creature how to gain human form in the first place, we're no nearer to finding out who is."

The rest of the drive south remained silent. Every once in a while, I'd sneak a peek at Calder and wonder what he was thinking. Then I'd have to remind myself it didn't matter and go back to staring at my hands.

When we came closer to College Park, Eamon took the exit for Berwyn Heights instead of continuing toward UMD. No. No way was I going to stay with them after what just happened.

"Eamon, could you drop me off at school?"

"I'm taking you back to our place."

"I can't. I have too many things to do."

He hesitated a moment. "All right. But you have to stay indoors unless one of us is with you."

I looked at Calder again. He glanced at me before looking away.

"Okay," I said.

Eamon took a road toward the college and soon turned onto Farm Drive.

"Just drop me off at—" I began, but as I pointed, my words failed and my finger sat in midair, pointing at a busy flash of red and blue. Eamon pulled over. As soon as the car stopped, I rushed out and hurried toward the whirling lights. An ambulance sat next to the police cars. The paramedics had someone on a gurney. I gasped as I saw a streak of blue hair.

"Darci!" I shouted, pushing through the standing crowds.

"Miss, I can't let you in." A police officer held me back.

"Olivia!" someone shouted. I turned. Jenna stood next to two officers, her eyes wide and her face furrowed with trauma. I ran to her. As I approached, one of the officers held up his hands.

"Please return to your dorm, miss," he said. Jenna stepped toward me.

"No, it's okay, she's my friend." Her voice shook.

"*What happened?*" I cried. "Was that Darci?"

"Someone attacked her! I was walking back to the dorm and I saw them struggling..."

"You don't remember what the attacker looked like?" the officer asked. She shook her head.

"It was dark. I think he wore a long coat," she said. "I s-screamed and whoever it was ran off. Other people came r-running and someone called for help. I thought Darci was..."

"What's happened?" Calder jogged up from behind me. Jenna's floodgates opened as she ran straight into his arms. He patted her back. I forced myself to look back at the cop.

"Is Darci okay?" I asked him.

"She's stable," he replied. "They're going to take her to the hospital for observation, but she should be back very soon." He turned to his companion and started talking about perimeters and unsubs.

"Can we go now?" Jenna asked from Calder's arms. The cop looked up.

"You can go," he said, "but we might be in touch. Do you have any family you can go stay with for a few days?"

She shook her head. "My family is all in Boston and I need to stay here. I've got midterms."

"We can post some officers here, but we can't guarantee your safety," said the officer.

"Why don't you go home for a few days?" I said. "I'm sure your professors will understand."

She shook her head again and took a deep breath. "No, I'll be fine. Darci's going to be okay. I'm sure you'll catch the guy who did this."

"If you're sure," said the officer. "Some advice: stay indoors after nightfall and go talk to someone. A therapist, counselor, something like that. Take it easy for a while. The shock might hit you hard over the next few days, and it's important to have someone there to help you sort it all out."

"All right," she said. He left her with a nod and walked away. She released a ragged sigh. "I can't believe this happened here. A killer, right outside our building!"

Right outside our building. I met Calder's eye. He knew, like I did, who the serial killer was. Had they been right all along? Was the creature really after me? And was Darci another unfortunate victim in her path? A wave of nausea hung over me.

"Why don't you head inside?" said Calder, guiding Jenna toward me.

"I don't want to be alone," she said with a simper, turning back to him. I wanted to barf. He stepped away from her embrace and held her by the shoulder.

"Why don't you stay with Olivia?"

She looked at me.

"You'd have to sleep on the floor." I gave an apologetic grimace. "Or I can come to your room if you want." She considered me for a second but closed her eyes as if trying to make a painful decision.

"No. No, I think I'll be okay. If I change my mind, I'll call you." She turned back to Calder and hugged him again. "Thank you for being there for me."

"Olivia," he said, gently sliding out of her grasp. "Maybe you should stay with someone." He gave me a pointed look. Did that mean I should go back with him or stay with Jenna? I couldn't go back with him. And Jenna didn't offer. So, I didn't ask.

"I'll be okay," I said, though I didn't feel okay. It took everything I had in me to keep it together as Jenna and I went inside. She went to her room on the third floor and I went up to mine on the fourth. Then I let it out. Worry about Darci, about Naia's loss, about Calder's anger, about school, and still about Samantha's indifference all came tumbling out of me. I pummeled my pillow, then buried my face in it and wailed. My phone buzzed with a new text, this time from Eamon.

Calder told us what happened. If you feel that you must stay at your school, please keep indoors as much as you can. Calder will be on campus during the day to make sure you're safe. We'll keep searching. Be careful.

I breathed, wiped my eyes, and wished my stupid pride hadn't kept me from staying with them.

The rest of the week continued in a drumming routine. Every night, visions of Naia haunted my dreams. She wailed at me, crying out that it was all my fault. Then she collapsed, gray and lifeless at my feet, until her eyes snapped open and she became the horrific creature, who snarled and snatched at my throat. I awoke gasping. Sheer exhaustion put me back to sleep every morning between four and five a.m. until I had to get up for class. Then, every day I walked down to breakfast with Jenna and watched for Darci's return.

Calder came every day too, but he kept his distance. The day after Darci's attack, I saw him sitting on a park bench as Jenna and I made our way to Footnotes. Jenna didn't see him. She had become more subdued and skittish since the attack. I couldn't blame her. Calder saw me notice him, but he motioned for me to keep going. Was he still mad at me? Right now, I didn't have the time or the emotional energy to find out. Just knowing someone was there watching out for me gave me enough courage to step outside every day.

Midterms arrived and I had a lot riding on them. I especially had to do well in Zoology. The internship still dangled ahead, like a cupcake in front of a hungry preschooler. Though I spent lunches with Nathan and Jenna, all of us kept busy in our books rather than socialize. Nathan avoided talking to me. I didn't press him. I deserved it for being such a terrible friend and a big coward for dodging a "determine the relationship—or lack thereof" talk.

And every evening, I shut myself in my room, studied, and sipped cocoa. But I wasn't safe from the persistent nightmares.

It wasn't until Thursday that Jenna finally brought up our social lives. She seemed better since the attack—back to her perky, friendly, Calder-obsessed self.

"We should go celebrate the end of midterms!" she said as we walked out of the library to go to Zoology. We made the out-of-the-way, but necessary route of walking past the bronze statue of a terrapin turtle standing on a plinth in front of the McKeldin Library. A rub on the turtle's worn nose was supposed to bring good luck. I had to smile every time I rubbed the statue's shiny face. My school's mascot could've been a panther, or a bear, or a tiger. But nope; Olivia Owens, future marine biologist, appropriately had an amphibious marine animal as her school's mascot.

"I can't celebrate yet," I said as testing nerves crept up my back. "I have two more midterms tomorrow."

"Ugh, Olivia, you worry *way* too much." Jenna pushed my arm with one hand and sipped an energy drink with the other.

"It's going to be fine," Nathan said. "Tell you what. Once midterms are over, Saturday night, all of us are going to the coast for dinner at sunset. I'll buy."

"Nathan, I—"

"Nope, nope, no arguing. I insist. It'll be great." He squeezed my shoulder as we walked up the steps of the Bio building for Zoology. A renewed effort to win me over? I didn't answer. When midterms were done, I could talk to him. Yeah. After midterms, my brain would have more space, and I could make it clear that we were just friends. After midterms.

22

Not Human

Friday afternoon, I finished the dreaded Literature exam, where I had to explain why I thought *Wuthering Heights* was an interesting representation of the human condition, or whatever garbage I tried to come up with. I needed a good grade, though, so I hoped my feeble analysis was enough to pull a B-minus.

After handing in the test, I left the classroom, made my way to the front doors, and pushed through them before I realized I didn't have my usual companions with me. Jenna and Nathan were off finishing up their schoolwork and Calder was nowhere to be seen. Students milled around, heading in and out of the building, walking the sidewalks, standing in clusters. I looked in the direction I needed to go. Nothing I could do about it—I just had to hurry back. Thinking of Eamon and my need to earn his respect, I set my shoulders and began walking.

As I went, my bravery solidified little by little. My midterms were done. The application for my internship was in progress. I breathed and made the long walk back to Cambridge Hall. But when I turned onto my dorm's street, I stopped. Up ahead, Calder sat on the bus stop bench across from the front entrance.

A sudden fluster crept up my neck. Did I have to do this now? Maybe I could avoid him by crossing the street. If I put the hood up on my sweatshirt and snuck by, he wouldn't see me. But before I could reach back for the hood, he looked over. I sighed and continued down the sidewalk.

"Hey," I said as I got closer.

"Hi." He stood. It felt a little like the day I first saw him when he had arrived in Maryland. We stared at each other for a second.

"You okay?" Calder asked.

"Yeah." Finally, I could say it truthfully.

"I just wanted to check on you."

"Haven't you been doing that all week?" I said, but had to smile. Even though we stood in shuffle-footed awkwardness, I realized I didn't mind having him one step ahead all the time. Seeing him now, looking tired, but not angry, lifted my spirits.

He smiled at the ground. "Yeah, I guess I have been. But I also wanted to tell you Cordelia came back early this morning. I could've just texted you, but I thought I'd wait until you were done with midterms and tell you everything in person."

"What did she say?"

He took a deep breath and sat back down. I sat next to him.

"She said your friend Naia was definitely from Coralium. She'd been missing from the ocean for several weeks. They think the creature was from Coralium too. Well, sort of."

"Sort of?"

"Cordelia said Naia's family was from another reach entirely, but they migrated to Coralium when she was a child. They got lost on the way. A big storm steered them off-course into Chesapeake Bay and one of the little merlings got separated from the rest of the family. They never found her."

"Oh," I said with a dispirited exhale. I shook my head. "That's so heartbreaking. I can't even imagine. Do they think the creature is the little girl who got lost?"

"Yeah. Loch Raven has a river connected to the bay that floods every few years. She must have somehow gotten washed into the reservoir and has been there ever since."

"So she isn't vicious. She's just…lost." I stared into space, unable to grasp how terrifying it must have been for a child to end up alone. Naia just wanted her sister back. And now… "What about Naia's body?" I asked.

"Uther and Walter returned her to the merpeople when they went to pick up Cordelia."

"How? I thought the morgue was keeping her during the investigation."

"They, uh, stole her body."

I straightened, both worried and a little impressed. "Oh. Are they in trouble?"

"No. Uther took care of it."

"Good." I bit my lower lip. "Are the Coralians upset?"

"I'm not sure," he replied with a frown. "But if I had to guess, I'd say they probably are."

"I didn't kill her," I said loudly, drawing stares from some students passing by. Calder waited until they turned their incredulous stares away before continuing.

"No one is saying you did. Not even Cordelia."

I pinched the bridge of my nose. "So what do I do now?"

"We find the creature. Once we do, we can take her to the merpeople. She'll be able to back up our side of the story."

I leaned back against the bus stop bench and sighed with frustration. "Where does she keep hiding? How does she disappear?" I turned toward him. "Have you checked the pool?"

"Yes. It's been drained for the last few weeks. They're refinishing it. Is there an indoor pool?"

"Yeah, but no one can get in without a key card."

He leaned forward and balanced his elbows on his knees.

"There's somewhere we've missed. We'll find it. Until then, we're here to keep you safe."

I tentatively looked up at him. The memory of our last conversation made my face burn. Did I want to bring it up? Not really. Would he?

"Where are your friends today?" he asked. I deflated. He wanted to know about Jenna. I frowned at the bus pulling up in front of the stop to exchange passengers.

"Um, I think they're still taking midterms," I said, folding my arms. "They wanted to hang out tomorrow night if you're..." I trailed off as the bus drove away and I noticed a familiar person shuffling up the front steps of Cambridge Hall across the street. A person with a blue streak in her hair.

"Darci!" I shouted. She didn't hear me. I turned to Calder. "That's my friend who got attacked. I'll be back." I stood and hurried across the street. She went into the building. I followed after her inside. "Darci!"

She stopped, turned slowly, and her face brightened.

"Hi, Olivia."

"Are you okay?" I asked, then shook my head. "Sorry. Of course, you're not okay."

She sighed. "No, I'm okay." She smiled, but it didn't reach her eyes. "Honestly, I feel lucky to be alive. How many people can say they survived the Loch Raven Strangler?" Her smile faded. Moving her whole body instead of just her head, she looked around the lobby with a fearful expression.

"What is it?" I asked.

"Could we talk for a minute?" she asked. "My room is just off the hallway."

"Yeah, sure."

She glanced over my shoulder. "Um...in private?"

I turned to see Calder. I hadn't heard him come in behind us. He nodded.

"Go ahead, I'll wait out here."

"This way," said Darci. She turned to go. Before I could follow, Calder stepped closer to me, took my wrist, and whispered in my ear. "Fill me in when you're finished."

The brief closeness sent my heart wild. I couldn't look at him. Surely, he saw my blush. I gave him a brief nod, followed Darci down the hall, and once Calder was out of earshot, I let out a slow breath to steady my firing nerves.

Darci unlocked the door to her room and went in. Or, apartment. It had a small living room and kitchen. She put her purse and keys on the kitchen counter, then sat on the little couch and rubbed her forehead.

"So how are you?" I asked. "You look good for what you've been through."

"My injuries were minor. Luckily. But—I'm freaking out," she replied with a long exhale. I sat in a plush chair next to the couch.

"I can understand that."

"I wanted to talk to you, because..." She paused and her eyes bore into me. "I know you saw it too. That snarling thing that tried to get you that night a few weeks ago?"

"Yeah," I said cautiously, wishing Calder were here to help me know what to say and what not to say. I couldn't tell her the truth about her attacker.

"The cops said it had to be the Loch Raven strangler. But it was like—" She stopped, rubbing her chest just below her throat, her face a haunted mask of pain.

"Like what?"

"Like it wasn't...human." She shut her eyes for a moment. "I know that sounds insane."

"It doesn't sound insane. I saw her too, remember?"

"No one believes me. I kept calling my attacker a 'she,' but they said it couldn't have been female because this kind of crime isn't typically done by females *to* females. Some behavioral analyst came to talk to me and she kept asking if 'he' tried to force 'himself' on me, if 'he' had a weapon." She sniffed and rubbed her nose. "I described her to them, but they made me take a drug test."

I grimaced and knotted my fingers together. The same guilt for freeing the mermaid raked at me.

"I'm so sorry this happened. I believe you though."

She gave me a gloomy smile. "Thank you." She sniffed again and staring toward the nearby window of her apartment. They let me come home after all my drug tests came back negative. But I'm scared."

"I know. I am too." How could I reassure her when I had no idea where the creature was, and when my own anxiety made me freeze in my tracks half the time? "But…I have friends trying to track her down right now, so she won't hurt anyone else."

Darci frowned incredulously. "Are they detectives or something?"

"No." How could I explain? "Do you mind answering a couple questions for me?" I asked. She shrugged.

"Why not? It's not like the police were any help."

"Okay. Just tell me what you remember."

She fidgeted with her glasses. "Well, I was walking back from the rec center the night it happened. I kept hearing someone behind me, but every time I looked, I didn't see anyone." Her words sounded bland and rehearsed, as if she'd said them a hundred times before. She probably had, after talking to the police. "Then I heard running footsteps. I turned and saw it—*her*." She stopped, her face screwing up at the grotesque memory. "I ran. I almost made it to the front steps before she…got me."

"And Jenna saw you?"

"Yes. Everything started going black when I heard Jenna scream. I guess she called 911 because the paramedics came soon after that."

"And you don't remember seeing anyone else? Maybe heard another voice or anything?"

"No. Wait, there was one other thing." She pointed a finger. "The woman, or thing, that attacked me—she was dripping wet."

I sat back. The creature had found a water source nearby. Lake Artemesia was too far and the pool didn't have water in it. If Darci was walking from the rec center…I straightened with a gasp.

"Campus Creek," I said. I hadn't thought of it before. The creek was so shallow and with it running through campus, people were constantly crossing over its bridges. But it had to be where she kept hiding.

"What?"

"Nothing. Never mind. I've got to go." I stood. "She won't come after you during the day, so just make sure you're inside before nightfall."

"What makes you so sure?"

"That's the only thing every case has in common. Do you have roommates?"

"Yeah. They're all gone for the weekend though."

"Okay. Don't go anywhere alone." I walked toward the door.

"Wait," she said. I stopped. She gave me a hard look. "What is she?"

I hesitated. "She's…not well. She shouldn't even really be here."

"So like an experiment gone wrong? I wondered what those biotech people were up to."

I gave a humorless laugh. "No, she's not from them. But I have friends who are going to find her and take her away."

She looked at me with narrowed eyes. "Who are these friends?"

"It's hard to explain. Just trust me." I gave her one last reassuring, and totally unconfident smile, then left. I needed to get to Campus Creek.

23

Campus Creek

I headed down the hall when laughter from ahead reached my ears. On the other side of the lobby, near the student lounge, Jenna and Calder stood close together. I backtracked and kept hidden around the corner. Jenna leaned against the wall. She touched Calder's chest and said something else. I frowned and turned back.

I couldn't approach them like that. But I could *not* go to Campus Creek to look for the creature on my own. Could I?

The sun was still up in the west. I'd be done well before nightfall. All I needed to do was rule out Campus Creek as the creature's hiding place. Chances are, the shallow little brook would be too small and thin for her to use as a retreat.

I mulled it over a minute longer, then decided to try to go through the side door alone. But the moment I opened it, my muscles threatened to seize. I grit my teeth.

"Olivia?"

I jumped. Calder strode up the hallway toward me.

"Where are you going?" he asked. "Why didn't you come get me?"

"You looked busy," I said, turning away so he wouldn't see the curl to my lip.

"I wasn't busy. I was waiting for you."

"Sorry, I just—" I didn't want to get into it right now, so I pushed the door open. "Come on." We went outside and I continued. "Darci said her attacker was all wet. She'd been walking back to the dorm from the rec center. Campus Creek runs right through campus, and it's on the other side of the rec center. I hadn't thought of it before because it's so shallow, but maybe it's where the mermaid has been hiding."

"Oh. Yeah, we thought of the creek too. We even checked a few areas, but it's so shallow. And in most areas, it was only a trickle."

We hurried up the sidewalk, passing Cumberland Hall adjacent to Cambridge, then crossed a parking lot and came to a series of concrete steps. A brick wall ran along the ride side of the stairs and a terraced community vegetable garden, used by the school's agriculture club, extended along the left. At the bottom of the stairs, an entrance to the recreation center went off to the left. Ahead, across another small parking lot, leafy bushes and trees overgrown with ivy and undergrowth hiding the creek from view were alive with fall colors.

We crossed the parking lot and hurried for the bridge spanning the creek at the other end. A smell that reminded me a lot of the Pirates of the Caribbean ride at Disneyland arose as we came to the bridge. My heart quickened with the excitement that we might find some clues. But despite the hope, and the comfort of having Calder there to help, I had to force down the fear and keep walking. The creek wound its way through thick vegetation, a carpet of fallen leaves, and dead twigs.

I leaned over the side of the bridge and looked down into the mostly dry creek bed. Though the banks were steep, the actual water levels were so low, it was no wonder the others didn't think the creature could be hiding here.

"Did you check around this bridge?" I asked him.

"No," he replied. "Damn, we got interrupted during the search and hadn't had a chance to come back to walk the entire length of it."

I took a deep breath. "Well, we're here now." I turned and tried to peer under the bridge, but the tall metal bars along the sides prevented me from seeing much. "I can't see anything."

"Look," Calder pointed at the bank on the other side, close to the water. "Come on." He hurried across the bridge and rounded the railing. I followed after him, but couldn't help thinking back on his distaste for snakes. If he worried about it at all, he didn't mention it.

He climbed down the bank, then stopped and held out a hand to help me down. I took it, hoping the shade from the trees hid my burning face. As soon as I found level ground, I let go. The smell changed from the nostalgic scent of an amusement park ride to a musty, rotting stench. I held one hand over my face.

"See that?" Calder pointed again. "And that?"

"Ew," I said with a frown, staring at the remains of two raw, half-eaten fish. Across the creek on the opposite bank from where we stood, the bridge created a sort of cave between the bank and the water. "Look at that."

Heaps of branches and leaves, along with old clothing, diverted the water to make a pool in the cave-like space, like a nest with water in the bottom. The nest wasn't visible from above. Even from where I stood, it looked more like the work of either a homeless person or smart beavers.

"She's not here," said Calder. "But she *was*."

Though part of me wanted to celebrate the find, the gag-inducing smell and the memory of her snarls made my hands shake. *She's unwell. And lost*, I reminded myself.

"But where is she now?" I asked. "And if she's spending a lot of time in the water, why hasn't she gotten her fins back? She should have been able to change back a long time ago."

"Maybe she can't remain fully submerged out here," he said. "Or maybe it's different for a mermaid who's been living in fresh water for so long."

I looked up when voices approached from overhead.

"Shh," I said quickly. Chattering students crossed the bridge, happily leaving their midterms behind. We listened for a minute, watching the wooden slats overhead until I realized how close Calder stood to me. I peeked at him, my chest tight. But because he watched the bridge above us, he didn't notice.

"Okay, let's go." He stepped up the side of the bank. I let out the air I'd been holding and stepped up, sliding on the leaves and debris. He reached out for me again. I took his hand again. I didn't want to let go. But let go I did. Again.

While we walked back to the dorm building, Calder pulled out his cell phone to call Uther, telling him about what we'd discovered.

"It was Olivia's idea to search the creek," he said into the phone. I smiled at the acknowledgment. He continued. "It made a sort of dam, hidden under a bridge. You couldn't see it unless you were right next to it." He paused for a second while Uther spoke. "Yes. But we have to do it humanely. Right. Okay." He finished his call and hung up. We passed the rec center and climbed the steps alongside the vegetable garden our way back to my dorm. I dug my hands into my jacket pockets. The sun had neared the horizon and with it went the warmth.

Soon we came to the sidewalk in front of my building, which was more crowded than usual. I stopped, struck with a sudden thought.

"Calder," I said.

"Yeah?"

"I've just thought of something. If the mermaid has been living down there, able to come and go whenever she wants, why haven't more people been attacked? Darci can't have been the only person to walk out here alone."

He frowned in thought. "That's a good point."

"And what about the person that freed her from Loch Raven? If someone helped her gain human form, they had to have known what they were doing. And you said they're probably close by."

He looked at me with an intense frown.

"I'm taking you back to the house." He grasped me by the shoulder and kept walking.

"Oh. Um…okay. Do you think—" I stopped as my cell phone buzzed. I pulled it out. A text message from Nathan glowed on the screen.

Did you get this? You got everything done, right? A screenshot of an email came up with the text. An email from Professor Seeley.

Thank you to all those who have turned in their paperwork for the internship. The final decision on interns will be made after midterms have been graded. We have had many qualified applicants. It will be a difficult…

I stopped walking. My vision blurred. Yes, I had turned everything in. Hadn't I? I opened my email and checked it. Then rechecked it. No email from Professor Seeley. Could there have been a mistake? Had I really missed the internship?

I stood, frozen in my cloud of utter dread. I couldn't talk. I couldn't even cry. How could I have let myself get so distracted?

"What's wrong?" Calder asked.

I couldn't say it. Saying it would make it real. He waited. I stared at the empty inbox on my phone. "I—I didn't get the internship," I whispered.

"What? Really?"

I didn't look at him. He sighed.

"I'm so sorry," he said. "I know you worked hard."

Tears stung my eyes. Did I work hard, though? Had I let too many other things get in the way? The merpeople, Calder, investigating, running around ponds and lakes and morgues… I must have missed something. I squeezed my eyes shut and cupped a hand over my nose and mouth. Maybe if I couldn't breathe, I wouldn't cry in front of him.

He stepped closer, but I stepped back. I lowered my hand.

"Would you just go back without me?" I said.

"What about the creature?" he asked.

"I'll be fine." I couldn't talk without my voice trembling.

"No, come on. It's not safe. We'll—"

"Just *go*!" I turned and ran the rest of the way to my building, fumbled with my key card to unlock the door, hurried up the many flights of stairs, and to my room. Then I pulled out my laptop to email my teacher, this time from an old account instead of my school one. My fingers paused on the keys. How should I word this? Dear Professor Seeley, you forgot someone? Dear Professor Seeley, how dare you exclude the one student who wanted this internship more than anyone?

In the end, my email centered more on the possibility of a technical error and a hope that I'd still be considered. I sent the email, changed into pajamas, and went to bed. But I didn't sleep.

24

Take That, Merworld Laws

The sun hadn't come up yet the next morning when I awoke with a start. Had Professor Seeley gotten my email? I rushed to find my phone, grappled, and nearly dropped it trying to open up my emails. My heart soared when I saw a new one from Professor Seeley.

Miss Owens—

I'm afraid I cannot offer you a spot on the internship team. Though I was impressed by your application, some serious circumstances make granting you a position impossible. If you do want to discuss it, please visit me during office hours next week, however, the decision has been made and remains unnegotiable.

Best,
Professor Roberta Seeley

My heart plummeted back to earth. Then it hadn't been a mistake. Professor Seeley hadn't just overlooked me; she'd rejected my application altogether. The words *serious circumstances* and *unnegotiable* jumped out at me. Unnegotiable. What circumstances could possibly have made me this ineligible?

I dropped my phone, lay on my pillow, and didn't move as the morning continued to lighten. Trying to go back to sleep was more of a languid refusal to open my eyes. What was the point? What was I supposed to do now that my last hope of achieving my goal was gone? What would Eamon think when he found out I'd failed?

The sun dawned clear and cloudless. The glorious sunrise shone in hues of pale yellow and clearest blue—as if my world teetered on the edge of ending. I glared at the view from between the blinds in my window then flipped over to face my wall.

My phone buzzed over and over. Texts from Nathan. Texts from Jenna. Texts from Calder. Even a text from my mom, though she had no idea what was actually going on. I replied to her with a generic, I'm-fine-school's-fine-everything's-fine text. I didn't want her to know. The other texts I ignored and turned my phone off.

I awoke again when someone knocked on my door. Disoriented, my eyes heavy and gritty, I looked around and read the clock. It was after ten am. I shifted. My head ached. Why did I feel like I'd been crying for hours? Oh, yeah. The internship. Gone.

"Olivia?" came Jenna's voice from outside. I didn't reply. "It's Jenna. Nathan told me what happened. I'm so sorry. Can we come in?"

I turned my head and stared at my orca poster. It didn't matter that I knew its diet, its migration patterns, or even its anthrozoological history. It didn't matter that there wasn't a soul on earth who understood how desperately lonely my world had become, or how the internship had offered hope for a cure to that loneliness. The facts were my life was still in danger, my best friend didn't care, and my so-called "friends," a.k.a. the merworld guardians, were never going to let me be part of them if all I did was make bad decisions and fail at achieving anything.

I shifted deeper under my covers. A carton of peanut butter fudge ice cream sounded nice right about now. But that reminded me of Samantha's letters, which made me think of Calder, which made me furious, which reminded me of the creature, which also reminded me of my lost internship. I sniffed twice and hiccupped. Another knock came at my door. I sighed, hauled myself to my feet, and opened it. Jenna and Nathan stood there.

"Hi," said Jenna. "Are you okay?"

I nodded, even though I wasn't.

"I'm sure if you talked to Professor Seeley, she could give you another shot," Nathan asked. A zing of anger throbbed in my chest. If only it could be that simple.

"It's...not just the internship," I said, my eyes filling up again. I turned away so they wouldn't see.

"What else is going on?" Jenna asked.

What else was going on? Ugh, so much. But it would be too hard to explain without revealing too many secrets and I didn't have the brainpower to talk around the truth.

"Nothing. I just want to be alone right now."

"Come on," said Jenna with a note of pleading. "Talk to us."

I stayed silent.

"Let's go," Nathan said. They walked out and closed the door behind them.

The morning wore on. Outside, it seemed like every student at UMD was out enjoying the October sunshine and the small window of freedom before the grind of prepping for finals began. Inside my dorm, I did my best to avoid everyone and everything. But since I had no food stocked up, I didn't stay much longer after Jenna and Nathan left. So I counted the spare change in my wallet for the vending machines, left the room, and went downstairs. As I headed for the lounge, someone called my name.

"Olivia?"

I looked around. Samantha stood just inside the lobby doors, twisting her hands.

"Hi." We faced one another for several weird seconds. During those seconds, I envied merpeople again. Or maybe I hated them. It was all way too confusing on an empty stomach.

"I was actually about to text you. You're probably wondering why I'm here, right?" Samantha asked with a laugh in her voice.

"Did they find the creature?" I asked.

"No. They waited at her little habitat almost all night. Still no sign of her."

I slouched. "Where could she have gone?"

"She'll have to go back there sometime. And when she does, they'll be ready." She looked at me for a second, her eyes squinting. "Sorry, can I just ask you something?"

I blinked. "Yeah."

"Do we know each other? I mean, did we ever meet back when…"

She looked around to make sure no one was listening to us. "...when I was human?"

I swallowed and shook my head. I hated this. Where was the chocolate?

"I'm sorry," she said again, "that must sound so weird. Ever since I came on land, I've had this," —she paused as if looking for the right word— "I don't know, empty space in my brain that makes me sound a little 'off' sometimes. But I swear you look so familiar, even though Cordelia keeps saying we've never met before." She waved it off and sighed. I wished I could wave it aside so easily. "Anyway, Calder told us you were upset about something," Samantha continued. "You weren't answering your phone. He had me come to check on you."

"It's just school stuff," I said, though it wasn't just the school stuff. I didn't want to get into it. Thinking about going to Professor Seeley and asking about my internship application made my stomach turn inside out. I should have been able to tell Samantha all of this—but I couldn't. That hurt too. She was my right-hand woman. She was always the one to talk me down from my freakouts.

Except she wasn't. Not now.

"Tell Calder I'm sorry I've been ignoring him," I said. "But I'm fine." I turned, heading again toward the vending machines.

"Well, there's something else too," said Sam. I stopped and turned back. "Seidon told me you could help me."

"With what?"

"I don't want to bother you. It's just that I needed a girl's help. I could ask Cordelia, but she's—"

"A pain in the neck?"

Samantha laughed. "I was going to say she's helping Eamon try to find the creature, but okay."

I managed a little smile. Sam went on.

"This is going to sound so dumb and I hope I'm not being awkward. But I have to do something about my wedding or I'll go insane. Seidon told me I should go pick out a wedding dress. So I'm going to go. But my mom is in Arizona and I have no one else to go with. Since we have to look out for you anyway because of the—"

"You want me to go wedding dress shopping with you?" I interrupted.

"If it's too much to ask, I totally get it. I mean, you barely know me. And it's kind of a big deal."

I bit my lower lip. "I'd love to go."

She raised her eyebrows. "Are you crying?"

I cleared my throat, ran my nose along the sleeve of my sweatshirt, and laughed.

"No. Um. Here." I handed her some change. "Would you grab me a couple granola bars from the vending machine? I just need to go up and change, then I'll meet you back down here."

I turned and ran up the stairs, simultaneously laughing and crying. Samantha might not remember all we've been through during our lives, but she still trusted me enough to ask me to go wedding dress shopping with her.

Take that, stupid merworld laws.

25

Old Samantha

I hurried up the stairs to my room. Once inside, I leaned over my laptop, did a quick Google search, and sent a few locations to my phone. Then I changed, ran a brush through my hair, grabbed my bag, and headed back down. In the second-floor stairwell, I saw Jenna going downstairs with a basket of laundry on her hip.

"Hey!" she called as I flew down past her. "Where are you going so quickly?"

"Uh, shopping."

"Shopping? Why?"

"My friend needs a wedding dress."

"Who?"

I paused. I'd never told her about Samantha.

"My oldest friend. Samantha." I walked down a few more steps.

"You've never mentioned her before."

"I haven't?" I said, even though I knew very well I'd purposely kept Samantha's existence on the down-low. It was easier not to talk about her than to explain a best friend who lived completely off the grid. I turned and looked back up at Jenna. "Huh. Well, she's…visiting."

Jenna scowled. "She's here now?"

"Yeah."

"Oh. So you're going to go wedding dress shopping with her, but you can't hang out with us?"

My mouth hung open in a stupor.

"I—"

"Forget it." She shook her head and instead of continuing down, she turned and walked up the stairs, leaving me in the stairwell with a new weight of guilt to accompany the rest of my baggage.

The frosty farewell with Jenna left a bad taste in my mouth. And if I'd hoped all awkwardness would suddenly melt away once I rejoined Sam, I must have been sleep-deprived. Silence dominated over the easy laughter and conversation we once had. Sam drove while I navigated. "Turn here," or "exit there," were some of the few things I said. I felt myself slipping back into the sad, muddy hole I fell into when Seidon first told me she'd lost her memory.

"So how's school?" Sam finally asked after ten minutes of nothing.

"It's fine," I said. "I'd rather not talk about it right now if that's okay." The sting and worry of losing the internship still hung around my neck like a deadweight. I should've just confided in Jenna and Nathan. I could've edited out the part about merpeople. Why did I push them away?

"No problem. We don't have to talk about school." She looked over at me. "Mind if I ask you a personal question instead?"

She wouldn't have asked like that before. Sam loved delving into my personal life. The more personal, the better.

"Go ahead."

"What's the deal with you and Calder?"

With my mind on what a terrible friend I'd been to Nathan and Jenna, I hadn't expected her to ask about Calder. "Wow. Um..."

"I ask because he's been all mopey lately."

"Mopey?"

"Yeah. Seidon tried to get it out of him, but he won't talk about it."

"Oh. Well," I began, wanting so badly to spill my guts, but I couldn't confide in someone who barely knew me. Then I realized: she'd remember one day. As soon as she went back to the ocean, she'd remember all of this. So I continued. "We had a fight earlier this week. I lost my temper because he's been flirting with my friend. That night, they were especially, uh, friendly. It sent me over the edge. And then I sort of ditched him last night. And ignored his texts today." I grimaced. What a first-rate friend I was.

"Really?" She gained a gleam in her eyes that was so like the old Sam, I felt a small leap of joy.

"Yeah. It sounds bad now that I say it out loud. It's so stupid. I'm actually crazy about him."

"*I knew it*," she said. There she was again! "Seidon told me you guys had history. Not so historical, is it?"

"Don't say anything. Because once all this is over, and you and Seidon go home and get married, Eamon and Calder and all the others will go back home too. The last time this happened, it didn't go well from my end." I looked down at my hands, working my jaw with the discomfort of the memories.

"Why not?" she asked mildly. I shrugged.

"I don't have anyone to talk to. At least, no one who gets it. All the merworld stuff, I mean."

"Oh. That must be hard. But, at least you can call them on the phone."

I looked at her in surprise, humbled by her words.

"You don't get to call your family?" I asked. She shook her head.

"No. Just letters. But I'm going to go see them before we head back to Zydrunas." She smiled, excitement giving her voice a lift. It somehow made me more ashamed. She was right. I did have all kinds of technology to stay in touch with people. How did I let myself get so isolated?

"I shouldn't have acted the way I did," I said. "Getting all jealous and stupid."

"Eh, we all get stupid when we're jealous. There was this mermaid Seidon was friends with a long time ago—she came for a visit last winter and wouldn't leave him alone. I wanted to strangle her. He finally had to tell her to get lost." She laughed. "And if it makes you feel any better, I don't think Calder is mad at you. Quite the opposite."

"Really?"

"Yeah." She smiled. Was she messing with me? She and Seidon had once gone to ridiculous lengths to throw Calder and me together. I sighed.

"Well, for now, our job is to focus on fixing the mermaid problems. Then—I don't know. We'll see."

"And in the meantime…it's okay for us to go wedding dress shopping today, right? Let the others handle capturing the creature. Something tells me we both could use a little fun."

The old Sam shone through again. I smiled. "Yeah."

We went to the few stores my Google search had found between College Park and Washington DC, but Samantha didn't like anything she tried on. After the third store, we both slumped back into the car just as the sun was setting. She sighed.

"They're all trying to force me into lace, rhinestone, or mermaid dresses."

I laughed. "I'd have thought the mermaid look would suit a *mermaid*."

"But I don't want to look like a mermaid on my wedding day. I want to look like a bride. This is such a rare opportunity for Seidon's family to attend a human wedding. And my family will get to be there. I want it to be special."

"It will be."

She glanced at me with a small smile. "Thanks for helping me. I'm sorry I've been so picky."

"It's okay, you were always…" I trailed off, aghast, then tried to cover it. "Uh, Seidon said you've always been, uh, fashion-conscious."

She gave me a peculiar look.

I cleared my throat and looked at the locations on my phone. "We've got one place left. It's in Old Town Alexandria. It'll be a long drive back, but Alexandria is really cool. If we don't find a dress at that place, we can call it a day and try again another time."

"Okay. When we're done, do you mind if we get some food? I'm starving."

Do I mind? Old Sam would have assumed instead of asking. And she would have assumed correctly.

"Definitely. There'll be lots of places to eat near this last store."

Once we came into historic, picturesque Old Town Alexandria, we turned onto King Street and made slow progress through the many traffic lights and crossing pedestrians. Sam didn't seem to mind the slow-going though. She squealed with delight at the rows of old-fashioned townhouses, quaint alleyways, cemeteries, and elegant churches.

We pulled up in front of the bridal boutique. It had a gray brick exterior, with scrolling designs carved into the stone and wood, and white-framed windows. We parked and fed the meter.

"Oh, this place is so cute!" Sam exclaimed.

"Right? I will never get tired of visiting this place." We got out of the car and went into the store. A bell rang. A woman with liquid black eyes, shining hair, and olive skin looked up from behind a little desk.

"Can I help you?"

"Yes, I'm looking for a wedding dress," said Sam, "and my friend needs a bridesmaid dress."

"I—what?"

"You've been helping me all day," she said to me. "We might not know each other that well, but you're more a bridesmaid than Cordelia or Eamon ever were."

We both laughed and I could finally keep a real smile on my face.

"Well, you're in luck," said the sales clerk with a smile. "My last appointment for the day had to reschedule, so I've got a space for you. Follow me."

Still giggling, we followed the lady into the boutique, passing mannequins in glittering, gauzy gowns and rows of poofy white dresses on racks. Samantha began browsing with the sales clerk while I looked at the one rack with multi-colored dresses. I stopped for a second to watch Sam, her happiness, and her eyes lighting up as she saw one of the dresses the clerk pulled out. I felt a rush of gratitude. Note to self: Buy Seidon an extra-large pizza—his favorite human food—for arranging this shopping trip.

Samantha smiled at another dress, but for a second she paused. She looked around as though someone had just shouted her name. But there was no one here, other than us and the faint melody of Canon in D playing in the background.

"What's wrong?" I asked. She shook her head.

"Nothing. I'm going to go try these on. I need your opinion." She walked toward the back of the store, where three large dressing rooms stood, draped with velvet curtains. The store clerk closed the curtain behind Sam and waited with her hands folded. After a few minutes, Sam came out in a simple, flowing chiffon gown with spaghetti straps and a v-neckline. It hugged her waist as though cut and measured just for her. My mouth dropped open.

"Sam," I sighed, forgetting I needed to act a little less familiar. She grinned so widely, her face could have powered a lightbulb.

"Wow, the first one!" said the sales clerk. "Do we have a winner?"

"I love it," she said. As she gazed in the mirror, her face fell. She looked over her shoulder, out the window, then toward the back door.

"What is it?" I asked. She shook her head again.

"Sorry, I keep hearing things. Must be a dog howling outside or something."

I sat back. Her mermaid ears heard something mine couldn't.

"Maybe we better go," I said.

She moaned at her reflection and turned to the sales clerk. "Let me talk it over with my fiancé, and I'll call about the dress tomorrow. Did you find anything you liked, Olivia?"

"Don't worry about me, this is your day."

She smiled. "Okay. But keep on the lookout for a bridesmaid dress. Let me change, then we can go."

The sales clerk took the dresses Samantha didn't try on and went to put them back on the rack. I picked up our purses and waited near the front of the store, gazing at veils, tiaras, and shoes. What would it be like to get married? I didn't think much about it. Sure, in a "someday" sense—but what was it like to find one person you wanted to be with for the rest of your life? I'd known what attraction felt like—and crap, did I ever know heartbreak. But real love? It always felt so elusive to me. My soulmate was the ocean. The thought sent a spasm to my stomach as I remembered the internship. I shook it off.

The sales clerk went back to the changing room.

"Miss? Are you doing okay?" she asked through the drape. Silence. "Miss?"

I looked toward the changing rooms, but the rows and corners of displays blocked my view. I rounded the rows until I saw the clerk ease the drape open a bit and peek. She reached in and pulled out the dress Samantha loved. Where was Sam?

The sales clerk approached me. "Did your friend want me to set this aside? I can hold it for the next twenty-four hours."

"Where did she go?"

"I don't know. She's gone. I just saw the dress."

She continued toward the front of the store. I looked around and noticed another door, labeled "Employees Only," open just a crack.

I peeked through. It led to another room with a back door. This one stood wide open. A frigid breeze blew in.

Then I heard the screaming.

26

Sunlight Through Soreness

I ran outside, searching all directions for the source of Samantha's desperate shrieks. It echoed off the bricks of every shadowed building. I hurried one way, then another, trying to follow the sound. Terror dizzied my vision.

"Samantha!" I shouted. Where was she? The screams faded into snarls and guttural gagging. "*Samantha!*"

I hurried around a corner, to a tiny parking lot between the buildings. There, behind a car. A flicker of shadows and a pair of struggling legs. I rushed toward them. And screamed. Samantha lay on the ground, her eyes bulging as she scratched and pulled at the creature's fingers around her neck.

The creature looked at me over her shoulder. Her eyes flashed yellow from a reflected light. Her teeth stuck out from her gaping mouth. I screamed again, threw myself at her, and grabbed her around the shoulders.

The creature twitched and wriggled. Her thin bones twisted under my grip. She growled and whined like a rabid dog and broke free. I fell. Her hands went around my throat. Trying to breathe, fighting against the painful pressure of fingers digging into my windpipe, I struggled to push her away. Her hands tightened. She was too strong. Black spots appeared in front of my eyes.

"*Calder…help*," I said, but it came out as a strangled whisper. Several pops sounded in the distance. A sudden sting burned in my leg. My arms stopped working. I couldn't see anymore. I couldn't even feel the creature's hands anymore. Shouting, then…

I awoke in a shroud of pain. Even my eyelids hurt as I pulled them open. I lay on a bed, covered in blankets. Where was I? Dull light came from behind heavy curtains covering a window in an unfamiliar room. I tried to sit up. My neck throbbed. Mustering as much vigor as I could, I forced myself to a sitting position. My shoes and sweater lay on the floor next to the bed. The room had blue walls, a dresser, and a nightstand. A bottle of water sat on top of the nightstand, next to my cell phone. In the corner sat a reclined easy chair, piled with a bundle of blankets. I grabbed the water and started to drink but choked. It felt like swallowing shards of glass.

I got to my feet and shuffled to the door. It opened to a dim hallway in a quiet house I didn't recognize.

"Hello?" I said, my voice little more than a croak. Down the hall, more light came from under a closed door. I continued toward it and opened the door to find a white-tiled bathroom, lit up by sunlight through a window. I walked in. My reflection in the mirror made me jump. My neck was splotchy red. My eyelids drooped. Tiny red dots bloomed from around them like grotesque freckles. I looked away, noticing the bathtub in the other corner, full to the brim. Something lay inside. I peeked into it and shrieked.

Samantha. Pale and bearing the same marks I had, she lay unmoving, crunched in a fetal position at the bottom of the bathtub. My muscles seized in horror. Nausea churned my stomach. This couldn't be real.

"*No!*" I slipped to my knees, falling on the freezing floor. "She killed her! She's dead!"

Footsteps hurried down the hall and into the bathroom. Seidon appeared, looking frantic, and bolted for the bathtub. Calder came in behind him. He reached down and picked me up. I was too numb to react.

"Samantha's dead!" I cried. I couldn't stop sobbing despite how much it hurt my throat. My heart hurt worse.

"Shh," said Calder, carrying me out of the bathroom. "She's fine."

"Why is Samantha in the water?" My weak, hoarse voice got worse.

"She's resting. The water helps her to heal." He took me back into the bedroom and sat me on the bed.

"Try and relax," he said, his voice low and quiet. "Sip some water." He opened the water bottle and handed it to me. I sipped from it again. Ouch.

"What happened?" I asked. He sat next to me.

"We don't know how, but the creature found you down in Alexandria."

I took a few breaths. The memory came in flashes—terrible, nightmarish flashes. I touched my neck with a shaking hand.

"Did she follow us somehow?"

"We don't know. All we know is she went after both of you. We thought we were too late. But you're both going to be okay."

I cleared my throat. "It hurts to talk."

"You're going to be sore for a while. Eamon's got some meds if you need some."

I nodded, then looked at the light from the window. "What time is it?"

A little after nine am."

The door opened. Eamon walked in. He had a stethoscope around his neck. He smiled.

"Samantha is just fine," he said. "How are you feeling?"

"I've been better," I whispered. "How long was I out?"

"Well, almost twelve hours or so, total," said Eamon. "Since your last dose of pain meds? Maybe about six hours."

"You were crying out in pain," said Calder. "Do you remember any of that?"

I stared at him. "No."

"You've been in and out since last night."

"Why don't I remember?"

Eamon stepped forward and put his stethoscope into his ears. "The trauma. It can affect memory. Mind if I have a look at you?"

He listened to my heart and lungs, then examined my neck, my eyes, my pulse, and my breathing.

"Anything hurt?" he asked as he tested my reflexes.

"Everything. Mostly my throat."

"That's to be expected."

I hesitated, looking from Eamon to Calder. "When can I go back?" I continued in a whisper. Anything louder grated on my vocal cords. "I have to talk to my professor tomorrow. It's really important."

"Olivia, you were nearly strangled to death," said Eamon severely.

"I have to talk to Professor Seeley about my internship," I stood too fast. My head spun. Calder caught me and eased me back on the bed. I sat while the dizziness faded.

"Would you go get some ibuprofen?" Eamon asked him. Calder walked out. Eamon turned back to me. "I can't let you go back. You need to stay under observation for the next few days. Serious complications can arise if you're not careful."

I bowed my head under a fresh wave of misery. "I have to talk to her. I have to convince her to give me another chance." I said it more to myself than to Eamon, but he replied.

"You're young. You'll have lots of chances. For now, just rest. Heal. We can take you back to school once we know you're okay." He patted my shoulder and stood. "Tell me immediately if you feel any intense pain or any shortness of breath."

I nodded. The bedroom door creaked open wider and Calder walked in with a bottle of pain reliever. He opened it and handed me two pills. I took them with some water and another wince. The pills might as well have been covered in thorns.

"I'm downstairs if you need anything," said Eamon. "Come on, Calder. Let her be."

"I'll be down in a bit," Calder replied. Eamon stood there for a second before he walked out. I inhaled slow. Images of last night continued to rise to my mind. Samantha struggling. Hands around my neck. Losing my ability to breathe. The panic. The blackness.

"How'd we get out of that?" I asked Calder. "I thought we were going to—" I stopped talking and shuddered. He sat back on the bed.

"We caught the creature," he said. I stared at him.

"You caught her?"

"Tranquilized her. I'm sorry to say, you got hit with a dart too."

"You shot me with a tranquilizer dart?" I asked, almost laughing despite myself.

He grimaced. "It was an accident. I was aiming for the creature. But the tranquilizer might have helped your pain for the first couple hours."

I had to smile at the look on his face. "How'd you find us?"

His frown turned to a half-grin. "Did you think we'd let you and Samantha go shopping alone?"

I scowled. "I should've known. So you were following us? The whole time?"

"Pretty much. Seidon and I thought you could use some girl time. And I think he wanted to go check out more human stuff."

I laughed, but it came out short and whispery. "So you gave him a grand tour of the DC area through our shopping route? That must have been boring. We weren't there to see any landmarks."

Calder chuckled, but then his face fell. "We thought you'd be okay in that last store. We ran to grab something to eat down the street. We even got you two some food." He looked down. His brows knit. "Seidon heard the screaming first. When we got there, that thing was on you." He rubbed his face. "I shot first and asked questions later."

He saved my life. My hand twitched, aching to reach out for him. I longed to confess that he was the last hope I had before everything went dark. But what would it accomplish? And what if he didn't care about me that way? I had too much to work out already. I couldn't wade through this too. I kept my hands in my lap.

"Thank you," I said, trying to hold back the bloom of emotion before it leaked out my eyes. I looked at his forearms resting on his thighs.

Slowly, I raised my eyes to meet his. He gazed back at me. I couldn't do this again. But I wanted him. I wanted him so badly I couldn't stand it. His eyes flicked down at my lips. The silence crackled between us. He leaned closer. Was he going to—

"Samantha is awake," said a voice from the hall. Calder looked to the doorway, where Seidon appeared. "Oh. Uh. Sorry." He grinned and walked away. I closed my eyes as my pulse calmed and the palpable magnetism between Calder and I evaporated. I took a long breath.

"I can't stand pretending she's just an acquaintance."

"Shh. She might hear you."

I turned my head away, which hurt my neck. I couldn't live like this anymore—acting like Samantha wasn't important to me, trying so hard to impress Eamon, then looking over my shoulder, worrying if my next breath would be my last. Trying to live half in the real world and half in the world of rescuing merpeople would either drive me to insanity or kill me.

Maybe it was time to move on.

"If I have to stay here for the next few days, could you at least take me back for a few minutes to talk to my professor tomorrow?" I asked, still not looking at him. "I still have my future to worry about."

"Sure. Come on downstairs when you're feeling up to it. We can get something for you to eat if you're hungry."

I gave a small nod. He stood and walked out. I looked around the little bedroom, to the curtained window, and got up from the bed. Sunlight on my face would feel nice. I opened the curtain. It looked out to the house's front yard. Down on the ground, Uther walked around the perimeter, gazing in all directions with a cigarette hanging out of his mouth. Just like old times. I wanted to smile, but couldn't.

I turned away from the window. The light from outside lit up the room and I saw the easy chair in the corner more clearly. What I had thought was a pile of blankets had only been a single quilt cast aside. Someone had been sleeping in it. I had a good idea of who it was. Which hurt worse, my throat or my heart?

The internship. Think of the internship. It'll get you through this.

The thought of having to confront my professor brought a new wave of exhaustion over me. I ran a hand over my sore neck, walked back to the bed, and sat down. On the nightstand, my cell phone lit up and buzzed. I picked it up. I had several missed phone calls and even more texts. I shut my eyes. If I wasn't careful, I'd lose not only my reason for going to school, but also the friends I needed to keep me going.

27

An Unorthodox Idea

A whole-body twitch awoke me. Had I fallen asleep? I opened my eyes and looked around. The pain in my neck had lessened. I sat up and took another drink of water. It still ached going down.

My stomach growled. I checked the time on my phone. Forget breakfast—it was closer to lunchtime now. I slid off the bed and stood, testing my balance. Then I hobbled out of the room and headed to the bathroom first. The bathtub was empty. I shut the door, used the facilities, washed up, and ran my fingers through my hair. My clothes from last night still bore the marks of struggle. I plucked at the shirt and sighed, then went out of the bathroom and down the hall. I gripped the railing as I descended the staircase to the little foyer at the front of the house. On the back side of the foyer, voices filtered through the hallway leading to the dining room. I followed the sound but stopped when another set of voices came from the other side of a door to my left, open a small crack.

"I'm just saying you need to keep your distance," said Eamon.

"I don't know what you're talking about," Calder replied. His tone of voice sounded defensive, almost defiant.

"I'm not an idiot. I can see it's not just friendship between you two."

He huffed. "You never cared before."

"Of course I did. I warned you about this last time you got too close to someone we were trying to protect. It did not end well, as you may recall."

"This is not even remotely the same situation. Olivia is not Aeronwy."

The sound of my name sent a cold tingle down my core.

"Maybe not, but I still have to insist that you keep your distance. If you hadn't been better able to blend in on a college campus, I'd never have assigned you to be her security in the first place. Because I was afraid this would happen. If you get emotionally involved, it can have disastrous consequences."

"We're not MI6, Eamon," Calder replied with a sneer.

"No, but we do deal with life and death situations and heavy world secrets. I care about both of you. Please, for both your sakes, end it now, before it gets any more difficult."

"I never said anything was going on."

"Good. Keep it that way."

I gripped my arms around my middle and backed away before they could come out and see me. Nothing going on. The spark between Calder and I? Either it didn't exist for him, or I just imagined it. I swallowed down the threat of tears. I shouldn't waste any more emotion on him. He was never mine to begin with. And Eamon didn't want us to be together. Not only that—he didn't want me to be part of them at all. If he had any thought of letting me join their team, why would he care whether or not Calder and I had feelings for each other? A tear broke through. I wiped it quickly. My chest heaved with the effort of holding back my heartbreak.

I turned and went back upstairs. Halfway up, I stopped as Seidon started coming down.

"Oh," I said, my breath hitching. He smiled, met me in the middle of the staircase, and hugged me.

"Thank you for saving her," he said into my ear. I hugged him back.

"I'd do it again every time."

He let me go. "You all right?" he asked, his eyes darkening as he looked at my face. I shook my head and stepped around him. He stopped me. "What's wrong?"

"Keep your voice down," I whispered and peeked downstairs. Calder and Eamon hadn't come out of the room yet.

"Why?" Seidon asked, also in a whisper. I pressed my lips together and tried to go up the stairs faster, but it made my head swim. He followed, taking hold of my forearm. "Go slow. The gravity on these stairs is pretty intense."

He almost made me laugh. I stopped at the top of the staircase to let my dizziness abate. He folded his arms and tilted his head, watching as I sniffed and breathed and made every other futile attempt not to cry.

"Samantha is all right, you know," he said. "She's downstairs with the others. You can come see her."

"That's not it," I said, my voice thin. He looked at me a second longer, then understanding dawned on his face.

"You heard them talking," he said. "Eamon and Calder."

I frowned. "Did you?"

He shrugged. "I can't help it. I eavesdrop on just about every conversation within a three-fathom radius."

I lowered my chin. "Would you do me a favor? Could you go down and ask one of the others to take me back to school?"

"Why?"

"Really?" I said with an eye roll. "You just heard—"

The door downstairs opened and Eamon and Calder walked out. They both looked annoyed. I turned to go to my room, but Seidon grabbed my elbow and pulled me back.

"Look who I found," he said. "She was just telling me she was ready for some pizza." He put his arm around my shoulders and squeezed.

Eamon smiled, all annoyance gone. "Come have something to eat, Olivia. Seidon, you are limited to four slices this time."

"What?" Seidon removed his arm, held a hand to his heart, and descended the steps in front of me. "I need my sustenance. I'm a growing merboy, Eamon."

"A growing merboy?" Eamon laughed. "Save some pizza for the rest of us, or soon you'll grow *outward.*"

"More of me to love," Seidon replied with a grin. Eamon chuckled again and retreated down the hall. Calder followed him without looking at us. Seidon stopped on the stairs and looked up at me.

"Come. Samantha wants to see you."

I lifted my head. "She does?"

He held his hand toward me. I came down the stairs and took it. He helped me down the last few steps, then released my hand and put his arm around my shoulders again.

"Don't let them get to you," he whispered with a brotherly squeeze. "You're our friend. Not just a person we're protecting."

I gave him a small, close-lipped smile. He let his arm drop and went into the hallway ahead of me. With a deep breath, I followed him but paused at a large window in the hallway that faced the backyard. Outside, the surface of the swimming pool rippled. It was October. Was someone swimming? Seidon backtracked and looked out the window as well.

"Don't worry," he said. "The creature is caged. She's not going to escape."

"She's in the pool?" I asked in alarm.

"It's the safest place to keep her."

"What about the chlorine? Will it hurt her?"

Seidon frowned in puzzlement. "What's chlorine?"

I shook my head and took a steadying breath. "Were you able to talk to her?" I asked. "Does she know who helped her take human form?"

He shook his head. "She hasn't spoken yet. I don't know if she can."

I gazed at the water a moment longer.

"Come on," he beckoned. "You can tell me all about the chlorine."

I looked away from the pool and trailed behind Seidon to the dining room. Everyone sat around the table talking and eating, except Uther and Walter, who stood in the nearby kitchen, piling slices on their plates. Seidon made a beeline for the open boxes on the counter.

"What's chlorine?" he asked them as he grabbed a slice and stuffed a corner of it into his mouth. "Olivia seemed worried it would hurt the creature."

"Nah," said Uther. "She'll be fine."

"Olivia," said Walter. "Come get some pizza before Seidon eats it all."

Samantha turned from the table and saw me. Her welts had healed more than mine had. She got up and came toward me.

"Are you o—" I began, but she wrapped me in a bone-crushing hug. Even though it hurt, I didn't move. My tears rose to the surface again, so close I had to squeeze my whole face to keep from crying.

"Thank you for stopping her," she said. "She would have killed me." She let me go. I nodded stiffly, holding my mouth in a hard line. She turned away to sit down. I swallowed and took a moment to curb my emotions.

"Come, sit," said Cordelia. She didn't eat any pizza. "We need to brief you on the most recent developments. Did Calder inform you of the creature's origins?"

"Yeah," I said and went to sit next to Walter. Samantha sat next to me, with Seidon next to her at the end of the table. On the opposite side sat Eamon, Uther, and Calder. Lieutenant Adrian stood against the wall behind Cordelia's chair at the head, still looking as broad and unpleasant as ever.

"Here is what we haven't yet discussed. King Enamerion was reluctant to talk, but he did confirm that the Coralians sent a special ops team to assess the situation when the creature first escaped. They were able to capture her and contain her before Olivia mistakenly set it free again. They've been trying to find the creature ever since, but their search has been focused north of here." I looked down at my hands. Though Cordelia hadn't spoken of me releasing the creature with any blame, I still bit my lip and kept quiet.

"How did they know the creature transformed if she wasn't in the ocean?" Walter asked.

"They can track unauthorized transformations," she replied. "But it's still a mystery how she did it. There are other parts to the ritual that should have made transformation outside a temple of Nereus impossible."

"So the Coralians don't know who showed the creature how to take human form?" Samantha asked. Cordelia shook her head.

"No one knows. The Hedron is going to discuss the freeing of the creature at the CHASM meeting, along with Samantha and Seidon's match."

Seidon slipped his arm around Samantha.

"They can't keep us from getting married," said Seidon. "I'll give up my fins if they try."

"Seidon," said Cordelia severely. "This isn't about you. This is about the security of our world. The creature going on a rampage looks bad for our human allies."

Again, she didn't speak with any accusation, but I still felt it. The creature's release looked bad for us because a human let her go when they had her contained.

"But it couldn't have been a human who showed her how to transform," said Seidon. "No one but Olivia knows the Prayer."

"I don't know it at all," I said quickly, my back straightening. "I heard it *once*, over a year ago. There's no way I could tell it to some wild mermaid, much less teach her how to use it to turn into a human."

"Nonetheless," Cordelia continued, "if we can't figure out why and how the creature was released in the first place, and restore alliances with all the reaches in the merworld, I fear that we will have no choice but to sever ties with humanity permanently."

Sever ties? I exhaled. Two warring thoughts cropped up in my head at once: a stab of dismay that the merpeople could close themselves off from humans forever and a strange, opposite sense of relief. Perhaps cutting off all contact would be a better solution for everyone. It would certainly decrease the death toll. We could move on with our lives. Then I looked up at Samantha. She gazed at Seidon, her face drawn in heartbreak. Trepidation in my own heart increased.

"Does that mean merpeople like Samantha would live on land as humans?" I asked. "Or would they just return to the ocean and never see their human friends or family again?"

Cordelia laced her fingers together and looked down at them.

"There are no other merpeople like Samantha. Closing the oceans would more likely mean she would remain as she is now." Cordelia brought her eyes up to meet mine. Her intense gaze said what her mouth didn't—Samantha would remain *exactly* as she is now, in mind as well as in body. She'd never remember our lives before her forgetting. And with her on land and Seidon at sea, she'd never marry him. I clenched my teeth. I couldn't let these things happen to her.

"So, we need to figure out who *first* released the creature," said Eamon. "And we need to prove that keeping humans as your allies is in the best interest of everyone involved."

"I agree," said Cordelia. "And I have a proposal. A rather... unorthodox one." Everyone's attention fixed on her. "As it stands, there are ten reaches in the ocean. Therefore, there are ten members of the Hedron. Historically, there have always been eleven. However, we cannot suggest any reach to contribute two delegates to CHASM. It would cause an unfair advantage. So, to help sway the vote in a direction we want, I propose we nominate an eleventh member to the council from among our human allies."

My jaw dropped. A ripple of surprise crossed every face in the room. Lieutenant Adrian stepped forward. "Permission to speak, Captain."

"Granted."

"You cannot nominate a human to a merperson council. It's against our laws."

"Actually, it's not," said Cordelia. He glowered. She either didn't notice or ignored it. "Centuries of distrust and hatred do not equal law. I consulted with a specialist at the Coralian archives. She said there has been a human member of the Hedron before. Hundreds of years ago. A queen. I believe her name was Elizabeth."

"Queen Elizabeth?" said Calder. "As in, Elizabeth Tudor?"

"According to my source, yes," Cordelia replied.

"Wow," I breathed. Queen Elizabeth was part of a merworld council? History books never covered that part of her life. Goosebumps tingled up and down my arms.

"So we have the precedence," said Walter. "We have the need. Who do we nominate?"

Cordelia's eyes locked with mine. Everyone else followed her gaze until they all stared at me.

My face flushed. My heart beat in my throat.

"What? No. You're kidding, right? I can't be part of some merworld council. I don't know anything about this kind of stuff."

"Olivia's right, Cordelia," said Eamon. "Are you certain you want to go ahead with this plan?"

"Yeah," I said. "Why don't you do it, Eamon?"

Eamon shook his head. "No."

"Why?"

Cordelia replied before he did. "Because the Hedron is more likely to ratify the nomination of a woman than a man, no matter their experience. No offense intended to present company, but merpeople trust women more than they trust men."

A matriarchal society. I remembered Linnaeus discovering that fact.

"Why don't we ask Natasha, then?" I asked.

"Natasha has chosen to remain at home at this time," said Cordelia. "You, Olivia, are the only logical choice."

"No, I'm not," I said more forcefully. "I'm twenty years old! I don't even have a college degree." The exertion hurt my throat. I cleared it and sat back.

"Age has nothing to do with it," said Cordelia. "Princess Meraud of Eldoris is barely eighteen and she's a member of the council."

I shook my head. "I'm not Princess Meraud."

"At least think about it," said Seidon, his eyes pleading. I dropped my chin, overwhelming pressure weighing on me.

I couldn't think about it. Because it wasn't going to happen.

28

Infraction

I had to get out of here. Between Seidon's failed attempts to hide his disappointment, Samantha's imploring face, the memory of Calder and Eamon's conversation, and the ominous knowledge that a murderous mermaid lay in the pool nearby, the house felt more like a prison cell. But Eamon insisted on keeping me until he was sure no complications arose from my injuries. So I kept to my room the rest of the day to avoid everyone.

After answering all the texts from my worried friends, I lay on my bed, the same questions running obsessively through my mind. Why did they have to put the burden completely on my shoulders? I couldn't do what they wanted. Growing up, I never even wanted to run for student council at school. To suggest I nominate myself for some merworld United Nations wasn't just laughable. It was downright impossible.

A knock sounded at my door. I didn't want to talk to anyone right now, especially if they were going to talk about CHASM.

"Olivia?" came Uther's voice. "I got something I need to ask you."

I sat up. “Come in.”

He came in slowly, as though worried he’d catch me getting dressed or something. When he saw me, he came in, holding a laptop.

“This is your email, is it?” He handed me the laptop. I looked down. There was my inbox, with all the emails I hadn’t yet deleted.

“Yes. This is it.”

“How long have you had it?”

“The school sent me the account name and password right after I got my acceptance letter. I used it to email Eamon to thank him for the scholarship.”

“And who is ‘admin?’” he asked, pointing to the word *Admin* listed below my username in the upper corner of the webpage.

“I…don’t know. It’s always been there. I figured it was part of having a school email. I didn’t think…” I trailed off and looked up at Uther. “Is that the person spying on my emails?”

“It could be. I tried to find out who it was, but it’s a completely anonymous name on an anonymous server. Most likely, it’s someone with access to your school’s internet servers.”

“Someone from my school?” I asked with unease.

“Yes. From now on, don’t use this email account. Begin a new one.”

I sighed. “Okay. Thank you. I’m sorry for all the trouble.”

He made a fist and tapped my chin with it. “You’ve always been trouble.” He laughed. “Haven’t kicked you out yet.” He turned and walked out. And oddly, he made me smile.

By Monday morning, Eamon granted my wish to fly the coop, and only after another checkup and my assurance that I felt fine, even though my neck was still a little sore.

I came downstairs in some clean clothes, courtesy of Samantha and Seidon running out to my dorm room to gather me some extra things. Calder came into the foyer.

"Are you sure you want to go back?" he asked.

I came down the last step. The conversation I overheard between him and Eamon rang in my ears.

"Yeah. I have to," I said. The dejection on his face made me want to throw something. Why did he have to do that—say one thing and then act differently? He turned to go out the front door.

"Come on, then," he muttered. I scowled and followed him. We walked outside, down the front steps, to the car in the driveway. I buckled my seatbelt and avoided his gaze.

It took a few minutes of silence before he finally spoke again.

"You're not even going to consider Cordelia's idea?"

I rolled my eyes to the car ceiling. "You know I can't do it. I'm terrible with people. I don't even know anything about human politics, let alone the merpeople's. And they don't trust me."

"It was a good idea," he said mildly. "It would be nice to have a say in some of their decisions. *We share the same planet*, after all." He gave me a pointed look. I sighed. Using my own words against me now, huh?

"What would you do in my place?" I asked.

"I'd listen to Cordelia," he replied without hesitation. "Isn't that what you want? To work with us?"

I ground my teeth together. "Even if I did, I still need a day job, don't I?"

"I guess so," he replied, then kept quiet the rest of the short drive to UMD.

We pulled into the drop-off lane in front of Cambridge Hall. I had less than fifteen minutes before Professor Seeley's office hour ended.

"Thanks for the ride." I got out of the car and shut the door, then crossed my arms in front of me and started walking.

"Liv, wait," Calder said, also getting out. "I almost forgot." He shut his door and came around to me, holding a bundle of blue tartan fabric. "You don't have much bruising, but you'll want to hide the scratches." He unrolled the fabric, which turned out to be a long scarf. He wrapped it loosely about my neck. But instead of letting go when he finished, he held on to the scarf and looked down at me. More of that electricity sparked. Or maybe it was only my imagination. *Twelve minutes. You have twelve minutes.*

"I have to go."

"I know. It's just…"

"What?"

He set his jaw and looked me right in the eye. "You've been through a trauma and I get that you need time to recover. But if my best friend didn't remember me—and I had the chance to change the laws that took her memory—I'd jump at it."

I blinked.

I hadn't thought of it that way. His words burned through me. Was he right? Could I really have Samantha back? Would it work? As I contemplated the possibilities, Lieutenant Adrian's cold stare and the cruelty of the Coralian merpeople rose to my mind. The elation that rose in my chest extinguished.

"You know they'll never let someone like me on their council," I said. "And even if they did, they'd never listen to me."

"At least think about it. What have you got to lose?"

I nodded. He moved closer. The gray buttons on his jacket shone in the sunlight.

"The creature is caught," I said. "You won't have to hang around anymore."

He lowered his voice. "What if I want to?"

I looked up. He wanted to? What was all that talk with Eamon? His eyes roved over my face. It would be so easy. I could give in. Who cared about a long distance anyway? I pulled my hands out of my sweatshirt pockets and lifted them to his chest.

Eight minutes.

I gently pushed him back and walked around him. "I have to go."

"Olivia..." he murmured.

"Hey, Calder!" Jenna waved and trotted up to us. She grinned at him, then turned a concerned gaze on me. "Are you okay? When I got your text, I freaked out!" Relieved she wasn't still mad at me for going shopping with Samantha, I smiled back.

"You don't mind walking with her, do you, Jenna? She's got somewhere important to go."

"Of course!" She put her arm around my shoulders. "Come back and hang out with us later, Cal."

"I'll try."

"You better!" Jenna smiled at him again and walked with me down the sidewalk. "So where do you need to go?"

"Professor Seeley's office."

"Are you okay?" she asked again. "Did they catch the guy that mugged you?"

That was the story I gave them. A mugging. "Um. Yeah. They caught the guy."

"Good."

Jenna continued a long string of questions about the mugging and about Calder. I looked back at him only once. He stood next to the car, watching us for a second, but climbed in when he saw me looking. I didn't want to talk about him. I'd rather keep lying my face off about the "mugging."

"Do you think he'll come hang out later?" she asked. She kept glancing back at him too.

"You know what? I don't think you should go after Calder."

"Why not?"

"He's going back to Scotland soon. You'll never get to see him." I clenched my teeth to keep my lip from trembling.

"I don't care. I gotta live in the moment, girl!" she said with a mischievous glimmer in her eye that reminded me so much of Samantha, my irritation spiked again.

"I can go to Professor Seeley's on my own; you probably have a class to get to."

"You sure?"

"Yeah."

"Okay. I'm here if you ever need to talk, though."

I nodded. She smiled and waved as she turned and walked back toward Cambridge Hall, where we left Calder. I sighed and tried not to think about it while I hurried to the Atlantic Building, where Professor Seeley had her office. I had less than five minutes.

I knocked on the open door. Professor Seeley looked up from typing something on her computer.

"Good morning," she said. She did a double-take. "Are you okay?"

"I'm fine. Did you get my email?" I asked with some trepidation. I'd sent it before Uther's warning not to use the email account.

"I did. Thank you for coming. Please have a seat." She gestured to the chair opposite her desk. I came in and sat. "You wanted to talk about the Hawaii internship?"

My heartbeat cranked up a few notches. Now, what was I supposed to do? Grovel? Or argue? I swallowed. It still hurt.

"Yes. I thought I had everything turned in on time."

"Yes, Miss Owens." She got my name right, which gave me hope. "I did receive your application. But I'm afraid I can't accept you into the program because of the incident earlier this semester."

My blood chilled. Incident? Was she talking about Naia and the creature? How could she know about that? And what did it have to do with the internship? I tried to breathe the calm back into my body.

"Um, what incident?" I asked.

"The plagiarism," she said, as though it were obvious.

Plagiarism? What?

"I never plagiarized anything," I said.

Professor Seeley lifted her hands in a brief gesture of futility. "You should have gotten a letter about it."

"I haven't gotten anything like that. An email or actual letter?"

"I'm fairly certain they do it electronically nowadays. The professor who informed me said she had alerted the dean's office. They should have gotten in touch with you."

I pulled out my phone and checked my emails. Aside from a few advertisements from the aquarium and some junk mail, nothing. I shook my head. Could it have been lost with the other emails that had mysteriously disappeared?

"There's no letter." I looked up at her. "Even if there was, I didn't do it."

She sighed and gave me a rare look of compassion. "I'm sorry, Miss Owens. I still can't allow you on the internship team."

"But..." Desperation rising, tears forming yet again, I sputtered, "but I need this."

"I understand. If you feel like you've been falsely accused, you can take it up with the professor who brought it to my attention."

"Who?"

She shook her head with a sympathetic wrinkle between her eyes. "I'm afraid it's not up to me to disclose that information. You can talk to the dean or your other professors." She took her briefcase, walked around her desk, and opened the office door. My cue to leave. I could barely feel my legs as I walked out.

Professor Seeley closed the door and walked away.

Now what? I shut my eyes with a weary exhale, then started walking. Whoever had accused me was lying. The thought burned like a swallow of bitter coffee running down my throat. Who would lie to ruin my chances of doing this internship? Which of my professors disliked me that much?

Cunningham? Briggs? Morales? It couldn't be Professor Trafford. She...wait. I stopped walking in the middle of the hallway. Professor Seeley had referred to the professor who reported it as a "she." Professor Trafford was my only other female teacher.

Professor Trafford. She had always been so nice to me, so supportive.

Why would she do this? I'd never copied work from another person in my entire life. Professor Trafford was supposed to have written me a letter of recommendation. Instead, she lied and called me a thief, jeopardizing not just the internship, but my entire college career. Why didn't she ask me about it first before taking such drastic measures?

Unless she had made a mistake. My heart perked up. Professor Trafford was extremely unorganized. She must have confused me with someone else. I picked up my pace. I had to talk to her. If I could fix this, I might have another shot at the internship.

I looked at the clock on my phone. My class with Professor Trafford had ended already. Oh great. Missing her class—that'll soften her up. I couldn't wait until her next class though. I hurried across campus to the Tawes building and Professor Trafford's office. But when I finally arrived, her office door was shut. I knocked. No answer. I tried opening it—locked. Maybe she was in another lecture? I hurried down the hall to her classroom, but the lights were off. She must have gone out to lunch. I sighed. This wasn't over yet.

With weariness tugging at my body, I made the walk toward the dean's office. If Professor Trafford had accused the wrong student, I could straighten it out. I could still go to Hawaii, be closer to Samantha, and find my path and my career without merpeople, or anyone else, messing it up.

29

Nothing

I walked out of the dean's office an hour later, too numb to cry. He told me the same thing Professor Seeley had. Not only that, but I was in danger of failing the class altogether, which would also result in a suspension of my scholarship.

He even gave me the letter from Professor Trafford outlining my "infraction." Specific things. So specific, it plunged my heart back into the thorny pit of hopelessness. Professor Trafford knew exactly what she had been doing. Only none of it was true. And I had no way of proving otherwise. How could she do it?

I trudged back to my dorm.

My appetite gone, I slumped over to my bed. I had just drifted off when I awoke to someone knocking on my door. I didn't want to move, but I got up anyway and opened the door. Nathan stood there.

"Hi," he said. I looked down, saw that I still wore the tartan scarf Calder had given me, and took it off. I didn't want to see anyone, but judging from the way Nathan had been lighting up my phone with endless texts, he wasn't going to back down until I talked to him.

"Can I come in?" he asked.

"Sure." I stepped aside.

"What happened to you this weekend?" He asked. "I tried calling when I got your text."

I continued the same lie I'd been telling everyone else. Lying was getting old. After I finished the fake story, he sat on my chair with a concerned frown. I sat on my bed.

"So they caught the guy?" he asked.

"Yeah."

"Was it the serial killer?"

"Umm…" How should I answer? Yes, it was the serial killer? Would he notice the lack of reports in the media? "I'm not sure," I replied. He swore under his breath, shook his head, got up, and wrapped me in a hug. I felt…nothing. Nothing but the pain in my neck and a wish for him to let go.

"Nathan, you're hurting me."

"I'm sorry." He let go at once. "Are you okay?"

"I'm fine." No, I wasn't. His eyes roved over my neck.

"I can't believe someone did that to you."

Wishing he'd stop looking at me like that, I raised a hand to my throat.

"I'm fine, really." Why did I keep lying? "I've had a doctor look at it. I'm just a little sore."

"So, what's going on with you?"

I looked down at my hands. The shame burning in my chest crept up to my face. "I just need alone time."

"I get it. But you've been acting weird all week. I thought we were—

you know—starting something. You *acted* like you were okay with it. Do you want me to…give you more time?"

I sighed with impatience. "Nathan—"

"I like you, Olivia. I want us to be more."

I looked up at him, marveling at his boldness. I should have been able to say it back. Any girl would be so lucky to have a guy like Nathan earnestly declare his feelings. Why couldn't I be like that? I wanted to like him the same way. Maybe if I lived in a world without mythical creatures at my neck and their human protectors in my head, I could like him the way he wanted me to. But even if I tried, I couldn't force myself to feel something.

"I can't."

He clenched his teeth and looked away.

"It's Calder, isn't it?" He barely moved his lips. His assumption didn't surprise me. But it pained me all the same.

"Calder is…not in the picture." I sighed. "Honestly, it's been a crazy semester. I just got mugged and after all this stuff with the internship…"

He looked back at me. "Yeah, what happened with that?"

I didn't want to get into specifics, especially since the accusations were untrue.

"I didn't get in. Professor Seeley wouldn't change her mind."

His shoulders sagged.

"That sucks. I'm sorry."

I shrugged, holding my breath to keep from breaking into renewed tears.

"So there's nothing else you can do?" he asked.

I swallowed. "I'm not sure about anything right now. I just need some rest," I said, hoping he'd take the hint. He nodded and looked down at my hand as though wishing he could take it. Then he stood and went for the door.

"Just one question." He paused before going out. "Tell me straight." He hesitated, furrowed his brow, then spoke fast. "Would things have turned out differently if Calder hadn't shown up?"

"Nathan." I rolled my eyes. "There's a lot of other issues right now."

"That doesn't answer my question."

I huffed, my temper rising. "No. Or…maybe. I don't know." He shook his head and walked out without another word. The silence he left behind stung. Would I be able to patch up our friendship once I got all my school stuff figured out? After Eamon and the others left? I sighed again. By the look on his face, I doubted it.

30

Doubt Aside

I sent an email to Professor Trafford that evening, asking why she accused me of plagiarism in such an aggressive and completely made-up way—edited down to more respectful wording. I didn't dare use my school email after Uther's warning, so I used an older account.

The next morning, I awoke early and grabbed my phone next to me to check my emails. No reply from Professor Trafford. I slumped back on my pillow and rubbed my neck muscles. The pain had gotten better—it should have brought me hope. But I had none left. So I mindlessly scrolled through my phone until the battery died. I plugged it in but left it off to charge.

On my shelf, Minerva's fins waved at me as though to say *get up off your butt and quit being a slacker.*

"What's the point?" I snarled at my fish. "I have no internship. The one teacher I trusted to help me turned around and ruined everything. My friends are all pulling away. What do I do?"

Minerva's swirling, midnight blue tail undulated in the water.

You could stop being a coward and maybe do what Cordelia suggested.

"Oh, shut up," I said aloud, even though the suggestion had come from my own thoughts. "You know I can't do it."

Everyone else is pretty sure you can, my thoughts continued. I shut my eyes.

"I'm not good enough. Or smart enough. Or brave enough."

Saying it loud cut like a knife. I wasn't brave enough. Not for any of this. My mind, my heart, my body all carried a weight so heavy, it took every ounce of willpower I had to get out of bed. I needed a shower, but once I managed to drag myself to the bathroom, I could only wash my face and brush my teeth.

Still, even that small effort made me feel just a little bit better.

I went back to my room and lay back in bed. My stomach rumbled. Maybe I could order out for a breakfast sandwich or something.

Someone knocked on my door. Ugh, why can't everyone just leave me alone? I wanted to ignore it and wallow some more, but I got up. Maybe it was Jenna. Or maybe a prepaid sandwich, whose delivery person showed up at the wrong door. It could happen. I opened the door and found Calder standing on the other side. He didn't have a sandwich.

"Hi," I said. "How'd you get in?"

"Walked in when someone walked out."

"Oh." I tried to discreetly run a hand over my hair to smooth it down. "Why'd you come?"

"We've been worried. You haven't been answering your phone."

I looked down.

"I'm fine. Just busy."

"Too busy to recover from almost being strangled to death? Or to answer texts?"

I shut my eyes, then realized something. Calder had never been up to my dorm room before. "Wait, how did you know where I lived?"

"Samantha told me."

"Oh." Right. She and Seidon had been here before. Calder stood there, looking cute and awkward in the long silence. "Did…you want to come in, or just check on me?"

"I'll go if you want me to."

I stepped aside. He came in. I couldn't help comparing the way my heart reacted when he brushed past me, as opposed to when I'd let Nathan in earlier. I half-heartedly pushed the door to close and sat in my desk chair. He sat at the foot of my bed, facing me.

"Did you get your internship?"

I didn't answer. Somehow, the question turned my depression into rage. I clenched my teeth, heaved myself off my chair, and went to my closet, where I pulled out a duffle bag and started taking shirts off the hangers.

"What are you doing?" Calder asked.

"Going home." Saying the words aloud made angry tears burn in my eyes. "I'm done. I almost died last weekend. My best friend, who also almost died, doesn't know who I am. Eamon doesn't think I'm good for anything but getting into trouble."

"No, he doesn't, he's just—"

I interrupted him. "And I didn't get the internship. Not only that, I'm in danger of failing Literature and my scholarship could be taken away."

"What?" He straightened. "Why?"

With many vicious tosses of clothing into my bag, I related the details of what the dean had said.

"...and then I find out that all the work I did, all the studying, all the homework was for *nothing* because some stupid professor accused me of cheating!" I rolled a pair of pajamas into a wad and threw them at the floor near the duffle. I covered my face with my palms and breathed as the seething anger, fear, and frustration all churned in the pit of my stomach. A moment later, a pair of hands came around the sides of my shoulders. His touch released the stress and despair, making it all flood out my eyes. I tried to hold it back; crying made my neck ache.

Calder slowly turned me around. I hiccupped, wrapped my arms around his waist, and cried against his chest. The growing heat in my heart, the sense of safety I felt in his embrace, made the lack of it with Nathan all the more blatant. Calder held me close, but not tight. One of his hands stroked my back, the other held my head. We stood there until I could finally sniff and swallow away my tears. Afraid of my monstrous, post-sob-fest appearance, I let go of him and tried to turn away from his tear-soaked shirt. He took my chin to stop me. I closed my eyes so I wouldn't have to see his face. His thumb traced over my skin. I raised my eyelids. His face was close. So close, I noticed things I'd never seen before. He had a tiny scar just above his left eyebrow and brown flecks in his gray eyes.

"You know you're not going home," he said. "You want to be a marine biologist."

"But what about this whole thing with Trafford? She's ruined everything."

"You'll get to the bottom of it. And you'll make it right. Because you're the smartest person I know."

I frowned. Not out of sadness, but out of awe. Here stood this guy I admired, pushed away, misjudged—and yet, he supported me. Believed in me. Called me the smartest person he knew, even though he hung around geniuses like Uther.

I couldn't take it anymore. Throwing aside every worry and doubt, I whimpered, threw my arms around his neck, and smashed my lips against his. He tensed, but only for half a second. Then he grabbed my waist, pulled me closer, and deepened the kiss. The urgency, the closeness—it overwhelmed me. I couldn't believe it. He wanted me. He wanted me as much as I wanted him, even though I was an emotional, blotchy, swollen mess. The explosion in my chest, the rush of breathing Calder, of tasting Calder, went beyond floating or even flying; I shot like a bullet to a place I never knew I craved so much.

He hummed as I entwined my fingers through his hair. The stubble on his chin scratched my face. He gripped me so hard, my toes lifted off the floor. My neck hurt, but I didn't care.

After several long moments, I pulled back to catch my breath. He lowered me down and gazed at me, a new light in his eyes. He didn't let go and I was glad. My legs held all the strength of room-temperature pudding.

"You don't know how long I've wanted to do that," he said.

"Really?"

"Come on," he said, as though he couldn't believe I'd question it. I loosened my grip around his neck but didn't step away.

"Honestly, you kept giving me mixed signals."

"So did you," he replied with mocking accusation. "With that Nathan guy hanging around." I opened my mouth to argue but stopped. The awkward double date, the arguments, the refusal to acknowledge what we both knew.

I looked down. "I guess you're right. It's just that last time this happened, we didn't work," I said in a small voice. "I didn't want to hurt again. And Eamon said…"

He pulled me in again, stroking the small of my back. Then he leaned close, whispering.

"I don't care what Eamon says. I'm not letting you go this time."

I closed my eyes, reveling in his words. His lips found mine again. Softer, lingering, sweet. For about five seconds, there was nothing but unbelievable bliss. Then the door opened. I was so distracted when Calder showed up, I hadn't shut it all the way. We both looked, our arms still wound around each other. Jenna stood there, her hand on the knob and her mouth open in surprise. Calder and I let go of one another just as Nathan came into view. By the look on their faces and the bags of fast food clenched in their fists, the scene Calder and I made was the last thing Jenna and Nathan expected to see on the other side of my door.

31

Finally

I lowered my arms and stepped away, but the damage was done.

"Not in the picture, huh?" Nathan's fury lowered his voice. He glared at me, turned, and stalked away. Jenna looked like she wanted to say something, but instead, she frowned and followed him.

"Ah," said Calder. "Whoops. They're not going to be happy, are they?"

I stared at the empty space they left in the hallway. I needed to go after them. To say…what? I closed my eyes. Calder touched my shoulder.

"He wanted a relationship," I said. "We…went on a date together before you came. The double date we went on was our second date."

"Really?" he said, sounding amused. "Hm."

"I swear, it didn't mean anything. I don't feel that way about him."

"What did he mean, 'not in the picture?'"

"That's what I told him. Because I thought you weren't." I covered my face. "I'm sorry. I messed up. And now my only friends in this school hate me."

"They'll get over it."

"No, they won't. I've been avoiding...this"—I gestured between us—"because I can't stand the thought of being left alone. You're going to run back to Scotland, Samantha is going back to the ocean with Seidon, and now Nathan and Jenna are never going to speak to me again."

He stood, arms folded, waiting for me to finish my rant.

"What do you want me to say? That I'm sorry?"

I sighed. "No. It's not your fault at all."

"Good. I'm sorry your friends are hurt, but I'm not going to apologize for...this." He made the same gesture I did.

I looked up at him. He stood, unabashed—almost proud. It made me want to step closer to him and kiss him again. But Jenna and Nathan's faces drifted in front of my eyes. The astonishment. The betrayal. So I stayed back.

"Maybe I should go," he said. "I think you've got some things to figure out."

"No," I said quickly, grabbing his hand.

"I'll be back. I'm not going anywhere."

The thought of sending him away made my heart ache. But he was right. I needed to salvage my life.

"Okay." I tried to smile. Didn't work.

"Get some rest."

"I'll try. I have a huge mess to try and fix with the school."

"And your friends."

I sighed and frowned.

"Just tell them the truth," said Calder. "If they care about you, they'll understand."

"You make it sound so easy," I grumbled. A smile tugged his lips. He leaned into the hall and looked both ways. Then he looked back at me.

"Don't forget," he said, "we have the creature locked up. You're safe." He lingered in the doorway. I bit my lower lip. Having him near me, knowing how he felt, gave me the best dose of courage I'd ever had. He gave me one last half-smile, then turned to go down the hallway. Was this what Samantha and Seidon felt? Could it be the beginning of becoming something as real as what they had?

Samantha and Seidon.

What was it Calder had said before he dropped me off yesterday? I had the chance to change Samantha's fate. Could I really do it? What had held me back before? Self-doubt. Feelings of inadequacy. Of failure. Right now, the things that had weighed on me so hard seemed insignificant. I felt like I could do anything, from fixing the situation with my school and earning back the internship I deserved, to changing the course of my best friend's life.

"Calder," I said before he made it to the stairs. He stopped and walked back.

"Tell the others…" I shut my eyes as my confidence waned. "Tell them I've changed my mind. If they want me to do the whole CHASM thing—I'll do it."

He shook his head. "It won't make any difference to me what you decide."

"I know. That's not why. But if I can help Samantha and Seidon—if I can get her back and help keep the merpeople safe at the same time—I want to do it."

He smiled and stepped closer. "I'll tell them."

"I do need to get my school situation figured out first, though."

"Fair enough." He stepped closer again.

"And I can't do it full time. I still have my career to think about."

"Of course you do." He leaned in, his nose brushing mine.

"And it's..." Oh, his face was so close. Breathe, Liv. "It's not like a for sure thing anyway, right? It's not like the merpeople will even let me be part of—"

He shut me up with another kiss. I wrapped my arms around his neck and held on tight. I couldn't let go. Maybe if I didn't, he'd have no choice but to stay. But soon, he moved away just enough to whisper in my ear.

"I have to go," he said. "I told Eamon I wouldn't be gone long." I groaned in complaint. He ran his hands softly up the sides of my neck and held my face. "I'll be back soon, okay?"

I nodded. He stepped back. I wanted to shout how I felt about him, how I couldn't stand the thought of him going back to Scotland, or even back to the house in Berwyn Heights. But I stayed quiet as he slid away, turned, and walked back up the hall. I shut the door and leaned my forehead on the jamb. For a moment, I relived the feeling of Calder's lips on mine, the intense joy, the tangible feeling of '*finally*' pulsing through me. Why did I ever try to push him away? How did I ever doubt him? I turned to the window and hurried over to peek through the blinds. A minute later, he walked out of the dorm building and strolled over the sidewalk. From where I hid behind the blinds, I saw him grin up at the sky. I giggled and reveled in the rush of elation, so potent, I wanted to cry—this time, in a good way. He walked down the sidewalk and vanished around a corner. Then I ambled to my bed and sat down, the kaleidoscope of feelings whirling like a mini tornado in my chest. How could I be so happy, so broken-hearted, so full, and yet so empty all at the same time?

I couldn't sit around daydreaming about Calder's lips all day. I grabbed my shower things and headed to the bathroom. I needed to look more like a professional and less like a mugging victim. Today, I was going to confront Professor Trafford.

I showered and got myself dressed and ready. I donned Calder's scarf to ward off the cold, and because it reminded me of him. I needed the extra courage. I hurried down the sidewalk toward the Tawes building.

After winding my way through the halls, I came to Professor Trafford's office and knocked. No answer. I knocked again.

"Professor Trafford? It's Olivia Owens. I need to talk to you."

Still no answer. I tried the knob. It opened. I peeked inside, but no one was there. I walked in and sat down in one of the chairs. She couldn't avoid me here and I would skip classes to wait all day if I had to.

While I waited, I gazed around her disorganized office. This woman was in serious need of a TA. Or a maid. She had bookshelves lining the right and left-hand walls. Books sat on the shelves, but almost none of them stood upright. Several more stacks of books lay in columns along the back wall. Papers covered the desk and the filing cabinet.

Behind her desk, a big bulletin board covered with outdated fliers, notices from several semesters ago, and a few posters with English-y quotes hung on the wall. A flowery sheet of paper tacked to the board read: *"The person, be it gentleman or lady, who has not pleasure in a good novel, must be intolerably stupid."* —*Jane Austen.* And peeking out from behind it, something caught my eye: a folded piece of fine linen paper, embossed with black calligraphy. I stared at it, my jaw tensing. I jumped to my feet, grabbed the paper from the bulletin board, and stared at it in disbelief. The calligraphy spelled out words I thought I'd never see again: *Tu ad cognoscendam veritatem.* It was an invitation. I knew because I'd been at that party. A party that took place a year and a summer ago, where Doran Linnaeus had intended to expose merpeople to the public.

32

Hans Christian Andersen

My breath stopped. I stared at the invitation, memories of that summer in San Diego hurling back to my mind. Had Trafford been at that party? She clearly knew Linnaeus well enough to receive an invitation, even though they lived on opposite sides of the country. If she had been there, she'd have seen me dressed as a mermaid in that fish tank. She'd have known…

And Uther—he said whoever was messing with my email had to be someone with access to UMD's servers. Could it really have been my Lit professor the entire time? I had to know.

I turned to the door and locked it, even though Trafford would undoubtedly have a key. Then I hurried around her desk to look at her computer. I pressed a button on the monitor and the screen awakened. To my surprise, everything looked…tidy. I marveled at the neat rows of electronic icons amid the chaos of Professor Trafford's office. I looked for an internet browser, but a file on the desktop caught my eye.

One of the folders was open, its little window taking up space on the right side of the screen. Its title: *Hans Christian Andersen.* Professor Trafford taught literature; a folder on Hans Christian Andersen shouldn't have given me pause. Except the files within the folder had titles like *The Beginning*, *Contacts*, *Debunked*, *Encounters*...and at the end: *Project Fathom.*

My jaw dropped open.

I grabbed the computer mouse and clicked on the *Project Fathom* file. Scans of the exact information Doran Linnaeus had in his paper files came up on the computer. Pictures, descriptions, everything except for the Prayer. I covered my mouth with both my hands.

How did she get all this? My heart raced. I had to show it to the others. I reached into my bag and felt around for a flash drive I kept on hand for school assignments. Then I plugged it into the computer's hard drive.

As I transferred the files from the *Hans Christian Andersen* folder, I looked through others on her computer to make sure I had everything on the merpeople. All the other files had academic-sounding names like *Analyses of Hemingway from Various Lenses* and *Shakespeare Deconstructed.* No hint of merpeople.

The computer moved slower than a food court line during finals week, so while I waited for the transfer, I clicked on another file: *The Beginning.*

It was on my fifteenth birthday that I saw it.

My family always picnicked at Loch Raven Reservoir on our birthdays. This one was no different. I stormed away from the spread of sub sandwiches and cupcakes after my brother made fun of my acne. I walked down the lane where a hundred gigantic oak trees grew. The sun sank low and I barely heard my mom call after me not to wander too far.

My brother was such a jerk. My acne wasn't so bad. Okay, yes it was, but why did he have to point it out to me so much? I knew I wasn't pretty—the cheerleaders at school reminded me of that fact more often than my brother did—and I knew that cute Bobby McFarlane thought me nothing but a pizza-faced wildebeest. My brother told me that too.

Tears ran down my face as I choked on my breath. I folded my arms to shut out the balmy summer breeze, as though it too called me ugly. Down the lane I walked, the lake close by on my left. Late afternoon mists already created a ghostly veil over the trees. The massive branches met over the path like a tunnel, a portal. Maybe to a parallel dimension—one where I was pretty and porcelain-faced and kissed by Bobby McFarlane.

Splash.

I jumped and looked around. I couldn't see my family. Hidden behind the rows of oaks, my brother probably pigged out on cupcakes so I wouldn't get one. Or maybe he was hiding behind one of the trees trying to scare me.

I looked to the water. The surface rippled, as though a stupid, gangly someone had disturbed the water. I walked through the trees, searching.

"I know you're there, Gregory," I said, stomping toward the wavering surface of Loch Raven.

Another splash. I looked for Greg. In the distance, now that I was out of the lane of trees, I could see my family. My mom's prematurely white hair. My dad's embarrassingly purple baseball cap. And beside them, sat Gregory in his red sweatshirt.

I looked back at the lake. Maybe a fish had jumped. I liked seeing them do it, so I stared, waiting, until something broke the surface. Something round and shiny, like a rock the size of a cantaloupe.

I stepped closer. I squinted. I leaned over the water. The rock didn't move. I waited.

Then I saw the eyes. Just as I recoiled and fell onto my butt, the head disappeared, followed by the flick of something shining and sinuous.

I stayed where I landed, my backside wet from the grass and my eyes glued to the mirrored surface of the lake, until my parents called me back. Then I ran.

If I saw what I thought I saw, it could only mean one thing:

Gregory, the cheerleaders, the jerks could all go to hell. I had a secret. One that would change the world.

She knew. She knew about merpeople. How much did she know? How deep in it was she? Did Eamon know about Professor Trafford? No, he'd have said something. I closed the document. The other folders on the flash drive stared at me. I clicked on the one labeled *Contacts*. When the folder opened, a few documents came up, one labeled *Elspeth*—Elspeth! The name Mr. Hawkins had heard when the creature had attacked him. I went to click on it, when I saw the title of the last document in the *Contacts* folder and my stomach folded: *Olivia Owens*. I moved the mouse away from *Elspeth* and clicked on the file with my name.

It looked like journal entries, the first dating back to last year. Before I was in Trafford's literature class.

August 1st: I've succeeded in bringing Olivia to UMD. Aside from Doran, she's the only person I've been able to find who has had direct contact. Finding her wasn't easy. It took me an entire summer. They forced me into sabbatical this year because I'd neglected my summer classes to search for her. And I had to squeeze her into a closet converted into a dorm room because her admission was so last minute. But I got her here. And when I'm finished—when the literary masterpiece of our time is published, revealing the truth about our world and the beautiful creatures with whom we share it—they will thank me. She will thank me. I can't wait to get started.

My mouth hung wide open. A feeling of horrible, intrusive violation crept over my skin. Trafford's journal entries went on and on, talking about my scholarship, my classes, my schedule, and my emails. Trafford gave me the scholarship. Trafford brought me here. Trafford had been stalking and filtering my emails. I scrolled through more entries, perverse curiosity outweighing my repulsion.

September 12th: School has started. Olivia is doing well in her classes. She excels in biology. She tried to register for Literature, but I managed to change her schedule. I need her to wait until my sabbatical is over. I want to teach her in person. She's my real link to learning more about the merpeople.

December 3rd: I had to write a letter to Olivia. Her grades have suddenly taken a turn for the worse. I'm not sure what's going on in her life, but if she doesn't get those grades up, I'll have no choice but to revoke her scholarship. I took a risk bringing her here since she isn't an English major. If she screws this up, I'm finished.

That was the semester Calder and I had stopped communicating—

the semester I bombed half my finals. She knew everything.

The files finished copying to the flash drive. I went to delete the entire Hans Christian Andersen folder, then paused and went back to the *Elspeth* file. The date at the top was from August of this year. I had to know.

She's a beautiful creature, it began. *I've gone to see her every year since I found her in Loch Raven. I longed for a way to communicate, to help her trust me. Then, shortly after this school year began, a strange man came to me. A man with beautiful eyes and purple fingernails. He showed me his gills. He told me he was a merman in human form and he'd found me worthy. He told me I could have the little mermaid for my own. He wouldn't tell me his name but promised I could keep her if I agreed to two conditions. One, I must tell no one. And two, I had to set my little mermaid free. He gave me a beautiful piece of mermaid poetry and told me to read it to her. So, I did. Day after day. Then, one day, it happened. She emerged from the water. She was strong. Too strong. She didn't understand her own strength. But I'm determined to help her.*

I called her Elspeth. I did it. I'd been found worthy. And I did it all without Olivia Owens.

I gasped. Trafford had freed the creature. The poem—it must have been the Prayer. Someone—a man—had given it to her. Linnaeus? No. He'd been dead for a year before any of this happened. I shuddered and closed the document.

I pulled out my phone—which I just now realized was still off—and turned it on. I waited, shaking it as though that would make it turn on faster. When the screen finally came to life, I pulled up my contacts to call Calder. But before I could press the button to dial the number, my phone pinged with several notifications.

Missed calls—all from Calder. Two voice mails. Several texts. None of them were from Jenna. One was from Nathan. I opened it, but when I saw the lengthy paragraph, I resolved to read it later. The texts from Calder all said the same thing: *Is your phone off? Where are you? Are you okay? Please answer me.*

I pressed the call button. Calder picked up before the first ring ended.

"Where are you?" he asked without any other greeting.

"I'm fine. You won't believe what I found." I pulled the flash drive out of the computer and made my way around the desk.

"*Listen.* The creature is dead," he said, his voice growing urgent.

"What?" I stopped. "How? What happened?"

"We don't know. When I left to come see you, I didn't realize anything was wrong until I got back. Eamon found it in the pool with its throat cut."

"Are you serious?"

"I'm on my way to get you right now. Are you at your dorm?"

"I'll be there in ten minutes," I said, then hung up. I went to unlock the door but stopped again. I'd forgotten to delete the Hans Christian Andersen folder from the computer. I dashed around the desk, deleted the folder, and emptied the computer trash so the files couldn't be recovered again. Outside, a class let out and chatting voices passed by the office door. Time to go, *now.*

I took two running steps toward the door, but it opened in front of me. I gasped. Trafford came in, saw me, and smiled as if seeing me in her office was a regular, pleasant occurrence.

"Hello, Olivia," said Professor Trafford.

33

Her Favorite Student

Professor Trafford shut the door behind her and flipped through a stack of papers. She'd left her reading glasses on top of her head again.

"Was there something you wanted to talk about?" she asked. I clutched the flash drive in my hand. My throat too dry to swallow, I tried talking, but my voice didn't work. I cleared my throat, my pulse pounding in my neck. She looked at me again.

"Are you all right, dear?"

My teeth clenched at the endearment. She had the nerve to ask if I was all right after what she did to me?

"No. I mean, yes I'm fine. And no, there's nothing I wanted to talk about."

"Can I ask why you're in my office then?" She gave me a sideways, mildly scolding look. I backed away. The flash drive dug into my palm. It took some serious deep breathing to keep from telling her what a vile human being she was.

I turned to open the door, but the handle wouldn't move. She'd locked it. A shock of foreboding froze me for a second before I turned the lock and tried the handle again. I had the door open a crack before it slammed shut. Professor Trafford's hand lay on the door. I turned. She watched me with a strange, serene smile, one that increased the surge of dread in my heart.

"So. What did you find out?" she asked, her voice as calm as a lecture on the Romantic Period. I didn't reply. I backed away and looked around in case I missed seeing a window, another door, maybe a secret passageway under a rug. Answer: D, none of the above. I slipped the flash drive into my bag and rummaged for my phone. Once my fingers closed on it, I blindly pushed the screen, hoping my thumb would hit my call list, hoping she couldn't see what I was doing, hoping she'd stay away from me.

"Why'd you bring me here?" I whispered, not sure I wanted the answer. A low buzz of a voice came from inside my bag; someone had picked up my call. Who, though? I spoke up, hoping whoever it was would hear me and figure out I needed help. "Why did you do this, Professor Trafford?"

Her face softened. "Please don't be afraid. All I want is to work together. I'm not out to get rich or hurt anyone. I'm not like Doran Linnaeus."

The name jolted my pounding heart.

"Never heard of him. And I'm sorry about being in your office." I had to give my listener a clue to where I was.

"Why don't you sit down?" She pointed to the chair.

"I don't want to sit down."

"No, I think you should." She gripped my shoulder and pushed me into a chair. The force sent pain through my healing neck. Then she reached into my purse and pulled out my phone. I made a grab for it, but she hung it up, put it back in my purse, and threw the whole thing aside. It landed with a flop near one of her messy bookshelves. Everything inside spilled out. She turned back to the door and locked it again. Then she moved the other chair in front of the door, sat in it, and surveyed me as though I were her favorite student. Was I? I shuddered.

"You've gained so much during your time here. I couldn't be more proud of you."

Proud? I closed my stinging eyes.

"If you're not going to explain," I said, "I think I'd like to go now."

"Oh, I don't think so. We have a lot to talk about."

"No, we don't. I don't have anything to say to you." I tried to stand. She pushed me back down, her face still and serene. Somehow, her tranquility made it worse. "I can scream for help, you know."

"Go ahead. There's no one in the building until after lunch. By then, I think I'll have you convinced."

"Convinced about *what*?"

"About how beneficial we can be to one another. I've given you your education and I can continue to provide it. I can even make sure you get your internship if you behave."

I scowled. "So, you did tell Professor Seeley I cheated?"

Her eyes shone with pity. "You have to understand. I wanted to give you a good recommendation. But it's best if you know how easily these things can be taken away."

"You could have ruined everything! I could have been expelled!"

She laughed and shook her head. "Oh, you'd never be expelled. No, this is just a little, bitty reminder of who's in charge here."

I glowered in disgust and slumped back. The whole thing, the whole twisted situation, made me sick. And yet I couldn't help but let my curiosity take the reins.

"What do you want from me?"

She swallowed, a tick of vulnerability on her face. "We have the incredible opportunity to introduce the world to something so great. Only this time, we can do it right. Together, we can change the world. But before we can, I need your help. Some...*unsavory* people have blackmailed me. I've lost a mermaid, and I know you can help me get her back."

She didn't know her mermaid was dead.

"Mermaids aren't real," I replied quickly.

Her demeanor changed like a light switch. The calm, sweet professor who could never find her reading glasses disappeared as her eyes narrowed. She stood over me.

"My sources tell me differently."

"Your sources are wrong." I tried to hold my voice steady, but she stood too close.

"I don't think so, Olivia Owens, friend of the Zydrunas royal family."

My skin went cold. She smiled and continued, "Oh yes. I know about Zydrunas. And Coralium. And Tetra. And Eldoris. I love the names of their reaches. Don't you?" Her smile widened so much, I could see silver fillings shadowing her back teeth. "I saw you that night at the Grant Hotel in San Diego. In that fish tank? With the mermaid costume? Remember? For a while, I thought Doran Linnaeus really *had* caught a mermaid." She chuckled. "Doran. He knew nothing. You pulled a brilliant escape that night, by the way."

She *had* been there. I clenched my jaw. She got up and walked around her desk. Would she check for the files on her computer? I looked at the door. The chair sat in the way, but I could move it, unlock the door, and run. But my stuff lay scattered several feet away, the flash drive with it. Trafford slung a large purse over her shoulder and came back around.

"Now," she said, "we have a lot more to discuss, and because you somehow got a hold of someone on your phone, I think it's time to go. We'll go to my condo. You know the place. Has a lovely pond nearby? I believe you were there a few weeks back." Her light tone was back, her suggestion like a cheery invitation. I gaped at her in horror.

"How did you…" I stopped before I gave anything else away. And because it didn't make any sense. She lived in the apartment building near the pond? What about the house Eamon investigated—the one up for sale, where the man had come out? Instead of explaining, Trafford leaned over and took my arm. "We're going to be an incredible team." I pulled my arm away.

"No. Please leave me alone."

"Now, don't be difficult."

I still didn't move. "Stop."

She sighed. "All right. I didn't want to do it this way. But if you don't come with me quietly, right now, you'll never get your internship and you'll never see your friend Jenna again."

I looked up at her in horror. "Jenna? What does Jenna have to do with this?"

She laughed, but it was a light laugh, as though I'd told her a cheesy joke. "Come on now, dear. Don't tell me you don't know the truth about your little friend?"

34

The House in Hanover

The truth? What truth?

"*What did you do to her?*"

"Come quietly and nothing will happen to her. And I'll send a little email off to both Roberta Seeley and to the dean to let them know this scatterbrained old lady got her students mixed up." She started digging in her purse. "And I'm sorry about this, but it is necessary."

She grasped my arm and pulled me up to stand next to her, then brought something out of her purse. Before I could react, she stuck a syringe into my arm. I gasped and tried to pull away, but warmth spread from the sting of the injection and for the second time in less than a week, some kind of drug flowed into my system. She gripped me hard to keep me beside her and put the syringe back in her purse. I expected to feel something, but nothing happened. At first.

I stared at my phone, my lifeline, scattered with all the rest of my stuff as she pulled me into the hallway. She took my arm, wrapped it through the crook of her elbow, and strolled down the hall.

"So, you really don't know about Jenna?"

She was baiting me. I stayed quiet. She smirked and walked, waving at people passing us in the hallway like she hadn't a care in the world. Once we were outside, she steered me toward the parking lot.

My eyesight started to fog around the edges. I searched for someone, anyone I could flag down to help me. Or maybe I should just kick Trafford in the shins and make a run for it. If she had Jenna, I could run back to the office, get my phone, and call Calder before whatever drug she gave me took effect.

"Here's my car," she said cheerfully, pointing to a black Mercedes Benz.

A black Mercedes. Was it the same one Timothy Hawkins had seen the night he was attacked? I gaped at the car. Along with everything else, had Trafford been the one telling the creature to attack all those people? My vision swam. My stomach churned. I yanked my arm away from her.

"Take it easy, dear," she said calmly, reaching for me. I swatted at her and took a few staggering steps away. She gripped my arms and tugged me back to the car. My head and eyelids grew heavier.

"No."

"You'll be okay." She spoke the way someone would to a crying child. "Come on. Sit down."

I pushed her away again and took two running steps before my legs gave out. Then I crawled.

"Well, really, Olivia. You're going to hurt yourself." She took me by the waist and hauled me back to my feet, half-dragging me toward her car. She opened the back door, shoved me in, placed my feet inside, then shut the door behind me. I sat up, but it took a lot of effort.

Drowsiness fell over me, along with a sense of calm I fought to resist.

I need to get out. The engine turned. I slumped sideways. *No, get up!*

"Why are you doing this?" I asked, my words slurred.

"Everything is going to be fine, dear," said Trafford in a soothing voice that made me want to vomit. "I promise. Just rest now. You're safe. And you'll see Jenna very soon. We all have so much to talk about."

The hum of the car's engine, the classical music playing on the radio, and whatever drug Trafford had injected me with pulled me further and further under. Maybe if I closed my eyes just for a second, the dizziness would...

I didn't want to wake up. Where was I? The bed I lay on was softer than my dorm room bed. The blanket covering me kept me warm. My fuzzy brain begged for more oblivion. My arm hurt. Ouch, why did my arm hurt? I groaned.

"Olivia?"

I opened my eyes to a blurred room lit by weak light. There was another bed across from mine. Someone sat on it. Someone with long brown hair. I blinked. Jenna came into focus, her arms encircling her folded knees. A cut marred her lip.

"Jenna? Jenna!" I sat up, but it made me dizzy. I grabbed my head and groaned again. The memory of what happened in Trafford's office pulsed back in pieces: the invitation from Linnaeus. The files on her computer. The psychotic calm in her face. She took my phone. She wanted something from me.

"Are you okay?" Jenna asked. Her voice sounded a little raspy.

"I don't know. Where are we?"

"Professor Trafford's house," she replied. I looked back at her, straining to remember the rest of what happened. Trafford caught me in her office. She threatened to hurt Jenna if I didn't comply and held the marine biology internship over my head. The pain in my arm had been from a drug.

"Did she hurt you?" I asked.

"I'm okay," she replied. She stayed shrunk in the corner. I took a deep breath, trying to clear my head a bit more, and stood. A whirl of vertigo made me sway, but I steadied my stance and stepped toward the door.

"It's locked," said Jenna.

I turned back to her. She rested her head on her arms, blocking her bloodied lip from my view.

"You have a phone?"

She gave a humorless laugh. "Do you?"

I sighed and went to sit on her bed. "No. She took it away and left it behind. I can't believe she dragged you into this. She's insane."

Jenna shrugged and stared straight ahead, still huddled in the corner with her chin on her knees. I studied her in disbelief. Shouldn't she be more scared or confused? She lifted her eyes to look back at me.

"I'm sorry," she said behind her folded arms.

"No, we're going to get out of here," I said. "My friends will figure out where we are. I know they will."

She didn't answer at first. "I should have been ready," she finally mumbled.

"Ready? What do you mean?"

She sighed, wriggled off the bed, walked over to the light switch on the wall by the door, and flipped it on. I blinked from the sudden brightness. Jenna kept her back toward me as she spoke again.

"I meant that I knew something like this might happen. I should have been more prepared." She sighed again. "When Trafford brought me here, she told me what she did to you. About your scholarship. Bringing you to the school. I didn't know until now."

"How could you have known? I didn't know until now either."

She didn't move and didn't speak for several seconds. "I'm sorry I failed you."

"Failed me? What?"

She slowly turned to face me. Then I saw it. The cut on her lip. The blood wasn't red. It was blue.

35

Black Moray

My jaw slackened.

"Jenna...you're—you're a mermaid?" I stammered, trying to grasp the new information that had hit me in the face. She lifted her hair to reveal the gills on the side of her neck. I laced my fingers through my own hair and gripped my scalp. How did I miss this? I'd suspected Nathan—a full, red-blooded human—before suspecting the actual mermaid living, going to school, hanging out right next to me! All this time and never even a hint. She knew everything about human life—nothing like Seidon, with his child-like ignorance of the human world, or even the hardened and battle-ready Captain Cordelia.

"Yeah. And my name isn't Jenna. It's Meriana." She rubbed her arms.

I sputtered a bit more. Then took a deep breath to try and calm the renewed dizziness. "Why didn't you tell me?"

I waited a second before answering. "I had to keep it a secret."

"But I *know* about merpeople. Calder does too. That's why he's here."

"I know," she said with a breath of her own.

"You do? Why didn't you say something?"

"I've been here these many months as part of an assignment to watch over you, because of people like Trafford."

"Wait, does Trafford know who you are?"

Jenna cringed and nodded.

"How?"

She looked down. "She's…been studying us. You and me and Nathan. I didn't realize it until it was too late."

"Is Nathan okay?" I asked.

"Yes," she said quickly, as though jumping on the chance to give me some good news on something. "He's fine. He has no idea about any of this."

"Why would Trafford study him?"

"She's been watching everyone who has ever gotten close to you. She's been monitoring your emails, hoping to learn more about merpeople, deleting anything that might give her away."

The email I'd sent to Eamon, thanking him for the scholarship. She'd deleted it. How much information did she get? Things that I thought were private? I had to put my head between my knees. I tried to take even breaths, but it didn't help.

I scooted off the bed and started to pace, only stumbling a tiny bit from the fading effects of the drug. Jenna rubbed her arms and moistened her lips nervously.

"I'm sorry I kept the truth about me from you," she said. "I see now that I shouldn't have. What do you want to know? I'll tell you what I can."

I turned to her, opened my mouth, then closed it again, trying to figure out which of the thousands of questions I wanted her to answer first. I settled for the one I'd already asked several times.

"Why didn't you tell me?"

"I had orders. Blend in with the humans, keep an eye on you, and don't tell anyone."

"Orders from who?"

"My superior. I'm part of a covert ops team called Black Moray."

"Black Moray?" I asked. "I've never heard of it. Is that the same military Cordelia is part of?"

She looked at me. "Captain Cordelia? From Zydrunas?" She gave a little, amused laugh. "No. It's a little above her pay grade."

Above her pay grade? Holy crap, who was this person that had once been Jenna?

"So you're like some kind of secret agent for the merworld?"

"You might say that."

"But you're so…young. Do merpeople train their secret agents as teenagers?"

"I'm older than I look. Living under the ocean, rarely seeing the sun will do that to you. I'm actually thirty-seven."

I gaped at her. Though she looked twenty years old, she was closer in age to my mom than to me.

"So all this time you've been pretending to be human. Pretending to be my friend. *All this time, Jenna.*" I couldn't bring myself to call her by any other name. "Everything you've said and done was fake." Why couldn't she have told me? All the things I'd been through. Helping Naia. Running from the creature. Dodging hostile Atlantic merpeople. All of it could have been avoided if she'd only been open with me.

"Not everything has been fake," she said quickly. "I have always been your friend."

"But you know so much about humans. You know about...college majors and cell phones and energy drinks."

"They weren't energy drinks. They were cans of energy drinks, sodas, and coffee cups filled with water. I've been living on land a long time. Well, off and on. I've learned how to blend in. And on a personal note..." She hesitated. "You don't need to worry about Calder. I was only acting the part of a human young woman when I was with him. I thought maybe if I earned his trust, he'd lead me to the rest of his friends who know of the merworld. I needed to keep tabs on them."

I stared at her. "First of all, that's not what I was talking about. Like, at all. And second, do you think lying is the best way to earn someone's trust? All you had to do was ask me and I'd have taken you to them in a second. Is this your first assignment with Black Moray?"

I'd meant it as a joke, but she flinched and looked away.

"No, it's not my first assignment."

I sighed. "Okay, look, I'm not mad that you flirted with Calder. Maybe I was, but not anymore. Right now, I'm more worried about everything that has happened because you didn't tell me who you were."

She frowned and dropped her eyes. She swallowed hard and rubbed her arms again.

"I came in January to keep an eye on you. It was supposed to be an easy mission. Then I stayed because of the creature's escape. They wanted me to find out if you were behind it."

"It wasn't me. Well, yeah, I set her free one time, but that was before I knew what she was capable of. Trafford is the one who helped her transform in the first place. Someone taught her how to do it."

Jenna stared hard at me.

"Who taught her how to do it?"

"I don't know," I replied. "A man. I've got all the information on a flash drive, but Trafford took that too." I didn't want to tell her about everything I saw on Trafford's computer. Not until she earned back some trust. "When we get out of here, you can go back and tell all your Black Moray friends that I've never been anything but trustworthy." My voice rose as I went on. "All the merpeople have done in return is steal my best friend's memories, accuse me of betrayal, and threaten my life and the lives of my friends."

"Steal your best friend's memories?"

"Yeah. Samantha. The one I went wedding dress shopping with. She became a mermaid that summer we both saved your people from Doran Linnaeus. She's engaged to Seidon. I'm sure you know him too?" Jenna nodded, so I went on. "Well, I've been friends with Samantha since we were both really little. But she doesn't remember any of it. She only invited me to go shopping with her because Seidon told her to. And now, any time she takes human form, she has to sacrifice her memories." Bitterness coated my words. "But you probably already knew all that too, didn't you?"

She didn't say anything at first.

"I'm sorry they've treated you with so much contempt."

I clenched my teeth. "Contempt doesn't even describe it. Why do merpeople have to act like humans are all out to murder them? Ever since I found out about them" —I paused and glanced at Jenna with lingering disbelief— "about *you*, I've kept the secret. I've risked my life. I gave up my best friend. Then there's Trafford, who decided to go and...*collect* me or something and screw with my entire life. All because I knew about merpeople. And *then*," I continued in a rant while Jenna watched me from her corner of the room, "along comes Naia, begging for help, so I helped her. And still, the merpeople blame me for everything bad that has happened ever since. I've lost Eamon's trust because of this."

Jenna rubbed her eyebrows with her fingertips.

"I'm sorry. I didn't want it to be this way," she said. I frowned.

"I'm not exactly thrilled about it either."

She sighed. "I wish that were the extent of it all."

What did that mean? My anger fumed again.

"What more could there possibly be?" I glared and waited for her answer. She raised her chin, then turned to look at me.

"I was the one who told Naia to come to you for help."

For a moment, all I could do was stare. My brain flashed through every memory I had of that night, trying to make sense of it.

"What? No, she told me Eamon had sent her."

"I told her to say that to maintain my cover," said Jenna. "I'm so sorry it brought you so much trouble."

"Trouble?" I cried. Freeing the creature had been the cause of murderous rampages. I'd hated myself for it. "Jenna, *people died.* Does that even matter to you?" Her eyes shone with remorse.

"Of course it does! Do you think I'm happy about what has happened? I made some mistakes. But I promise you, I did have your safety as my main concern."

"You pretty much failed on that. The creature almost killed me and Samantha."

"Wait, what?"

"When we were in Alexandria. The creature attacked us."

"You told me you got mugged in Alexandria!"

I huffed. "If you'd told me who you really were, I wouldn't have had to lie. Luckily, Calder and Seidon were finally able to catch her."

"They did?" Her eyebrows rose.

"Yeah. But she..." I grasped my head as I remembered what Calder had told me. "She's dead." I never got the chance to ask Calder more. Why didn't I just leave Trafford's office when I had the chance? The silence stretched on.

"Olivia, I am so sorry," Jenna said again. I fiddled with the ends of my hair instead of looking at her.

"Were you ever going to tell me?"

"I intended to tell you once my assignment was finished," she replied.

"When would that be?"

She blinked. "Um. Whenever they call me home."

"Any way they can track where you are?"

She frowned. "No. They don't know I'm here, and they won't know I'm in trouble until I miss my next check-in."

"When is that?"

"At the end of the week."

Deflated, I leaned back against the wall. "Anything else you wanna tell me?"

She rubbed her arms yet again. "I need some water."

I looked around the bare room. Aside from the two beds, the nightstand between them, the hideous lamp sitting on top of it, and a small, open closet, there was nothing else. Trafford had to have known merpeople needed water often. Why didn't she leave any in here? As angry as I was at Jenna, I couldn't let her get too dry. I stood and started searching. Under the beds, in the closet—no water. Then I tried the doorknob, even though Jenna said it was locked. The knob had been reversed, so the lock was on the outside. I jiggled it, jerked it, then pounded on the door.

"Jenna needs water!" I shouted. I struck the door again. "Trafford! You can't let her go without water for too long." The seconds ticked by. I looked back at Jenna. She lay on her bed with her eyes closed. "How long has it been since you've had something to drink?"

She swallowed. "A couple of hours." Worry slipped down my spine. Even humans would get thirsty if they hadn't had anything to drink for a couple of hours. She wouldn't last much longer.

36

A Wall of Information

"Trafford!" I shouted. There was no using the word 'professor' anymore. "Trafford, Jenna needs water *now*."

I waited. Still nothing. Either she was ignoring us, or she wasn't here. I turned away from the door and looked around the room again, as though a bottle of water would magically appear. There had to be a way out. I darted to the window and threw aside the heavy curtains. Bars covered the outside. Frustrated, I almost turned away. But then I looked back. The back window faced a grassy lawn, which led down to a lily pad-covered pond. The same pond I'd swam into several weeks ago to free the creature.

"Wait…" I said. "You said this is Trafford's house. That's the pond where the mermaid was kept after the Coralians captured her the first time. She knew about it." I turned back to face Jenna. "This doesn't make any sense."

She sat up. "Huh?"

"This is Trafford's condo, right?"

"I assume so." The rasp in her voice had gotten worse.

I scrunched my nose in complete bewilderment. "Naia brought me to an address near the pond. To a house that was supposed to be empty, but a man came out and chased her off. I freed the creature after he went back inside." I looked at Jenna. "You're the one who sent her to the address. Who was that man?"

Could it have been the mysterious man who told Trafford how to help the mermaid transform?

"I only knew the nearest address…I don't…" She lay back down. She needed water. Now. I turned away from the window and went back to the door. The knob had a hole in the center, but I had nothing to pick it with. I searched the room again, spotted the lamp on the table, grabbed it, and pulled hard. The plug flew out of the socket. Then I hurried to the door and slammed the base of the lamp down on the knob over and over again until it jarred loose. I looked down at it, jostled it, then lifted the lamp again and pounded the knob until it broke free. I pushed the other knob out, peered through the hole in the wood, and pulled the door open.

"I'll be back," I said and peeked into the hallway. There were other closed doors in the hall. I crept out. If Trafford hadn't come running already from my screaming and banging on the doorknob, she had to be gone. Still, I tiptoed, my nerves on high alert. At one end of the hall, a carpeted staircase led to the first floor. On the other end were a few closed doors. I opened one and found the bathroom. I hurried in, turned on the shower, and rushed back to the bedroom to help Jenna off the bed.

"Come on," I said. "I've got the shower running."

"Thank you," she whispered. Supported by my arm around her waist, she hobbled at my side until we reached the bathroom.

"Just get in," I said, helping her, fully clothed, into the stream. She sighed in relief, opened her mouth, and drank. Satisfied she would be okay, I stepped away. "Stay here."

I went back into the hallway and crept down the stairs, listening, watching, waiting to hear a door open or a car pull up from outside. Nothing.

I came to the ground floor and found sparse furniture and cardboard boxes. Trafford had either recently moved in, or she hadn't bothered to unpack anything. That wouldn't surprise me.

I went back upstairs and started looking in the other rooms. In the one across from ours, an unmade bed sat in one corner, and a desk covered in papers sat in another. A bulletin board hung in front of the desk. It looked like a wall belonging to a police profiler or maybe a conspiracy theorist. Maps, strings connecting spots in the ocean to the names of reaches Trafford knew about, and even photographs covered the bulletin board and the wall space around it. I followed the string labeled "Zydrunas" to a spot in the Gulf of Mexico, and the one labeled "Coralium" to…Loch Ness? Even though I didn't know Zydrunas's or Coralium's exact locations, I knew they weren't where Trafford thought. I let go of a breath. She thought she knew everything about the merpeople, but she was so far off.

She also had pictures of humans. Eamon. Calder. Natasha. Several pictures of people in fancy clothes, including Linnaeus himself. And, in the background of one of the pictures: Seidon and Cordelia. She had circled their faces and put question marks next to them. I leaned closer when footsteps outside the room froze my blood.

The door creaked open. I whipped around. But it was only Jenna standing in the doorway, dripping water. She saw the wall and her eyes widened.

"What is all of that?" she asked. I turned back to the wall and started tearing everything down.

"Most of it is wrong, but we can't leave it here. Help me." I crumpled everything I could into a giant ball of paper and yarn. Jenna pulled things off the wall, until she stopped, staring down at a post-it note.

"What's the matter?" I asked, ripping more stuff down in a big sheet of taped and stapled papers.

"Not all of it is wrong," she said, showing me the post-it. I read the words, written in Trafford's handwriting.

World leaders meeting in New York City. Thursday. Stranded Siren.

"What does that mean?" I asked. "What's Stranded Siren?"

But Jenna didn't seem to hear me. "How did she get this?" she murmured as she gazed at the note in alarm.

"What is it?"

She looked up at me, her eyes wide. And for the first time, I realized her normally brown eyes had become a deep, violet-blue. Had she been wearing contacts all this time?

"It's the meeting place for CHASM," she replied. "*The Stranded Siren* is a place in New York City—a dive bar, really. But the bar is only a front."

"The council meets in New York City? On land?"

"It's always been the place where CHASM convenes," said Jenna. "The Hedron meet on land so no one has the home-water advantage."

I looked down at the post-it note. "Trafford got so many things wrong. How did she get this one thing right? And wait, Thursday… does that mean *this* Thursday?"

"It must," said Jenna. "I knew they were meeting soon, but I didn't think it was this soon."

"What day is it today?"

"Wednesday."

My stomach dropped further. CHASM was meeting *tomorrow.*

"Do you know how to find this place? *The Stranded Siren*?"

"If I had a cell phone, sure," Jenna replied. "Why? Did you want to go there?"

I huffed. Would she believe it if I told her Cordelia had wanted to nominate me for a spot on the council? Then it hit me—if CHASM was happening tomorrow, surely that meant Calder and the others would be heading there too.

"We have to get back to UMD," I said. "My cell is still in Trafford's office. If we…" I trailed off as a sound stopped me cold: a door opening from downstairs.

"Run," I whispered. "Back to our room."

Jenna and I flew out of the bedroom, leaving the papers in clumps and pieces all over the floor, and went back into the other room. I tried to put the broken doorknob back into place, but there was no way Trafford wouldn't notice.

I leaned close to the door, listening for any sounds. Footsteps sounded on the stairs.

"We need to get out of here," I whispered.

"How?" Jenna asked. I bit my lower lip, my heart racing. Any second, she'd come upstairs and see the broken doorknob.

"Olivia," Trafford cried out in a sweet, motherly voice. "Meriana. Are you girls doing okay?"

I held my hand over my mouth and leaned my shoulder against the door.

"Why'd you break my doorknob?" she asked, her voice just outside the door. "It was only locked to keep you safe."

My fear morphed into fury and revulsion. She'd locked us in that room and left us—left Jenna without water.

"Olivia," she said again. "I know you're scared. But you have to understand why. If you let me in, I know I can convince you to help me." She pushed on the door. I held it shut even though I had no idea what it would accomplish. Trafford pushed harder. I pushed back. "Olivia, get away from the door."

Jenna moved to stand half inside the closet, her body tense, her wet hair hanging limp over her shoulders.

"You'll never get away with this," I said. "They'll find you."

Trafford slammed against the door, bouncing me back for a second. I pressed hard.

"I brought you all this way to make you my partner!" she shouted. "We can learn so much. We need each other. *I need you to help me.*"

"No."

"Is Meriana in there?" Trafford asked. I looked over at Jenna. She shook her head. I didn't answer. Trafford banged on the door harder, her voice getting louder, almost manic. "You can't trust her, Olivia. Now open this door right now! Open the door! Meriana, if you're keeping her from me, I have a gun and I'm not afraid to use it."

Panic raced up my spine. I clenched my teeth. We couldn't hold out forever.

"Open the door," Jenna whispered. She held the ugly lamp in one hand. I shook my head.

"She's got a gun," I whispered.

"Do it now."

Aggravated and afraid, I grunted and jumped back. The door flew open. Trafford stumbled in. She held a small handgun clutched in one fist. She looked at me.

"Just hear me out," she said, holding up her free hand, but with a huge *crack*, Jenna swung the lamp across the back of Trafford's head.

37

Grand Theft Auto

Trafford crumpled. My jaw fell. I stared at her unconscious form while Jenna stood over her, a flash of triumph on her face until she looked at me. Then her expression melted into fear. She let out a shaky breath and dropped the lamp.

"I can't believe I did that."

I looked back down at Trafford. "Did you kill her?"

"I don't know." She stepped away. I moved to where the gun fell and kicked it away from her hand. Should I check for a pulse? Should we run for it? I bent down and reached my fingers toward her neck when she moaned and stirred.

"*Run*," said Jenna, pointing out the door. I jumped back from Trafford and ran as fast as I could out the door and down the stairs. Jenna followed a moment later, holding a bundle of papers and string. "We have to get out of here," she said. "She's dazed, but not for long."

I hurried toward the front door, where I found a set of keys hanging on a hook. I couldn't steal her car, though. There had to be some other way we could escape.

Another groan came from above. I looked up and saw Trafford stumbling down the stairs, holding the gun in one hand and the stair railing tight in the other. Ugh, why hadn't we grabbed the gun when we had the chance? Her face pale, she looked down at me.

"Don't..." she said, but I didn't listen to the rest. I grabbed the keys, flung the door open, and pulled Jenna out with me. Along the curb in front of the condo sat the black Mercedes. I was about to steal a car. For a second, I stopped as I stood there, staring at the black, shining metal.

"Olivia! Hurry!" Jenna shouted. "She's coming!"

I jolted back into action, unlocked the car, and got inside. Trafford, limping but right on our heels, rushed toward us. I started the car before Jenna had her door shut and stepped on the gas pedal. Trafford dove for the hood, an insane gleam in her eyes. I screamed and pressed on the brake. Trafford slid off the hood and tumbled to the pavement. I cried out again and threw the car into reverse.

"Go, go, go!" Jenna slapped my arm. Several yards away, I stopped, put the car in gear, and screeched around until we were heading away from the condos and away from Trafford, who lay writhing on the ground, glaring after us.

Once we got to a main road, I finally breathed. My fingers white-knuckled the steering wheel. I drove completely on autopilot, not caring what street we were on or the direction we were headed. Jenna said something, but I didn't register what it was.

"I just stole a car," I said, still unable to believe I'd done it.

"She took us captive, Olivia," Jenna replied. She began dismantling the wad of papers and string, tearing it up, and throwing pieces out the window little by little.

"Don't do that," I said.

"I don't want anyone else to find all of this."

"No normal person is going to care about that stuff. We can throw it in a dumpster or something."

She stopped throwing the paper out the window but kept tearing it up as we drove.

"What do we do now?" Jenna asked. "If Trafford calls the police…"

"Breathe." I did it as I said it. "Just keep breathing."

She nodded and heaved a shaking breath.

"I have another question," I said, though my heart still beat fast and my rattled mind wouldn't calm. "We know the creature was originally from Loch Raven and that Trafford was the one who freed her the first time. But then Naia wanted me to help free her from the pond near Trafford's condo. But if you guys had her contained, why would you keep her in the pond instead of taking her somewhere safe?"

Jenna stayed quiet for another moment. "Because—and don't tell anyone else I told you—we weren't the ones who caught the creature after she first took human form. Trafford did. That house? Number 8? It belongs to her mother. We tracked the creature to that pond and kept her there until we could hear back from Captain Samudra on what to do with her."

"Captain Samudra?" Where have I heard that name before? "Is that the head of Black Moray?"

Jenna shook her head. "No. She's the captain of King Enamerion's armies. We had to get her permission before bringing a feral mermaid into our reach."

"But Naia somehow found out about it and came on land to get her sister back?"

"She came to me first. I felt so sorry for her. The poor thing only wanted her sister back. It was a risk, but I know how important family is, and I wanted to help her. We weren't allowed to do anything until we received orders from our captain. I told her if she wanted to take back her sister without having to wait for the captain's approval, she needed your help. I knew you well enough by then. I knew you'd help her, and that you'd keep it a secret. But I told Naia to say Eamon sent her instead of me. Partly to protect myself and partly because I knew you trusted him. I needed to keep my cover."

"Why didn't you tell me any of this?" I whispered, kneading my forehead. "All this time, you've known about everything. You could have saved us from so much frustration. From danger. *Why didn't you tell me?*"

"I told you. I couldn't. I'm sorry."

I sighed. So did she.

"I need more water," she said. "And we both need food. Pull into that McDonald's over there. I have a little bit of money I keep hidden in my sock." I pulled into the McDonald's drive-through, ordered a meal for each of us—and several water bottles for Jenna—then stopped near the restaurant's dumpster to throw away the torn-up paper and string.

I got back into the car and pulled onto the road. The smell of fast food constricted my empty stomach. I shoved several french fries into my mouth as I drove.

"We need to go back to UMD," I said around my fries. "I need to get my cell phone. Eamon and the others have got to be worried sick." Especially Calder. I told him I'd call him back and never did. He was supposed to come for me, but I wasn't there. And what about the person I had called in Trafford's office? I didn't know who it had been and had no way of checking.

"No." Jenna gripped my arm. I jumped at the sudden action and stared at her in disbelief.

"Why not?" If I wanted to abandon all sense and go to New York for an international merworld big-wig summit, I needed a change of clothes.

"We can't go back there," she said. "It's too dangerous. And if you're going back to get your phone so you can call Eamon…I can't let you do that either."

"What? Why?"

She sighed and bit her lower lip before replying. "There's another reason why my superiors wouldn't let me tell you who I was."

"Which is?"

She hesitated, a pained look on her face. "Eamon. There's more about him you don't know."

38

Scars

I held my breath, unsure if I could handle another bombshell. Then I pulled over.

"We can't stay in one place too long," said Jenna. "If Trafford calls the police, they could catch up to us."

"I'm not going anywhere until you tell me why I can't take us to Eamon," I said. A flicker of pain crossed her face before she looked at me with a resolute angle to her jaw.

"He might seem like a trustworthy friend to the merpeople, but he's keeping secrets from you."

"What secrets?" I asked. I knew Eamon. He had always been trustworthy, always told me the truth. But foreboding and reluctant curiosity tingled the hairs on the back of my neck. Did I really know him?

"I wish I didn't have to be the one to tell you all of this. But"—she took a deep breath— "he is responsible for the collapse of an entire reach."

My eyebrows shot up. "Eamon? No. That's impossible."

"Tell it to my parents," said Jenna. "Tell it to the many others who died in the explosion he was supposed to have prevented."

I gaped at her, horror and sympathy weighing heavily on my shoulders.

Jenna took a deep drink of water. "Let me start from the beginning." She wiped her lip. "It'll help you understand. About a year ago, there was a lot of unrest in Okeanos Ektasi, my home reach in the Mediterranean. A human industrialist had found oil. Eamon came to try and stop the humans from setting up an oil rig there and putting my people in jeopardy. But rather than shut down the operation, Eamon sided with the human and forced the entire reach to evacuate."

I stared through the windshield, horrorstruck. "Are you sure? Eamon would never—"

"I was there, Olivia. There was so much chaos. So much fear. But instead of going back to rectify the situation, Eamon set off an explosion under the water, which killed several of our people. My family included."

The explosion in the Mediterranean last year. I remembered it being on the news. I had asked Samantha about it in our letters. I had no idea Eamon was involved. My heart squeezed in sorrow but held onto denial.

"I'm so sorry," I whispered. I shook my head. "But it couldn't have been Eamon. He would never do something like that."

"I know it's hard to accept, but it's true. He's been covering his tracks ever since."

I brought one hand to my face.

"I wasn't given clearance to give you any information. But circumstances changed. Now that you know who I really am, you can't be left not knowing who he really is. Eamon is dangerous."

I couldn't believe it. Eamon? The solid, kind, careful Eamon? He couldn't be what Jenna claimed him to be. And yet, he had been so distant ever since he came here. He'd objected to Cordelia nominating me to the council too, which hadn't seemed weird at the time—I'd objected myself. Was he worried I'd learn what had happened in the Mediterranean if I became part of the Hedron? Had he been hiding all this time? I lowered my hand and glanced at Jenna.

"Do you think Eamon is worried about the Hedron finding him?"

"I believe he's been avoiding them. Keeping his activities a secret, muddying the waters to hide his whereabouts. He may have come here to help you, but he doesn't care about the merpeople's best interests."

The crack in my heart widened. This didn't sound anything like the Eamon I knew. Jenna put her hand on my shoulder. I shrugged away.

"They're still my friends," I said. "And Calder…"

The memory of when he came to my dorm room yesterday morning returned, vivid and earnest. I shut my eyes for just a second. The thought of his kiss, his embrace, his words nearly broke me.

"I know you care about him a lot," said Jenna. "But he's close to Eamon. We just can't trust anyone right now."

I shook my head. She was wrong about not trusting Calder. I needed to get back to him. I needed him to know I was okay. And if I was in trouble, what about him? With all of Eamon's problems with the Hedron, would they go to New York? Eamon would likely want to stay as far away from it as possible.

"Can I please just go get my phone?" I asked. "I have to talk to Calder."

Jenna sighed. "We can go try and get your phone. But we have to be careful. If the police find this car, or if Trafford somehow finds her way back there, or has accomplices, we're finished."

I nodded and pulled onto the road toward the freeway that would take us back to UMD. Along the way, I filled Jenna in about Cordelia's idea to nominate me as a human representative on the Hedron, and why.

She gawked at me.

"Are you serious?" she asked, but with awe instead of derision.

"I know. It's ridiculous. But we're desperate. I have to help Samantha and Seidon. And I can't let Samantha lose her memories permanently."

"No," she said, blinking and staring straight in front of her. "It's not ridiculous. Well, maybe a little ridiculous. But brilliant."

I couldn't help a smile. "Really? You're okay with it?"

"Olivia, we've been friends for almost a year. And I've been aware of you even longer than that. Of course, I'm okay with it."

I straightened in my seat, surprised at how much her support lifted my spirits.

"Thanks, Jenna. Or...what was your real name again?"

She smiled. "Meriana."

"That's such a pretty name," I said. "But I don't think I could ever get used to it."

She laughed. "There's something else you should know."

"Oh, great. Now what?"

She bent her elbow to show me her jagged scar. "The scar on my arm? I told you it was barbed wire, but a guy in one of my classes thought it looked like a shark bite. Remember?"

"Yeah."

She sighed and dropped her arm. "In the spirit of earning back your trust, I thought I'd tell you the truth. It is from a shark bite. I was being stupid once and got too close to one. Had to fin like hell to escape the frenzy once it smelled my blood."

I stared at her for a second. Then, I laughed. The situation we were in was so not funny, but I couldn't help it.

Soon, we pulled into the parking lot near the Tawes building. Jenna and I got out of the car, back on high alert. As we walked away from the parking lot, I looked back at the Mercedes. We needed to get rid of it sooner rather than later, before Trafford reported the theft. She was probably tracking its whereabouts right now.

Jenna led the way into the building. Though other students and even a professor or two passed us, no one gave us a second glance. We arrived at Trafford's office door and waited until the hallway cleared before I reached for the knob and opened it. Unlocked. Good.

I looked to the corner near the bookshelf where Trafford had thrown my bag, but it wasn't there. Everything that had spilled out was gone. Had she come back for it while I was unconscious? Could it be back inside her car? I walked out of the office, where Jenna waited and watched.

"It's gone," I said. I shut the door behind me and hurried up the hall. Jenna jogged in my wake.

"Your phone?"

"My bag, my phone, all of it. If Trafford took it, maybe it's still in the car somewhere, like in the trunk."

We jogged back to the front doors, rushed down the front steps, and made our way back toward the parking lot. But when we came within sight of the car, I stopped and grabbed Jenna to keep her from going any further. Two security guards walked around the Mercedes. One of them examined the back of it, the other looked around the parking lot.

Our transportation was a no-go.

"Keep walking," I said. "Don't look over there."

We tried our best to look casual. I watched the security guards from the corner of my eye but had to lose sight of them as we walked by unless I wanted to attract attention to myself.

"Let's double back and get some things from our dorms," I said, "then we can—"

"There!" someone shouted from behind. The security guards, one of them on a cell phone, started walking toward us.

Jenna grabbed my arm and ran—in the opposite direction of our dorms. The security guards kept up the chase. My lungs burned. A stabbing pain ached in my side. I looked back. The security guards kept coming. Soon they'd get either the police or more security guards to hem us in. I looked ahead, to where a bus sat at the stop along the street.

"Get on the bus." I pointed toward it.

We picked up our speed and raced across the street just as the bus started moving.

"Stop! Stop!" I cried, holding up my hands. The bus slowed and stopped. We raced around the front of it, skidded around to the doors, and scrambled on.

"Go," I said to the disgruntled driver. I didn't have my bus pass, but Jenna dug some more money out of her sock to pay the fare. The security guards kept running, waving their hands and shouting, but the driver ignored them.

"Sit down or I'll leave you to them," he barked at us. "I'm on a tight schedule." Jenna and I sat in the nearest seats, gasping for breath.

"I need water," she said. I frowned in sympathy. We'd left her water bottles in Trafford's car.

"We'll get you some more. Hang in there. We need to get to the train station."

"Why?" she asked, clutching her chest.

"We're going to New York."

39

The Train to New York City

The bus arrived at the train station. Standing in line, wearing two-day-old clothing, without a bag or a phone, to buy a ticket to one of the biggest cities in the world, made me feel completely naked. Jenna bought the tickets and eight bottles of water with her last bit of cash. I hoped the train would take us right where we needed to go.

We wearily found our seats on the train, not speaking. Jenna held her water on her lap like a strange bouquet.

"You ever been to New York before?" Jenna asked. She twisted open a bottle and drank.

"No," I replied. "I've always wanted to though. There's an amazing aquarium."

Jenna smirked.

"What?" I asked.

"You. Of all the things a city like New York has to offer, you want to see the aquarium."

I smiled and shrugged. "Have you ever been to New York?"

"No. But I'm interested in seeing it."

The train began to move. Out the window, the city passed in a humming lull, and by and by, gave way to the countryside. I lapsed into quiet mode, still unable to completely accept my new realities.

The pain of it hit me like a gut punch. I wouldn't be going back to school at UMD. Trafford used the scholarship to get me to help her. And because I didn't do what she wanted, my scholarship, my classes, everything I'd worked for the last year and a half—they were all gone. Even if I could afford an education at UMD, I still had the false accusation of plagiarism on my record. Trafford wasn't likely to give me any glowing recommendations after all that had happened. My future, one that had been so certain, now faded behind like the passing forested hills of Maryland. I shut my eyes.

"What's wrong?" Jenna asked.

"Oh, you know," I began with fake serenity. "My entire education has screeched to a halt, I just escaped kidnapping by my sociopath professor, and now I'm sitting on a train, with my black-ops mermaid friend, heading to a covert merworld council."

She laughed. I smiled wryly. How many people in the world had ever been in this very weird position? Fear, inadequacy, awe, and restlessness spun circles within me. I'd felt like this before: when I had first met Cordelia and Seidon. Only now, the feeling was multiplied by ten. One for each member of CHASM.

"Tell me about the Hedron," I said. "Do you know any members?"

"Not all of them," she replied with a shake of her head. "My king, Enamerion, is one. Prince Seidon's mother, Queen Hydria, is another."

I knew this, but still, my heart skipped. I'd get to meet Seidon's mother.

Jenna went on. "There's a reach in the south Atlantic called Tetra. Their member of CHASM is General Glaucus. And there's one in the Antarctic, on the Atlantic side called Varuna. Its member of CHASM is Captain Tempus. I don't know any others. But they all either hate or barely tolerate humans. You'll want to be on your guard at all times."

I expected that. But I didn't say anything more. The minutes passed. Every time I thought of asking a question, a cold fear would drop on my head and choke the question out. Most of the questions revolved around the same things—the only things Jenna couldn't answer: how in the world was I going to convince a group of powerful, human-hating merpeople to agree with me? And what was I going to do with my shattered life once CHASM was over?

The sky slowly darkened as the train continued north. I couldn't see anything beyond the trees, still full of yellowing and blushing autumn leaves. Neither of us spoke. I wished Calder were here.

Jenna looked around.

"I've got an idea. Be right back," she said, then got up from her seat and approached a woman seated across the aisle and a few rows ahead of us. I couldn't hear the conversation, but Jenna gestured toward me and held her hands up helplessly. The woman gave her a sympathetic smile, then scooted over so Jenna could sit down. They bent their heads toward the woman's cell phone while she tapped on the screen. A few minutes later, the woman wrote something on a scrap of paper and handed it to Jenna with another smile. Jenna then got up and came back.

"Okay," she said, showing me the piece of paper. "I told her our phones were dead, but that we had to meet some friends at the *Siren*. She looked it up and wrote down some directions for us."

On the sheet of paper were handwritten steps on how to get from the train station to a place on West Street. In my already emotional state, her kindness made me want to blubber like a baby. I sniffed.

"That was nice of her," I said. I sniffed again and leaned against the window. At least there was some kindness left in this insane, strange world.

A few hours later, a halo of city lights full of skyscrapers finally appeared in the distance. I exhaled all my breath, my heart filling with wonder at the massive, glittering city I'd heard of my whole life but never seen in person. It took us a lot longer to get there than I thought it would. One minute, the lights sat far in the distance, then the next, they were all around us. Then, we zoomed beneath them as the train entered an underground tunnel. Lights on the tiled walls sped past. When would this road trip end? And what was I going to find when I got there?

"Next stop, Penn Station," said a voice from a loudspeaker.

The passing tunnel lights slowed as the train decreased its speed. A few minutes later, it squeaked to a gradual stop.

"This is it," said Jenna. She stood. I followed her off the train and looked around. The station, with sparse passengers making their way through the platforms, looked a lot like an airport.

"Now what?" I asked. Jenna looked down at the written directions.

"We take the subway heading south."

After a lot of turning around and more walking, we emerged into Manhattan. The train and station had been quiet, but the city was alive. The honking cars, the lights, the people walking the streets—everything assaulted my senses. I smelled cars and hot dogs, though I couldn't see a hot dog stand anywhere.

Jenna tugged me by the arm. "Come on." She pointed to a nearby sign pointing to the steps leading down to the subway. I barely blinked as we descended. A faint scent of urine and river water greeted me. I cringed, both in disgust and in fear of being mugged for real.

Any thief who attacked us would be disappointed. We had nothing but the clothes on our backs—a point that drove home as soon as we followed the trickle of passengers toward the turnstiles that separated us from the subway platform.

"How are we going to—" I began, but Jenna looked around and vaulted the unattended turnstile.

I heaved a sigh and followed suit.

After a ten-minute subway ride, we emerged from the subway pit and onto the surface sidewalk. The buildings here didn't stack as tall as the skyscrapers of upper Manhattan. They were made of different colors of brick, with window after window facing the street. We crossed a cobblestone intersection, the tires from passing cars rumbling from the uneven surface.

"There it is," said Jenna.

Ahead, a neon sign stuck out from the corner of a building of black-painted brick. The letters spelled *The Stranded Siren Tavern*, a section of the word *Tavern* winking. We passed a parking garage on our way to the corner. I rubbed my eyes, weariness tugging down my shoulders. My neck ached from sitting so long, with muscles that hadn't healed from my attack yet.

"You must be hungry," Jenna said. "They've got food here."

Hungry? I think the lingering smell of pee and sausages made me lose my appetite. Still, I ambled along as Jenna walked toward the neon lights.

They buzzed and flickered overhead as we passed. Around the corner where the two streets met, the pub entrance sat facing the Hudson River. Lights from the city reflected on the dark water. Buoy bells sounded in the distance. Some people walked out of the pub, one wearing an NYPD sweatshirt. We walked in.

Dim lighting and muted jukebox music, the long bar, and scattered tables all lent the place to a typical, seedy dive bar. I looked around for a bartender, a host, anyone who might try to card me since I was still underage. A few people sat at the bar, a couple of others in a booth with a plate of fries between them. With the absence of the stench outside, the scent of fried food sent my empty stomach into hunger pang mode. But instead of approaching the bar, Jenna walked around it and headed toward the back of the pub.

We passed some empty pool tables. I stared at grimy posters of old rock bands, classic cars, and New York cityscapes decorating the walls before turning to see Jenna approach a man seated at a tiny, round table at the very back of the bar. A pitcher of water and a glass sat on the table. As she got closer to him, he stood and embraced her, engulfing her small frame with his considerable height.

"Meriana," he murmured. "Thank Nereus you're all right." His hair was long, dark gray, and streaked with premature white. He wore it with the top half tied into a ponytail behind his head. He wore simple black clothing, looking like a hipster poet on open mic night.

"I am now," she said as she released him.

"What happened? I tried calling your cell phone."

"It's a long story. I'll fill you in later. We're both exhausted."

"Of course." He smiled, wrinkles deepening in the corners of his eyes and creases of his mouth. He clapped her on the shoulders, then looked at me with eyes a startling shade of aqua blue. "And this is?" he began, dipping his chin toward me in greeting.

"Olivia Owens," said Jenna. "My friend."

His eyes widened a little. "Oh. Yes. Olivia Owens. Our newest nominee."

Did he say nominee? Then it was official. I swallowed, my nerves crawling back in full force.

"We weren't expecting you until tomorrow, but we're happy to offer you accommodations."

They expected me to come? How? We didn't know about the time change for the council until earlier today. Jenna and I must have missed a lot during our short stay at Trafford's house.

He gave me a small smile and motioned toward a black door in the corner. "Come."

"Water first," Jenna said with a trace of breathlessness. She went straight to the pitcher, lifted, and drank it empty, even though she'd downed eight bottles on the train. She put it down, gasping, then turned back.

"Feel better?" the man asked. She nodded and wiped her chin with the back of her hand. He guided us to the door. Jenna opened it and held it so I could walk through. The man followed. The door led to a small foyer, with a set of stairs on the left and a hallway continuing straight on. The man closed the door and both he and Jenna stood in the square space, facing me. She gestured to him.

"Olivia, I want you to meet my uncle, Pelagius."

"Are you a part of CHASM?" I whispered in awe. He chuckled.

"No. I am head of Black Moray and an alternate for CHASM, should the Hedron require one. But please, allow me to show you to a place where you can rest while you're here. Come this way." He beckoned toward the staircase. We went up the creaking wood stairs, the plaster walls lit by a naked bulb hanging overhead.

"Has anyone else arrived yet?" Jenna asked.

"His majesty is coming in the morning. The ambassadors from Tetra, Vellamus, Cansu, and Zydrunas have all arrived."

"Zydrunas?" I asked with some excitement. "Who's here from Zydrunas?"

He stopped on the stairs and looked back at me. "Queen Hydria and her delegation."

Seidon, Cordelia, and the others must be with her.

"Can I see them?"

"I'm afraid not. They, too, requested rest and refreshment after her long journey. Come. The council convenes first thing in the morning."

40

The Stranded Siren

Pelagius and Jenna left me in a tiny room with a thin bed and a communal bathroom down the hall, which I utilized with relief after our long train ride. After I finished, I went back to the bedroom. It looked cleaner than the rest of the place, but I still lifted the blankets and sniffed them warily. Once I confirmed they were odor-free, stain-free, and bug-free, I finally sat. Alone in my thoughts, I marveled at Pelagius's kindness. The absence of the typical merperson hostility calmed me, but I still missed Calder. Would he and the others come?

A knock sounded on my door. Too tired to get up, I said, "Come in."

Jenna opened it. In one hand, she held a plate of french fries and a hamburger. In the other, she held a change of clothes.

"I've brought you some food." She handed me the plate. "And some clothes. I hope they fit," she said. "*The Siren* keeps a good stock of clothing on hand for visitors, but with the Hedron arriving, they have a short supply." She set the pile on the end of the bed.

"It's fine. Thank you." I picked up a fry but didn't start eating.

"I know this place looks awful from the outside," Jenna went on, "but it's safe and comfortable here. The pub downstairs is run by humans, but they don't know the truth about what goes on here. They're well paid to protect every person that walks through the back door."

"It sounds like the mafia," I said with a huff. She laughed.

"Nope. Just merpeople. Get some rest. If you need anything, there's always someone around. Just say the word."

"Thanks, Jenna."

She nodded and moved to walk out.

"Hey, Jenna?" I asked. She looked back. "Your uncle is nice. If he's the head of Black Moray, why doesn't he just take the eleventh spot instead of just being the alternate?"

She smiled. "That's sweet of you. But he can't. He's a citizen of Coralium. There can't be two delegates from one reach. He can vote only if another standing member is unable."

"Oh. Okay."

She nodded and left. I started on the fries. Salty, hot, and crispy. Even though it was my second hamburger-and-fries meal of the day, I downed everything.

As I ate my burger, I listened. Out the bedroom window, even through the glass, the sounds of New York echoed: sirens, horns, voices, screeching tires, seagulls. With the constant noise, the worry over what would happen at the CHASM council, and the anxiety about Calder and the others, I'd never get any sleep. And oh, how I wanted to sleep. I lay down on the bed, my body heavy but my mind full.

The door opened again and Jenna entered, holding a bottle of water.

"I went downstairs and realized you didn't have anything to drink." She came in and set the water bottle on the nightstand.

"Thank you." I took the water, unscrewed the lid, and sipped it. "So can you tell me how this is going to work?" I asked. "This whole CHASM meeting?"

"Well, I've never been to one before, but my uncle has." She sat on the other end of my bed. "The Hedron will have to ratify your nomination first. After that, your number one priority is to protect the secret. As long as you keep that in mind, you'll do fine."

"But what if they need me to make a decision on something I don't understand?"

"Ask questions. There's no law against that. Although I can't promise they'll be very nice about answering." She frowned apologetically.

"Huh. Right." I yawned. My eyes grew irresistibly heavy.

She smiled and patted my shoulder. "I'll leave you to go to sleep." She yawned herself. "You're probably exhausted. I'm happy to answer any questions you have tomorrow."

I sipped my water again. "Thank you."

She smiled and walked out. I took another drink of water, pulled my shoes off, and changed into the pair of pajamas in the stack of clothing Jenna had brought. The soft sweatpants and shirt soothed my skin. I crawled under the covers. Even though my mind was still full, and the bed wasn't much better than my dorm bed, I quickly fell asleep to the lullaby of New York City traffic.

It felt like only a few minutes had passed when someone shook my shoulder hard. I awoke with a start and looked around, barely able to keep my eyes open. I blinked a few times in the dark.

"What's the matter?" My speech came out in a syrupy murmur. A hand closed over my mouth. I squealed and fought hard against the strong hands pulling me out of the bed. My muscles moved too slow, too weak. I elbowed my captor several times and cried out again, though his hand muffled my words. My mind went back to Loch Raven, where Kai had held me in a similar position. I fought again to free myself from him and tried to scream.

"Blood of Nereus, be quiet!" said a hoarse voice in my ear. "I've been sent to warn you. But if you'd rather die, or watch your friends die, by all means, keep using your obscenely sharp elbows."

It wasn't Kai. It was Adrian.

41

Rigged

I relaxed. He let me go.

"What do you want?" I whispered.

"Eamon needs you to come," he said. A tiny bit of light from the window allowed me to see the faint outlines of his face. "Now."

"Eamon? He's here? What about Calder?"

"Just come."

I took a step back. "No, I'm not going anywhere with you. Why couldn't Eamon come himself?"

"No one is allowed near you. I was able to get to you only because I was assigned guard duty at your door. You have to come now, while everyone is asleep."

"Why should I trust you?" I asked with a scowl.

"I told you. If you don't come now and hear what Eamon and the rest of your friends have to say, people are going to die."

He had to be lying. He didn't care about humans. This had to be some kind of trick to get me away from the council. He wouldn't want me voting to allow Samantha and Seidon to get married. The prejudiced merman had made his hatred for humans clear from the moment I met him.

I stepped back again and bumped the back of my legs on the bed.

"I don't believe you."

He gave an impatient sigh. "Then I'll have to prove it to you, but we don't have much time. If they suspect I've been speaking to you, I could lose my fins." His shadowed eyes darkened fiercely. "And if I lose my fins because of you, *human*, you'll live to regret it."

"You're not making any sense."

"I'll take you to Eamon. But I'll have to carry you. If any of them hear two footsteps on the stairwell, they'll know you've left your room."

I frowned in repugnance. "They can probably hear everything we're saying now."

"No, they can't. The bedrooms are soundproof. And I'm the last guard patrolling the stairwell until morning."

I still glared at him in suspicion. He had to be lying. This had to be a trap. He shook his head and turned away.

"Fine," he said, throwing his hands up. "If you're so confident about the real reason you're here, then by all means, stay." He reached for the doorknob. I stepped forward.

"Okay, okay. I'll come."

He came back, turned his back to me, and squatted down. I wrapped my arms around his neck and got on his back, cringing as he stood. This was so stupid. Part of me was sure he only wanted to take me to a back alley and slit my throat, but another part prickled with curiosity. What if he was telling the truth?

He eased the bedroom door open without a sound and walked into the hallway. Then he locked the door with a key—one-handed. His other arm held me up on his back. He walked slowly down the hall and to the stairwell, ascended two floors, and came into another empty hallway. I had to hand it to him. The dude was strong. He approached one of the doors and made light scratching noises on the wood with his fingernail. The door opened.

Eamon stood there, lit by the lightbulb in the ceiling. Once he saw us, he held a finger to his lips, opened the door wider, and let us in. Uther, Walter, and Calder all stood inside. Calder had dark circles under his eyes and his facial hair was especially scruffy. I let out a fervent breath of relief, but Eamon reached out and grabbed my shoulder. His eyes wide, he again raised a silencing finger, then shut the door.

"You have to be quiet," he whispered.

"But he said the rooms were soundproof." I tried to pull away so Adrian would let me down, but he didn't loosen his hold.

"We cannot take any chances," said Eamon. He nodded to Adrian, who finally put me down. I turned to find myself engulfed in Calder's tight embrace.

"What happened to you?" he asked in my ear. "How did you get here?"

"It's a long story."

Eamon cleared his throat. "We don't have much time. There's a lot to explain."

I begrudgingly slid away from Calder but held his hand with both of mine.

"We tried to get a hold of you to tell you," Eamon said. "The creature is dead."

"I know. Calder told me. What happened?"

"We don't know," said Eamon. "We found her body lying in the pool."

"Why would someone kill her? She couldn't even talk."

"She could," said Calder. "Well, sort of."

"She could? What did she say?"

"Cordelia used telepathy," Calder continued. "The creature couldn't use words, just images and emotions. Cordelia said the creature communicated terrible fear and sadness. And the images that came up in her mind were a cage in the pond and the face of a woman."

"A woman? Who?"

"Cordelia didn't know," said Eamon. "Never seen her before. But there was something else. The creature communicated *reluctance.* Regret. She didn't want to hurt people anymore. Cordelia felt her plea to make it stop."

I shut my eyes with the sudden surge of dread and sympathy. The creature had feelings, thoughts, and intelligence. Fear. Remorse. I gave a shuddering sigh. Despite all she had done, she wasn't just a mindless killer. Someone had been controlling her. And now, someone had silenced her. The same person? Could it have been…

"Did you see who killed her?" I asked.

"No."

"I wanted to post a guard," said Uther, "but Cordelia assured us it would be safe."

"I didn't find out until I got back."

"Maybe if lover-boy didn't put his cell on silent, you would have gotten the message sooner," said Uther. Calder scowled at him.

"It's not his fault," I said. "He tried to warn me. I should have hurried back to my dorm the second he told me to."

"Where've you been?" Calder asked. "When you called me back, it sounded like you were in trouble, but you couldn't hear me."

"I called you?" I asked. Then I remembered. "Oh! In Trafford's office. Yours must have been the number I dialed."

"We came looking for you, but all we found was your bag." He reached down, rummaged through a pile of luggage, and pulled out my purse. He handed it to me. I let out a breath.

"Thank you." How to begin explaining what had happened? I pressed my lips together and breathed some more. "It was all my professor. She's the one who gave me the scholarship." My voice shook. "She knows about merpeople. She knew Linnaeus. She was at his big party in San Diego. Remember? She saw me at the party and—I don't know—somehow figured out who I was."

"Your *professor* did all this?" said Eamon.

"I went to her office to talk to her about a problem with my internship. I found an invitation from Linnaeus on her wall."

"She kept it out in the open?" Calder asked incredulously.

"She's a hot mess. She had all kinds of outdated stuff on that bulletin board. But when I saw it, I decided to try and log onto her emails to see what else I could find. Instead, I found other stuff on her computer. She caught me snooping and threatened to take my scholarship away if I didn't help her with—I don't know, getting in touch with the merpeople or something. I think she wanted to write a book." The more I explained, the worse I felt. My hands began to shake. "She stuck me with some kind of drug and took me to her house. It's near the pond where...where I freed the mermaid." Calder grasped my shoulder and rubbed it with his thumb until I could swallow and compose myself. "She took Jenna too."

"Jenna? Why?"

Oh, boy. So much. I quickly explained Jenna's true identity, what happened at Trafford's house, and how we'd made our way to *The Stranded Siren*. Calder let me go and began pacing. Walter came closer and hugged me.

"You going to be okay?" he asked, giving my shoulder a few pats. I shrugged.

"I don't know what to do now that the mermaid is dead."

"Whoever killed her wanted to eliminate your only defense," said Eamon. "But that's the least of our worries. Right now, we need to focus on CHASM."

The mermaid's murder was the *least* of our worries? I gaped at Eamon. "What else is there?"

Calder stopped pacing. "They wanted you on the council," he said.

"But it was Cordelia's idea," I said.

"She nominated you so you could help defend human rights," said Eamon. "But the other side, the ones who opposed the nomination the most, suddenly changed their minds and approved it."

"Why?"

"They know they can manipulate you," said Calder.

"Manipulate me?"

"They're certain you'll vote yes. But they've changed the vote to move in their favor. You have to vote no, or people will die."

"Vote no for what?"

"Seidon and Samantha's engagement," said Walter. "You have to vote no."

"What? No! I can't do that to them."

"You have to," said Eamon. "The whole thing is rigged."

"What do you mean, rigged?" I asked. "Rigged how?"

"There's a clause to the proposition," said Uther. "If you vote yes, you also vote yes to a Purge."

"What's a Purge?"

"An extermination," said Eamon. "Many members of the Hedron believe Seidon's engagement is the result of being too lax on merworld security. Too many humans know about them. The vote is a draw. Half want a Purge, the other doesn't. It just so happens that the same ones who want the Purge don't want Seidon to marry Samantha. They struck a compromise. The only way the Hedron will allow Seidon to marry a human is to purge the rest of the human world of all knowledge of the merworld."

Something in me snapped like a glass vial, spreading fear from my head to my feet. I couldn't believe it. It couldn't be true.

"How can they do that?" I cried. Adrian shushed me. I lowered my voice. "They can't kill everyone who knows about the merpeople. That's all of *us*. Who's going to help them with human issues if they ever need it?"

"It isn't just us," said Calder. "It's our families. My mum. My brother. Your parents. Samantha's family. Even old enemies. Anyone they suspect of knowing."

I shut my eyes and shook my head.

"Why can't they just make us forget?" I asked. "They took Samantha's memories. Why not do that rather than kill innocent people?"

Adrian shook his head. "The sacrificing of memories works only on a merperson. Otherwise, we'd have scrubbed all your minds years ago." He cocked an eyebrow as though wishing he could scrub our minds right now. I frowned.

"The least you could do is look sorry," I snapped at him.

"Hey," Calder said gently. "He's helping us."

"No, give me one good reason why we should believe any of this." I turned to Eamon. "The Hedron want to kill us all, so they put me on their council to vote for it? Why would I vote for my own death?"

Eamon glanced at the others. "Queen Hydria was told that every member of the Hedron would be informed of all the aspects of the vote, including you."

"But they never told me."

"Right. Whoever wanted the Purge tried to keep it from you on purpose. That way, they could ensure the vote passed and they could get what they wanted."

"This is insane," I said. I rubbed my face. "I never wanted to be here in the first place, and now you're telling me I have to vote down Seidon and Samantha's marriage to keep the Hedron from murdering every human who has ever heard of them? Do you know how crazy it sounds?"

Eamon sighed. "You should never have been put in this situation. I'm sorry."

"Where'd you get all this information?" I asked, looking around at them. Calder, Walter, and Uther all looked at Eamon. He looked at Lieutenant Adrian, then back at me.

"Queen Hydria told me," said Eamon. I frowned.

"And I'm supposed to believe that? How do I know you aren't trying to manipulate me?"

Eamon looked aghast. "Why would I do that?"

"You haven't wanted me around. You haven't trusted me. You thought I released the mermaid on purpose and lied about it. And what about that reach in the Mediterranean, Eamon? The one you blew up to cover your tracks?"

Eamon's face paled as though I'd slapped him across the face. Calder, Uther, and Walter all looked at him.

"You said the explosion was an accident," Calder said. Eamon ignored him.

"How did you know about that?" he asked me.

"Jenna told me," I said, lowering my head under his piercing gaze. "Her family died in the explosion. She said it was your fault."

"Your friend, who has been pretending to be a human for months, told you it was my fault?"

"What else am I supposed to believe?" I blinked away the tears gathering in my eyes as I confessed the ugly truths I'd been bottling up. "She told me what happened. It made sense."

Eamon sighed. Then he took a step forward and slowly grasped both my shoulders in his hands. I turned my face away.

"Listen to me, Olivia," he said, his voice gaining a severe edge I rarely heard from him. I looked him in the eye. "What happened at Okeanos was a terrible tragedy. Mistakes were made, but I worked *with* the merpeople to evacuate everyone. The explosion was meant to keep humans from discovering Okeanos Ektasi. If I hadn't done it, they would have found hard proof that merpeople exist. The ones that stayed? They disobeyed orders. They couldn't do what was asked, not because they didn't want to leave their homes, but because the orders came from me."

I sniffled and wiped my face. Eamon took a deep breath. "And as far as not wanting you around?" He shook his head and let go of my shoulders. "I never intended to make you feel that way. I'm sorry. We all care about you."

"I need to take her back," Adrian interrupted. "They could come for her at any time now."

Eamon closed his mouth and nodded. Calder stepped forward and wrapped his arms around me again. I stood, unmoving. All the information dumped on me at once froze me to the spot.

"None of us intended for this to happen," he whispered. "All you have to do is vote no and it'll be over."

I clutched his shirt. I couldn't leave him.

"We need to go," said Adrian.

"I don't want to go," I said to Calder. "I don't want to do this."

"You can do it. I know you can do it. Beat these bastards at their own game."

I let go and looked up at him. My eyes stung. Heaviness weighed on my heart.

"If I don't get a chance to see them, tell Seidon and Samantha I'm sorry."

He nodded. "They'll understand."

"We must go, now," said Adrian. He turned and lowered himself down. I reluctantly stepped away from Calder and without taking my eyes off him, climbed onto Adrian's back. Then Adrian took me out of the room, down the hall, down the stairs, and back to my room, leaving me with my turbulent thoughts.

42

The Hendecahedron

I sat on my bed, watching the sky outside slowly grow lighter and the lights in the city wink out. My eyes didn't close the rest of the early morning. I longed to be back with Calder, to sleep, to feel safe.

Everything they told me came down to one thing: Someone within the Hedron thought they could trick me into sentencing my friends and family to death. This body of powerful merpeople didn't want a human on their council. They had only their agenda. Who was it pulling all these strings? Someone told Trafford to release the mermaid from Loch Raven. Someone tried really hard to keep the truth from getting out. Someone orchestrated the Purge. I sighed, then clenched my teeth as I stared through the window to the river's glittering surface.

I didn't know who was behind it. But I did know their plan would fail. Samantha and Seidon wouldn't be allowed to get married, but the alternative was unthinkable. They'd understand. We'd find a way.

A knock sounded on my door.

"Olivia?" came Jenna's voice.

"Come in."

She opened the door. When she saw me, she frowned.

"Didn't you get any sleep?"

I nodded. "Some."

"I've brought you some breakfast." She came in, holding a plate of bacon and eggs.

"Thanks." I took the plate from her.

"You're welcome. Eat fast though. You need to come to the CHASM chambers soon. The vote for your nomination is taking place as we speak."

I froze mid-bite. "Now?"

"They convened about an hour ago."

Thank goodness Adrian had brought me back when he did. I gazed at my bacon and eggs as though it were my last meal.

"You can finish eating and freshen up first, of course," Jenna continued. She looked at the side of my bed, where my purse sat, and gestured toward it. "Where'd you get that?"

I looked down. I wasn't supposed to have gone anywhere last night. "Oh, um…uh…Lieutenant Adrian brought it to me. C-Cordelia found it and brought it."

"Oh. Okay." She looked back at me. "I'll come back in a few minutes to take you down to the chambers." She stepped out and shut the door. Curious, I went over to the door and peeked out. A burly merman with wild tangles of brown hair and scars on his massive biceps stood opposite my door. Jenna looked back from down the hall.

"Was there something else?" she asked. "You should probably hurry to get ready."

I shook my head. "Right. Sorry." I shut the door. Adrian had been right about the guards posted by my door. Had I misjudged him?

No time to worry about it now. I finished eating my breakfast and picked up the pile of clothing Jenna had given me last night. A plain white button-up shirt, a pair of jeans that were a size too big, and even a sports bra and new pair of underwear were all tucked into the stack. A small bag contained a toothbrush.

I changed, ran my fingers through my hair, used my toothbrush and water bottle to rinse my mouth and wash my face, and hoped it would be enough. Soon, Jenna came back.

"Ready to go?" She smiled.

"I'm not sure," I replied. She patted my back.

"You'll do great."

We continued past the merman on guard duty and started down the stairs. On the ground floor, we turned left down the passage and came to another stairway heading downward. My heart pounded harder with every step.

We soon came to the ground floor, which consisted of a short hallway. At the end of it stood Pelagius in front of a door.

"Miss Owens," he said with a small bow. "Welcome. They're ready for you."

He opened the door and stood aside. I swallowed, took several deep breaths, and walked in. Feeling as though a set of high-beam headlights shone on my face, I laid eyes on the people in the room.

They sat at a round, wooden table. One guy even kind of looked like King Arthur, complete with shoulder-length, silvery-white hair and a trim beard. Each of them had a glass of water in front of them. Sinks with faucets lined the walls on one side, so anyone sitting at the table could easily fill their glass if they needed. I looked to my right and with a jump in my heart, I saw a long pane of glass spanning the upper half of the wall. Behind it, a myriad of people sat, watching through the window. Seidon smiled and waved when I saw him. Samantha sat beside him. She waved too. Cordelia, Adrian, and about a dozen other people I didn't recognize sat in there too.

"Olivia Owens," said King Arthur, pulling my attention back to the table. "Please." He held a hand out to the only empty chair at the far side of the table. I moved slowly, feeling so inferior and out of place I could have died. As I went, I studied each face with a combo of fascination and trepidation.

All of them were of different ages and colors. Dark skin, light skin, and shades in between. Long hair and short. Pale eyes, bright eyes, and eyes dark as shadows. They held me in their gaze as I circled to my chair. Some faces held suspicion, some downright malice—others seemed only curious. One was different though. She watched me with her arms gripping the sides of her chair, as though to keep herself from rising. The moment I saw her, I knew: she had to be Seidon's mother, Queen Hydria. Her eyes were the same deep blue, and huge like his. Their noses were the same. Her silvery brown hair fell over her shoulders in thick waves. Her chin came to an elegant point, her face more angular than Seidon's.

I held back a sigh of awe and immediately wanted her to like me.

The empty chair sat between King Arthur—whatever his real name was—and Queen Hydria. I lowered myself onto the chair, feeling overwhelmingly small and plain in this room of wild-eyed merpeople. Not only merpeople but royalty and dignitaries. I looked down at the table and noticed it wasn't a circle, but a polygon that had eleven equal sides.

Pelagius went out the door and shut it behind him. King Arthur then rose to his feet. Everyone in here really needed name tags. I couldn't keep calling him King Arthur.

"As the elected herald for this session of CHASM," he began, "the Hedron welcomes the human, Olivia Owens."

He didn't look at me. The rest of the group nodded, except for one mermaid with long, ice-white hair sitting across the table from me. She lifted her chin in defiance, her eyes narrowing as she stared at me. My first impulse was to cower, but I resisted. I clasped my hands together to keep them from shaking.

"The council has come to a decision regarding the nomination of said human," King Arthur continued. I looked up at him. He hesitated, as though an unpleasant smell had just reached his nose. "Due to your actions in defending our people and protecting our secret, the nomination is granted. Pending a swearing-in, you will be counted among the Hendecahedron."

Whoa. It worked. I should have felt victorious. The hardest hurdle had been crossed. But instead, I felt a plunge within me, like I'd jumped off the high dive at the public pool. I was in. I was part of this now.

I looked at Queen Hydria—the only person whose name I knew. Her eyes bore into mine and I heard a voice in my head: *Vote no.*

I gave her the tiniest nod. She looked away. The door opened and Pelagius came in, holding a small bundle wrapped in black fabric.

"All in order, your Majesty," he said. He stood in front of the door, looking like a middle-aged bouncer at a club.

"Then we are back to business," said King Arthur. "Olivia Owens, please stand."

I did, my legs trembling. Was I really here? Was I standing in a room with a secret merworld council, now a part of it? Me, a nobody, a college student with barely half a degree to my name. How did this happen?

Pelagius approached with the black bundle and set it before me.

"Before the swearing-in," said Queen Hydria, her voice quiet, yet somehow still piercing, "I think it only fair that we introduce ourselves to the nominee. Name, reach, and ocean, by human reckoning."

King Arthur nodded. "Very well. I am King Enamerion of Coralium. North Atlantic." He sat.

Enamerion. A human-hater. My fear of him doubled. Next to him, a young mermaid with long, fiery hair and translucent eyes stood.

"I am Princess Meraud of Eldoris. Arctic." She sat delicately. Cordelia had mentioned her. She was only eighteen. She turned to the merman sitting next to her for his introduction. He looked like a pirate with his scraggly, black-and-gray-streaked hair hanging down his back and a long, unkempt beard.

"I am General Glaucus of Tetra. South Atlantic," he said. I remembered Jenna mentioning him too.

"I am Queen Minali of Arulius. Indian Ocean," said the mermaid on the other side of General Glaucus. She had long, black hair, russet skin, and striking eyes the color of the ocean. She sat. Another mermaid stood.

"I am Queen Asherah of Cansu. Caspian Sea. The only landlocked reach in the world," she said with pride. Her gray hair flowed in waves down to her thighs. Though her face held the most wrinkles of all the members, she carried herself with the most dignity. An Asian mermaid stood next. Like Queen Minali, she also had black hair, pulled back in intricate braids.

"I am Captain Ula of Sunil. Pacific," she said in a deep, rich voice. The merman sitting beside her, who I could only describe as Tongan, stood.

"I am General Vasa of Maristela. South Pacific." He sat. How was I supposed to remember all these names? A merman with dark skin and salt and pepper locks stood next.

"I am Prince Arik of Anquanhai. Antarctic, Atlantic side."

Did he say Prince Eric? At this, I had to press my lips together. A merman named Prince Eric. He didn't look like his Disney namesake, more like someone's Rastafarian grandpa. But then the white-haired mermaid who sat beside him stood and glared at me with so much hatred, it chased the amusement away like a scared rabbit.

"I am Captain Tempus of Varuna, Antarctic, Pacific side," she said, still staring daggers at me.

"And I am Queen Hydria of Zydrunas. North Pacific." said Hydria to my right. She sat. I waited. What was I supposed to say to all that?

"Um...good to meet all of you."

General Glaucus chuckled. Some of the others scowled at him.

"Olivia Owens," said Enamerion. The lack of a title before my name felt all the more striking after hearing the names of the dignitaries surrounding me. "At this time, you can make your choice. You may accept the nomination, or you can be dismissed."

Every eye in the room looked back at me. Oh, crap. Did they want me to give some kind of speech?

I looked through the window and met gazes with Cordelia, then Seidon, then Samantha. I wished the merpeople would let my human friends come too. I could use their support.

"I know humans haven't done much to earn your trust." My voice shook. I took a quick breath to try and steady it. "But I'm here. And I'm going to try. I'm planning a career in ocean research. I'll make it my mission to conserve oceans and divert exploration away from your reaches."

A silence followed. Some looked at me like I was a little kid saying something cute. Both Captain Tempus and Prince Arik still bore fiery death stares. My face burned. I looked down. I should leave. I didn't belong here. Tempus looked like she would love nothing more than to end me right here and now. But I couldn't leave. I had a job to do. Calder, Eamon, my family—everyone I loved and cared about needed this.

I could do it. Like Calder said, I could beat them at their own game. They expected me to vote yes.

I cleared my throat and, with some effort, looked up at Enamerion's majestic face.

"I accept the nomination."

His brows twitched. "Then please take the vessel in your hands."

I reached for the bundle, unwrapped the cloth, and found a white clam the size of both my fists. It looked exactly like the one I'd handled in San Diego. Touching this one would leave my imprint on a second merworld vessel. I hesitated.

"Go ahead," whispered Hydria. I slowly picked it up. Cold, heavier than it looked, and smooth as glass, I held the vessel in both hands and waited.

"Open the shell and repeat the words," said Enamerion. I slid a fingernail between the lips of the clam and opened the top. At the center, a large pearl began spinning, giving off golden light. The clam warmed in my hands. Smoky wisps came from it, forming into an insubstantial figure above the vessel. High, shrieking sounds like whalesong chorused from inside the vessel, along with words.

"I come before this council." It paused. I repeated the words. "Elected and chosen." I repeated them again. "I now swear fealty to the Hendecahedron during this council for the Concealment, Harboring,

Armament, and Security of Merpersons. I will protect the secrets, the rights, and the safety of the oceans. Every decision I make, I make for the good of our people. Should I betray this Hendecahedron, my life is forfeit. By the blood of Lord Nereus, I vow."

43

One Thousand Clicks

Pelagius rewrapped the vessel in the black cloth and took it out of the room. I sat in silence and scanned the faces around me. Some looked resigned. Others looked like they'd just eaten something gross.

"This session of CHASM will now convene," said Enamerion. "The first issue at hand is to inform this body that the feral mermaid has been destroyed."

"Destroyed?" said Glaucus. "When did this happen?"

Hydria straightened. "By reasons and persons unknown, the feral mermaid was murdered the night before last. Captain Cordelia can confirm."

"What of the humans?" The old, silvery-haired mermaid turned her glassy eyes on me. "Have they done this as retribution for the creature's victims?"

"No, of course not," I said. "I mean, yeah, they—or *we*—want justice. But no one suspects a mermaid has been behind all this. They think it's a serial killer. And a male," I added, thinking of Darci and what the police had said to her.

"But are we certain a human didn't kill the creature?" asked Captain Ula. "A mermaid life for a human life?"

"At this point, there is no way of knowing who killed the creature, but justice has already been served," said Enamerion. "I've been informed by one of our operatives that the human Lisa Trafford, who admitted to harboring the creature, has suffered a massive brain injury and lies comatose in a hospital."

"Wait, what?" I said. "She's in a coma?" How hard had Jenna hit her?

"Should she regain consciousness," Enamerion said loudly over me. "We can revisit the issue of her penance."

I gaped at him, looked at the other somber faces around the table, then glanced through the window where the others sat. Cordelia watched me with stoic composure. Seidon looked worried. And Samantha held the same expression I saw her make when we sat in the dining room in Berwyn Heights. Hardened, intense, and commanding, she gazed at me. She believed in me, even though she didn't know the real me. Her look, her very presence, gave me courage.

"Someone else told Trafford how to release the mermaid," I said. "Only merpeople know how to do that. And even though the creature couldn't say it, she knew the truth. Whoever killed her wanted her silenced."

Everyone in the room stared at me.

"Are you defending the human?" asked Enamerion.

"No. She's done a lot of terrible things. But—"

"Then you're suggesting a merperson is at fault for all this mess," sneered Tempus. Based on the information Trafford had on her computer, I had to agree.

"I know it sounds unlikely, but—"

Before I could finish, the rest of the Hedron all began talking at once, until Enamerion stood again.

"The Hedron will come to order," he said. "Based on our most recent intel, the human Lisa Trafford freed the creature and allowed her to wreak havoc on the humans, risking our exposure to the world."

"Because someone told her to do it," I insisted. "And *how* to do it.

His gaze bore down on me. My courage snuffed out.

"Someone must be held accountable," said Enamerion. "So, unless you have proof otherwise, when she wakes, the human will pay."

Proof. All the information from Trafford's computer was on a flash drive, in my purse a few floors above me. I couldn't believe I had the nerve, but I stood.

"I have proof."

Every eye turned my way again.

"You have proof?" Enamerion seemed taken aback at first but soon smoothed his expression and gestured to the table with one hand. "Then present it."

"It's upstairs," I said. "I can go get it."

He studied me for a second then turned to address the rest of the table. "We will have a short recess. Olivia Owens will retrieve her… evidence. Then we will meet back here and review it before moving on to our second issue at hand. Pelagius, one thousand clicks, if you please. Provide Miss Owens with an escort."

The second issue. He meant Samantha and Seidon's engagement and the Purge. Would the evidence on the flash drive be enough to have it dismissed entirely? Could I actually succeed in ending all of this?

The rest of the delegates scooted back from their seats, drank from their glasses, or began talking to one another in low voices. Tempus kept casting me nasty looks.

"One thousand clicks?" I asked Hydria. She pointed to Pelagius, who sat something on the table that looked like a sundial. It clicked like a time bomb. Or maybe a clock? Were clicks like seconds? I tried to do the math in my mind on how long a thousand seconds was, but it made my head spin.

"Come, Miss Owens," said Pelagius. He opened the door. I got up from my seat, sought out Samantha and Seidon through the window again, and smiled at the look of pride in their faces—even Cordelia's. I turned and hurried out the door. Jenna came around the corner. She didn't look at me though, only at Pelagius. Her face was expressionless, her eyes unblinking.

"Olivia has some important evidence she needs to retrieve," said Pelagius. "If you could escort her and obtain it?" He gave her a stern look. She nodded. Then she looked at me and smiled. She seemed a little on edge but linked her arm around mine like she had done on many occasions before.

"Where do we need to go?" she asked.

"My room," I replied. "I need the flash drive in my bag. And I need a laptop too. Uther should have one."

"Consider it done." She guided me toward the stairs. "How are you?"

I gave a sullen chuckle. "Way out of my league. But I'm okay."

"What are you going to do?"

"The flash drive has everything on it. Trafford kept a record of everything she did. If I can show it to the Hedron, they'll have to drop all this."

"Trafford kept records?" she asked.

"Yeah."

She stared at me for a second, then smiled again. "Well then, we better hurry up and go find it." She pulled at my arm and increased her pace. We hurried up the stairs and to my room. I found my purse on the floor where I'd left it, grabbed it, and dumped everything out on the bed. Wallet. Cell phone. Key card to my dorm room. Old receipts. Old ChapStick. Several coins. Pens. Where was the flash drive? My heart plunged. I panicked and rifled through everything on the bed again, then looked back into my bag. Nothing in the pockets. No flash drive.

"No. No, no, no! *Where is it?*"

"It's not here?" Jenna asked.

"Has anyone been in this room?" I asked, turning to look at her.

"No. I don't think so."

I gripped my scalp with both hands and began to hyperventilate. "I have to have that flash drive!"

"Could it have fallen out?"

I dropped to the floor and looked under the bed. Nothing. I tore the covers off. No flash drive. Had Eamon taken it? Calder knew about it, didn't he? They found my purse and brought it with them. Maybe they had it and were looking through it now. I turned back to Jenna.

"I need to see Calder. *Now.*"

She smiled. "I will take you to him."

I sighed. "Thank you."

We hurried out of the room and back to the staircase. Jenna went up. I followed her up one flight, then another, then another. What floor was Calder's room on? I didn't remember it being this high but she kept going.

"Are you sure we're going to the right place?" I asked.

"I'm sure."

Several more flights later, Jenna opened a door. Bright sunlight made me blink. We emerged onto the roof of the building, where industrial ductwork ran the length and low, pyramid-shaped skylights lay in intervals.

"What are we doing way up here?" I asked.

"I'm taking you to Calder," she said with a weird smile. She pulled me again.

"What's he doing on the roof?"

She guided me around some of the ductwork.

"Jenna, what's going on?"

She didn't reply but put a hand on my back and pushed me around a big, metal box.

"What are you—" I stopped. On the other side of the box, someone lay unmoving, with tied hands and feet.

"*Calder?*" I shrieked, darting forward. Jenna grabbed me by the collar and stuck a knife next to my face.

"Quiet, or he dies."

44

An Impossible Choice

"Jenna, *what are you doing*?"

She moved her face close to mine, her knife blade cold against my skin. Any trace of mirth or mercy were gone.

"Stop calling me Jenna," she hissed, her eyes narrowing in fury. "My name is Meriana. And I told you to be quiet."

"Well done," said another voice from the corner behind me. I turned my head to see Pelagius coming around the metal box. He smiled at me. I couldn't breathe. What was happening?

Pelagius came around to stand in front of me.

"Did you find your evidence?" he asked me, but Jenna replied.

"No," she said. "It wasn't there."

"Good." He looked at me. "So. They got to you."

"Who got to me?" I asked, in a terrified whisper. "Why are you doing this?

He smirked. Jenna took a few steps toward Calder lying on the ground. He watched her, his face full of livid anger. She looked back at me.

"Because your vote is needed. You're part of the Hendecahedron now." Her voice became syrupy.

Pelagius walked behind me. "Who told you about the Purge?" he asked.

I tried to move to keep him in front of me, but I didn't want Jenna—Meriana—at my back.

"Why does it matter?"

He put his hands on my elbows and jerked my arms behind me.

"Just let her go, please," Calder begged from where he lay.

"Answer the question, Olivia," said Jenna. Or Meriana. I couldn't come to grips with the shock of her blade pointed at Calder, much less use her real name.

"Um..." I struggled to swallow with my parched throat. "No one. I overheard it."

"Do it," said Pelagius. Jenna walked over to where Calder lay, pulled something from her pocket, and jammed it into his thigh. I screamed and lurched toward him, but Pelagius held me back. He jerked. Jenna pulled it away. He looked down at his leg, breathing heavily.

"What did you do to him?" I shouted, still trying to tug myself out of Pelagius's grip.

"Here's how this is going to work," said Pelagius. He gripped my arms harder. "Meriana has just injected your boy with a paralytic. Tetraodontidae venom. It does not have an antidote. Without medical attention, his lungs will soon seize and his heart will stop."

Wild with terror, I tried again to rush toward him, but Pelagius stopped me. I couldn't hold back the ragged tears no matter how hard I tried. Tetraodontidae was pufferfish venom. I'd heard about it before.

Pelagius was right; there was no antidote. Only medical intervention could help someone with pufferfish venom in their system. How could this be happening? Maybe if I screamed loud enough, someone downstairs would hear and come to help. I opened my mouth.

"You can help him," said Jenna. "But you have to hurry. You must do exactly what we say if you want to save his life."

"What? What do I need to do?" I said, urgency shaking my voice. I looked back at Calder. He held his tied hands to his leg, pushing hard as though trying to stop the paralytic from spreading.

"All you have to do is go down and vote to allow Prince Seidon to marry your human friend," said Jenna.

I looked away from Calder to gape at her.

"You want the Purge to pass," I said.

"You don't have to worry," she said. "As a member of the Hedron, your life will be spared. Just go down and vote yes."

"If you refuse," said Pelagius's voice in my ear, "I'll kill you right now, in front of him, and make it look like an accident. The Hedron won't lose sleep over it. They never really wanted you anyway."

"No, Olivia," Calder murmured. "Don't."

"How can you do this?" My heart beat out a breakneck rhythm. "Jenna, we're friends. You know me. You know Calder. You can't—"

"Don't tell me what I can and can't do." She ground her teeth as she spoke. "Not when everything I have ever loved has been ripped from me. All because of humans."

"The explosion wasn't meant to hurt anyone. He was trying to protect them. They didn't listen—"

"Shut up!" she shouted.

"Meriana," said Pelagius. "Hush." He came to face me. "It'll take a while for the poison to reach his heart. In the meantime, I will accompany you to the vote. We don't have long. Try anything foolish and he'll be dead long before anyone can reach him."

I choked back a sob. If only I could somehow lure both Jenna and Pelagius away from the roof. I could find Eamon and bring him here to save the guy I loved.

The guy I loved. I loved him.

I loved him.

Taking a deep breath to steady my unraveling nerves, I looked down at Calder again.

"I'll be right back," I said. "You just hang on. Just hang on, okay?"

"You can't, Olivia," Calder cried. "I'm dead either way!"

"*Shut up*," said Jenna, kicking him in the ribs. He groaned and curled his torso.

"Stop it!" Shaking, I stepped away to go find the stairs. "I'll do it. Just—just please, please don't hurt him."

Pelagius gripped my arm and looked at Jenna. "I'll take her back down and make sure the vote passes. As soon as it does, I'll send word. You know what to do."

"Please don't hurt him!" I sobbed, torn between my need to be by Calder's side and desperation to hurry downstairs before the poison stopped his heart.

Inside the hall, Pelagius let go of my arm and grabbed me by the chin. He leaned close to my face. "Gather your senses. Don't say a word about what has happened, or he'll die. If you cooperate, I'll try and talk the Hedron into letting him live despite the Purge." He let go of me and started down the stairs. I followed, gripping the handrails for dear life.

"Why is this happening?" I whispered, mostly to myself, but

Pelagius answered.

"You must see our point of view. We can't ensure our secrecy, and therefore our safety, if we remain known to your people. There will always be another Doran Linnaeus. Another Lisa Trafford. My niece has had to live with the knowledge that humans took everything from her. As have many merfolk."

"But without our help, Doran Linnaeus would have put you all on display."

"If my Black Moray team had been given the mission to stop Doran Linnaeus instead of the amateurs from Zydrunas and that idiot Eamon O'Dell, he wouldn't have gotten as far as he did. We'd have killed him the moment he threatened our people. Your pathetic leniency toward human life might have cost us everything. But no matter. In the end, we'll get what we want."

I tried to dry my face as I quickly stumbled down the steps. How could I have gotten into this mess? How could I have let Jenna play me this entire time? Was this CHASM thing all a big act to allow the merpeople to rid the world of any human who knew about them? Whether they planned it this way or not, they couldn't do it without a majority vote. My vote. Easily swayed, naïve little me.

People will die.

We had only been pawns.

If I voted no, Calder would die. If I voted yes, Samantha could marry Seidon, but every person who knew about the merworld would die. If only Eamon were here, even passing by in a hallway. Where were they? If they knew what was happening on the roof, they could stop it.

Step, step, step. Every hurried step down took me closer to the basement room where the vote would take place. Above me, Calder sat at Jenna's—Meriana's—mercy. In front of me, Pelagius descended, a bob in his step as though he didn't have a care in the world. Below, the rest of the Hedron waited for me and my stupid vote.

Hydria knew. She told me to vote no. Why didn't she do something about it? Couldn't she challenge the vote, or try and change it somehow?

I stopped at the top of the staircase and shook my head to clear it. I needed to focus on the now—how to save Calder from Jenna. Meriana. How to change the vote without Pelagius knowing.

"Hurry up," said Pelagius.

"Please," I said. "Please don't do this."

"You would think differently if you'd watched your family die, all because a couple of humans thought they knew what was best for a race of people they couldn't possibly understand."

"I'm sorry."

"Hmph. No, you're not. You're terrified. And you should be."

"Killing innocent people won't solve the problem."

He yanked on my arm. I lost footing on the stairs, but his hard grip kept me upright.

"Remember, double-cross us, and your boyfriend dies." He let go. Blood rushed back into my arm where he'd held it, making my skin tingle. I rubbed my arm and tried to breathe and gain composure before walking back into the CHASM chambers.

45

The Casting of the Votes

"Where in the great blue world have you been?" Enamerion asked. How long had I been gone? It must have been longer than a thousand clicks.

"I'm sorry I took so long," I said, my voice small. I couldn't let them suspect anything was wrong. Everyone shuffled to their place at the table. I avoided looking at the glass window. I couldn't bear to see the disappointment in their faces. Pelagius shut the door behind me and took his stance in front of it.

"Well?" said Captain Tempus impatiently. "Where is this evidence?"

I lowered my head.

Look up. Stand your ground, came a stern voice to my mind. I lifted my chin. Who had spoken to me? I couldn't tell from all of the faces waiting and watching. I tried not to cower. Then I looked through the glass. Cordelia stood right on the other side, her arms crossed, a look of formidable focus on her face. I straightened.

"No," I said. As hard as I tried, I still couldn't keep my voice completely steady. "I had it among my belongings and now it's gone. Let's just move on to the vote." I walked around the table and took my seat beside Hydria.

"Are you all right?" she asked quietly. The other delegates looked on.

"I'm fine." A lie. Shouldn't I just tell them what happened? They couldn't allow Pelagius to threaten me like this. It had to be illegal. I looked at Hydria, ready to tell her to stop the vote, but Pelagius stared me down. As though he knew exactly what I was about to do, he met my eye and shook his head. I looked away. If only I had merpeople telepathy.

"Well, then, after that waste of our time, I hope we can proceed," Enamerion said in derision.

We couldn't vote until the Hedron had seen the evidence. The information on the flash drive proved merpeople were behind the attacks, not humans. But one glance at Pelagius's glare was enough to keep my mouth shut. I had no time.

"Our next issue at hand is whether to allow Prince Seidon, son of Hydria and Llyr of Zydrunas, to wed the former human Samantha Abernathy, daughter of Crystal Abernathy of Arizona. A vote in favor will allow the match to take place. Furthermore, to preserve the purity of our race, and to prevent this situation from occurring again, the stipulation of additional security measures will be enforced to the fullest extent of our law."

I ground my teeth together. Additional security. Is that what they called the murder of dozens of people?

"A vote against the betrothal, and both merpeople will resume their lives in Zydrunas."

I snuck a peek at everyone sitting at the table. Glaucus looked bored. Tempus smirked at me. Arik looked ravenous. On the other side of

Enamerion, Meraud gazed at me with sympathy. The others all sat still, unmoving, unemotional. Through the window, Samantha, Seidon, and Cordelia watched. Samantha wrung her hands. Seidon's face blazed with defiance. I noticed none of the other people in the room sat near them and kept casting them looks.

"Pelagius, the pearls, if you please."

Pelagius nodded and left the room. I released a breath, as though Pelagius's presence had sucked extra oxygen out of the room.

"What happens when something gets voted down?" I whispered to Hydria, even though I knew every ear could hear me.

"The proposal is dropped."

"Can it be brought up again?"

"Not until the next CHASM meeting."

"How often does it meet?"

"Every five years, except in cases of emergency." She looked at me.

Vote no. Her voice came in clear. I nodded. People weren't going to die on my watch. But how to save Calder? I looked back through the window. Cordelia got up and left the little room. I stared at Samantha.

Calder's in trouble. On the roof. Find Eamon, I said in my mind. *Please hear me.* She didn't respond. The minutes ticked by. Every second brought Calder closer to cardiac arrest. Where was Pelagius? Was he delaying on purpose?

I looked at Hydria. If I whispered it to her, Pelagius wouldn't hear me. But what about the rest of the Hedron? What if one of them were on his side?

"I'm sorry, I—" I began, unable to stay in my seat, when the door to the council room finally opened. I looked to the door, where Cordelia stood, holding another black bundle in her hands. A rush of relief came over me. Had she heard me? Had it worked?

"Where's Pelagius?" Enamerion asked.

"Took a fall," she said. "Your Black Moray team doesn't navigate gravity very well."

I wanted to scramble around the table and hug her to pieces. Had she captured Pelagius? Was there hope for a way out of this? If there was, it needed to be quick.

"We can proceed to the vote without him," said Hydria. "My captain may serve as security."

"The CHASM herald chooses the security," said Enamerion.

"And the security you chose is unavailable," said Hydria. Enamerion frowned.

"Come on now, Enamerion," said Glaucus. "Let us proceed with the vote and go home. I'm starting to itch." He scratched his arm and took a long drink from his glass.

Enamerion looked like he suppressed a growl. But he nodded to Cordelia, who brought the black bundle over to the table. She reached inside it, pulled out a big pink and white conch shell, and gave it to Enamerion. Then she reached into the bag again, brought something out, and dropped it into his open hand. Moving around the table, Cordelia gave something to each member of the Hedron. When she came to me, I held out my hand. She dropped two pearls into my palm: a white one and a black one.

"Please add your vote to the shell as it is passed to you," Enamerion continued. "A white pearl signifies a vote in favor. A black signifies a vote against."

He began by dropping a pearl into the conch shell. I couldn't see which one. Then he passed it to Meraud. She cast her vote, passed it, and the conch went around the room. Everyone kept their votes hidden. As the shell passed closer and closer to me, I glanced again at Seidon and Samantha. I knew what I had to do. I hoped that somehow, my thoughts were able to reach my friends' minds and that Calder was getting help.

Hydria dropped her pearl into the shell and handed it to me. I felt every eye in the room on me as I chose a pearl and dropped it into the shell.

"Security will now count the votes," said Enamerion. Cordelia took the shell from me and stood between me and Enamerion. One by one, she dropped a pearl into her hand and placed it on the table in front of her.

Hurry, Cordelia.

"One in favor. One against. Another against. One in favor. A third against." She kept going, the pearls forming little groups until there were five white and five black. Cordelia rotated the conch shell to get the last rattling pearl out. I watched, holding my breath.

A black pearl dropped into her hand.

"The proposal has been voted down," said Enamerion, looking a little bemused. From behind the glass, both Seidon and Samantha stood, looking both hurt and angry. I jumped up from my chair.

"Olivia?" Hydria said in surprise. I didn't say anything as I hurried for the door. The Hedron started talking, but I ignored them and ran out into the hall…and right into Pelagius's arms. His hair was mussed and he had a swollen bump on his head.

"You think you've saved your people, Olivia," he said. "You and your traitorous little Captain Cordelia?" I pulled free of his grasp and ran up the hallway. He called after me. "You've saved nothing. You've saved *nothing*!"

I ignored him and ran. I wanted to call for Eamon to come, hoping he'd hear me, but what if Jenna heard? She'd kill Calder. If he wasn't already…

No. I couldn't think like that. Up the first set of stairs, then the second. Suddenly grateful I'd been living on the fourth floor of a dorm building for the last year and a half, I hurried up the third flight, the fourth, and fifth, up and up. Insane with worry, I pushed through my heaving lungs and burning legs and rushed up the last flights of stairs. On the final step, I tripped and fell, then scrambled back to my feet and pushed through the door onto the roof.

I crept around the ducts and the metal box blocking Calder and Jenna from my view, then peeked around it. Jenna was nowhere in sight. Calder lay in the same place where he had been before I went down. He didn't move.

"NO!" I cried and ran. I skidded to a stop, fell to my knees, and shook his shoulder.

"Calder!" I shouted. "Wake up!"

Nothing.

"No, Calder. Come on, breathe!" I shook him again. I slapped his face. He still didn't move. How long had he been like this? Tears flowing, fingers shaking, I felt for a pulse, but couldn't find one. I thought back to old CPR classes, put my hands on the bony center of his chest, and pressed hard a couple times, then pinched his nose shut and breathed into his mouth.

Over and over, I breathed and compressed, breathed and compressed. Had it worked? I bent my face close to his mouth to feel for breath while I watched his chest for movement.

"Come on," I whispered. "Come on! Come back to me." I checked his pulse again. Nothing. I did more compressions. Adrenaline kept me going. But my hope drained as Calder's body didn't respond. I wept and pounded on his chest.

"Don't leave me! Don't you dare leave me!"

46

The Failure

I could barely breathe for him through my sobs. My arms began to tire, though I couldn't have been doing this long.

Breathe. Compress. Breathe. Compress.

"Wake up. Please wake up."

Breathe. Compress. Don't stop.

"Eamon!" I screamed as loud as I could. "Eamon, help me!" I pinched Calder's nose shut to breathe for him again, when he arched his back, gasped, and opened his eyes. I recoiled, watching as he caught his breath and blinked up at the sky. Once he recovered enough, he looked up at me.

"Liv."

I sniveled loudly and flung my arms around him.

"Thank you," he whispered. I kissed his face over and over, moving closer to his lips until I kissed them too. He gently pulled away.

"Listen," he interrupted, shifting with a wince. "You need to get out of here."

"No. I'm not leaving. The vote is done. You're safe." I untied his hands.

"No, please. You have to go, *now*."

"Come with me. I'll help you." I untied his feet next and grabbed his arm to help him sit up, but he moved at a snail's pace.

"I can barely move my legs." His voice turned to pleading. "Please, just go. It's not over. They kept talking about some kind of failsafe, and it has to do with you."

"What is it?"

"I don't know, but you have to go before they try and use you again."

"I am not leaving you!"

A gun clicked from behind me. I turned. Pelagius stood pointing a handgun at us.

"You recovered nicely from the toxin," he said in a silky voice. I sat in front of Calder to shield him, but he slowly sat up and pulled me back.

"Takes more than that to finish me off."

Pelagius laughed. "Boy, if we'd intended to kill you, you'd already be dead. Now. Where is Meriana?"

I could ask the same thing, though I didn't care what the answer was.

"I don't know," said Calder. "But you can't hurt her anymore."

"What?" I said, looking from Calder to Pelagius.

"She did her duty," Calder continued, ignoring me. "And Olivia did hers. Now let us go. Your vote has failed. To kill us now would break your laws."

"I can assure you, none of the Hedron give a damn about killing humans," said Pelagius.

"Then why don't you just kill us?"

"Calder, no!" I cried, grabbing his arm. Pelagius stared down at us, the barrel of his gun aimed at my head. My breath and heartbeat doubled. A cold drop of sweat ran down my back. But Pelagius, with an ugly frown, lowered the gun. Hatred burned in his eyes and heaved in his breath.

"Because you're not enough," he hissed. Spittle flew from his lips. "As tempting as it is, killing you now would only make you martyrs. No. You'll die as the creature died. Like the Trafford woman will die. As a means to an end." He smirked.

My mouth hung open.

"You killed the creature?"

He shrugged. "No. I didn't. That wasn't my part to play."

"Your part?" I asked. Had all of this been part of some twisted plan?

"Meriana!" he called out. He looked around the rooftop, then stopped. A breeze blew over us. Pelagius then turned to look toward the ledge of the rooftop, slow, as though listening for something I couldn't hear. Then he faced us again. He stepped closer, close enough for me to see his fist whiten around the gun. It took everything I had in me to keep from cowering. He didn't raise the weapon though. He only chuckled.

"This isn't over, Olivia Owens. You've saved nothing."

He turned and walked back around the metal box. The door to the rooftop shut.

I breathed again, deep and desperate, then began to tremble. I clung to Calder. He returned the embrace, but only for a second.

"Quick, help me up," he said. I nodded and tried to get up myself, but my knees shook too much. Together, we stumbled to our feet. He swayed. I held him around the waist to steady him.

"Why didn't he kill us?" I asked.

"I think he's got something worse planned." He took a step with a wince. "This was all Pelagius. He set everything up to try and get Samantha killed. It didn't work though. She's too well protected."

"Did Jenna tell you all of this?"

"She told me everything. I tried to talk her into letting me go. She got mad and walked away as the poison set in. If you hadn't come when you did..." He looked down at me, gripping my shoulders with an earnest eye. "But she could have just slit my throat. I don't think her heart is in it."

"Where is she?"

"I don't know," he replied.

"Can you walk?"

He took a few tentative, dragging steps. "It's getting better. Let's go look for Jenna." We limped our way across the roof. When Calder tried to head for the door to the stairwell, I stopped him.

"We can't go out that way. Pelagius is down there."

"Get behind me. I'll check the hallway before we go out."

"You can barely walk. *I'll* check the hallway." We took another step when a scraping sound came from behind. I turned. Another breeze blew by.

"Wait a sec."

Calder stopped while I walked over to the building's ledge, where the sound had come from. I peeked over. A wide balcony about eight feet down ran the perimeter of the building. Jenna sat on the balcony's banister, facing the one-hundred-foot drop with her feet dangling over the edge.

"I found her," I said over my shoulder. "Jenna. Er, Meriana. Why don't you move away from the edge?"

She ignored me. Calder shuffled up from behind.

"Come on, Jenna," he said. "Pelagius is gone. It's over."

She said something, but I couldn't hear her. I sat on the edge of the building. Calder grabbed my shoulder.

"I'm okay," I said. "I'm just going to go down there and talk to her."

"It's not safe."

"If Pelagius forced her to do all these things, she needs help."

His lips pressed into a line. "Be careful."

I slid slowly to the edge and eased myself over until I dropped onto the balcony below. Calder watched from above. I looked up at him for a second, then turned to Jenna.

"Why don't you come inside with us? We can go down and tell the Hedron what happened."

She turned her face toward me, a weird smile on her face. "Do you have any idea what it's like to fail?"

"To fail? Of course I do."

She shook her head and looked back toward the river. "I failed so many times. I failed to save my family. I failed to get Seidon. I failed in my plan to use the creature for our purposes. Well, at least I didn't fail to destroy it before it ruined everything."

"You killed her?" I couldn't imagine Jenna, my friend, harming anything. She saw my face and rolled her eyes.

"Stop it with your self-righteous pity, Olivia. None of that matters now. I failed to get you to vote for the Purge." Her speech sped up as she spoke. "Plan A turned to plan B, C, D, E, all the way to plan Z because I couldn't hack it."

I shut my eyes for a second, trying to let the new information sink in. Something else struck me. "Wait, you wanted to get Seidon?" Didn't

Samantha mention a mermaid who had been hanging around him? "Did you...want to marry him?"

She didn't answer, which gave me answer enough. Jenna was a lot older than him. I frowned at the weirdness of the revelation. But merpeople lived longer than humans. Maybe things like courtship and marriage worked differently. Still, I exhaled in surprise. "I'm sorry you had your heart broken, but—"

Jenna laughed. "My heart had nothing to do with it, Olivia." She spat out my name like a curse. "With a place in the Zydrunas royal family, I could convince the rest of the Hedron to finally get rid of every human on earth that thought they could butt into our business."

Had Pelagius programmed all of this in her mind? I frowned and stepped closer.

"Come on," I said. "You're going to go down to the Hedron and explain all of this now. You have to make things right."

She shook her head and gave a maniacal laugh. "No. Because things will never be right. Not anymore. I don't belong here. And I don't belong in the ocean. My home is gone. My family is gone. I had sisters. They had children. I've failed them all."

My heart rate began to rise again. She was really making me nervous.

"Just come inside," I said, reaching for her.

She looked at my hand but didn't take it.

"It wasn't supposed to end this way," she said. "I wish I could say I was sorry."

"Jenna, what—"

"For my people. For my family, who I will see soon." She looked at me. A tear dropped down her cheek. She smiled. "Say farewell to your life, Olivia. Because I'm about to ruin it."

Alarm bells in my brain rang out.

"No, Olivia! Don't do it! Help me! *Help!*" she shouted as loud as she could. I grabbed for her arm. She pushed me away and jumped.

47

Wherever You Go, We'll Find You

I screamed. Jenna's body fell. I stared as she disappeared over the ledge and leaned forward when a pair of hands grabbed me from behind.

"*No*," said Calder. How'd he get down here? "You don't want to see that."

"She—she fell. She fell!"

My legs gave out. Calder tried to support me, but in his weakness, we both sank to the floor. For a moment, I couldn't move. Jenna jumped from ten stories up. There was no way she'd survive that. The image of her face as it disappeared over the ledge replayed before my eyes over and over.

"We have to get out of here." He dragged us both to our feet. "Let's go try and find Eamon."

Shock kept me from speaking. Calder pulled me toward the door, but I didn't go. Instead, I did what he told me not to: I looked over the side. In spite of the dizzying height, I could still see someone bent over

Jenna laying on the sidewalk. Above them, the awning covering the entrance to the pub was broken as though she'd hit it on her way down. Had it broken her fall enough to save her? Could she have miraculously survived that fall?

Below, whoever knelt beside Jenna began shouting. Over and over. More people came out of the pub to surround them. One of them pointed up and the rest of them looked. I pulled myself away. Calder grabbed my hand and pulled me along.

"We need to go. Now."

"Why? I didn't..." I trailed off, unable to grasp the unthinkable truth.

"They'll think you did. She shouted your name before she fell."

"I had no reason to kill her. They can't actually believe—"

"Listen to me. *You* were the failsafe. She jumped to implicate you."

I didn't want to believe it. How could she do this?

"This way," he said, walking with a dragging limp. We got back into the building and headed down the stairs.

"Find them," someone said among a group of people several floors below. "You take that floor. The rest of you go up."

Calder pulled me away from the stairs and toward the hallway. I followed him into a bedroom similar to the one I'd been staying in. He shut the door behind us and stood with his head next to it.

"There's no lock," he said. I leaned against the wall, trying to breathe, my face twisted in grief and horror.

The doorknob turned. I gasped. Calder held the knob.

"It's me. Seidon," said the voice from the other side of the door. Calder let go and stepped back. The door opened. Seidon's face appeared.

"You can't stay here," he said. "Pelagius is on the rampage."

Calder took my hand and together, we hurried after Seidon. For a moment, I hesitated. Jenna and Pelagius had betrayed me. What if Seidon did the same? What if he'd been pretending to be my friend all this time and now that I'd voted to not let him marry Samantha, he was going to throw me right back into the Hedron's jaws?

I clung to Calder, who still walked with a slight hobble. But he followed resolutely after Seidon, and I wasn't about to leave without Calder, so I went along. Seidon took us toward the other end of the hallway, which ended with a door leading to the building's fire escape. Seidon ran toward it. We followed, struggling to keep up when the door opened.

Seidon shoved us sideways into one of the rooms in the hallway, then shut us into darkness.

"Not in there," said Seidon. "I've been checking these rooms along this floor."

"Any idea where they may have gone?" came a voice that sounded like Enamerion.

"Probably hiding. Or if they're smart, they're using the ventilation."

Whoa. Seidon learned a new word. How did he know about ventilation systems, when things like laptops were a complete revelation to him? And since when did he get so good at lying?

"Keep looking. Report back if you find them."

A few seconds passed, where all I could hear was mine and Calder's breathing. Then the door opened again.

"He's gone," Seidon whispered. "But I don't know if he believes me. You have to hurry."

"Seidon, I'm so sorry about the vote," I said as we emerged into the hall. "I had to, I swear I didn't want—"

"Quiet," he snapped. "Uther said for you to meet him on the corner of West and Watts."

"Where's everyone else?" I asked.

"Uther, Walter, and Eamon were in the pub during the meeting. They didn't know Meriana had fallen until Pelagius ran outside. He was the first one to reach her. Eamon said he ran out and tried to help her, but she was dead. They got away during the confusion when the rest of the Hedron came outside to see what had happened."

We reached the outside door. Seidon opened it and waited without looking at us. Calder walked out. I stopped in front of Seidon.

"I didn't kill Jenna," I said.

He raised his eyes. "I know. But this is the last time I can help you. I've got to get Samantha back to the water before they turn on her."

"We can take you," said Calder. "Go find her and bring her here. We can take you to the coast."

"No. If they find out we helped each other, we'll never be safe. Just go."

I grabbed his arm. "Seidon, please. I'm so sorry. I had to vote no."

He scowled, his eyes watering as he gazed at me.

"You did what you had to. Now go."

Calder pulled me with him. I didn't look away from Seidon as we rushed onto the fire escape.

"Stop!" someone shouted from the stairs above us.

"Go, go!" Calder cried. We half ran, half fell down the stairs. More enraged shouts bellowed overhead. We descended, faster and faster, stumbling down each step. I looked up. Someone came down after us. I couldn't tell who.

We descended the ladder at the end of the fire escape and jumped the last few feet to the ground. We broke into a limping run, with

Calder still weak from the poison, and emerged onto the street running alongside the river. I looked to my left, where a crowd of people stood looking at something lying on the ground. I wrenched my eyes away, gnashing my teeth, and ran again.

"There they are!"

I looked back. Pelagius broke away from the group and hurried after us. We tore down the street as hard as we could. I glanced back. Pelagius wasn't fast, but he looked dangerously determined and didn't slow down.

"Where were we supposed to go?" I asked, trying to keep my voice low so Pelagius wouldn't hear us.

"Keep going," said Calder. We ducked down a side street and into a parking garage. He pulled me behind a parked car in the garage and held a finger to his lips, his breath heaving. I tried to swallow. My cotton shirt clung to my sweaty skin. My heart refused to slow.

"I know you're in here," came Pelagius's voice. "You can't hide. Wherever you go, we'll find you, Olivia Owens. You and all your human friends are dead."

I covered my face with my hands. Footsteps came closer to where we hid. Calder looked around, then his eyes landed on the handle of the car on our other side. He reached up and pulled the handle. The alarm rang out long and loud. Pelagius cried out.

"Under the car," said Calder, looking me hard in the eye. "Like we did in San Diego." Then he pushed me to the ground. I flattened myself to the oily concrete and slid under the car next to the one wildly screeching and beeping. He came behind me. We slithered and wormed our way beneath the first car, then another, until coming out the other end. I looked around, trying to see where Pelagius was but couldn't find him.

I came into a crouch and waited until Calder got to his feet. Then we both ran out of the parking garage and back toward the street labeled *West.* At the corner, Calder stopped me. He looked left and right.

"Which way?" I asked.

"I don't know." He looked back and forth, then behind us. "Go!"

With renewed dread, I saw Pelagius on our tail again. We bolted down the sidewalk, heading away from *The Stranded Siren.* Pelagius remained on our heels until a beat-up blue car stopped right in front of us. Uther rolled the window down.

"Get in!" he shouted. I hurried to open the back door and threw myself in while Calder rounded the hood and jumped into the front seat. Uther shifted the gears, pounded the gas pedal, and screeched around the corner. I looked out the back windshield. Pelagius stopped running. But he didn't look defeated. Before his form receded behind us, I saw a smile twist his face.

48

Facing the Future

Uther drove the car down several streets and around a ton of corners until stopping fast beside a subway entrance. My heart thudding, my body swayed with the car's momentum.

"Are you both all right?" Uther asked. Calder nodded. I didn't reply.

"What happened?" Calder asked. "Seidon said you saw Jenna fall."

"It was fast," Uther said, retelling the same story Seidon had. "When Pelagius started screaming that Olivia killed Meriana, the rest of the Hedron came running out."

I exchanged a worried look with Calder.

"I didn't do it," I said.

He huffed. "Course you didn't. Walter and Eamon know it too. I don't think she was dead when she landed. The awning broke her fall. I could have sworn I saw her move before Pelagius got to her. But before we could make sure, he started shouting. As soon as I heard him accuse you, I told Seidon to find you and get you out. Eamon and Walter escaped out the back. I took Samantha and left her in a safe place by the water. Seidon should have reached her by now."

I let out a sigh of relief. Uther continued.

"But you've got to get out of New York. Don't tell anyone where you're going. They're going to come after you. And all of us."

My heart dropped. I shook my head and put my hands over my face. Uther's door opened. I looked up.

"Where are you going?" I asked.

"Going to see what I can find out. Then I'm getting out of here. Keep your phone until I can update you. Then, get rid of it." He got out.

"Uther!" I cried. He stopped. I climbed out of the car, ran to him, and squeezed him in a tight hug. "Don't go back there."

He patted my back.

"I'll be fine, *meine freundin.* I got ways of finding things out." He stepped away, clapped my shoulder, then walked into the subway entrance. I sighed and turned back to the car. Calder had moved to the driver's seat. I got into the front. We sat in silence until he reached over and put his hand on my shoulder.

"You okay?" he asked. Eyes glazed, I shook my head. How did everything go from bad to so much worse in such a short time?

Pelagius had started it all. Jenna was dead. And now the entire Hedron thought I had killed her. I buried my face in my hands.

"You did the right thing," said Calder.

"What right thing?" I muttered numbly. "I didn't do anything but make things worse for everyone. Our friends have to run. The Hedron all think I'm a murderer. You almost died." My voice rose as the reality and trauma clutched my throat.

"You didn't give in. You chose to protect everyone instead of just me."

Tears teemed in my eyes. I hiccupped several times trying to hold them back. Calder put his arm around me. I dissolved into my hands. He rubbed my back. I turned into him. He held me while I sobbed.

A few minutes later, Calder stopped the car along the sidewalk near Central Park, where the fall colors created a haven in the middle of the bustling city. There, we waited. Time ticked sluggishly by. We got out of the car and went into the park to get off the street, the sun setting over the towering New York skyline.

Finally, Calder's phone rang.

"Uther," he said, then pushed the button to put it on speaker.

"Are you safe?" Uther asked. Calder looked at the park around us.

"For now, yes. What's happened? Are the Hedron still at *The Siren*?"

"*Ja*. They called an emergency revote. Pelagius insisted on taking his spot as an alternate. With his vote, the Purge passed."

"How do you know?" Calder asked.

"I waited in the pub until the Hedron came out."

"And they didn't see you?" I cried in disbelief.

"Hiding in plain sight, *junge*. But Hydria recognized me. She told me about the Purge."

"But…my parents. Samantha's mom and sisters. What about my friends at school? My teachers? Do the Hedron think everyone who knows me knows about them?"

"For now, I can only guess. I don't know who they'll go after. All of us, for sure. Calder, Eamon has already contacted your mother. I'm heading out to Arizona to help Samantha's family hide. I'm happy to extend the invitation to your family as well, Olivia, if they're willing."

I felt a small measure of relief. "Yes. Thank you."

"Why did Jenna do this, Uther?" Calder asked from behind me. "Does anyone have any idea?"

"Some hurts…run too deep to heal," he replied. "I don't think the mermaid ever intended to live through this."

"But why drag everyone else down with her?" I asked, wiping my streaming eyes. "Why force the Hedron to come after us?"

"The key now is finding proof of what her intentions were. If we can find proof that she meant to frame Olivia and bring about the Purge, then it'll be overturned."

"*How?* I've lost all the evidence."

Uther was silent for a moment. "I don't know. For now, all we can do is stay alive until we can figure out a way to clear your name. Stay hidden. Don't trust anyone with fins. I'll do what I can on my end. Calder, you know how to reach me without using a cell phone if you need to."

I walked a few more steps away. I couldn't bear any more. Calder continued talking to Uther, but I couldn't hear what he said. I stared across Central Park, so beautiful, so recognizably iconic—but my broken heart withered at the unknown before me.

Where to go. What to do. How to do it. So many questions. None of them had answers.

A moment later, Calder came up behind me. He put his arm around my shoulders. I looked up at him. Alive. Constant. I slipped my arms around his waist and nestled into the safety of feeling him beside me.

We had a long road ahead. But I didn't have to face it alone.

THE END

the story continues in . . .

For the latest updates and book news, subscribe to the
L.L. Standage newsletter at WWW.AUTHORLLSTANDAGE.COM

Or follow her on Instagram, Twitter, and TikTok
@AUTHORLLSTANDAGE

Acknowledgments

This book has been so many years in the making! I can't believe it's finally in the hands of my readers. To all of you who took a chance on me, I thank you. You are part of what makes this job so amazing.

A big, giant, squishy thank you to Anna Marie Roberts, Melanie McMillan, Dayna Slack, and Karli Denton for helping with my kids during the 2021 Summer and beyond. Without so many helpers, I'd never have been able to meet my deadlines.

To my incredible alpha and beta readers: Kylie Pond, Kate Gomm, Marie Parker, Marni Cochran, Cassie shields, Alyssa Sellers, Patti Hulet, Michelle Taylor, and Crystal Birdno. Thanks for all your time and talents, advice, and catching the little typos!

To my Editing Goddesses (yes, you can put that on your resume), Rebecca Blevins, Jeigh Meredith, and Neha Patel at Salt & Sage Editing: you've done it again. You took my mess of a manuscript, combed through it, and helped me braid it all up beautifully. Your encouragement helps me continually conquer that stinky old Imposter Syndrome. And your critiques help me to keep learning. I can't thank you enough!

To my ANWA friends, especially my Red Mountain Writers: I. LOVE. YOU. I love our chapter meetings where we laugh, share, and learn together. Thank you for always being such fantastic cheerleaders!

A big thank you to Molly Phipps for her continued brilliance in cover design and formatting. I will still tell people about you even though I worry you'll get too popular and busy for me. Haha. Thank you for your talents, lady!

To the really cool people I met on my trip to Maryland: Dan and Marijen on the airplane, Courteney, Isabel, and Charlie from Jimmy Johns (thank you for the sandwich and cookie, guys!), and those very nice people I met in DC whose names I never learned. You guys all made me feel like a million bucks and cheered me up when my laptop crashed and I thought all was lost.

And to Blake, Amanda, and little "Prima:" thank you for opening your home to me. Alexandria is amazing and I will always treasure that trip Back East!

To the University of Maryland: I hope I did your beloved school the justice it deserves. The choice to make UMD my story's setting might seem strange and random, but I'm glad I did it. It's a beautiful place and it just...worked, ya know?

Here's to hoping you can reopen Footnotes one day. And sell blueberry muffins there.

And Bret—I am grateful every day that you chose me. I'll choose you every day from now until eternity.

...You are a rock star.

And of course, I have to thank my Heavenly Parents. A lot of prayer goes into every book I write and I couldn't do it without divine help. I owe it all to Them.

About the Author

L.L. STANDAGE (Amy to her friends), has been making up stories her entire life. In high school, she decided she wanted to be an author and began writing the most cringe-worthy epic fantasies, which, sadly, will never see the light of day. When she isn't writing, she enjoys laughing with her husband, playing Zelda with her kids, drinking herbal tea, getting pedicures, traveling, mountain biking, and eating food. She loves chocolate and geeks out over anything having to do with England. She lives with her family in the very sunny, cactus-infested fire hazard known as Arizona.

Chasm is her second novel.

Made in the USA
Columbia, SC
19 November 2024